W9-BIA-139

YOU DID THIS

JAMIE MILLEN

FEB 2024

TITLES BY JAMIE MILLEN

CLAIRE WOLFE THILLERS

YOU DID THIS
YOU MADE ME
YOU ARE NEXT

JAMIE MILLEN

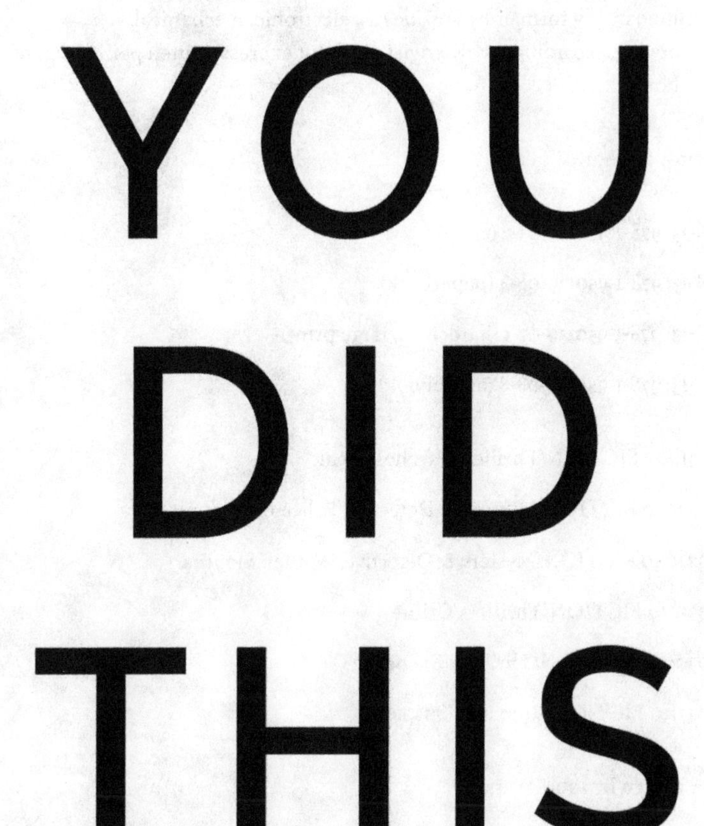

This book is a work of fiction. Names, characters, organizations, places, events, and incidents are either products of the author's imagination or used fictitiously. Any resemblance to actual events or actual persons, living or dead, is purely coincidental.

Copyright © 2022 by Jamie Millen

All rights reserved.

No part of this book may be reproduced, or stored in a retrieval system, or transmitted in any form or by any means, electronic, mechanical, photocopying, recording, or otherwise, without express written permission of the author.

jamiemillen.com

ISBN-13: 978-1-950139-05-7 (ebook)

ISBN-13: 978-1-950139-06-4 (paperback)

ISBN-13: 978-1-950139-07-1 (hardcover, large print)

ISBN-13: 978-1-950139-08-8 (audiobook)

FIC031080 FICTION/Thrillers/Psychological

FIC022020 FICTION/Mystery & Detective/Police Procedural

FIC022040 FICTION/Mystery & Detective/Women Sleuths

FIC031010 FICTION/Thrillers/Crime

FIC030000 FICTION/Thrillers/Suspense

FIC027110 FICTION/Romance/Suspense

Cover design by 100 Covers

First edition

CHAPTER 1

Claire had blood on her hands when she limped home from school that afternoon. Tears blurred her vision. An October breeze ran icy fingers through her hair. Hurt and anger pumped in her veins as her sneakers pounded the cracked sidewalk. Claire had promised herself she wouldn't let Tina get to her again. Now she had broken that promise.

She turned a corner, and a two-level house came into view. The kitchen windows glowed with yellow light. For another girl from a different family, home meant warmth and safety. But the sight of her house filled Claire with dread, and on this day more than any other.

Sisters should love each other. Claire knew this the way she knew parents shouldn't fight and a mother shouldn't favor one daughter over the other. Life was never as it should be. Claire had tried to love Tina. But each time she opened her heart, her little sister drove a dagger into her soft, sensitive core.

Claire alone saw Tina for what she was—a cruel little witch. Her sister hid her true nature well. To the rest of the world, Tina was a blonde-haired, blue-eyed angel with dimpled cheeks. Everyone fell for her disguise. Claire, too. Tina flashed that cherubic smile, and hearts melted. Every time.

But not anymore. Today, Claire had learned her lesson. Tina had gone too far. She had broken Claire's heart one time too many. Claire was done with Tina. The little bitch was dead to her.

Claire paused on the welcome mat, sucking in air and blinking back tears. *You can do this, Claire.* She'd keep her head down and go straight to her room. With luck, Tina and her parents would forget she existed until the party was over.

Armed with that miserable hope, she eased down the door handle with her elbow and shouldered her way inside. She inhaled the sweet scent of melted chocolate, and the knife blade in her heart twisted. Mom had baked her favorite treat, but the cake was not for Claire. It never was.

Claire made for the staircase and stole a glance at the kitchen. Balloons floated in the air, their ribbons anchored to kitchen chairs. Streamers arched from the ceiling. Gift-wrapped boxes waited on the counters beside salad bowls and trays of cookies. In the center of the display sat the cake. Two number-shaped candles crowned the dark icing. Today, Tina was fourteen years old.

Claire's mother smiled to herself dreamily while she sliced carrots on a cutting board. An apron covered Mom's new floral-print dress. Her blonde curls fell to her shoulders. She'd had her hair done for the occasion. But when she spotted Claire sneaking across the hall, her smile faded. Her mother saved her smiles for others. Teachers. School moms. Strangers on the street. And Tina. Always Tina.

Mom dropped the knife onto the cutting board. "Where is your sister?" The question was an accusation. *What have you done to her?* She always spoke to Claire as though she was addressing a mass murderer.

"How should I know?"

"You were *supposed* to walk her home."

"I waited *ten minutes* for her."

Her mother's gaze moved to Claire's cheek. Suspicion turned to fear, and her mouth dropped open.

"What happened to your face?"

Claire had forgotten about the blood. Her fingers were still sticky. She must have touched her face, smearing her cheek with a red mark of Cain.

Mom charged at her. "Claire, why are you covered in blood?"

She was exaggerating, but the question choked Claire up. Where *had* the blood come from?

Mom stood face-to-face with her. They were the same height now. Soon Claire would overtake her like her father. Under her mother's paralyzing stare, Claire tried to remember what had happened. A knife had glinted in the sunlight. Tina had hurled insults, her lips curling into a snarl. And then...a gaping hole in her memory.

The searing pain in the calf of her leg jolted Claire back to the present. She looked down. Blood still oozed from the fresh gash in her skin.

"I cut my leg...I slipped on the curb." *Yes. That's what happened.* But would Mom believe her?

The distress in her mother's eyes eased a little. She crouched on one knee and inspected the bloody tear in Claire's leggings. Then she straightened and breathed a sigh of relief. The blood was Claire's, not Tina's. There was no need to fuss. And the blade in Claire's heart twisted again.

"Can I go now?"

Mom didn't answer. She returned to the kitchen and the birthday party preparations.

Claire climbed the staircase. In her room, fresh tears slid

down her cheeks. *It isn't fair*. Claire did everything her mother expected of her. She aced her exams. She had qualified for the track team at her new high school. Claire never complained about the move. But no matter what she did or didn't do, Mom had only one daughter, only one that counted.

A door opened downstairs. Her parents raised their voices —Mom's shrill questions and Dad's gruff replies. He had come home from work early for the party. Claire headed for the bathroom. Her mother would expect her to stand at attention and sing her sister "Happy Birthday."

"Then, get in the car," Mom yelled as Claire crossed the hallway, "and go find her. They'll be here any minute."

Claire swung the bathroom door shut behind her with her foot. She washed her hands in the sink, and the swirling water turned red. The shower head hissed when she pulled the handle. She waited for the water to heat. In the mirror, a sad girl with a red smudge on her cheek glared back. She had her father's inky-black hair and obsidian stare. Only Tina had her mother's golden curls and dazzling blue eyes. *And every drop of Mom's love*. A steamy mist wrapped her like a shroud.

She stripped and stepped under the flow of scorching water. The cruel smile on Tina's angelic face flashed in her mind. Her sister's hateful words rang in her ears. *Ugly. Stupid.* Tina had walked off, swinging her hips and shoulders. *Let her go. Who cares?* But Claire *did* care.

After school, Claire had waited outside Newburgh Middle School. She shifted on her feet while kids poured out of the gates. *Where was Tina?* If she came home late, Mom would blame Claire. She always did. Ten minutes passed on Claire's wristwatch before she gave up. Tina was probably home already, counting her presents. Claire would have to endure another agonizing birthday party for that spoiled brat. Tears had welled in her eyes on her walk home, distorting the world around her. She didn't notice the broken curb of the sidewalk until her foot slipped, the world falling from beneath her, and the exposed metal edge slicing into her soft skin.

Claire worked the shampoo into her hair, the lather sliding down her shoulders. She hated Tina. She wished her sister was dead. Better yet, she wished her sister had never been born. The thought shamed Claire. She cried again, but this time the warm rain from the showerhead washed her tears away.

She scrubbed the dried blood from her leg and face. Claire wasn't ugly. The eyes of boys at school followed her when she walked by. She'd had a boyfriend in Boston. Well, sort of. Robbie Cline had invited her over to study for biology class. One secret kiss didn't make him her boyfriend, but he might have been. She'd never know for sure. Their family's move to Newburgh last year had cut that relationship short. Claire wasn't stupid either. She had the grades to prove it. Tina might fool the entire world, but she would never fool Claire again.

Claire toweled off and stuck a Band-Aid over the cut on her leg. She dressed in her bedroom, selecting a clean skirt, shirt, and underwear from her closet. Downstairs, the doorbell rang. High-pitched voices floated upstairs—greetings stuffed with phony cheer and the murmurings of grown-up conversations. Claire sat at her desk. She had a calculus exam tomorrow. Any minute, her mom would call her downstairs to face the firing squad. Until then, she'd study in peace.

Minutes passed. Claire lost herself in her penciled calculations. Her stomach rumbled. Mom still hadn't called for her. Maybe she'd forgotten about her? *Good.* Claire clenched her jaw and focused on her schoolwork. When she looked up again, the hubbub had settled. The house had grown quiet. Outside her window, night had descended on their street. Had her mother cut the cake without her? Claire had not heard the birthday songs.

She dropped her pencil on her workbook and got to her feet. The pain in her leg had faded to a dull ache. She opened her door and peered over the banister into the hall. The guests had gone. Her parents sat on the couch in the living room below. Two strangers sat on the armchairs facing them. Brown suits hugged their frames. The fat one spoke in low tones and recorded her parents' answers in a notepad. Tufts of wispy gray hair protruded from his brown fedora. His thin companion listened in silence. How long had they been sitting there?

Claire's mother crossed her arms over her chest. Her father placed his hand on her shoulder. Claire hadn't seen her parents touch in years. Dark clouds swirled within her. Who were the visitors? And where was Tina?

Her mother's body convulsed as she wept. Her father hugged her and whispered in her ear. Then the strangers got to their feet. The fat man handed her father a business card and tipped his hat. They left the house and closed the door behind them.

Mom clung to Dad, her hands clenched. She sobbed and sobbed, her body quivering. Claire froze at the banister, watching her mother cry, black dread pooling in her gut like spilled blood. *No, this can't be happening.*

Dad pulled free from her embrace and stood. "Come, Diane. We need to go."

He fetched their coats from the closet and helped her mother into hers. They were leaving the house without her.

Claire descended the staircase, the wooden panels creaking beneath her shoes. Her parents looked up.

"Mom, Dad, what's going on?"

Her father's face was pale and blank. "We have to go to the medical examiner's office. We need to..."

What was a medical examiner? Claire didn't know. But a visit to his office seemed like a terrible thing.

"Why? What's happened?"

But Claire knew what had happened. Her darkest, most shameful wish had come true.

Mom stared at Claire, her eyes hardening, and she aimed a shaky finger at her daughter.

"You," she growled, her nostrils flaring. "You did this."

A chill swept through Claire. She shook her head. "I didn't do anything—"

"Don't deny it!"

Her mother lunged toward the staircase, but Claire's father held her back.

"Easy, Diane. Calm down."

"I won't calm down," Mom wailed. "She killed Tina!"

"Diane, don't say that! Don't you ever say that."

Her father wrapped her mother in a tight embrace. Rage gave way to grief, and another fit of tears racked her body. Over Mom's shoulder, Dad glanced up at Claire. His eyes filled with pain...and an unspeakable question.

Claire snapped out of her trance and bolted up the stairs. She fled to her room and locked the door. Without taking off her shoes, she leaped onto her bed and huddled in the corner. She rubbed her thumb over the ghost of dried blood on her palm.

Tina was not coming home. Not tonight or ever again. And it was all Claire's fault.

CHAPTER 2

TWELVE YEARS LATER

Detective Claire Wolfe stood at attention before the desk of Newburgh PD's investigations captain. She hoped he wouldn't ask too many questions. The wrong question might expose the true reason behind her job application.

Behind the desk, Captain Charles Emmerso riffled through her file. The stout fifty-year-old's hair thinned atop an expressive face with kind eyes. Claire had a sixth sense for people. Her former partner and mentor had called her the Mentalist for her uncanny ability to read minds. Her intuition whispered that she and Captain Emmerso would get along just fine.

"Graduated top of your class at the Academy," he said. "Made detective after only two years on the beat. Joined homicide after four." He closed the manila folder. "That's an impressive resume, Detective Wolfe."

"Thank you, sir." Claire ran her hands over her thighs, smoothing the fabric of her trousers. She did not regret trading her police uniform for the cheap business suits of the Boston PD Investigations Bureau. Three years of working homicide in the capital had more than qualified her for this smaller city job.

He grunted. "You first applied for this position, what, two years ago?"

"Yes, sir. I reapplied every six months."

Emmerso looked her in the eye. "Tell me, Detective, why is a bright, rising star so eager to leave the Hub of the Universe for our humble city?"

Her intuition had not failed her. Emmerso was a good guy. On her first day at Boston PD, her captain had asked why "a girl like her" had become a cop in the first place. He had meant a "pretty face." Claire had deflected the compliment, a habit she was still trying to shake. Men liked her. There was no use denying it. Instead, she used that knowledge to her advantage. Men always underestimated a "pretty face."

Her transfer request had nothing to do with her former captain or any of her coworkers. Claire had enjoyed working at Boston PD, and she had learned more than she had hoped to during her three years in Major Crimes. But Newburgh PD had always been her ultimate destination.

Claire understood what Captain Emmerso was asking—would this new rising star cause trouble in his bureau? She had to put his concerns to rest. "My parents live in Newburgh, sir. My mother has health problems, and I wanted to move close to home."

The half-truth made Claire's conscience squirm. Her mother's issues had little to do with her physical health. But full disclosure would have jeopardized her true goal and complicated their working relationship.

Her answer seemed to satisfy Captain Emmerso. "I spoke with your colleagues at Boston PD."

Claire's shoulders stiffened. Her current captain had not looked kindly on her desire to transfer. Had he sabotaged her new career path? Her fears were unwarranted.

"They all spoke highly of you, especially your partner. He

said you're a talented detective and a crack shot. He also said you took down a hardened bank robber, single-handed. How did you manage that?"

Claire grinned. Detective Ned Brooks, her partner and mentor, had not missed the opportunity to put in a kind word. *Thanks, Ned. You're the best.*

She knew what Captain Emmerso was thinking now. How *had* this skinny young woman overpowered a career thug? The truth was anticlimactic—Claire had talked the big guy into submission—but she left the details to her new captain's imagination. "He underestimated me, sir."

Captain Emmerso smirked. "I'll try not to make the same mistake. When can you start?"

Two weeks later on a Tuesday morning, Claire stood before his desk once again, ready to begin her duties...and her secret personal project.

Captain Emmerso glanced at the holster and badge secured to Claire's belt. "I see you've already visited the armory. For a change, IT got your workstation ready on time." He handed her a printed page with her initial log-in details. "You'll partner up with Detective Jared Wallace, your FTO."

Wallace. Claire had heard the name of her Field Training Officer before, but where?

"Everyone calls him Jed," Emmerso continued. "You're about the same age. He grew up in Newburgh and knows the lay of the land. He'll introduce you to our training materials for the city's ordinances and the department's SOPs. You also need to qualify with your weapon."

"I already scheduled that." Claire had expected some paperwork on arrival but assumed the department's Standard Operating Procedures would resemble those of Boston PD.

"Good. We're a small investigations bureau. Six officers, including you. Lieutenant Washington and Detective Gomez are upstate with the DEA on a special task force. You'll report directly to me for the time being. Our other lieutenant passed away a month ago after thirty years in the department. You'll see his name on the reports—Brian O'Leary."

O'Leary. Claire's smile faltered. The name conjured ghosts from beyond the grave. O'Leary had handled Tina's murder investigation. The overweight detective had delivered the news of Tina's death and continued to drop by Claire's home for weeks after the funeral. Claire's parents had never allowed her to hear his updates. What she knew about her sister's death she had gleaned from news reports and rumors. Tina was the victim of a brutal murder. Her body was discovered near Newburgh Middle School. The police never arrested her killer. And in the twelve years since her death, Detective O'Leary had become Lieutenant O'Leary.

Claire had wanted to confront O'Leary about his investigation, and now she never would. It didn't matter. Claire could blaze another trail to her destination. And today, she would take the first step toward finding justice for her sister.

Captain Emmerso rose from his chair. "I'll introduce you to the rest of the team."

The squad room contained three pairs of office desks, head to head. A whiteboard covered a wall, and a kitchenette—complete with a water cooler and a large, shiny coffee grinder—occupied one corner of the room.

"Gentlemen, join me in welcoming Detective Claire Wolfe."

Three men raised their eyes from their computer screens and gave her the twice-over. *Great*. She was the only female detective on the team.

"She earned her chops at Boston PD, so be nice and she might teach you a thing or two."

The two detectives got to their feet, a disheveled, puppy-faced Caucasian and a stocky Asian.

"Brendan Mahoney," said the one.

"Haruto Nakamura," said the other. "O'Leary left big shoes to fill."

"Yeah," Mahoney said. "Size twelve, if memory serves."

Claire returned their smiles and shook their hands. The jokers of the Bureau had revealed themselves. "I'll do my best."

"Last but not least, Detective Jared Wallace."

Detective Wallace sprang to his feet and walked around his desk. Younger than the other detectives, Wallace had a handsome boyish face beneath a crewcut. His gray necktie hung like a plumb line over the buttons of a creaseless shirt, which he'd tucked neatly into his gray trousers. He gave Claire's hand a vigorous shake.

"Call me Jed." He looped his thumbs in his belt and slouched against the desk. The nickname and entitled body language clashed with the initial impression of order and conscientious eagerness. "Welcome aboard."

"Thank you."

"Make yourself at home," Emmerso said. The curt inflection in his voice implied he had other matters to attend to. "Detective Wallace will show you how to work the coffee machine. You need a PhD in engineering to operate that thing, but your partner has it all figured out."

"Yeah," Mahoney quipped, already back at his computer screen. "Jed's great at making coffee. That's all he does around here."

Jed made a chattering duck impression with his hand. "Don't listen to him. Mahoney's delusional. He thinks he has a sense of humor. Now, how about that coffee?"

"I'd love some." Claire itched to start her private investigation, but she'd better invest in her relationship with her new partner. Soon, she'd need friends she could depend on in the department.

In the kitchenette, Jed took two paper cups from a dispenser on the wall and placed one beneath the spout of the coffee grinder. The chrome juggernaut belonged in a Starbucks, not a police department. He pressed a button, and the grinder moaned. He pulled levers, loaded filters, and emptied used coffee grinds into a bin, then heated milk in a tin beaker. Finally, he presented her with a cup of steaming coffee topped with a thick layer of foamed milk.

"Captain Emmerso wasn't kidding," she said. "I think I'll need a three-day course before I try that myself."

"It's easier than it looks. Sugar?"

"No, thanks." Claire took a sip. "That's a good cup of coffee."

Jed smiled. He repeated the process for the second cup. "I don't know any Wolfes in Boston."

"We're an endangered species."

Jed's hospitable grin chilled. He'd been digging for information, and Claire had offered none. Small talk was not her field. Since Tina's death, she'd learned to shrug off personal questions with humor. She didn't like to talk about herself or her family.

Her family. Claire had moved into a rental house a few days ago but still hadn't visited her old family home. Her parents didn't even know she was back in town. She couldn't put that off forever.

Jed sipped his coffee. "You a Celtics fan?"

"Celtics?"

"You know, Boston's basketball team."

"I don't follow sports."

"Pity. They're on a winning streak."

They sipped their coffee. Claire felt like she was on a bad blind date. Not that she'd dated in Boston. A few of her fellow officers had shown interest, but she'd kept her distance. An on-the-job romance would complicate her work environment.

Instead, she had focused on advancing within the force so she could transfer to Newburgh PD's Investigations Bureau and pursue the mission that now lay one coffee away.

Jed gave her another tight grin and sipped his coffee. They waited for each other to lead the conversation. Was having a female partner awkward for Jed? By handling her with kid gloves, he only made her uncomfortable.

Claire missed Ned Brooks from Boston PD already. He had respected her reserved nature and appreciated her sense of humor. And his eyes crinkled when he smiled.

Claire broke the silence. "What's on our table for today?"

"I'm putting the finishing touches on a domestic homicide, an open-and-shut case. The DA's office should have the arrest warrant ready any minute now. You're welcome to review the murder book and see if you have any suggestions."

"I'd be glad to."

Claire had used murder books at Boston PD. The software, designed for the needs of law enforcement, collected the interviews, forensic reports, and crime scene photos of a homicide investigation into a single electronic interface.

"We also have two fresh robberies and one suspected identity theft to check out. Fate's given us an easy honeymoon."

Claire forced a brief smile. She disliked the metaphor, which implied their relationship would go beyond their professional roles. Luckily, Jed's desk phone rang, and as he walked over to answer, Claire grabbed her opportunity.

At her desk, she nudged the computer mouse. A log-in screen appeared over the backdrop of the Newburgh PD emblem, which matched the police badge they had issued her that morning. She chose a new password and opened her email. Jed had already forwarded links to the training materials. Claire opened the links and scanned the contents.

"Yes, Dad," Jed whispered into his phone. "I realize that."

Claire suppressed a smile and opened the investigations interface. A single murder book appeared on her list of active cases—the homicide Jed had mentioned. Claire double-clicked the murder case and skimmed through the summary. In a crime scene photo, a slender woman in her thirties lay lifeless on a kitchen floor.

After three years in Major Crimes, the sight of a dead body no longer aroused horror, only curiosity. A jealous husband kills his cheating wife. Open-and-shut, as Jed had said. Most cases were predictable. Follow the procedures, ask the right questions, and voilà—the wheels of justice turned.

"Yeah, Dad," Jed continued, his voice irate. "I'm on it. This isn't a good time."

Unable to shake his nagging father, Jed seemed to want to crawl into a hole and die. Again, Claire pretended not to notice.

Leaving the active murder book open on the screen, Claire entered the department's search portal. At Boston PD, Claire had located the case number for her sister's murder file, but nothing more. Only authorized homicide detectives at Newburgh PD could access that murder book. Three years later, Claire finally had access to the Newburgh PD system.

She typed in the case number from memory and clicked the search button. Blood pulsed in the arteries of her neck as the hourglass icon turned. The search returned a single result.

Claire held her breath. She had waited twelve years to reach this day. Transferring the files to Boston would have raised unwanted questions, as would visiting Newburgh PD, so Claire had applied to join Newburgh PD. She'd needed to transfer anyway to claim jurisdiction and pursue any leads she found. Now the day had arrived. But was she ready to see what lay within Tina's file?

She double-clicked the murder book. An error message appeared on the screen. No digital records for the case existed in the system. The message referred her to the Department's Archive to get a hard copy.

A hard copy? Only once before had Claire consulted paper records—for a cold case from the eighties. Tina's case was only twelve years old. Why was her file not in the digital system?

She minimized the computer window and got to her feet. "I'll be right back," she told Jed, who was still wrestling with his father on the phone. Abandoning her coffee on her desk, Claire made for the elevator down the hall. When she had visited the armory that morning to sign for her standard-issue Glock 22 and other equipment, she had passed a sign for the evidence room and archive.

At a service window on the second floor, an elderly black officer read the morning newspaper over a mug of coffee. Rows of filing cabinets crammed the room behind him. Sealed evidence boxes lined the shelves on the far wall. The air smelled of mothballs and the same powerful coffee beans she'd enjoyed in the Investigations Bureau. This police department took its coffee very seriously.

Claire read his name tag. "Morning, Officer Freeman."

Officer Robert Freeman raised his head of short salt-and-pepper hair, his face wrinkling with surprise. Then he smiled, revealing rows of white teeth. "Please, call me Bobby. Everybody else does. You're that new detective, aren't you?"

"Word travels fast." She held out her hand. "Claire Wolfe."

He gave her hand a short but vigorous shake. "How are you finding your new partner?"

Claire gave a dutiful smile. "He sure knows his way around the coffee machine."

The smile lines on Bobby's face deepened. "You're diplomatic. That will serve you well with his daddy."

When Claire bunched her eyebrows in confusion, the

officer leaned in and dropped his voice to a whisper. "Jed's daddy is Harry Wallace. *Chief* Harry Wallace."

So that's why the name Wallace had sounded familiar. Jed's pesky father was none other than the department's top cop. Claire had better watch what she said around her new partner.

"People used to call him Dirty Harry," Bobby added, "but you didn't hear that from me."

"Thanks for the inside information." There was a story behind that nickname, but Claire didn't pry.

Bobby frowned. "Pity about O'Leary. He was one of the older faces in the department."

This time, Claire didn't tense up at the name. "What happened to him?"

"Heart attack, so they say. What they mean is 'too many donuts.'" He chuckled, then grew serious again. "I don't know about that. He'd been drinking again. Must have done in his liver. Over the years, this job can get to you." He glanced at Claire with grandfatherly concern. His words were a friendly warning. *Don't let that happen to you.*

Claire nodded. "I'll keep that in mind, Bobby."

Officer Bobby Freeman got around to business. "How can I help you, Detective?"

"I need an old case file."

"How old?"

"Twelve years."

"Closed?"

"Cold."

"Ha!" Bobby grinned. "The new detective shakes the dust off the old unsolved cases?"

"Something like that."

Bobby shifted a computer mouse and glanced at his monitor. "Do you have the case number?"

"I do." Claire dictated the number.

Bobby clicked his tongue with surprise. "Gotcha. Well, what do you know? One of O'Leary's cases. He hated computers, worked with hard copies when he could get away with it. Old habits die hard. I say you have to move with the times. That's what keeps me young."

To prove his youthful abilities, he got to his feet and hobbled toward a row of filing cabinets. Claire's guts clenched as Bobby opened a drawer and his fingers walked the folders within. The tension was unbearable. Twelve years since Tina's murder, the moment of truth had arrived.

Bobby slammed the drawer shut and trudged back to the service window, empty-handed.

"Sorry, Detective. The file isn't where it's supposed to be."

Claire perked up. Tina's file was missing. "Did anyone check it out of the archive?"

Bobby squinted at the computer monitor. "Nope, the log is empty. It's probably in the basement. We cleaned up before the renovation last year, and I haven't gotten around to sorting through the boxes. So much dust and all."

"Oh."

"I can check the basement if you like." He had noticed her disappointment and would go the extra mile.

"I don't want to put you to any trouble."

"It's no trouble. This is my job, and I've been putting off that basement way too long. I'll get your file, Detective. But with all that mess, it might take a few days."

"No problem. It's an old case. A few days make no difference."

Bobby smiled. "OK then, Detective Wolfe."

"Please, call me Claire."

Claire returned to the elevator, her fingers trembling. She was so close now. *Don't worry, Tina. I won't let you down. Your murderer is going to jail.* She rubbed her palm. The nervous tick had begun the day Tina died, and now Claire willed her hands to stop.

When she returned to the squad room, Jed stood at his desk. He was pulling on his gray suit jacket, his face pensive. Something had happened.

"We're heading out."

"What's going on?"

"Dispatch called. We have a Jane Doe."

The honeymoon was over.

CHAPTER 3

Weary single-level homes decayed on the streets of suburban Newburgh, the leafless front-yard trees scratching at gloomy skies. Claire eyed them from the passenger seat of Jed's unmarked police cruiser, a silver Dodge Stratus. The news of a fresh murder scene had killed their appetite for small talk.

Newburgh Middle School glided past the window in ghostly silence. So did the shadowy woods on Park Street. The scenery of Claire's childhood was both darkly familiar and disturbingly foreign, the warped dreamscape of her formative nightmares.

An ambulance had beaten them to the scene, along with two squad cars and an unmarked sedan. Jed pulled into the emergency lane, adding his vehicle to the line.

At the sight of the dark woods, Claire's stomach tightened. Most of the death scenes she had encountered in Boston were indoors. The rusty scent of blood and death clung to the walls and floors. Despite that morning's crisp fall breeze, something in the tall jam of trees and wild shrubs triggered a primal dread.

was OK." His face crumpled at the memory, and a sob escaped his mouth. "She looked Julie's age."

"How old is Julie?"

"Fourteen."

Claire's breath froze in her chest.

"Do you know her?"

Michael shot the detectives a nervous look and swallowed. Horror flickered in his eyes. "I...don't know."

"You don't know? Could she be one of Julie's friends?"

"I couldn't tell, man. Her face...her face." He struggled to put the shaking cigarette between his lips.

If the descriptions disturbed Jed, he hid those feelings well. "What else did you see?"

"Nothing. I threw up. Then, I called nine-one-one."

"You didn't see anyone else here, anyone leaving?"

He shook his head. A paramedic stepped between the detectives and handed Michael a steaming cup of tea. "Thanks."

"Michael, did you touch anything?"

"No, I just wanted to get away."

Jed glanced at Claire—did she have any further questions?—and she shrugged.

"Your mom is on her way," Jed said.

He jotted down Michael's phone number and his home address. Then, he handed the boy a business card and instructed him to call if he remembered anything else. Jed's handling of the interview had been professional and thorough, and Claire regretted her comment to the archive officer about Jed's coffee-making talents.

Claire lightened the mood. "Nice cards."

Jed grunted with pleasure. "They're one of the department's few perks. I can order some for you if you like."

"Thanks. I'd like that."

They ducked under the yellow crime scene tape and followed the well-trodden path among the trees. Leaves crunched underfoot as they negotiated broken branches and exposed roots.

A uniformed black officer stood at the edge of a clearing. "Watch your step!" He pointed to a patch of chunky vomit.

"Thanks," Jed said.

"Del Freeman," the patrol officer told Claire, by way of introduction.

"Claire Wolfe."

"Yeah, I know. Welcome aboard, Detective."

"Thank you, Officer."

Freeman. The young patrol officer's name and face recalled Officer Bobby Freeman at the Department Archive. Claire had found another family connection at Newburgh PD, but she said nothing. Jed did not need to know she'd dug up old cases on her first day.

Jed and Claire stepped around the acrid puddle, then another. Blowflies buzzed in a clearing the size of a small room. The forensic specialist, an Asian in a white surgical suit, went about his work.

The body lay at the foot of an old willow with a gnarled, forked trunk. The white soles of the girl's running shoes faced them, her feet pointing heavenward. In her blue jeans and pink sweater, she looked as though she might sit up at any moment. Was that how Tina's life had ended—alone in a forest, her feet extended, her arms at her sides, as though she'd settled down for a nap?

The forensic tech photographed the body. His blue rubber gloves matched the baggies over his hair and shoes. Captain Emmerso and a middle-aged patrol sergeant had taken the same precautions to avoid contaminating the crime scene. Numbered circles marked items of interest to the investigation.

The detectives helped themselves to disposable gloves and booties from the box at the edge of the clearing.

"Sergeant Eckhardt," Emmerso said when the detectives drew near. "You know Detective Wallace. Detective Wolfe joined the department today."

The sergeant's arched eyebrows gave him an expression of continual surprise, although Claire was sure he'd seen it all.

"Not much of a welcome," he said, displaying the dark humor typical of seasoned officers.

Claire nodded. When she glanced at the victim's head, she stifled a gasp. The girl's face was gone. A dark-red pulp of congealed blood and mangled flesh appeared below the fringe of golden hair where the face should be. This girl would never wake from her nap.

The flash of a camera flared. The forensic tech snapped close-ups of the girl's head and hands.

Sergeant Eckhardt called Officer Freeman over. "It's time for that walk-through."

The officer described the dispatch call and what he and Officer Jenkins had found at the crime scene. "The victim's name is Grace Miles, according to the tag on her schoolbag." He pointed to the red backpack three feet from the girl's head. "Eighth grade. That makes her about fourteen years old."

Emmerso said, "Detective Wallace will lead the investigation. Detective Wolfe, I hope you'll speak freely. We can all benefit from your experience."

Claire nodded again, feeling self-conscious. Her captain expected her to justify his recruitment decision by adding value to the investigation.

"Detective Wallace," Emmerso said. "Over to you."

Jed cleared his throat and activated the digital recorder. "The victim is a female, approximately fourteen years old. The body is lying on its back, about two feet from a large willow tree. The victim's face shows many overlapping chop wounds, possibly severe blunt-force trauma. A small backpack is on the ground about three feet south of the victim's head. It bears the name Grace Miles. There are no visible signs of struggle."

Jed turned to the tech. "Do we have a time of death?"

The forensic tech slipped paper bags over the girl's hands. "Judging by the blood coagulation, blowflies, and lack of maggots, I'd say about eight to twenty-four hours ago. Nothing definite yet."

Claire scanned the undergrowth while Jed resumed his monologue.

"OK. The estimated time of death is between eight and twenty-four hours ago. No visible signs of sexual assault either. An autopsy will have the last word on that. The killer cleaned up pretty well. The victim's face shows extensive trauma with a blunt object, but there's no sign of a weapon."

Claire stepped toward the thick foliage at the edge of the clearing. "Detective Wallace. Over here."

Jed joined her, then spoke into the recorder. "We found an ax with a curved handle in the brush, about ten feet away. Red, sticky fluid is visible on the chopping blade." He stopped the recording. "Can we get a photo of this?"

The forensic tech walked over, labeled and photographed the ax, then bagged the weapon in a paper evidence bag.

"Can I move the body now?"

"Sure."

Captain Emmerso turned to his detectives. "Anything else? Detective Wolfe?"

Claire considered the dead girl. The voice of Ned Brooks of Boston PD echoed in her mind. *Look for what's missing*. Claire's intuition squirmed. Something *was* missing, but what? She turned to the tech. "What about the cause of death?"

The officers glanced at her with surprise. The bloodied ax and destroyed face seemed to provide an obvious answer. But Claire had learned that in death, as in life, appearances often deceive.

"Good question," the forensic tech said, adding to the other officers' surprise. He kneeled over the girl's destroyed face. "The mutilation took place post-mortem. There are no defensive wounds, and the bleeding from her head isn't as extensive as you'd expect." He pointed. "See the contusions on her neck? That thin, horizontal furrow is a sign of ligature strangulation. I'm betting the autopsy will list asphyxiation as the cause of death."

Jed turned to Claire. "Why bash in her face if she was already dead?"

She shrugged. "Anger?"

Jed nodded slowly. "They knew each other. The killer surprised her and strangled her. Then, he laid her body out carefully."

All at once, the missing detail surfaced in Claire's mind. "Too carefully. She didn't die here." Claire pointed. "There's no dirt or leaves under her shoes. The mutilation took place somewhere else, too. Her sweater shows some blood spatter but not the surrounding ground. The ax would have made a mess. And then there's the lividity of her skin."

A Boston forensic pathologist had explained the decomposition process to her. At death, blood circulation stops, and gravity pulls the blood in the body's organs downward. The blood at the lower regions colors the skin purple a few hours after death. This livor mortis remains even if the body is turned over later.

"The killer kept her facedown," Claire continued, "for hours after death, then moved her here. That deep purple color also indicates asphyxiation."

The forensic tech beamed at Claire. "This one's a keeper, Captain."

"I agree," Emmerso said. He turned to Sergeant Eckhardt. "We'll need to canvas the neighborhood. There are few houses on this street, but maybe somebody saw the drop-off."

"We'll take care of that."

Emmerso spoke to his detectives. "Notify the girl's family. Check out her school, too."

Jed answered. "We're on it, sir."

The bosses exited, leaving the detectives to process the scene. While the ambulance team placed the body in a bag, Claire considered the facts of the case. Most murderers panicked, leaving heaps of evidence at the scene. This killer had acted rationally, cleaning up and depositing the girl away from the murder site along with the ax and her schoolbag. Unless he had screwed up, this killer would not be easy to catch.

CHAPTER 4

Jed parked his silver Dodge Stratus outside a two-level Cape Cod house that afternoon. With its tidy mowed lawns and chrysanthemums in pink, red, and white, the Miles family home was a picture of suburban order and tranquility. Claire and Jed got out of the car, the doors slamming shut with ominous finality. The homicide detectives were about to shatter that tranquility forever.

As they followed the short, paved path through the yard to a white door, a fresh wave of déjà vu washed over Claire. The house, with its slanting roof tiles pierced by upper windows, resembled her own childhood home. This exact scene had played out before Claire's eyes in the past. But last time, she'd been on the receiving end of the visit.

Jed reached for the dolphin-shaped knocker, then rang the bell instead. He jiggled his eyebrows at the crucifix above the door. The Miles family were religious. They'd need the comfort of faith now more than ever.

A carrot-haired man answered the door. He looked older than his forty years. The dark rings under his eyes told of a sleepless, worry-filled night.

"Are you the officers?" A note of desperate hope slipped into his voice. The hope was the worst part. He still believed his little girl was alive.

Jed showed the man his badge. "Detective Jed Wallace. This is Detective Wolfe. We're from the Newburgh Police Department. Are you Gareth Miles?"

He nodded. "Yes. Please, come in."

The Miles family was not alone. A handful of women hovered in the kitchen. The concerned friends and neighbors whispered among themselves. Last night, their husbands had helped the father search for his daughter. Today, they had returned to work while their wives comforted the teary mother on the couch and told her everything would be all right. But nothing was all right. Things would never be all right again.

Fewer people had stuck around at Claire's parents' home after Tina's death. The Wolfes had moved to Newburgh from Boston only a few months before, little time to lay roots. Claire's maternal grandmother, Tessa, had rushed over from Boston to mourn her granddaughter, despite having fallen out with Claire's mom years ago. A few months later, she passed away, too. Misfortunes triggered each other like dominos. Sometimes, they left nothing standing.

A boy of twelve—Grace's younger brother, Claire assumed—sat on an armchair, idly kicking his feet, which dangled above the carpet.

Jed glanced at the somber onlookers, then turned to Gareth. "Could we speak with you and your wife in private?"

The husband swallowed hard. "Sure."

As Gareth approached his guests, Claire noticed the framed photo on the coffee table, and her heart pounded. Except for the devout, tight plaits, the girl with the golden hair, blue eyes, and dimpled cheeks looked exactly like Tina, Claire's dead sister.

The consolers muttered parting words of encouragement and filed out of the house. Gareth sent the boy, Paul, upstairs to his room. *Paul. Grace. And the crucifixes.* After today, would the girl's family still believe in divine justice?

The detectives sat opposite Grace's parents on the couches. Dispatch had called with their home address and general details. Gareth and Candace Miles paid their taxes and had never missed a mortgage payment on their home. Neither parent had a criminal record. Had Grace simply been in the wrong place at the wrong time or had she known her killer?

"Mr. and Mrs. Miles," Jed said. "I'm very sorry to inform you we've found Grace's body."

The wife shook her head slowly.

Gareth said, "Are you sure it's Gracie? Couldn't it be someone else?"

Claire and Jed glanced at each other. Did the father know about the victim's mutilated face, or was he in denial, the first stage of grieving?

"We're quite certain. We found her schoolbag at the crime scene. Her dental records and DNA will say for sure."

Grace's father blinked at them, waiting for them to provide more information, hoping they would change their minds and annul the verdict. His wife's sobs tugged him back to reality. He put his arm around her, holding her as his eyes glazed over.

"We need your help with some questions," Jed continued. "We're investigating her death as a homicide. The first forty-eight hours are critical to finding whoever is responsible. Do you mind?"

A slew of dark emotions crossed the mother's face. Exhaustion gave way to shock and pain, then anger. Candace Miles clenched her jaw but nodded. The guilt would come later.

"It's best if we speak with you separately."

Gareth and Jed moved to the kitchen, while Claire pulled

out her new Sony Digital Voice Recorder, a parting gift from her former partner, Ned Brooks. She placed the device on the coffee table.

"When did Grace go missing?"

"Yesterday afternoon," Candace said. "Gracie didn't come home from school."

Gracie. Claire noted the nickname. With all the paperwork, forensic science, and law enforcement jargon, a detective could forget the victim was a thinking, feeling human being with hopes and dreams of her own. Gracie would help her remember.

"That would be Newburgh Middle School?"

"Yes. Gareth drops her off every morning on his way to work."

"But the middle school is only a few blocks away."

"We like to see that she gets there safe and sound. I usually pick her up after school, but yesterday Gareth did." She glanced at her husband in the kitchen. "He took the day off to fix things around the house. She wasn't at the school gate, so Gareth went inside to look for her. None of her teachers or friends had seen her. She must have disappeared that morning, but we didn't even know..." She trailed off, sobbing.

Grace's parents had been protective of their daughter, just as Claire's mom had tried to protect Tina. Despite their best efforts, their worst nightmare had claimed their precious daughter. Claire knew what the mother was thinking. If only she had been more vigilant, maybe she could have saved her daughter?

"Was Gareth the last person to see her alive?"

"Yes. We called everyone we know. I drove around the city searching for her. My brother- and sister-in-law helped, too. We tried the hospitals."

"And when did you call the police?"

She studied her hands. "Only later that evening. We were so sure we'd find her."

The part of Claire that still mourned Tina wanted to comfort Gracie's mother. She wanted to tell her she could have done nothing to save her child, but Claire didn't know that for sure. The detective in her focused on finding the killer.

"Did she have any enemies?"

"No. Gracie was a sweet girl. Why would anyone hurt her?"

"Did she receive any unwanted attention from strangers or other adults?"

"Not as far as I know. She was only in touch with family and friends from school. We all go to church every Sunday, the New Baptist Church on Starlet Avenue. Gracie has ballet class twice a week. *Had*," she corrected herself. "She *had* ballet class."

Claire noted the name of the dance studio. "Could anyone have contacted her on social media and lured her away from school?"

"She didn't use social media. Gareth installed a child safety app on her phone—"

"She had a phone?" They had not found one at the crime scene.

"Just for calls. In case of an emergency. The app blocks sites that aren't safe for kids. Gareth tried to track her location yesterday, but her GPS was off."

"Is the phone here?"

"No. We looked for it everywhere."

Claire jotted down Gracie's phone number. She reviewed the mother's movements over the past forty-eight hours.

Jed returned to the living room with Gareth.

"We'll send someone over soon to take your fingerprints."

"*Our* fingerprints?" Gareth seemed alarmed at the possibility of becoming a suspect.

"It's standard procedure. We eliminate the prints we'd expect to find and focus on the others."

"Oh, I see."

"Do you mind if we take a look at her room?"

"No, of course not. I'll take you."

As Claire got up, she glanced at Gracie's framed portrait again, and a cold shudder crawled down her spine. The resemblance to Tina was uncanny. Claire and Jed followed Gareth up the staircase, floorboards creaking softly under their feet.

"This is Gracie's room," Gareth said. A sign on the door with glittery, flowing letters bore her name. There were no "keep out" warnings. Gracie's teenage-rebellion phase had not started yet and it never would. They followed Gareth inside.

A fantasy print of a unicorn hung on the wall above the bed. A full moon reflected in the still waters of a lake. Books and princess figurines filled the desk and shelves of white enameled wood. She had quite a collection. Claire wondered whether the Miles parents doted on their son the same way.

Jed pointed at the white MacBook Air on the desk. "We'll need this for our investigation."

"OK. She didn't use it much, just for school projects and stuff. You know how kids are with their phones." He laughed, then remembered his little girl was gone, and his lips squirmed with suppressed emotion.

Jed unfolded a plastic evidence bag from his pocket and slid the laptop inside. Then he scribbled details on the bag and a notepad and handed Gareth the receipt. They searched the drawers and closet but did not find the girl's phone.

"Do you need anything else?"

"Do you mind if we look around the house?"

"No. Go ahead."

"Do you have a shed?"

"Yeah. Out back."

Gareth led the way downstairs. Claire knew what Jed was thinking. It was a long shot—Gareth did not seem like a killer—but they had to rule him out.

Gareth cut through a narrow kitchen and opened a back door. Like the front garden, the backyard had received ample attention. They trampled neat squares of grass until they stood before the narrow wooden shed in the far corner. Gareth unlocked a rusty padlock, and the door swung outward. The two detectives could barely squeeze inside.

Gareth waved his hand at gardening and woodwork implements hanging on the wall. "I don't use the tools much anymore."

He was extremely well-organized for an amateur handyman. Each tool hung within an outline drawn on the wall with a thick black marker pen. The handsaw looked shiny and unused, unlike the hammer and the set of wrenches.

"I used to mess around with bits of furniture. Now it's just the occasional picture frame."

One outline stood conspicuously empty—an ax with a curved handle. The detectives exchanged meaningful glances. For one long, tense moment, Claire thought Gareth might slam the door and lock them in the shed.

The moment passed. Claire and Jed stepped outside. Either Gareth had no idea about the bloodied ax or he thought he'd disposed of it in the woods. As casually as possible, Claire checked that her Glock was within easy reach.

Jed cleared his throat. "Mr. Miles, where's your ax?"

Gareth bunched his eyebrows, then peered back inside and scratched his pumpkin-colored hair. "It was there last time I checked. Why?"

Jed shrugged. "No reason."

CHAPTER 5

Crickets chirped as Claire's feet hammered the sidewalks of Newburgh. Her nightly jogs helped clear her head, and tonight her head was full of dead girls.

The parents' accounts of their daughter's disappearance matched. After interviewing the Miles family, Jed and Claire had visited their neighbors, who had shared only kind words for Gracie and her family. The detectives picked up tuna sandwiches at a local deli on the way back to the station.

Jed called T-Mobile's forensics department and requested they email him the call list and tower locations for Gracie's missing phone. He made a note to send them the court order within three business days.

Back at the squad room, Gracie's schoolbag revealed her middling grades and love of Twinkies. Her MacBook contained school projects and a YouTube playlist devoted to Ed Sheeran. Neither provided leads for solving her murder.

A fourteen-year-old victim severely narrowed the detective's avenues for investigation, and the results of the forensic analysis might take weeks. To make matters worse, the patrol officers canvassing the neighborhood of the crime scene had discovered no eyewitnesses or household security camera footage.

Claire scheduled a meeting at the victim's school for the next day, then she inquired about street camera footage for the area. The killer would have used a vehicle to transport the body to the woods. Assuming the drop-off had taken place early that morning, Claire could flag any vehicles sighted during that time as suspicious. But as fate had it, the only red-light camera on Park Street had broken months ago. Newburgh was not Boston.

A visit to the few stores in the general vicinity provided three closed-circuit camera recordings. Designed to catch shoplifters, they had limited views of the street. By late afternoon, Claire's eyes watered from squinting at illegible registration plates captured in poor lighting conditions. She and Jed had only a shortlist of car makes and colors to show for their efforts. Had the killer known the area was a surveillance blind spot?

Seeing that Claire was new to the Department, Jed offered to write up the reports for the crime scene and initial investigation. Now *that* was the gallantry Claire appreciated. She needed to cut her new partner some slack. Newburgh PD was turning out better than she had expected.

A short drive in her beat-up white hatchback took her home to Harrow Street, a quiet lane hedged with red-brick buildings. The furnished rental had two bedrooms, a fully equipped kitchen, and a basement to boot. After living for years in a pokey downtown apartment, she'd satisfied her urge for wide living spaces. And quiet. In Boston, her upstairs neighbor had been both a concert pianist and a traditionalist. No electronic keyboards or headphones for him. Most nights Claire had fallen asleep with cushions clamped to her ears. There was only so much Chopin she could handle at one AM. She remembered that blessed silence whenever she thought of moving to smaller digs to save money.

Claire had changed into her running clothes and hit the streets of Newburgh, and now the rubbery thumps of her white Nike Air trainers on the sidewalk echoed off the residential homes.

Grace Miles had worn white sneakers, too. A fourteen-year-old girl, murdered. Just like Tina. Claire's first case had set an ominous tone for her new job. Two homicides, two fourteen-year-old girls, separated by twelve years. The girl's body in the woods rose in the theater of her mind. Just how similar were the murders? Claire knew very little about her sister's case. The way things were going, she'd learn nothing more.

Tina's case file was missing. The fact was another gloomy portent. But her experiences at Boston PD calmed her. The amount of paperwork a police department generated boggled the mind. It was a minor miracle that any case files survived the archaic manual filing process before modern technology digitized the paper trail.

Her years in law enforcement had prepared her for other disappointments, too. Most homicides resolved easily. The victims often died while engaged in other criminal activity. But if no promising leads emerged within the first few weeks, the Bureau would shelve the case. Police departments had to focus their limited resources on the warm cases the detectives were more likely to solve.

To the teenaged Claire, the lack of progress in Tina's investigation had seemed like a government cover-up or gross negligence. She had focused her anger and frustration on Detective O'Leary. Her muscles tensed at the mention of his name. But the reason Tina's killer had escaped justice was probably more mundane. Claire should blame municipal budget limitations, not the invisible hand of criminal conspirators.

She jogged on the spot, waiting for a red Honda Civic to pass. Claire knew about cars. Her dad would test her on the makes and models when he drove her around Boston. She'd helped him fix a 1957 Chevrolet Bel Air back in their good old days before they moved to Newburgh.

She crossed the street. Claire was glad Tina's file was missing. Was she emotionally prepared for the crime scene photos and ME reports in all their stark and impersonal detail? Was that how she wanted to remember her little sister?

Claire came to a halt and rested her hands on her knees. She had wandered further from her rental than she had intended. While thoughts of work and Tina had distracted her mind, her feet had carried her to Pine Hills and deposited her outside her parents' home. Her childhood home. The scene of the crime.

Lights flickered behind the living room drapes, the strobe effect of a television set. Was her dad home? Slick with sweat and empty-handed, Claire was in no state for a family reunion. *Family reunion.* Claire gave a short, mirthless laugh at her wishful thinking. What family? All traces of functional family life had disappeared into a dark lifeless hole along with Tina's coffin.

Claire knew one thing for sure. Her mother would not celebrate her return. Again, Claire's conscience twinged with guilt for not telling her parents she was back in town. Her dad would be happy to see her, wouldn't he?

She pulled out her phone and, catching her breath, dialed her old home number from memory. The number rang in her ear before it jingled in the house across the street. The shadows beyond the curtains shifted. What if her mother answered? Speaking with her would open the can of nasty worms Claire had kept sealed for years. She moved her thumb to the Cancel button when a gruff voice said, "Hello?"

"Dad, it's me, Claire."

"Claire!" The word animated his voice. "Where are you? Are you in Newburgh?"

"Yeah, I'm back."

"That's wonderful!" Her father's voice became distant as he turned away from the receiver. "Diane! Claire is back. Are you coming over now?"

"I can't tonight. But I will. Soon."

"Come over for dinner, Friday night. I'm cooking."

Today was Thursday. "Tomorrow night?" Claire had made no plans. She had no excuse to decline, and her father sounded so happy, so desperate to see her. "Um, OK."

"Excellent, Cub." *Cub*. Her dad had given her that nickname. *My little Wolfe cub*. He hadn't called her that in years. "We'll see you tomorrow."

He put down the phone. That was her dad—no frills or hesitation. Always to the point. His voice had sounded older and raspier than she remembered. Since leaving for the Academy, Claire had called only a handful of times. She had ended half of those calls when her mother had answered. Claire had faced hardened criminals in the streets, but she still fled from her mother. Her mother had loved Tina and Tina alone. Twelve years after Tina's death, Claire was still competing with her sister for their mother's love.

Claire drew a deep breath, turned around, and jogged back to her new home. Tomorrow. She'd open that can of worms tomorrow.

CHAPTER 6

Claire stood beside her dad as the ground swallowed the coffin. Gleaming in the dull sunlight, the polished wood descended slowly. The carved grooves and rounded surfaces seemed too beautiful to spend eternity in the ground. The halting movement reminded Claire of the mechanical puppy her father had bought her years ago from a stall at the Boston Harborwalk. Like the puppy, the funeral didn't seem real.

Claire didn't cry. She couldn't cry. Because Tina wasn't dead. Claire refused to believe it. She had seen burials on TV. In the funeral home, the casket was always open, allowing family and friends to say goodbye. The deceased would rest on white satin cushions, dressed in her finest clothes, her eyes closed, and a peaceful smile on her lips. But Claire had not seen her sister's body. The lid of the casket had remained shut the entire service. No, Tina wasn't in that box. She was too full of life to die. Her sister was playing another prank. Any moment, Tina would leap from her hiding place and laugh at their surprised faces.

No, Tina wasn't dead. Death was too boring for her. Newburgh could not contain her ambitions, so she had run off to find her fortune in the big wide world. Tina had fooled them all.

But her sister didn't show. Not during the service. Not at the graveside either. The priest chanted verses from the Bible in his sad voice while the coffin disappeared into the hole. Over the chatter of birds in the tall, leafy trees of the cemetery, a winch groaned and Claire's mom sobbed. Her dad stood by Claire, his tall, broad frame a warm, reassuring presence under cloudy skies.

Tina had abandoned them. She cared nothing for the hurt and heartbreak she had left behind. Years later, she might deign to think about them while she sipped a cocktail on a tropical beach. She would pity them and their small, ordinary lives. She'd laugh with disdain at her old family who still mourned her loss. Tina had no time for mourning. Why should Claire cry for her?

A dozen people stood around the grave. Claire's grandmother. Mothers from school. Strangers. When she caught them staring at her, their eyes darted to the gaping hole. One of them did not avert his gaze—the fat man with the brown suit and hat and wisps of gray hair. The stranger had broken the news of Tina's death to her parents in the living room. Despite his ruffled appearance, his eyes were sharp, and they studied Claire with interest. What was he searching for? Anger? Pain? Or was he wondering why Claire couldn't shed a tear for her dead sister?

The diggers shoveled earth into the hole. The clods thumped on the wooden box, and the pitch of her mother's sobs rose. Hands gripped Claire by the shoulders, pulling her away from the open grave and guiding her toward the car.

Five silent minutes later, they were home. Claire and her mom got out of the car. Her father did not. He had to drive Claire's grandmother back to Boston.

Mother and daughter stepped into the house. The living room seemed vacant and strangely unfamiliar, as though they had returned from a long vacation and had to readjust to their home. They hung their coats in the closet.

Claire was her mother's only daughter now, her only child, as she had been during the few sweet years before her sister's birth. Perhaps now Mom would love her again.

Mom lingered in the hallway. She seemed to have forgotten where she was or what she had wanted to do. Claire longed for her mother's touch. She yearned to comfort her and to be comforted.

"Mom, can I get you something to drink?"

Her mother glanced at her, but there was no glimmer of recognition in her eyes. She snarled.

"You little bitch!"

"Mom?"

Mom lost her temper often, but never like this.

"You think I don't know what you did?"

"I didn't do anything, Mom."

"You always hated her, always tried to hurt her. And now you've done it. You finally killed her."

Claire gasped. "What? No! Mom, I—"

"Don't act stupid! I know my own daughters. Tina was an angel, but you...you're the Devil!"

Her mother rushed at her. Claire turned and ran to the staircase.

"Murderer!" Mom yelled at her back. Her heavy footfalls hounded Claire while she climbed the steps. "Murderer!"

Claire raced down the corridor, her shoe sliding on the wooden floor as she dived into her room. She locked the door behind her.

The handle rattled. Fists hammered the door. "You killed her!"

Claire stepped away from the door, her legs trembling. What would Mom do to her?

"No, Mom. I didn't do anything."

This was unfair. Claire had done nothing wrong. Behind the door, her mother sank to the floor and moaned like a wounded animal.

"You were supposed to look after her."

"I tried to."

"The hell you did! I saw the blood. *Tina's* blood."

Claire remembered the blood, too. On her hands, her face, her leg. She'd slipped on the curb. That was *her* blood, not Tina's. Why wouldn't her mother believe her?

"Murderer." Mom no longer yelled, she just repeated the word over and over.

Claire hadn't killed Tina. She would remember doing *that*. But suddenly Claire wasn't sure. She rubbed at her palm, trying to wipe away the invisible bloodstain.

Claire's legs bumped into her bed frame, and she sat on the mattress. She'd never leave her room or look her mother in the eye again.

"Murderer." Mom's voice was a raspy groan of despair. "This is all your fault."

And then, Claire cried.

CHAPTER 7

"Think the father did it?" Jed asked Claire, Friday morning, from the driver's seat of his car.

Claire turned Jed's question over in her mind. Most female homicide victims knew their murderers. But Grace Miles was a teenager, not a battered wife or ex-girlfriend. She did not fit the usual profile, and Claire's gut insisted that Gareth had told the truth.

"He doesn't seem like the murdering type to me," she said, eventually.

"Did you see how jumpy he got when we mentioned the fingerprints?"

"That's not surprising. Most civilians think the police only fingerprint criminals. And it would upset any father to become a suspect in his daughter's murder."

"Not every father took the day off work the day his daughter turned up dead. He was the last person to see her alive, and he didn't report her missing until late that evening. I bet the ax at the crime scene has his prints all over it."

"That won't prove much. Anyone could have stolen the ax

from his shed. That lock was a joke. If he had killed her, he would have known not to use his own ax."

They cruised along the streets in silence. Everybody knew about fingerprints. Thanks to CSI shows on TV, civilians had learned a lot about forensic science. Or thought they had. The scriptwriters got much of their forensic science—and police procedures—wrong.

Gareth might know the fingerprints on his ax were useless in court. It didn't matter. If he had killed his daughter, Forensics would find other indications yet unknown to Hollywood. Law enforcement owed those scriptwriters a thank you. By grossly simplifying forensic science, they unintentionally provided a useful service to real police detectives and, by extension, the law-abiding public.

Either way, she and Jed shouldn't toss about such theories lightly. Losing a child was devastating enough—being accused of her murder would be unbearable. Had Detective O'Leary considered Claire's dad a suspect in Tina's murder?

Jed turned a corner but remained silent. Had she wounded his pride by questioning his theory?

Claire played Devil's advocate. "Assuming he did it, he had the means and opportunity, but what's his motive?"

Jed shrugged. "Maybe he abused her, and she threatened to tell her mom or social services."

Claire glanced at her partner. "I don't know. They're a religious family and they doted on Grace. That fancy laptop is proof enough."

"Maybe they're compensating. A religious family might cover up the abuse. I wouldn't be surprised if the wife is his accomplice."

Claire had to laugh. "Congratulations, Jed. You're even more cynical than me."

He smirked. "Thank you, Claire."

Claire sighed inwardly. She had sensed no friction between the parents. If Gareth had abused their daughter, the wife knew nothing. Soon, the detectives would test those suspicions.

They pulled into a cobblestone parking lot beside a blocky administrative building, and the ghostly fingers of déjà vu touched Claire again. The brown walls and tin roofs of Newburgh Middle School seemed frozen in time and reeked of tragedy.

Claire had never attended Newburgh Middle School, but she had walked her sister there and back every weekday. Every day but one. And on that day, Tina had died.

The long, uniform hallways conjured the familiar scents of waxy sandwich wrap and broken chalk. Posters on the walls promoted friendship and dental hygiene. An aura of order and calm radiated from the school. This was a safe space for young teens. But it was also one of the last public areas two fourteen-year-old girls had seen before meeting violent deaths.

The secretary at the reception counter had a corona of gray hair and black horn-rimmed glasses. She welcomed the detectives and led them down a corridor to the office of the principal, who awaited their visit.

Ms. Delores Maynard had an aquiline face that seemed too large for her petite body and thin neck. She rose from her desk to shake their hands, while Jed made the introductions. The principal had tied her black hair in a tight bun. A pair of horn-rimmed glasses sat on her nose. Were hornrims a requirement for all school staff?

"What a tragedy," she said. "My heart breaks just thinking about Gracie."

Despite the stern facade, her voice was warm and empathetic. A measure of earnest formality befitting the circumstances restrained her speech.

"Did you know her well?" Jed asked.

"I meet with each of our students."

"Are you aware of any issues at home?"

"No, but Ms. Evans can tell you more. She was Gracie's class teacher."

"Thank you. We'd like to ask her classmates a few questions, too. Individually."

"What questions?"

"The usual. When did they last see Grace? Did they notice anything strange over the past few days? Obviously, we won't mention any details of the actual homicide."

Ms. Maynard looked from Jed to Claire and seemed to weigh her options. "I suppose that's OK, but I might need to get their parents' permission before you question them further."

"No problem."

Detectives did not need parental consent to ask minors questions, but the principal was granting them access to Gracie's classmates, and Claire did not want to create obstacles.

"We'd also like to see her locker."

"Of course. We can stop there on the way to her classroom."

They followed her past the doors of brick-walled classrooms. The ghosts followed, too. The murdered girls had walked these corridors. Had they known their lives were about to end?

Gracie's locker contained a few schoolbooks and spare stationery, but no phone. They continued toward the classroom.

Claire took advantage of the stroll to scratch a mental itch. "How long have you been at Newburgh Middle School?"

"Seven years. Two as principal. I moved here with my family from Brookline to take the job."

Ms. Maynard had not taught at the school in Tina's day, and so she had not connected the two dead girls. With a gap of twelve years between the murders, the connection was very weak. Still, Gracie's resemblance to Tina had startled Claire, and her detective's sixth sense tingled.

"Have you spoken with the students about Gracie's death?"

By now, the students had heard about the murder from the media and their parents. But had the principal primed Gracie's classmates for the detective's questions?

"I only found out yesterday afternoon. Gracie's teacher broke the news to her class this morning. Our social worker will speak with each of her close friends to help them process their feelings."

Claire didn't remember getting any help "processing her feelings" at school when Tina had died. Times had changed. Maybe she could have used that.

"Is there a date for the funeral?"

"Not yet. We'll know in a few days." Claire did not mention the word autopsy.

They arrived at room 8B. The principal rapped her knuckles on the door and waited. A blonde woman about Claire's age opened the door, a book in hand. Like the principal, she sported spectacles and a tight hair bun. These glasses, however, had rounded gold frames. So much for Claire's theory about hornrims.

"These are the detectives," Ms. Maynard told the teacher softly. "May I speak with the class?"

"Yes, of course. Thank you, Ms. Maynard."

The teacher stepped into the corridor while her boss slipped into the classroom and closed the door. Claire didn't blame the teachers for their dominatrix dress code. Claire would rather enter a lion's den than teach middle school. And if forced to do so, she'd wear riot control gear. Jed introduced them to the teacher.

She shook their hands. "Lisa Evans."

Her skin was soft, her grip solid—the handshake of a

teacher on the front lines. Ms. Evans held the book to her chest and glanced at the floor. Was she blushing?

Jed arched his back. "Sorry to meet you under such sad circumstances. We need to ask you a few questions about Grace Miles."

Ms. Evans seemed to remember something, then opened the book at a dog-eared page. "Here she is. That's our Gracie."

Gracie. She pointed to a smiling girl, one headshot among rows of smiling children in the yearbook. Claire recognized Gracie at once from the framed photo at her parent's home.

"This is last year's class, but they're the same kids."

"Did you teach her last year as well?" Claire asked.

"No, this is my first year at Newburgh."

Jed shifted on his feet. "Fresh out of teacher's college?"

Again, Lisa blushed. "Yup. Fresh meat."

Claire observed her partner and the teacher. Their body language spoke loud and clear. Something was going on between these two. *The pretty young teacher meets the dashing detective*. Claire wanted to roll her eyes and tell them to get a room. She herded the conversation back to the case.

"You called her Gracie?"

"Everybody did. She was such a sweet girl."

Claire studied the photo. Gracie Miles looked every bit the part. But angelic appearances could deceive, as Claire knew only too well. "Did she fight with the other kids?"

Lisa shot Claire a glance, a flash of cool blue eyes. "No, she got along well with her classmates. Everybody seemed to like her."

Jed cleared his throat. "Had she been having any issues at home?"

"Not as far as I know. Her parents are good people."

"You know them?"

"Sure. They came to the parent-teacher meetings. Both of

them. Usually, just the one parent attends, but they said the meeting was very important to them."

The doting parents strike again. Or was Gareth concerned about what his wife might say if she attended the meeting alone? Claire dismissed the thought. He could have told her to stay home if he was a control freak. Again, Claire could not picture Gareth as a killer.

"Did you see Gracie at school on Tuesday?"

Lisa shook her head and frowned with regret. "She wasn't at school that day."

"Didn't that seem suspicious?" Claire had slipped easily into the "bad cop" role. Gracie's parents had not noticed she was missing until the end of the school day, but her teacher must have known much earlier.

"No, not really. Grace had cut class often these past few weeks."

Claire's ears pricked up. "She cut class?" Maybe Gracie wasn't the model daughter after all.

"Just a few times. Usually toward the end of the day."

Finally, Jed got back into gear. "Do you know why?"

Lisa shrugged. "They're teenagers. The rebellious phase passes eventually. I didn't make a big deal of it."

"I understand." Jed turned to Claire. "Anything else?"

"Do you mind if we borrow that?" Claire glanced at the yearbook, now firmly pressed against the teacher's chest.

"Please. Keep it. Anything that might help the investigation. We have other copies."

Claire accepted the book. "Thank you."

Jed pulled a card from his breast pocket and handed it to the pretty teacher. "This is my number. If you remember anything else, call me. Don't hesitate."

Another blush, another demure glance at the floor, and she

took the card. "Thank you, Detective Wallace." The teacher swayed her hips.

This time, Claire did roll her eyes.

"Is the class ready for us now?"

Ms. Lisa Evans gave her a tight smile. Did she see Claire as the competition? "Let's see."

They followed the teacher into the classroom. Claire had never seen such a quiet and well-behaved group of teenagers. Ms. Maynard joined the principal at the front of the class and in a crisp, commanding voice introduced the police detectives. The kids' eyes sparkled. The detectives had the full attention of twenty-five fourteen-year-olds. They moved a few desks and chairs to opposite corners of the room and interviewed Gracie's classmates one by one while the teachers looked on and the kids traded whispers.

None of the children had seen Grace on Tuesday, nor had they noticed her talking to strangers on the school property. Claire made a mental note to interview the school's janitors and groundskeepers.

Some kids asked questions of their own. "How did she die?" the boy with the immense black fringe had asked. He seemed to have spent the morning blow-drying his hair. Claire had brushed off the question, saying the details were not public knowledge. A girl asked whether she was in danger, seeing the killer was "still on the loose." The girl was parroting her parents' concerns. With a comforting smile, Claire told her not to worry.

"That is all for today," Ms. Maynard said once the interviews had concluded. "If you have any additional information, contact the school office and we'll be in touch with the detectives. You have free time for the rest of the lesson."

An excited hum passed among the kids. The detectives thanked Ms. Maynard and Ms. Evans and followed them outside. The corner of Claire's mind itched. An important detail was missing.

"Anything else, Detectives?" the principal asked.

Claire said, "We'd like to speak with the janitors, gardeners, and other adults who work on the grounds."

"Of course. I'll call them to the staff room."

"Thank you. We'll be right along."

They watched Ms. Maynard's back recede down the corridor.

"Anything interesting?"

Jed glanced at his notepad. "Not from her classmates. But skipping class might be a sign of trouble at home. Or it might mean nothing. Let's hope the forensic report finds something solid. If not, we can return to the Miles home with a warrant. I'd like to see what he's got in his basement."

"Detective Wolfe?"

They turned. A girl stood beside them, her hands clasped together, her fingers fidgety.

The principal had disappeared and so had Ms. Evans. There was no harm in fielding one more question. "Yes?"

"About Gracie. It's probably nothing, but I don't want to get into any trouble." She glanced down the corridor.

Claire gave her a reassuring grin. "You won't. What's your name?"

"Drew. Drew Ellison."

"Nice to meet you, Drew. What did you want to tell us?"

"Gracie was acting weird the last few weeks."

"In what way?"

"I don't know. She became very quiet like she had secrets."

Jed met Claire's gaze. This was just the information he'd been hoping for.

"I think she had a boyfriend."

"What's his name?"

"I don't know. I never saw him, but Grace would meet up with him after school. Sometimes she'd leave school early to see him." Drew's face scrunched up like she was going to cry. "Gracie was my friend."

Claire touched the girl's shoulder. A hug from a homicide detective on the case would be inappropriate. "Thanks for telling us. You did the right thing."

Jed handed her a card. "Call me if you remember anything else."

The girl took the card in both hands and hurried back indoors.

"Bingo," Jed said. "The parents didn't mention a boyfriend."

"Neither did the neighbors. Gracie hid him well."

"The brother might know something." Jed consulted his notepad. "Paul."

"Her phone," Claire said. "We have to get that phone."

Forget the eyes—the cell phone was the window to a person's soul. And Gracie's phone held the key to her last hours and her mystery boyfriend.

Jed's phone beeped, and he swiped it open. "T-Mobile sent the phone records to my email. I'll check them when we get back."

"Excellent." Claire smiled. For the first time, things were looking up.

Their meetings with the two janitors and gardener proved less fruitful. None remembered Gracie, and school rules prohibited them from talking with students. They had noticed no suspicious older boys or men.

By the time Claire and Jed returned to the car, a TV van had parked across the street, and camera operators were setting up their equipment.

"The hyenas don't waste any time," Jed mumbled.

"Aren't they supposed to be vultures?"

"Nah. Vultures can fly, and I'm not a dog person."

A young woman got out of the van and adjusted her mane of auburn hair using a small makeup mirror. When she spotted the detectives, she grabbed a digital recorder from her tote bag and ran toward them at a brisk, determined pace.

Jed fastened his seatbelt. "Bella Winters. She writes for *The Newburgh Herald*. Watch out. She bites."

Claire often found speaking with the press easier than evading them. Reporters were just doing their jobs, and some served as useful assets. But she didn't argue.

"Detective Wallace," the reporter yelled through the glass of the closed window. "Have you made any progress in the Miles murder?"

Jed started the ignition, mimed the words "no comment," and pulled off.

Claire agreed. So far, all they had was conjecture. But one thing was certain. Gracie Miles had secrets.

CHAPTER 8

Captain Emmerso's blood pressure spiked when his boss stormed into his office that afternoon and slammed the door behind him. Chief Harry Wallace only materialized in the captain's office if something went wrong. Emmerso braced himself for the worst. They didn't call the chief "Dirty Harry" for nothing.

Chief Wallace skipped all pleasantries and slapped a folded newspaper on the captain's desk. "How do you explain this?" The headline read, "No Leads on Newburgh Teen Murder."

Chief Wallace leaned his bulky frame on the desk, his knuckles whitening on the surface, so he could tower over his subordinate like a uniformed King Kong. Ten years his senior, the chief had used that time to cultivate a beer belly and a permanent scowl, both of which he now aimed at the Investigations Bureau captain.

Emmerso cleared his throat. "We're making progress."

His boss cut him off. "Progress isn't enough. We need an arrest."

Emmerso believed that progress often led to the arrest of

the true culprit, whereas skipping the investigation did not. But his instinct for self-preservation told him not to argue the point.

"A little girl was butchered in our city," Chief Wallace grumbled. Then, in case Emmerso had misinterpreted his words as moral indignation, he added, "The press is all over this like maggots. Mayor Thornton is up for reelection in six months. I remind you that the mayor appoints the chief of police. A new mayor might show his concern for citizen safety by lopping off heads down the chain of command. Have I made myself clear?"

"Crystal, sir."

When angry words didn't do the job, throw in the casual threat of summary firing. Emmerso guessed that the chief's early career had included a long stint as a drill sergeant. Old habits die hard.

"Now I understand your detectives have got something on the kid's father."

A lump of annoyance swelled in Emmerso's gut, weakening his survival instinct. Detective Jed Wallace had taken his theory straight to the chief. Under normal circumstances, Emmerso would have hauled the detective over the coals for insubordination. But Jed was also the chief's son, a small but important detail.

"Gareth Miles." Emmerso had studied the detectives' reports.

"So, what are you waiting for?"

"Evidence. And—"

Chief Wallace cut him off. "Then get the evidence. We need an arrest pronto before this case turns into a cluster."

Emmerso forced his lips shut. According to The Innocence Project, the United States penitentiary system housed twenty thousand wrongfully convicted inmates, and Emmerso had no desire to add to their number.

"He's not a flight risk. We'll surveil him and see what happens."

"Good." Chief Wallace rose to his full height and lumbered out of the office, swinging the door shut behind him.

Captain Emmerso sighed. As much as he hated the chief's aggressive management style, he understood the pressures he faced, too. Those pressures were the reason Emmerso had no ambitions for further advancement. He preferred to serve here, his ear close enough to the ground that he could measure his success by the number of lives saved and perps locked away instead of approval ratings and budget allocations.

He got to his feet, opened the door, and called Detectives Wallace and Wolfe into his office. Emmerso perched on the edge of his desk.

"What do we have on the Miles murder?"

Jed tried to hide his smirk. "The ax belongs to the father. The prints match him. We're still waiting on the full forensic analysis."

"When will that be ready?"

"I don't know. The county forensics lab has a chronic backlog."

Emmerso eyed his officers. "Do you think he did it?"

The detectives exchanged silent glances. Did they disagree on that point?

Jed answered. "The father has no alibi. He took the day off work to fix things around the house. But the case isn't airtight."

"Motive?"

"We found no indicators of domestic abuse. The decedent had cut class, allegedly to meet a boyfriend. Maybe the father found out and confronted the victim? For now, the boyfriend is just a rumor. Her bag and laptop gave us nothing. There's no relevant camera footage either. We're still trying to locate the girl's phone. Recent calls trace to the general area of the school and her home. A prepaid number appears on several calls—a burner phone or just another kid."

Emmerso chewed his lip. They had a weapon and conjecture—not enough to convince the DA to press charges and certainly not enough for a conviction.

"Anything else?"

Claire pursed her lips but said nothing.

Jed placed his hands on his hips. "Sir, let's bring the father in. I'll get him to talk. And an arrest will get the media off our backs."

Emmerso clenched his jaw. The media was the mayor's problem, not theirs.

"Do you know how many people burned at the stake for witchcraft in the Middle Ages?"

The detectives blinked at him. The police academy's course list did not include Medieval history, but Emmerso was making a point.

"Far more than you think. Most denied the charges at first but confessed later under torture. Apply enough pressure and people will admit anything. Thankfully, those days are long gone."

Emmerso sighed. "You know how things work. Once we arrest him, the clock starts ticking. We must bring him before a judge within forty-eight hours. Seeing that today is Friday, the bereaved father will spend the weekend in jail. When we eventually have to let him go, the media won't forgive and forget. And neither will the jury of public opinion. People will think he got off on a technicality. We'll have ruined his life."

Emmerso let his words sink in. Shoehorn a man into a conviction and you're the criminal. But Jed wasn't ready to give up.

"Sir, we can at least search his home. He might consent

without a warrant. That will show the city we're making an effort, and we might get a lucky break."

Emmerso turned to his recruit. "Detective Wolfe, what do you think?"

Her eyes widened. She seemed startled that he'd asked her to take sides. Jed's lips stretched thin and white, but he didn't look at his new partner. Was he worried about what she might say? Would she question his judgment in front of their commanding officer?

"You're both right. We don't have enough information. Can Forensics speed things up?"

Emmerso smiled. Claire had wriggled out of that one with a diplomatic response, satisfying both sides and neither. Along the way, she'd given her boss some homework. He deserved that for putting her on the spot. He'd underestimated her. Claire was good at politics. She'd rise high in the department someday.

Emmerso glanced at his wristwatch. *Friday evening already?* "Grace Miles died two days ago," he said. "The first forty-eight have passed. I'll speak with Forensics and see what they can do. Meanwhile, do the paperwork for surveilling the girl's father. His phone, too. That's all, Detectives."

Jed and Claire filed out of his office. Emmerso drummed his fingers on his desk. He had one dead fourteen-year-old girl and zero solid leads in a gruesome murder case that was becoming more high profile by the minute. The chief was breathing down his neck, and Emmerso had sensed a rift between the detectives leading the investigation. The county forensics lab might not be enough to save his neck. He needed to hedge his bets.

Emmerso reached for his desk phone. It was time to call in favors.

CHAPTER 9

With the sun setting over Newburgh, Claire prepared to face her fears. She parked her white Ford Focus hatchback on the curb outside her parents' home. Sitting behind the wheel, she drew two deep breaths. *Get out of the car and knock on the front door*. Why did that seem so difficult?

A thick fog hung over her childhood memories, and she had trouble distinguishing facts from fantasy. As day transformed into night, Claire prepared to cross a forbidden threshold, entering a murky realm where reality was less than certain. In that sinister Twilight Zone, the ground beneath her feet could disappear at any moment.

You can do this, Claire. The girl who had grown up in that house had feared her own shadow. During the ten years since she'd left home, Claire had graduated from the Academy, patrolled the mean streets of Boston, and won her detective promotion. She had returned to Newburgh as a successful, independent woman with a purpose. Tonight, she would take another step toward exorcising her past. Claire would complete that process when she put Tina's killer behind bars.

Still, this visit terrified her more than Grace Miles's crime scene and the Miles family house of mourning put together. Her childhood home combined the horrors of both.

Claire got out of the car. She forced her legs to walk down the short driveway and onto the front porch. The place seemed smaller than she remembered. The wood-board walls had recently gained a fresh coat of paint. Her father had been keeping himself busy around the house. A television projected flickering light onto the drapes along with the murmuring of recorded voices.

She pressed the buzzer. The sound echoed within above the hum of the television. Her father would be at home. He was expecting her. Something moved indoors. *Too late to turn back now.*

The door opened. An old woman stood in the doorway. Gray streaks had invaded her untamed bush of blonde hair like weeds. Despite the sunken eyes, deep wrinkles, and hunched back, Claire still recognized her mother. Before Tina's death, Diane had taken pride in her appearance. She would never have answered the door in a threadbare bathrobe and mouse-gray slippers. The old woman at the door didn't bother with makeup or hair dye.

Diane Wolfe stared at Claire with shifty eyes, her head wobbling. Did she recognize her daughter after all these years? Claire, too, had changed.

"Well, well, well," Mom said. "The killer returns to the scene of the crime."

Without waiting for a response, she turned her back on her visitor and shuffled back indoors. Claire stepped inside and closed the door behind her. The paint on the kitchen cupboards had faded from years of use. Shuffling feet had created a path along the hall carpet. Her mother followed the path to the La-Z-Boy opposite the television and ignored her daughter.

Claire breathed a sigh of relief. *So far so good.* Mom had let her in. She had not yelled or hurled insults. Had Diane mellowed with time?

Her mother limped along. "Watch out for the spiders. Huge suckers."

Claire scanned the living room walls and ceiling but found no arachnids. *What was that about?* The La-Z-Boy groaned as Mom flopped on the padded seat. She had put on around thirty pounds since Claire had seen her last, and her ankles had swollen.

Claire approached the couch. She'd welcome an evening of watching TV with Mom. Wasn't that what normal families did? For years, a normal relationship with her mother had seemed impossible.

She sat on the couch, and her early optimism turned to stone in her chest. An old family movie played on the screen. Claire recognized the scene—Tina's tenth birthday party. There she stood, the golden-haired angel with the dimpled cheeks and sapphire eyes. Tina blew out the candles on the chocolate cake Mom had baked and made a wish. She tore open her birthday presents, all smiles. The camera shifted, and Claire floated across the screen for a split second, a gloomy, dark presence that haunted the backdrop.

Did her mother know she was coming over tonight? Had she selected the video to send Claire a message? *Don't think for a moment that I've forgotten. Or forgiven.*

Her mom knocked back a Bud Light, shaking the can to empty the last drops of beer into her mouth. Then, she crumpled the can with practiced ease, tossed it onto the carpet, and opened another from the six-pack beside the recliner. She didn't offer Claire a beer.

"Is Dad home?"

Mom didn't answer. She was exactly where Claire had left

her five years ago—older and heavier but still fingering the festering sore in her heart, a hurt she had learned to cherish.

But something else had changed. Her mother had never missed an opportunity to pounce on her only living daughter. Her supply of barbed words had been limitless. Now she seemed to have forgotten Claire was there. Add to that the talk of non-existent spiders and Claire arrived at an unsettling conclusion. Mom was still there in body, but her mind had faded. If Claire had sought to reconcile with her mother, she had returned home too late.

Claire got to her feet and climbed the staircase. The wooden steps creaked beneath her pumps, but Mom didn't budge from the television and her beer.

Claire opened the door to Tina's room. Her bed was made, the frilly white linen decorated with red hearts. The fantasy posters of Grace Miles were too innocent for Tina. A single studio shot of Orlando Bloom hung on the wall. He struck a James Dean devil-may-care pose, his leather jacket flapping casually over a white undershirt. A row of Barbie dolls stood at attention on a shelf, all blonde-haired, blue-eyed, and perfect. Like Tina. Her sister had controlled the dolls with possessive fury, and God help those who dared touch them.

Eighth-grade workbooks lay in a tidy pile on the desk. Tina had printed her name on the labels in her round, exact handwriting. Her sister's headshot smiled at her from a frame on the center of the desk, a devotional image at the heart of a sacred shrine.

Claire picked up the framed photograph. For weeks after Tina's funeral, Claire had clung to the belief that her sister hadn't died, that she had run away from home. Standing in Tina's room, preserved exactly as Tina had left it, Claire almost believed that Tina might walk back in. "Hi, everyone, I'm home!" she'd call, blowing inside with tales of travel and conquest as though she hadn't abandoned her family twelve years ago.

Tina was never coming home. Claire had. She had grown up and made her way in the world, and she had the bruises to prove it. But Tina would remain forever blonde-haired, blue-eyed, and fourteen years old. Perfect.

Other recollections surfaced, troubling memories Claire had buried deep in her mind. A storm of conflicting emotions raged within her. On the one hand stood the heavenly, dimpled angel, the Tina who offered Claire chocolate chip cookies fresh from the oven in her mittened hands. But Tina had a dark side, too. Only Claire had glimpsed this Tina, the cruel demon who knew no limits and sprang on Claire without warning, its claws and teeth bared.

Claire placed the photograph back on the desk. Had she imagined that version of Tina? Sibling rivalry was as old as Cain and Abel. Had Claire projected her worst desires on her little sister? She could no longer tell.

Claire left Tina's room and opened the door to her own. Or she tried to. The door caught halfway and refused to budge. She reached her arm inside and turned on the light. The corner of a brown packing box peeked around the door. Claire shouldered her way forward, creating an opening wide enough for her to slip inside.

The box had company. Stacks of them, some taped shut, others overflowing with old magazines, defunct desk lamps, and light fixtures rose from the carpet and occupied the bed. Plastic sheeting, now gray with dust, covered the naked mattress. Tina's room awaited her sister's immediate return, but Claire's had become a storage space. The message was obvious. Nobody was hoping for Claire to move back.

"Claire," someone said behind her.

She spun around, her hand instinctively reaching for her

holster. A tall, thin man stood in the hallway, flecks of gray hair at his temple.

"Dad. Geez, you startled me."

He spread his arms. Claire slipped back through the narrow opening of the door and into his embrace. She lingered in his arms, a little girl with her daddy. Only this little girl matched her daddy in height. Claire surrendered to the warm, comforting sensation. A tear materialized in the corner of her eye, but she didn't care. When had someone last hugged her?

"Welcome back, Cub. It's so good to see you."

"Same here." Claire wiped the tear from her eye and pulled away. "I see you put my old room to good use."

Her dad gave her a sheepish grin. "Your mom wanted me to tidy things up. Back in the days when the mess bothered her." His expression darkened for a moment, then he found a happy thought. "But I kept your books. Go on, have a look."

Claire poked her head back inside. A pile of thick textbooks rose on her desk. *Police Operations: Theory and Practice. Forensic Science: An Introduction. Law Enforcement Field Guide.* Those subjects had not featured on the Hannover High book list.

When Detective Brian O'Leary's visits to the Wolfe home ended, Claire had made a decision. If the police were ineffective idiots, she'd solve the crime herself. She devoted every moment of her free time to studying police procedures and forensic science.

Her dad buried himself in his work. Her mother sank into a pit of alcohol and self-pity. Claire dived into the world of law enforcement. Each member of the family coped with Tina's loss in his and her way. Two years later, Claire's coping mechanism had become her career.

With her high grades, Claire could have studied anything. Scholarships had fallen into her lap. The pathways to lucrative careers in law and medicine beckoned. But to her teachers' horror, Claire applied at the police academy instead. If her dad regretted her wasted potential, he never showed it. He had kept her old textbooks on her desk, the well-thumbed pages now crusted with dust.

"I want to show you something," he said.

She followed him downstairs and into the kitchen. Her mom, still glued to the television screen, didn't stir as they walked by. He opened a cupboard door, withdrew a hardcover from among the cookbooks, and opened it on the counter.

Newspaper cuttings covered the pages. "Boston PD Foils Bank Heist." "Respected Journalist Found Dead." "Mayor Celebrates Drop in Crime." In each article, a yellow marker highlighted Claire's name, first as Officer C Wolfe, then Detective Claire Wolfe. Her father had created a scrapbook of her every media mention.

"You've been stalking me."

"Guilty as charged. And there's this." He slid a newspaper over, *The Newburgh Herald*, and pointed to a brief article on page eight. "Newburgh PD welcomes new detective."

Claire scoffed. "Must be a slow news day."

Her stab at humor masked her guilt at not letting him know she was back in town.

"You could have stayed here, you know?"

Claire laughed. "No way. Have you seen my room? It's a mess." As one person, they glanced at her mother in the living room, the real reason she could never move back home.

Her father nodded with silent understanding. "I'll get started on dinner."

"I'll help."

They got busy in the kitchen. Her father chopped vegetables and basted a whole chicken, while Claire set the dinner table. During her absence, her father had learned to cook, and soon the house filled with the warm smells of microwave chicken.

Her dad turned off the television set and led her mother to the table. They tucked in, the clatter of busy cutlery punctuating the silence.

"Claire has transferred to Newburgh PD," her dad said. The glow of the light fixture above the dinner table emphasized the liver spots on his forehead and the creases at the corners of his eyes. The years had chipped away at him, too.

Mom looked up as though seeing her for the first time. Claire rummaged for details of her new job she could share with her mom, details that did not involve the murder of a fourteen-year-old girl.

"I'm closer to home now." She hazarded a smile but braced for an attack. None followed. Instead, her mother's eyes widened with fear.

"Have you seen the spiders?"

Claire shot her dad a glance. He stared at his plate of food, and his chewing slowed.

"No, Mom."

"Big suckers. All hairy legs. They climb the walls and ceiling. Bill thinks I'm crazy, but I see them." Then, she laughed, louder and longer than was comfortable.

Her dad touched her shoulder. "Diane, there's no need to worry Claire about that."

Her mother ignored him. "There's a pink one. A red one, too, the brightest red you've ever seen." Her face folded in terror. "They're horrible!"

"How are your coworkers?" her dad asked.

Claire pounced on the change of topic. "I like my boss. The other detectives seem nice enough, too."

Mom glanced at them in momentary confusion. Then, she picked up her knife and fork and resumed eating. The diversion seemed to have succeeded. Her dad had learned to work around her mother's hallucinations.

"Easing into things slowly?"

"No, not at all. We got a homicide on the first day and are getting busier by the minute. But the department runs by the book, and I think—"

The thump of a fist on the table cut Claire off mid-sentence. Plates rattled in the aftershock. Mom glared at her across the table, her knife clenched in her fist.

"You want a murderer?" She pointed the knife at Claire. "There's one sitting right here."

"Diane—"

"Don't Diane me. Can't you see what she is? Don't you know what she's done?"

Claire's knife and fork clattered onto her plate.

Her dad grabbed his wife by the arm. "Diane, it's time for your pills."

"I don't need any pills!" Diane shook free of his grip and pointed the knife at him. "You're trying to poison me!"

Slowly, her dad reached out and removed the knife from her hand. "Calm down, Diane. You're making a scene."

"I don't care!" She turned on Claire again, her eyes burning, her cheeks wobbling with rage. "Murderer!" she cried. "Murderer!"

Claire sprang to her feet. The chair crashed to the floor behind her, but she didn't stop to pick it up. With chicken churning in her stomach acids, she marched to the front door.

"Claire," her dad said. "Please, wait..."

But Claire didn't wait. She opened the door and fled into the night.

CHAPTER 10

Claire sat in the driver's seat and cried. The glow of the ceiling light dimmed, and the car's interior merged with the cold darkness outside. She had never felt so alone.

This was a mistake. She should never have come home. What had she been thinking—that she could turn back the clock? That Mom would change? She had raced back to Newburgh expecting to solve Tina's murder and make everything right. But Tina's file was missing. Claire had no hope of finding the truth. And even if she did—what good was that? No matter how many killers she put behind bars, she would never bring Tina back. What was she doing there?

Claire punched the steering wheel. She hated her mother. She hated herself for loving her, for needing her approval. After all the disgust and anger Mom had heaped on her over the years, Claire should know better. *Stupid girl. Stupid, stupid, girl!*

Knuckles rapped on the glass at her ear, startling her. Her father stood on the sidewalk. Claire wiped her eyes and rolled down the window.

"I'm sorry about that, Claire. She seemed calm today."

"It's OK. We'll try another time." *In another ten years.*

"Please don't go." Before Claire could protest, he added, "I'm taking her up to bed now. We should talk. Please. Stay awhile."

Claire should have driven home already instead of crying in the dark like a little girl, but she couldn't refuse him now. "OK."

"Thanks, Cub. Give me a few minutes."

Claire drew more deep breaths to cool off. Then, she got out of the car and let herself in. The floorboards shifted overhead as her parents moved about. The dinner table was a battlefield of chicken bones and dirty dishes. Claire packed the leftovers into Tupperware and placed them in the refrigerator. She cleared the table and washed the dishes in the kitchen sink.

Claire was the lucky one. She had escaped to Boston and started a new life. Her dad had stayed home. His daughter's death might have broken him inside, but he had put on a brave face for them all. He had weathered the dark years while her mom sank into depression and tried to drown her sorrows in a sea of beer. Now he had become her mother's nurse. Claire pictured him upstairs, dressing her mom and combing her hair, ensuring she took her pills and telling her everything would be all right.

That was real love. Claire found a kitchen towel and dried the dishes. She wasn't sure she was capable of that level of devotion. After Tina's death, finding love and settling down had seemed selfish. How could she think of romance when her sister's corpse decomposed in the ground and her murderer walked free?

The only hint of carefree romance in Claire's life lay buried in the distant past—before the Wolfes had moved to Newburgh and their lives had gone to hell. In her Bostonian middle school, Robbie Cline had not been her boyfriend, but he might have been. While studying biology together in his bedroom late one afternoon, they had kissed. A few days later, her parents had packed up their household and relocated to a small city with a name Claire had never heard before.

Tessa, Claire's maternal grandmother, had not approved of the move. She had not approved of Claire's dad either, but she had seen them off. Claire would have looked her grandmother up in Boston when she'd joined the police force, but Tessa had passed on a year after Tina. "Dead from heartache," Claire's mother had said. Tessa had reunited with Tina, and Claire's mother longed to join them.

Claire hung the dish towel to dry, then searched for another distraction. From her car, she fetched the middle school yearbook that Lisa Evans, Gracie's teacher, had given her, and she curled up with the magazine on the living room couch.

She found the picture of Gracie Miles, her blue eyes flashing with youthful innocence. Claire traced the familiar, perfect smile with her finger. Her similarity to Tina was uncanny and a little disturbing. If Claire had believed in reincarnation, she would have suspected that Gracie was Tina's reborn soul. But Gracie had entered this world two years before Tina's death. So much for reincarnation.

Claire flipped the pages and read the text. Gracie enjoyed ballet and apple pie. Under the section entitled "Twenty years from now...," Gracie had predicted that she'd have a husband and four kids. Two boys and two girls. Tina would never have chosen that future for herself. *Sorry, Gracie. Twenty years from now, you'll be bones in a box.*

Again, the similarities gave Claire pause. Two homicides of identical fourteen-year-old girls in Newburgh, twelve years apart. Did Tina and Gracie share more than perfect smiles and tragic ends? Had Tina's killer murdered Gracie, too? Why had he waited twelve years to kill again?

Claire dismissed the theory. For starters, Claire still knew nothing about Tina's death. Mentioning her sister's file would raise eyebrows. Captain Emmerso would shoot down the idea as wild conjecture, and rightly so. Gracie's murder was simply a weird but entirely random coincidence.

She studied the photos of Gracie's classmates. Twenty young girls stared back at Claire, but only a handful had her golden hair and deep-ocean eyes. Hypothetically speaking, if Gracie and Tina shared a killer, what new leads would that theory create?

Claire got up, the yearbook in her hands, and returned to the kitchen. She found a ballpoint pen beside the telephone on the kitchen counter and a notebook of yellow, lined paper. Paging through the yearbook, she found more girls who matched the dead girls' profiles. Karla Smith. Dana Wood. Amy Collins. Earlier that day, Gracie's classmate had asked whether she was in danger, too. Claire had told her not to worry, but now her gut itched. She jotted down the first girl's name, Karla Smith.

Footfalls sounded on the stairs. Claire tore the yellow page from the notepad, folded it into her pocket, and closed the yearbook on the counter.

"The baby is asleep," her dad said. He glanced at the clean dinner table and spotless kitchen. No trace remained of the meal. "Thank you, Claire. You didn't have to clean up."

"It's the least I could do. You've got enough on your plate, Dad."

His grin radiated appreciation, and his eyes drifted to the yearbook. "What you got there?"

"Just a...work matter. We shouldn't talk about it. I'm sorry about earlier."

"You have no reason to apologize."

"I should have seen that coming. She's always hated me. Even before Tina died."

"She doesn't hate you."

Claire gave her dad an are-you-kidding-me look, and he changed the subject.

"You want a smoke?"

Claire raised her eyebrows. "Since when do you smoke?"

"For the record, I don't smoke. But I might sneak a cigarette from time to time."

"I would never have guessed."

"There's a lot you don't know about me, Cub." He jerked his head toward the back door. "C'mon."

He extracted a lighter and a half-empty pack of Lucky Strike cigarettes from a kitchen drawer and made for the back door. Claire followed.

They sat on the backyard steps under the amber light of a naked bulb. Long tufts of wild grass broke through the cracked, hardened dirt. Judging by the well-tended front lawn, passersby would never imagine the sorry state of their backyard. Pretty on the outside but falling apart within. That summed up her family life well.

Her dad lit up, took a long drag, and blew smoke into the night. He handed the cigarette to Claire. She put the filter to her lips and inhaled. Having avoided nicotine all her childhood, she had smoked her first cigarette, ironically, in the Academy, egged on by her fellow trainees. After a long day of the Academy's grueling military-style regimen, a few drags had provided a dose of non-conformist comfort. Years had passed since her last cigarette, but tonight she puffed out a single perfect smoke ring on her first try. They watched the ring diffuse in the chilly air.

He grinned. "You've done this before, haven't you?"

She handed back the cancer stick. "There are things you don't know about me either, Dad."

A lump of guilt lodged in her throat, marring the intimate moment. She thought of other things her father didn't know—things she kept secret. Things relating to Tina. If he ever found out, he'd see Claire in a very different light. He might not share the back porch with her again.

Claire turned their minds to the good old days before Newburgh. "Fix up any old cars lately?"

Her father chuckled. "Nah, I've been too busy with work... and stuff."

Like nursing his wife. Again, her heart wept for her dad's situation. His job as a salesman used to take him far and wide, but now he needed to stay closer to home.

He exhaled a plume of smoke into the night. "Your mother wanted to be a singer," he said, apropos of nothing.

"A singer?"

"Mm-hmm. When we met, she sang in a band. Folk music mostly. They had a few gigs in bars. Nothing fancy."

Claire hadn't known that about her mother. She couldn't recall Mom ever singing. "Why'd she stop?"

"She fell pregnant with you, and we weren't married."

Claire looked at her dad. "You had a shotgun marriage?" Her parents were always so by the book, so conventional. She couldn't imagine her mother ever having sex, never mind getting pregnant out of wedlock.

He shrugged and smiled. "That makes you a love child."

He handed back the cigarette. Her father had a warm, rambling conversational tone like an old cowboy. This was the Bill Wolfe his customers knew and loved. It also made him a great salesperson.

"It wasn't your fault she stopped singing," he continued. "Diane could have gotten back to it after you were born. That didn't stop her from blaming you." The cigarette passed between them again. "She blamed me, too, saying we were part of some conspiracy to ruin her life. She was right, of course. We have more in common than you think."

Claire laughed at his ironic joke and blew another smoke ring. "I have to agree, Dad, now I've learned your dark little secrets."

He glanced at her. "And yet, you're still here."

"It'll take a lot more to chase me away."

She handed him the cigarette. Claire liked this—sitting with her dad, reminiscing, sharing secrets—and she wanted more.

Her dad sighed. "Then, Tina was born. Tina was *her* child, Diane said. The baby girl had blonde hair and blue eyes just like her. As soon as Tina could speak, she sang. As soon as she could walk, she danced. Tina was Mom's little protégé. She was going to grow up and fulfill all your mom's old dreams." He stubbed out the cigarette on the concrete step. "When Tina died, Diane fell apart."

A chilly breeze ruffled Claire's hair. She'd never heard the complete story or seen it from her father's adult point of view. "I'm sorry I screwed up your life."

"You didn't screw up anything, Cub. You're the best thing that ever happened to me. I was at college when Diane found out she was pregnant. I dropped out to get married and find a job. But I don't regret any of it. Things worked out just fine. Diane could have picked up where she left off." Her dad exhaled a deep breath into the night. "Your mother doesn't hate you, Cub. She hates herself."

Claire's eyes misted up. She had needed to hear that. For the first time since she'd moved to Newburgh, she was glad she'd come home. And now she wanted to let him know why.

"I came back for a reason." Her breath frosted in the chill

air. Speaking with her dad beneath the stars, her words sounded like a sacred oath. "I'm going to solve Tina's murder, Dad. I'm going to close her case."

He grinned at her, pride glimmering in his eyes. "Oh, I know you will, Cub. I always did."

CHAPTER 11

Sunday evening, Karla Smith dialed a number on her phone, her fingers quivering. The light faded outside her bedroom window, but Justin still hadn't called. Was he avoiding her? It was time to find out.

The sound of thumping from the next room started again. Karla rolled her eyes, hit the Send button, and waited for the call to connect. To ease the tension, she stroked Garfield's thick fur coat. The cat didn't mind, purring and closing his eyes with pleasure.

Justin, a high school junior, had opened Karla's eyes to a new world of experiences. But now he had stopped returning her calls. She had tried him twice since Thursday. The first time she dialed his number, she had felt vulnerable and insecure. She didn't want to seem desperate or pathetic. But his long silence frightened Karla. Had he grown bored with her? Did he have another girlfriend? She had left a quick message, trying to sound friendly and casual and confident that he'd return her call. He hadn't.

The line rang on the other side. At least this time his phone was on. When she had called on Friday, it had cut to voicemail right away. She needed to hear his reassuring voice. Last week, a girl in her grade had died, her body dumped in the woods near Karla's school. Two police officers had spoken with the dead girl's class, a man and a woman. Karla had walked past the detectives in the corridor. The woman had long dark hair. She had worn a business suit, not a uniform. A female detective was cool and all, but the visit reminded Karla that life was short. And fragile.

Karla's mother was no help either. Since Derek, her new boyfriend, had moved in, she didn't have time for her only daughter. Karla counted each time Justin's phone rang to help block out the soft but persistent bumping sounds that came from the thin wall that separated her bedroom from her mom's. She and Derek couldn't keep their hands off each other, even around Karla. *Ugh.* A girl in Karla's grade had been murdered, but all her mother cared about was making out. And Karla was supposed to be the teenager in the family!

What remained of her family? Karla's dad had left when she was five. She hardly remembered him. Her mom had destroyed all his photos, cutting his face out of the family photo albums as if he were a tumor. Karla didn't blame her mom for moving on, but she wished she'd be more grown-up about it. Karla got the feeling the lovebirds just wanted her out of the way.

The number had rung five times.

When Karla had met Justin, everything had changed. He *saw* her. She meant something to somebody again. Her life consisted of more than schoolwork and being ignored by Mom. Justin's happy-go-lucky attitude was just what she needed right now. His attitude...and his product.

She lit up every night to calm her nerves, waving the smoke out through her bedroom window. Down to her last joint, she was desperate for a refill.

Come on, Justin. Pick up!

Seven rings. Eight. If she got his voicemail again, she'd let him know she was angry. Pissed off, as Derek would say.

On the ninth ring, he answered.

"Karla." Justin's voice was like music to her ears, and all her frustration melted. "I can't talk now." Why was he whispering?

"Are you OK?" Had something happened to him?

"Yeah."

"I've been trying to call you since Thursday."

"Yeah, I'm sorry. Things are crazy. I have to lie low for a while."

Lie low for a while. What did that mean? Were the cops after him? Justin had never seemed worried about getting caught with weed. Had his mom found out?

"Are you grounded?"

"No. It's just..."

She waited for him to complete his sentence. What terrible thing had kept him away from her?

"Did you know the girl who died?"

"Grace Miles?"

"Yeah, Gracie."

Gracie? How well did Justin know her? Too well, it seemed. Now Karla was suspicious.

"Sure, I knew her."

How could she not? She and Grace Miles looked so much alike, Marlene had asked if they were cousins. The news of her lookalike's death had disturbed Karla, but hearing her name on Justin's lips aroused another emotion. Yep, Karla was pathetic. She was jealous of a dead girl.

"How do you know her?"

"I don't. It's just...when I heard she was dead I was just... shaken, you know?"

"Yeah. Me, too." Something wasn't adding up. Was he lying to her? No, Justin would never lie to her.

"It's crazy, you know. She was so..."

Karla tensed while he searched for the right word.

"Young."

Karla relaxed. She had thought he was going to say "pretty."

"Justin, I need to see you."

"I want to see you, too. But things are a bit complicated now."

"What do you mean?"

The line went silent. Justin's secrecy and talk of Grace Miles grated on her nerves. This was so unlike him.

"Like I said, I need to lie low."

"Are you in trouble?"

"No! No. Nothing like that."

He wasn't making any sense. She needed to see him, to feel his arms around her, his lips on hers, and inhale his scent. Why was he keeping his distance? Karla remembered her other need.

"I'm down to my last one."

Maybe the promise of money would convince him to risk a meeting. Karla had saved up some cash from babysitting the neighbors' six-year-old. Those savings were running low, too, but seeing Justin again would be worth it. She could always borrow a twenty from her mother's handbag if she needed to. Her mom wouldn't even notice.

Justin sighed. "I'll see what I can do."

"So I'll see you soon?"

"I'll try."

Karla hung up. She shoved Garfield from her warm, comfortable lap. The cat leaped to the floor, stretched his legs, and stalked off, switching his tail to show his displeasure. He'd get over it.

Karla showered and blow-dried her hair. She put on a push-up bra, a fresh pair of jeans, and a sweater. Adding lip gloss and a touch of glitter under her eyes in her bedroom mirror, she grabbed a handbag and stepped out of her room. The door to her mom's bedroom was still closed, the soft sounds of hushed voices within.

"I'm going out, Mom," she yelled. She ran downstairs, her boots pounding the stairs and drowning out any protest her mom would make. Karla had school tomorrow, and where was she going after dark? Karla had ten seconds before her mom threw on some clothes and followed her downstairs, and Karla used those seconds to escape.

The crisp night air chilled her skin as she marched along the sidewalk. Streetlights created widely spaced islands of yellow in the darkness. The neighbors across the street were home, their lights on.

She searched the road for Justin's small white car. Crickets chirped. Leaves rustled overhead. A few cars lined the road, but none of the dark, silent vehicles belonged to Justin.

Where was he? And why was he "lying low?" Had he'd gotten mixed up in something bad? Something illegal? Well, besides the weed. Or because of the weed? And why had he mentioned Grace Miles out of the blue? Grace had died on Wednesday. Ever since, Justin had blocked her calls. Did his sudden radio silence have something to do with Grace's death?

The shudder that gripped her had nothing to do with the chilly night air. Suddenly, standing alone on the street curb at night didn't seem like a smart idea.

A car engine hummed down the road. A white car cruised toward her and pulled over. "I'll see what I can do," Justin had said. Had he sent someone to pick her up? Was he injured and unable to drive?

Karla peered through the passenger window. The driver was not Justin. In the darkness, the silhouette of a woman glanced at her. The driver looked too young to be Justin's mom.

She didn't roll down the window. Karla opened the door, and a light turned on inside.

"Need a ride?"

Karla relaxed. She recognized the woman from her school. This was a safe bet. She was in luck!

"Yeah, thanks."

Karla climbed inside and told the woman her destination. A sudden thought froze Karla on the seat. She was bumming a ride to visit Justin and stock up on weed. What if the driver asked about Justin? It was too late to back out now.

"Seatbelt," the driver said.

"Right!" Karla gave a nervous laugh. "Safety first."

Karla buckled up, and the car drove off. She'd get out a few blocks from Justin's house to make sure the driver wouldn't tie her to him.

The car slowed down, and they stopped at a shadowy stretch along the roadside. Was the driver waiting for someone else? Of course, she was! She hadn't come here for Karla.

"You see that?" The driver pointed a gloved hand toward the street outside the passenger window.

Karla searched for whatever had caught the driver's attention. All she saw was a dark house. The lights were out. Whoever lived there was sound asleep or away from home.

Her vision blurred for a fraction of a second, then something thin and hard tightened around her neck. Karla couldn't breathe! Her hands rushed to her throat, and she tried to dig her fingers beneath the thin rope, but the driver was pulling back too hard.

This made no sense. The driver's job was to protect her, not hurt her! This was... But her thoughts flew away. Her lungs screamed, filling her mind with one desperate desire.

Air. She needed air. She tried to scream, but her lungs wouldn't inflate. The rope was so tight she feared it would cut into her neck and slice her head off. Karla lunged forward, away from her attacker, but her throat only burned more painfully. She flailed with her legs but found no leverage. Her fingernails tore into her skin around the cord, and her neck stung.

Karla reached for the phone in her bag. Her fingers ran over the smooth surface of the screen, like a blind person reading braille, but the phone slipped away.

Bright spots appeared on the dark ceiling of the car. The spots merged and clouded her field of vision. Her arms felt heavy. Her strength fled. Karla wouldn't see Justin tonight or ever again. She was going to die here. As her limbs went limp, the strangest thought flittered through her mind. She hadn't said goodbye to her mom. Then, the bright spots swallowed her world completely, and she knew no more.

CHAPTER 12

Claire regretted eating breakfast Monday morning as Jed drove her to the southern outskirts of Newburgh. Another crime scene. Another young girl. And all during Claire's first week on the job. Somehow, her instincts whispered, both murders would lead back to Tina.

Jed had said nothing the entire way, his knuckles tight on the steering wheel. She knew what he was thinking. On Friday, Captain Emmerso had prevented him from arresting their only suspect. Four days later, they had another corpse on their hands. Claire understood Jed's frustration even though she still believed Gareth Miles did not kill his daughter. Innocent until proven guilty. Captain Emmerso was right. That rule was all that separated law enforcement from The Inquisition.

So far, this second homicide had little in common with Grace Miles. The crime scene was far from Newburgh Middle School. And yet that premonition wouldn't keep quiet. Somehow, this murder was Claire's fault, too.

Incomplete office buildings rose from the construction site like giant skeletons, a far cry from the artist's impression of futuristic skyscrapers in chrome and glass displayed on a large sign. The label in a bold sci-fi font read Silicon Towers.

Jed's car raised dust clouds. He turned a corner and swore softly. A media van parked on the sandy new street beyond the police cruisers and ambulances. This time, the press had beaten the detectives to the crime scene.

A short female patrol officer waited on the sidewalk. Officer Dunn offered them the logbook wordlessly, her face grim.

Jed signed his name and handed the clipboard to Claire. The forensic tech, a patrol sergeant, and another patrol officer were already at the scene. At least this time the detectives had arrived before Captain Emmerso.

Officer Dunn seemed to read her mind. "Captain Emmerso's on his way with the chief."

A ball of stress burned in Claire's stomach. One dead girl was bad enough. Two dead girls within a week was a crap storm, and the detectives still had no solid leads on the first.

The patrol officer pointed to a pile of yellow helmets. "Use the hard hats. Site rules. Just follow the planks. The guy who found her is inside with the others."

The detectives ducked under the yellow police tape and did as they were told. Claire followed her partner, picking her way along loose wooden boards, piles of gravel, and shovels. In the distance, a jackhammer pounded the earth. High above them, drills whined.

Related or not, the unsolved murders would dominate the news. The media would want heads to roll. They would blame the Chief of Police, and the crap would flow downhill. A morning breeze kicked up the dust, turning their clothes gray.

Sergeant George Eckhardt was speaking on his phone when they arrived. He nodded at them and waved at the second patrol officer, Officer Daniel Hackett, his cue to walk them through the scene while the sergeant continued his conversation.

"The foreman called nine-one-one an hour ago." Hackett pointed a boney finger at two men in overalls and hard hats who stood twenty feet away. "It took time to understand what they wanted. They're Russian immigrants and have trouble with the language. We got here fifteen minutes ago and secured the site. The chief is on his way."

"Yeah," Jed said, "we heard. Let's have a look."

They made for the forensic tech crouched over a body on the gravelly path. Today, the tech added a face mask and a yellow hard hat to his blue-and-white surgical gear. The dead girl lay on her back, arms at her sides. The dust had painted her clothes and skin white. Despite the lack of foliage, the scene was all too familiar. Adrenaline churned in Claire's stomach. The dust could not hide the extensive damage to the girl's face. As they approached, the forensic tech looked up. The dust turned his patches of visible skin gray.

"No need for fingerprint powder today," he said. He got to his feet. "If we're going to meet so often, Detective Wallace, you might as well introduce me to your new partner."

Jed stared at the dead girl. He didn't seem to register the tech's words. Had the dust powdered her partner's face white? Or had the crime scene drained the blood from his face?

"Claire Wolfe," she said.

"Brandon Yang. Welcome to the party. Help yourselves to some latex party favors."

Jed pulled a pair of disposable gloves and booties from the box on the ground. "Let's get started." He glanced back at the street and the invisible media van. "The sooner we finish here, the better."

He spoke into his digital recorder. "The victim is a Caucasian girl found lying on her back, hands at her sides, legs extended. Ten feet from the retaining wall of an office building, still under construction. She looks about the same age as the first victim, Grace Miles. About fourteen years old."

He looked at Claire, and she nodded. Her gut clenched. Was the victim one of Gracie's classmates? Had Claire interviewed her at the middle school yesterday?

Jed crouched over the girl. "Blonde hair. Severe facial mutilation. No signs of a struggle or sexual assault. Again, like the first victim."

Claire's insides twisted in a knot. There was no denying it now. Gracie's killer had struck again.

"No ax this time," Brandon said. "I checked. But don't bank on any trace evidence. The dust has destroyed everything. Except for a few red hairs on her sweater."

Jed shot Claire a meaningful look. Gareth Miles had red hair. He spoke into the recorder. "There's dust everywhere and red hairs on the victim's body." He stopped recording. "Can you rush a DNA analysis for the hairs?"

"We're still processing the first crime scene."

"Give the hairs priority. Have you photographed everything?"

"Yeah."

"Any identifying marks or belongings?"

"There's a handbag." He pointed at a numbered circle.

Claire almost missed the bag. Dusted white, the handbag blended in with its surroundings. Jed fished around with gloved hands. "There's a phone. The screen is locked. Send it over once you've lifted any fingerprints."

"Aye-aye, sir."

Claire scanned the construction site.

"Anything to add?" Jed asked Claire.

She shook her head. Two guys in construction overalls stood at the gaping entrance of the building. The older one had a square jaw of thick gray stubble. Or was the gray hair also an effect of the dust? Jed and Claire approached the men, while a crane shifted far overhead.

Igor Kapilevich was new to the construction outfit. He lived on-site but spoke little English, so his friend translated. Living on-site was not strictly legal, and while he was happy to cooperate, he asked to have his name dropped from the record to avoid any unpleasant visits from Immigration and Customs Enforcement. Jed assured Igor he'd stay out of trouble if he told the detectives all he knew.

Igor had woken up early that morning and prepared for work. The moment he discovered the body, he called his supervisor, the translator who had notified the police.

"Did he see any strangers at the site last night or this morning?"

The manager translated, and Igor shook his head. None of their colleagues had seen or heard anything either. Jed handed out his cards.

"This is a nightmare," he muttered to Claire. "Where is Captain Emmerso?"

He glanced at the street where cameramen waited for them. Officer Freeman yelled at the reporters to stand back. Soon the detectives would have to run that gauntlet, too.

Jed shook his head. "Red hairs. We should have arrested the Miles father."

Claire swallowed her words. Truckloads of media pressure would rain on them soon, and they could not afford a fight.

Jed's phone rang, and he put the device to his ear. "Yes, sir. We're here right now." He listened a little longer. "Yes, sir. I understand." He slipped the phone back into his pocket. "Captain Emmerso wants us back at the station right away."

"I thought he was coming here."

"Change of plans. The chief went ahead without him to handle the press. Patrol will close up the scene."

The recall was like a slap across the face. "Is he pulling us from the case?" Emmerso might replace Claire, the new detective, to satisfy the media lynch mob.

Jed shrugged. "We'll find out soon enough. We have an ID for the girl. Her mother reported her missing this morning."

"What's the girl's name?"

"Smith. Karla Smith."

Jed dusted off his jacket and headed for the line of reporters with their cameras and questions. Claire hung back, frozen to the spot. The world wavered around her. For a dizzying moment, she almost fainted. She reached into her pocket and withdrew a folded sheet of yellow notepaper. A single name appeared on the sheet in Claire's handwriting. Karla Smith.

CHAPTER 13

The squad room buzzed with uniforms, and Claire knew she was in trouble. The hubbub was the death rattle of her career in law enforcement.

Detective Mahoney looked up from his desk and smiled when Claire and Jed walked in. "Good morning!"

Jed eyed the chatting uniforms in the squad room. "What's going on?"

"You tell me." He glanced at their dust-coated shoes and smirked. "Detective Wolfe joins the department and suddenly we're up to our necks in dead girls."

He was joking, but Claire's cheeks burned.

Jed looked at the closed door of Captain Emmerso's office. "Is the captain in?"

"Yeah and he's got company. Three suits. I'd wear a bulletproof vest if I were you."

"Thanks for the tip."

"On the bright side," Mahoney said to Claire, "your business cards arrived." He pointed to the shrink-wrapped tower on her desk.

Claire examined the pack of cards. She might never get the chance to use them. "They got my phone number wrong."

"That's your department-issue number. It redirects to your phone, then to your home line if there's no answer."

"So I'm always on call?"

"We live to serve."

"Nice." She dropped the pack onto the desk. "Not sure I'll be needing these after today."

Claire and Jed traded brave grins and prepared to face their doom. Jed knocked once on the captain's door, and they entered. Captain Emmerso gazed at them. Claire failed to divine her fate from his sincere but calm expression.

"Detectives, these are our new friends from the FBI."

Three suits sat in the visitor chairs, a woman and two men. Claire and Jed squeezed into the limited standing room. Emmerso needed a larger office.

Jed ignored the visitors. "Sir, we have evidence connecting the two girls."

His display of investigative competence was supposed to deter the captain from reassigning the case, but he was wasting his breath.

"Relax, Detective. I'm not taking either of you off the case. But the Bureau has kindly agreed to consult. I think we'll all be glad to benefit from their expertise."

Jed's posture relaxed as the words sank in. They had not lost the case—they had gained reinforcements. Somehow, the captain had wrangled a team of specialists on very short notice. Like the detectives, the FBI agents wore plainclothes suits.

"Detective Jed Wallace," Emmerso said, "and Detective Claire Wolfe, meet Dr. Sally Fleisher, a leading forensic psychiatrist at the FBI's Behavioral Analysis Unit in Quantico."

The woman nodded at Claire, a subtle gesture of female comradery in this male-dominated profession. Her head of long, silky hair belonged in a shampoo commercial photo shoot. The deep pools of her sensitive eyes drew Claire in, registering every detail. Dr. Fleisher's penetrating glance might have unnerved Claire were it not for her smile, which radiated approval and acceptance.

The other two agents had little in common. The older man's world-weary grimace reminded Claire of Tommy Lee Jones's character from the *Men in Black* movies, only this agent wore brown. His colleague, the third agent, was both younger and better looking—no offense, Mr. Jones. When his eyes met Claire's, a sudden spark of recognition parted her lips and froze her brain.

Emmerso continued his introductions. "Dr. Fleischer's associates are Special Agents Tom Brown and Robert Cline."

Robert Cline. His face had shed the soft curves of adolescence, but Claire recognized Robbie Cline, her high school biology study partner, the boy she had kissed in his bedroom. Since that kiss, he'd filled out into a trim and toned adult man. How had Robbie Cline landed up in the FBI?

Special Agent Tom Brown shook their hands. "Please to meet you." His mild Southern drawl reinforced the Tommy Lee Jones association in Claire's mind.

Special Agent Robert Cline shook her hand, too, and smiled. "Call me Rob."

He turned back to Captain Emmerso, and something sagged within Claire. Robbie featured prominently in her childhood memories of Boston. But the young FBI agent didn't seem to remember her at all.

The captain continued. "I've given them the big picture. Detective Wallace, send them the case files ASAP. Dr. Fleischer will build a profile for the killer to help narrow our focus. Special Agents Brown and Cline have extensive experience with complex violent crime on a national scale. To make the most of their expertise, I'm splitting them up among you. Special Agent Brown will assist Detective Wallace, who will continue to lead the investigation. Special Agent Cline will partner with Detective Wolfe. The County Sheriff's Department is available as well if we need them."

Agent Cline kept his eyes on the captain. Still no sign of recognition.

"Questions?"

"No, sir," Jed and Claire said as one.

Claire marveled at her captain. Emmerso had redirected control of the investigation without demoting his detectives. If the media complained about their lack of progress, he could refer them to the nation's leading experts on multiple homicides. But on paper, his detectives remained in charge. If the case resolved favorably, Newburgh PD could take credit. His maneuver had also sent Jed and Claire on separate trajectories. Not only had he sensed their clash about the homicide's direction, but he'd parted them without stepping on their toes. If Claire had worn a hat, she'd take it off to him.

"Good. Then I'll let you get to work. If Dr. Fleischer's initial assessment is right, this second girl won't be the last. We have a serial killer on our hands."

CHAPTER 14

"Listen up, everybody," Captain Emmerso said as Claire returned to her desk carrying a pile of photocopied papers.

Officers packed the squad room to capacity, the air thick with adrenaline. The captain had commandeered Patrol and Dispatch to help with the investigation, and the officers seemed eager to play their part.

After meeting the FBI agents in the captain's office, Claire had rushed to print copies of the case files while Jed, the captain, and the agents had huddled over their plan of action. Like the others, Claire was curious about the investigation's new direction. Jed stood beside Captain Emmerso, and they waited for their audience to settle.

"You all know why we're here," Emmerso continued. "Two young girls are dead. We need to stop the killer before he strikes again." He glanced at the FBI newcomers. "Join me in welcoming our friends from the FBI, Special Agents Tom Brown and Robert Cline, as well as Dr. Sally Fleischer. Our early theories about the killer are still on the table, but let's be open to new ideas."

Jed shifted on his feet. He still seemed to cling to his theory about Gareth Miles. Emmerso had humored him but asked the investigation to keep an open mind. *Captain Emmerso strikes again.*

"Detective Wallace is lead on this investigation, so keep him in the loop. Over to you, Detective."

Jed cleared his throat. "Both victims match a very specific physical profile. They are fourteen years old and have blonde hair and blue eyes. Both studied at Newburgh Middle School, though not in the same class. More girls might match this profile. We're going to put them under police protection until we catch the killer. We'll notify Patrol once we've compiled a list of names."

Claire remembered the sheet of yellow notepad paper in her pocket and raised her hand. "I can make that list. I have a yearbook from Newburgh Middle School." She did not tell them she'd already prepared that list before the second murder.

Jed flushed at the interruption. "Great. Detective Wolfe, write up a list of names on the whiteboard, and Patrol can work from that. We also need to increase our surveillance on Gareth Miles, the father of the first victim."

A patrol officer raised his arm. "The first girl's father is a suspect?" He sounded incredulous.

"Until we can rule him out for certain. His prints were on the ax we found at the first crime scene. We just received the forensic analysis for the first murder. DNA found at the scene matches nothing on record. We're still waiting on the toxicology report. Dust at the second crime scene, a construction site, contaminated any trace evidence. This time we have the girl's phone, and Forensics will send it over later today."

A loud groan drew their attention to the coffee juggernaut

in the corner where a balding and pot-bellied patrol officer had sneaked a shot of caffeine.

"Excuse me, Officer?" Jed yelled over the noise.

The caffeine junkie turned to the crowd of angry faces, his eyes wide and innocent. "Who me?"

"Do you mind? We're in the middle of a briefing."

The officer shrugged and paused the coffee machine mid-process.

"Thank you." Jed glanced at his notepad, the items he had discussed with the FBI team. "When the killer notices our efforts to protect the girls, he might expand his range. We'll compile lists of potential targets in other schools and neighboring towns and notify local PDs about the suspected danger. Detectives Mahoney and Nakamura, I'll ask you to handle that. Stop by Newburgh Middle School, too. Detective Wolfe and I were there last week. We spoke with the first victim's teachers, classmates, and the maintenance staff. The victim had skipped classes and displayed secretive behavior before her death. Let's find out about the second victim, but be ready for surprises. We didn't treat the first homicide as a serial murder and we might have missed something."

The detectives nodded their agreement. They had received the bum assignment but, for a change, they kept their snarky comments to themselves.

"Our contacts in the FBI ran a ViCAP search for similar crimes."

Claire held her breath. The Violent Criminal Apprehension Program, or ViCAP for short, maintained a database of serial, violent, and sexual crimes. Only a fraction of crimes entered the system, but ViCAP was still the best tool available. If the killer had murdered and mutilated before, his earlier victims might show up in the database, allowing the detectives to connect the dots.

But just as Jed raised their hopes, he dashed them. "So far, we've found nothing. The victim profile didn't match any missing person reports either. Not for the past two years."

The past two years. Those search parameters made sense considering the two recent homicides, but not if the killer had murdered Tina, too.

Claire said nothing. Even if they widened the search period to twelve years, Tina's murder probably wouldn't show up. If O'Leary hadn't bothered to digitize her case file, he would not have gone to the trouble of submitting the details to the FBI. Claire reminded herself to follow up with Officer Freeman at the archive. She hadn't heard from him since Thursday, her first day on the job. Chances were Claire would never see her sister's case file.

No, there was no point in mentioning Tina's murder. A personal connection to the crimes would suspend her from the investigation. Even so, Claire wondered, where had Gareth Miles lived twelve years ago?

Jed looked at his notes. "We'll also review the list of sex offenders and ex-cons in the area. Dr. Fleischer of the BAU is working on a criminal profile for the killer, and we'll want to cross-reference the profile with known offenders." Jed asked for volunteers, and two patrol officers raised their hands.

"Detective Wolfe and Special Agent Cline are to interview the victim's mother. Speak with the neighbors while you're there. Meanwhile, Special Agent Brown and I will review the victims' belongings and telephone records. The department will make a short announcement to the press. The ME's office and the county forensics lab are giving this case top priority. Their reports on the second victim should be available within the next few days. That's all for now. We'll touch base later."

The officers and detectives dispersed to their tasks. Claire took the yearbook and headed for the whiteboard on the wall.

She wrote the names in a column. Grace Miles. Karla Smith. Then, she leafed through the yearbook and added the others. Dana Wood. Amy Ellen Collins. The list would grow once she contacted more schools.

Claire drew a line through the first two names. Gracie Miles was dead. So was Karla Smith. Claire had written her name down on Friday night. If she had warned Karla's family, could Claire have saved her life? But last week, she'd had only a hunch based on a twelve-year-old murder. Gareth Miles had been their only suspect. She'd had no way of knowing the killer would strike again.

"You work fast," said a woman. A pretty young patrol officer stood beside her and copied the names onto her standard-issue white notepad. The officer had tied her strawberry blonde hair in a ponytail. The name "Long" appeared on the tag on her chest.

"Excuse me?"

She smiled. "The list. I barely had time to grab a pen and paper."

"Oh, right." Officer Long's comment seemed innocent enough, but Claire had to be careful. Why raise questions she'd rather not answer? "No time to waste, right?"

"Yeah." The officer glanced at the names and shook her head. "My little sister is fourteen years old." She fixed Claire with an admiring look. "I'm glad you joined us, Detective Wolfe. We need more women in the Investigations Bureau, don't you think?"

Claire relaxed. Officer Long wasn't suspicious of her, she just wanted to become a detective. Claire smiled. "I do, Officer Long."

"Please, call me Jess." She tapped her notepad. "I'll get right on these." She walked off.

Claire studied the names on the board. Her wild speculations had given her a head start on protecting the next potential victims. For the first time since her arrival, optimism welled inside her. A detective's worst enemies were time and budget, and the Newburgh Police Department was throwing all its resources at the investigation. If they followed the playbook, they'd find the killer in short order.

"There you are!" Claire turned to the speaker, an elderly officer with salt-and-pepper hair.

"Officer Freeman. I mean, Bobby."

The archive officer flashed his rows of pearly teeth. "Ready for some good news?" He held out a crumpled manila folder.

A sense of unreality washed over Claire as he handed her the case file.

"This is it?" she asked, although she knew the case number printed on the cover by heart. After she'd despaired of ever getting hold of the folder, the moment had arrived. Tina's file weighed unexpectedly little in her hands considering its contents—the details of her sister's murder, the mystery that had changed the course of her life and haunted her every step.

"You'll never imagine what I went through to get it," Bobby continued. "The folder had fallen behind a cabinet. Had to call in my son, Del, to help me shift that monstrosity away from the wall."

Del. Claire had met the patrol officer, Del Freeman, at the first crime scene.

"Thank you so much, Bobby."

"Just doing my job. I hope that helps."

"I hope so, too."

She stared at the folder, then held it away from her body, as though she was handling a venomous snake.

A man approached her, Special Agent Rob Cline. In her excitement at receiving Tina's file, Claire had forgotten that she had two other homicides to investigate and a new partner—her old high school flame.

Rob jingled a key chain in his hand. "Detective Wolfe, are you ready to head out?"

Again, his voice and body language betrayed no sign that he remembered the teenager he'd kissed thirteen years ago. That was probably for the best. If they were going to work together, Claire would prefer not to dredge awkward memories of her teenage self from the past.

Claire tucked the folder under her arm. "Yes."

Tina had waited twelve years. She could wait a little longer.

CHAPTER 15

"Should we talk about the elephant?" Special Agent Rob Cline asked Claire as he drove the Bureau car, a blue Toyota Corolla, out of the Newburgh PD parking lot.

Claire froze on the passenger seat. "The elephant?"

The unmarked FBI sedan was larger and more comfortable than her hatchback. But the turn in conversation made her doubt whether the FBI agent was mentally fit to sit behind the wheel of a vehicle.

"You know—the pink elephant in the corner of the room we've been ignoring."

Claire could find only one interpretation for his comment. "You remember me?"

"Those striped running tights were pretty hard to forget."

Claire laughed. "I'd forgotten about those." Her years on the school track team had not gone unnoticed.

"It's not as though I kissed every girl who came over to study."

Claire tried to keep a straight face. She stared out the window to hide the blush that must have painted her cheeks red.

"So, there were others?"

He grunted in the affirmative. "But only one I kissed."

Claire said nothing, unsure how this reflected on her. Was she the only girl he'd wanted to kiss or the only one who had let him?

"I guess you didn't enjoy it as much as I did," he continued. "A few days later, you disappeared into thin air."

Claire took the bait. "That had nothing to do with you. Or me. My parents moved us to Newburgh."

Rob, or rather Robbie, frowned. "You could have called."

He had her there. Claire had lost contact with all her classmates in Boston. Why hadn't she tried to stay in touch? The thought hadn't occurred to her. She'd been an insecure little girl, angry at her parents for disrupting her life. In some ways, she still was.

"I didn't know you were into long-distance relationships."

"Neither did I." He laughed. "I'm just messing with you. I understand completely."

Claire laughed, too. An hour ago, his failure to remember her had disappointed her. She couldn't fault him now for remembering her too well. "When did you know it was me?"

"The moment I heard your name. Before we arrived."

"You hid that well."

"One of the many tricks I learned in the FBI."

Claire breathed at ease, relieved to have evicted the elephant from the car. A lot had happened in the past thirteen years. They could reminisce about those crazy teenage days, secure in the distance of time.

"The FBI, hey? I never imagined you'd become a Fed."

"I never imagined you'd become a cop. A detective, no less."

"Well, life is full of surprises."

"It is."

"And how do you like the FBI?"

"Pretty well. I started in the Crisis Negotiation Unit."

"That sounds pretty intense."

"It was. Then, I moved around, going where they sent me. Hostage negotiation, mostly. Interesting work."

Claire would have liked to hear more about his exploits, but Rob pulled over. They had reached their destination.

The Smith family home, like many in the suburbs of Newburgh, was a two-level Cape Cod, with slanted tiled roofs and low chimneys.

A man answered the door. Tall and wiry, he glared at them with deep-set, suspicious eyes.

"Mr. Smith? I'm Detective Wolfe from Newburgh PD, and this is Special Agent Cline."

He blinked at them.

"May we come in?"

The hard facade broke. "Yeah, sure. Sorry, I thought you might be another one of those reporters." Smith had a mild Southern drawl. "The police called a few hours ago."

"We're following up. May we come inside?"

"Sure." He led them to the kitchen table, where Jean Smith sat in long gray pajamas, her head in her hands. The omelet on the plate before her remained uneaten.

The man touched her shoulder. "Jeanie, the police are here."

Mrs. Smith straightened. She sniffed and wiped her face with the back of her hand.

Claire repeated the introductions. "We're very sorry for your loss. May we ask you a few questions?"

Mrs. Smith composed herself and nodded her agreement. She swept her blonde hair from her face. Shabby but still beautiful, she had low-maintenance hair that looked good even without brushing.

Claire turned on her recording device. "When did you last see Karla?"

"Yesterday afternoon."

"And you reported her missing late last night?"

She glanced at the man. "Karla's very independent. We were just...lazing around at home. She went out around nine and never came home."

"Did she usually go out alone at night?"

"She didn't ask my permission."

"Where was she going?"

Mrs. Smith teared up again. "I don't know. She didn't say. I just heard the door close, and I figured she'd gone to a friend. When it got late, I called around, but nobody knew where she was."

Her language seemed off to Claire, using "I" instead of "we." "What about you, Mr. Smith—were you at home then?"

"Oh, Derek isn't Karla's dad. Her dad took off years ago. I don't know where he is. His number was disconnected last time I tried to call."

Claire turned to Derek. "What's your full name?"

"Derek Allen. Jean and I have been together for the past few months."

"Were you here yesterday?"

"We were together the whole evening," Jean said, pointedly. Had the reporters tried to paint Derek as the culprit? That would explain her defensive attitude.

"I see." So much for Mom's evil boyfriend. Claire could guess what had kept the couple busy the night of Karla's disappearance, but she didn't want to invade their privacy any more than was necessary. Still, she needed to rule out domestic issues.

"How did Karla feel about you two?"

The couple exchanged a sad glance.

"OK, I guess," Jean said. "We never really talked about it."

"Was she acting unusual recently? Did she have any trouble at school?"

"None that I noticed." There it was again—the guilt of the bereaved mother. If only she'd paid more attention, maybe she could have saved her daughter's life? "She kept to herself."

Claire jotted down the name of Karla's father and her two best friends. They should be able to corroborate the mother's story.

"Another girl in her grade died last week," Derek said. When all eyes turned to him, he added, "It's all they talk about on TV. Is this the same guy?"

"We're exploring all possibilities," Claire said. Derek's question sparked one of her own. "Did Karla know Grace Miles, the first victim?"

Jean's eyes searched for the answer on the wall. "I'd never heard her name until it was on the news. Karla never mentioned her, but she must have known her."

"I see." Claire would follow that up with Karla's friends, too. She handed Jean one of her brand-new business cards. "Call me if you think of anything."

Karla's mother accepted the card.

"May we have a look at Karla's room?"

Jean showed them the way upstairs. The dead girl's bedroom, the third Claire had observed within a week, was different from the others. Karla had neither Tina's ordered Barbies nor Gracie's laptop and unicorns.

"I'm sorry about the mess," Jean said.

Worn pajamas and dirty socks cluttered the floor. Lip gloss and a container of glitter sat on a desk of lacquered wood. The walls were white and bare. Neither mother nor daughter had bothered to decorate the room. It was a sad, loveless room. Jean made to pick up the clothes, but Claire held her back.

"Please don't. We might need to test for fingerprints."

Jean nodded. "I kept telling her to tidy up her room." She chuckled at her daughter's bad habits, then fresh tears overcame her as the realization set in. Her daughter was gone forever.

Derek materialized beside his girlfriend and touched her shoulder. "We'll wait downstairs if that's OK."

"That's fine."

Rob handed Claire a pair of white latex gloves.

"You came prepared."

"Never leave home without 'em. Nice business card, by the way. Any chance I can get one?"

"Maybe. If you're good."

They stepped into the bedroom.

"Do you think the killer was here?" Claire asked. It was hard to tell whether the disarray of clothes and papers counted as signs of a struggle.

"And risk alerting the mom? Unlikely. Not with serial killers."

Serial killers. Claire had investigated domestic murders and gang-related homicides but never that rare monster that made national headlines, launched Hollywood movie franchises, and inspired countless documentaries. What fascinated people so much about human predators? Was it the shock factor and the primal fear of being the next victim? She was glad to have the FBI on the case.

Claire peeked under a pile of school papers covered in math symbols. Karla's last bit of homework. No wonder she and Jed had made little progress on the case. They had trained to track regular killers, not monsters. Claire thought of the red hairs the forensics team had found on Karla Smith's body and the carrot-colored hair of Gareth Miles. Gracie's father had not seemed like a Dr. Jekyll. Would Claire recognize a Mr. Hyde if she stared him in the eye?

"I guess a crazed killer doesn't need a motive either."

Rob opened a closet door and searched the shelves of jumbled clothes. "Oh, they have motives, just different ones. There are two broad types of serial killers. Disorganized killers usually suffer from mental illness. Richard Trenton Chase killed six people, convinced he was being poisoned by dish soap, his blood was turning to powder, and he needed to drink his victims' blood to survive."

"Geez." Claire opened a drawer of the desk and poked around the notepads and pencils.

"Disorganized killers might wander into a house and kill whoever is home. They would not sneak in quietly to extract the victim."

Rob closed the closet door. "Organized killers are a different story. Killing is often part of a sexual fantasy they've nurtured for years. They plan the murders and select their victims carefully. But reality never lives up to the fantasy, so they kill again to get things right. That's their motive. The key to catching them is to understand the fantasy that drives them."

Claire found comfort in that idea. Motive meant logic, however twisted. Logic was a path she could follow. With the BAU's help and good old-fashioned police work, they might catch this killer after all.

Rob dropped to the floor and peered under the bed. There was a sudden, blood-curdling howl. A red ball of fur shot past Rob and vaulted out of the room.

Claire and Rob paused for a tense moment, then chuckled with relief. Claire gave Rob a hand up. The Smiths owned a cat.

Claire returned to the desk drawers. Her latex-covered

fingers bumped against a long, thin object wrapped in plastic at the bottom of the last drawer.

"Bingo," Claire said.

She held a clear Ziploc bag containing a single, thin joint. Gracie and Karla had more in common than Claire had thought. Both dead girls had secrets.

CHAPTER 16

Fear gripped Dana Wood as her father drove her home. That afternoon, Dad had shown up at her school. He never picked her up from school, but today he'd left work early and dragged her out of class in the middle of English Lit. She sat in the passenger seat, terrifying thoughts circling in her mind. First Grace Miles. Now Karla Smith. Was she next?

In class, Dana had sat two rows ahead of Karla Smith, a loner who dressed weird. Karla had never occupied Dana's thoughts, and Dana had barely even known who Grace Miles was. Now both girls haunted her.

"Are you OK?" her dad said from the driver's seat.

This was the second time he'd asked her. Normally she would have responded with a smart-ass comment. But today she just nodded and stared out the window.

She focused on the fluffy gray clouds that crowded the sky, anything to distract her from the dead girls. After a week of sunshine, fall had resumed. The rain would follow. She loved the carpet of red leaves on the ground—the colors and the soft crunching beneath her feet. But thoughts of fall did nothing to improve her mood. She didn't want to walk anywhere—she wanted to stay indoors, safe from faceless killers. But was anywhere safe anymore? Like the rain, the killer was on his way.

They arrived home, and Dana followed her dad inside.

Mom gave her a tight hug, longer than usual. "Are you OK, sweetie?"

"Yeah. I'm going to my room."

Her mom gave her dad a worried look, then relented. "OK, sweetie. I'll call you for lunch."

Dana dropped her bag on the floor of her room when her phone rang. She climbed onto her bed and hit Accept.

"Are you still alive?" The video chat app provided a fish-eye view of Lena's face and the red-brick walls of the school.

"Cut it out. I'm freaked out as it is. What is wrong with you people?"

"'You people?'"

"My folks. The cops who spoke with us today."

Ms. Maynard, the principal, had interrupted math class to introduce two police detectives, a white guy with messy hair and a beefy Asian. The detectives split up to question the students one by one. The Asian guy asked her when she'd last seen Karla. Had Karla been acting strange? Dana had noticed nothing. Messy Hair thanked the students for their cooperation. He scanned the rows of students, sizing them up like they were criminals. Then, his gaze lingered on Dana, and her breath froze in her lungs. Was there a bull's-eye painted on her forehead?

Dana shivered at the memory. "Everybody's acting like I'm next."

"Remember Karla?"

"Of course, I remember Karla. Like I can think about anything else!"

"What color hair did she have?"

Dana pictured her former classmate. "Dirty blonde."

"And Grace Miles?"

Dana rolled her eyes. "I get it—they were both blondes. But so are you."

"I don't have blue eyes. They did, and so do you."

A hard lump formed in Dana's throat. Lena was right. That's why the cop had stared at her. But the fact only angered her.

"Some weirdo's going to kill me just because I look like Grace and Karla?"

"Uh-huh. And because you're fourteen years old."

"That is so unfair!"

"It's got nothing to do with fairness, Dana. We're talking about a serial killer. It's all over the news. The FBI is searching for him. But look on the bright side. You always wanted to be famous."

"I wanted to be Taylor Swift famous, not *dead* famous."

"Sucks to be you."

"Thanks a lot, Leens."

"Oh, by the way, what flowers do you want at your funeral?"

"That's not funny."

Lena giggled. "C'mon. It's a little funny. Don't worry. *I* won't let anybody hurt you."

"Wonderful. Now I'm relaxed."

Lena changed the subject abruptly. "Are you still going to Dean's birthday party?"

Dana had been crushing on Dean Ward since third grade. Dana and Dean, their names rolled off the tongue, didn't they? They were made for each other.

"Yes, of course, I'm still going."

"I don't know. Your dad just pulled you out of school. I doubt he'll let you go to a party at night."

Dana scoffed. "I'd like to see him stop me. Why?"

Was Lena plotting to hit on Dean while Dana wasn't around?

"Just askin'. Thursday is still a few days away. Maybe they'll catch the killer by then."

"I hope so. It doesn't matter anyway. I'm grounded." Dana groaned. "This is so unfair!"

"Yeah, sucks to be you."

A loud knocking on her door startled Dana. She covered the mouthpiece with her hand. "What is it?" she called.

Her father spoke through the door. "Dana, we need you downstairs."

"Coming!" She spoke into the phone. "Gotta go. Talk to you later."

"If you're still breathing."

Dana ended the call and opened her door. What did Dad want now? While she was safe in her room, her fear had evaporated. Now her dad only annoyed her. Her parents couldn't force her to miss Dean's party. It's not as though the killer would attack her in front of all her friends, would he?

She stomped down the stairs, ready to give her parents a gutsy speech, when she halted. A uniformed black police officer stood in the living room. Had they caught the killer? The worried faces argued against that. Was Dana in trouble?

"Dana," her mom said. Her mom never called her sweetie around strangers. "This is Officer Freeman. He'll be watching over you for now."

Watching over you. Lena hadn't been kidding. The killer *was* out to get her. The lump in her throat ballooned.

"Hi, Dana," the cop said. "I'll be outside. You won't even notice I'm here. But you can't leave the house until further notice."

This was worse than Dana had imagined. Before, she'd had a fighting chance of convincing her dad to let her go to the party. But now she had a freaking police officer watching her every move! There was no way she was going to miss Dean's party. This was so unfair!

Dana swore, and her mother gasped. Dana didn't care. She was already grounded.

CHAPTER 17

The Investigations Bureau's detectives had gathered around Dr. Sally Fleischer when Claire and Rob returned to the station late that afternoon. The forensic psychiatrist had spread crime scene photos of the murder victims over the six desks, turning the squad room into her private workspace. Hope surged in Claire's chest. Had Dr. Fleischer made a breakthrough?

Captain Emmerso waved Claire and Rob over and sat on the edge of a desk. "OK, everybody. Time for show and tell. Detective Wallace, let's start with you."

Jed looked worn out. "We have the ME's report for the second victim. Like the first girl, she died from asphyxiation. Both victims were strangled with a general-purpose nylon cord. Both display post-mortem damage to the face with a large, edged weapon, like the ax found at the first crime scene. We still have no weapon for the second murder."

Rob said, "Any fingerprints or DNA?"

"The brown hair and skin flakes from the first scene drew blanks. And it turns out the red hair from the second isn't human."

"Let me guess," Rob said. "Persian cat?"

Jed eyed him with surprise. "Yeah." He glanced at a printed page. "An Exotic Shorthair, to be exact."

Claire smirked at the baffled looks from the other detectives.

After allowing the crowd to marvel at his extrasensory perception, Rob came clean. "We met the cat in Karla's bedroom. Scared the crap out of us."

The officers enjoyed a much-needed laugh. Claire now understood the reason for Jed's exhausted expression. He'd been banking on the hair connecting Gracie's father, Gareth Miles, to the second murder. The investigation was officially out of suspects.

Jed continued his briefing. "The ME estimates the time of death between eight and ten PM last night."

Claire said, "Karla's mom said she left the house at around nine o'clock that evening. She must have died shortly thereafter. That differs from the first victim, Grace Miles, who was last seen Wednesday morning but died between four and six PM that day."

"Which raises the question," Captain Emmerso said. "Where was she that morning until her death?"

"We have a lead." Claire raised the sealed evidence bag with the single marijuana joint in the air for all to see. "We found this in Karla's desk drawer. Her mom says she knew nothing about it. Gracie had been skipping class and acting strange until her death. I'm wondering whether the two girls had more in common than their physical appearance."

"They did," Jed said. "Phone records for the two victims show calls to and from the same mobile number, a burner phone, shortly before their deaths. The girls knew the killer, and this explained his access to them. We're still working on unlocking the phone of the second victim. The first girl's phone is still missing. Transmission tower logs place her phone in the general vicinity of the middle school before the signal cut out. Either the battery ran dry or the killer destroyed the phone. Either way, keep an eye out for that phone. It might be critical. What did the neighbors have to say?"

"Nothing useful. None saw Karla or anything suspicious last night."

Mahoney said, "Neighbors aren't as nosy as they used to be."

Jed glanced at Nakamura. "What about the schoolkids?"

Nakamura shrugged. "Nothing interesting. Karla kept to herself. Teachers said she had a complicated family situation. Her father was out of the picture."

Jed looked at Claire. "Anything on the father?"

"A name and a disconnected phone number. The mother said he took off years ago and hasn't stayed in touch. We'll look him up."

Special Agent Tom Brown spoke up. "We can send the joint to the FBI lab for analysis. They might be able to identify the source of the drugs."

Emmerso nodded. "Good idea." He turned to Jed. "What's the social media presence for the girls?"

"Very limited."

"What, no Facebook?" Mahoney said.

"Get with the times, pal," Nakamura said. "Facebook's for old farts like you. The cool kids are on Snapchat and TikTok."

"How would you know?"

"I'm one of the cool kids."

"Yeah, and I'm a unicorn."

Emmerso guided the conversation back to business. "That leaves us with local ex-cons and sex offenders. That's a long list. We'll want to narrow our search as much as possible, which brings us to Dr. Fleischer's profile."

Dr. Sally Fleischer sat at Claire's desk. She lifted her gaze from the crime scene photos at the mention of her name. The squad room fell silent, and all eyes focused on her.

In recent years, FBI profilers had become famous for the highly specific descriptions of killers they conjured from a handful of crime scene details. The assembled officers waited in anticipation for the specialist to pull the rabbit from her hat.

Dr. Fleischer's dark sensitive eyes glimmered, and her lips trembled. She seemed ready to cry. How did the delicate soul choose a career that involved staring at crime scene photos all day? She let out a pent breath.

"On the surface, this is a simple case. The victimology indicates a well-defined profile. Fourteen-year-old girls. Blue eyes. Blonde hair. They went to the same school. Same MO. But the mutilation of the face..."

"Yeah, what's with that, Doc?" Mahoney interrupted, his expression uncharacteristically horrified. "Is that some kind of ritual?"

Dr. Fleischer hesitated. "That's the unsub's signature."

"Um, excuse my ignorance. *Unsub*?"

"Sorry. Unsub is short for 'unknown subject.' The killer. As opposed to the modus operandi or MO, a killer's signature includes the aspects of the crime that are not technically necessary to complete the murder. Signatures aren't always present. But they can be very helpful in identifying the type of unsub in question. We classify serial killers loosely into two groups."

"Organized and Disorganized," Claire blurted, winning impressed looks from the officers and a knowing grin from Rob.

"Very good. This generalization often helps to focus our investigations. We've identified sets of characteristics that are typical for killers in each group. Extreme violence and mutilation are usually the signs of a disorganized killer. Facial mutilation especially serves to dehumanize the victims, making them easier to kill. Disorganized killers often attack on impulse and suffer from mental illness. Organized serial killers, on the other hand, choose their victims carefully. They plan the murders and clean up afterward.

"We can break down these categories further based on the killer's motivation: Visionary; Mission-oriented; Hedonistic, and Power/control. There are many subdivisions, too. Without getting bogged down in the details, these crime scenes point toward an Organized Thrill or Lust killer. The unsub has a clear victim selection profile. He prepared a nylon cord for strangulation and cleaned up the forensic traces. He prefers close contact with the victims."

Nakamura raised his hand. "What about the facial mutilation? Didn't you say that was Disorganized?"

"That's where the profile breaks down. Lust killers might torture and mutilate their victims, but only while they are alive. They lose interest in their victims after death. The facial mutilation we find here is post-mortem. In other words, these murders mix the characteristics of both Organized and Disorganized killers. Mixed Type murders make the job of profiling much more difficult."

The anticipation in the air faded. The magician's hat would produce no white rabbits today.

"Difficult," Rob said. "But not impossible."

"Correct. As an organized killer, the unsub is most likely a highly intelligent white male. He will have access to a car or similar vehicle, which he uses to surveil his victims and transport their bodies. He is familiar with police procedures and forensic science."

"A cop?" Nakamura said. The temperature in the room dropped instantly.

"That's possible. Or a forensics tech. Or a regular Joe. Most people know enough from CSI TV shows and detective novels to avoid leaving fingerprints at the crime scene. This killer might have a stable job and a romantic relationship. He has access to a private space where he processed the bodies and mutilated their faces." Dr. Fleischer swallowed hard and seemed on the verge of tears.

"Anything else?" Emmerso asked.

"There are some other general pointers. The killer might try to insert himself into the investigation. Be wary of Good Samaritans. Most known serial killers experienced severe emotional deprivation in early childhood. Flag suspects with emotionally cold and critical mothers."

Claire's heart skipped a beat. *Emotionally cold and critical.* The doctor had described Claire's mother. Obviously, not every unhappy child became a killer.

"We're dealing with a psychopath," the doctor continued. "He might display superficial charm but he lacks empathy and uses other people only to satisfy his needs. In childhood, he didn't learn to form genuine caring relationships. Instead, he developed violent sexual fantasies and he murders to play out those fantasies. He might take trophies or souvenirs of his victims—hair, clothing, or jewelry—which he'll use later to relive the crime and masturbate. You'll want to search a suspect's home for those items or photos of the victim."

Mahoney said, "Could the facial mutilation be a part of the killer's sexual fantasy?"

Dr. Fleischer pursed her lips. "That's possible but unlikely. Remember, the mutilation took place after death. A Lust killer would derive sadistic pleasure from torturing a live victim."

"Could the killer be her age?"

Nakamura emitted an incredulous laugh. "You think a kid did this?"

All eyes turned to Dr. Fleischer. "Twenty known serial killers were under the age of thirteen. Many more committed their crimes before their eighteenth birthday. But in our case, the unsub is most likely an adult. The precise execution of the murders shows experience. He's killed before. The first victim might have died many years ago. He keeps on killing to relive that fantasy. Identifying his first murder will make catching him much easier. Back then, he would have killed closer to home and made more mistakes."

Claire froze. Could the entire department hear the thumping of her heart? A fourteen-year-old girl *had* died before in Newburgh. Twelve years ago. And the victim's case file lay on the back seat of Claire's white Ford Focus.

The psychiatrist spoke to Jed. "Does the first victim's father, Gareth Miles, have a history of violent crime?"

Jed blinked at her, also lost in ominous thoughts. "No."

"Did the extended ViCAP search turn up any similar murders?"

"No young girls with facial mutilation."

"Try widening the search criteria further. Our unsub might have started with a different MO and honed his technique over time."

"'Honed his technique,'" Mahoney said. "You make the killer sound like an artist."

"To his mind, he is."

With dark thoughts clearly swirling in their heads, the team got back to work. Captain Emmerso found a conference room for Dr. Fleischer and her disturbing photos, freeing up his detectives' workspace.

Claire ran a background search for Karla's father, Clive Smith. He owned a bunch of credit cards and had defaulted on a mortgage in Nevada. Claire tried the number on file. This line still worked, but Smith didn't answer. She left a vague message on his answering service asking him to call her urgently but doubted that he would.

Claire reviewed the Medical Examiner's report and the forensics lab analysis. An hour later, the pathologist's toxicology report for Grace Miles arrived. The tests revealed traces of marijuana in her blood. *Bingo*. The finding vindicated Claire's hunch. Grace and Karla had more in common than their looks—they shared a drug habit. Did their dealer lure them with drugs only to strangle them while incapacitated? Claire shared her suspicions with the rest of the team.

Mahoney and Nakamura got up from their desks and said their goodbyes. The evening had snuck up on Claire and, on cue, she yawned. The time on her phone read 8:58 PM. The windowless squad room concealed the fact that darkness had fallen outside. After a day of intense investigation, her eyes unfocused over her computer screen.

Rob walked over, pulling on his jacket. "Tomorrow's another day."

Claire stretched her neck. "So they tell me."

"Tom is still with Detective Wallace. Can I bum a ride?"

The agents shared a blue Toyota Corolla. Claire had intended to head straight home to read Tina's file, but she could make a detour. "Sure." She reached for her bag.

"Got any dinner plans?"

That was the sneakiest dinner invite Claire had ever received, but she smiled. "I do now."

CHAPTER 18

Claire's shoulders tensed under the straps of her schoolbag as she walked down the street. Morning birds dived from the trees overhead, their shrill squawks momentarily blocking out the patter of two sets of shoes on the sidewalk. The daily stroll to school should have been calming and enjoyable. But Claire knew her sister would ruin the experience.

"Guess what day it is today?" Tina asked.

Claire recognized the playful lilt in her sister's voice. That sound always meant trouble. Cruel, self-centered mind games were Tina's specialty. Claire said nothing. By ignoring the question, she hoped Tina would tire of her tricks. But she never did.

"Come on, *Big Sister*. You should know. My birthday is the highlight of your year."

Claire hated being called Big Sister. The nickname made her feel awkward and self-conscious, and the irony in Tina's tone emptied the words of all sisterly love. *You're not older and wiser, just oversized and clumsy.*

Claire didn't bite. In a few minutes, they would round the corner to the middle school. Tina never acted up in public. She carefully guarded her persona—the blue-eyed angel who everyone adored.

"I wonder how many presents Mom and Dad got me. Hmm. Let's see. More than you on your birthday, that's for sure. Don't take it personally, Big Sister. They don't hate you. They just love me more than you."

Claire rolled her eyes but kept her lips sealed. All her life, Tina had been studying her older sister, scanning her for weaknesses and imperfections. Apply the right pressure in the right spot and the cracks appeared. Tina knew exactly what to say to provoke Claire into doing or saying something Tina could use against her later.

"Don't feel bad, Claire. It's not your fault you're adopted."

A gasp of incredulous laughter escaped Claire's mouth. That was a shameless lie even by Tina's standards. "You're so full of crap. I am *not* adopted."

"No, you're not. But they wish you were. You're just so unlike the rest of us, so ugly and stupid."

Claire's face warmed. Her hand itched to slap the idiot. *Ignore her, Claire.* But her sister had found that hairline crack. Claire was not stupid. She didn't have her sister's golden locks and sapphire eyes, but she wasn't ugly either. She was just regular. Nothing special. Tina, on the other hand, *was* special. Their mother pointed that out often—and in front of Claire—and Tina believed it.

After Tina had sprouted breasts over the last year, she'd added an extra strut to her step to best show off her new assets. She'd have a full, ample chest like their mother—yet another reason for her mother to dote on her carbon copy. The birthday party after school today would be unbearable.

"I can see why you're jealous," Tina continued. "You'll never amount to anything. Me? I'm destined for greatness."

Claire guffawed, but her sister's words were having their

effect. Tina had ruined Claire's mood. *Only another two hundred feet. One more minute.*

"I don't blame you for trying to kill me either."

That did it. "Oh, please, Tina. I did *not* try to kill you."

Tina smiled a toothy grin, a piranha tasting blood in the water. "Oh, yes you did, Psycho Girl. Don't deny it. But I'm ready for you."

Her arm became a blur, and Claire stepped away quickly.

"Geez, Tina! Be careful with that."

The kitchen knife whistled in the air. Tina switched the blade from side to side, and for a scary moment, Claire thought her little sister was going to skewer her. But Tina slipped the knife back up her sleeve.

"Mom will be pissed you took that." *No, she wouldn't.* Her little girl could do no wrong. She'd probably blame Claire if she ever found out. Everything was always Claire's fault.

"Just sayin'," Tina said. "Next time, you'll pay with your life. But there won't be a next time. You don't have the guts."

Claire shook her head and kept her distance. "Whatever."

One day, Tina would pick on the wrong person. Then, she'd get what she deserved. *Stuck-up bitch.*

They rounded the street corner, and their paths diverged.

"Just don't make me wait for you after school, OK?"

Tina didn't answer. She strutted toward the entrance, her perky breasts like horns on her chest, and she disappeared into the flow of kids. Claire never saw her sister again.

CHAPTER 19

Detective Jed Wallace glared at his nemesis. The mobile phone with the pink PopSockets grip sat at a rakish angle on his desk. For two hours, Jed had labored to unlock the screen, but the Samsung Galaxy was as uncooperative as a rebellious teenager. Like everything about this case, this task had gone sideways.

"You still busy with that?"

Special Agent Tom Brown stood over him. Jed had found his new associate's Southern twang amusing at first, but now the accent grated on his nerves. The older agent seemed to enjoy picking out Newburgh PD's faults. "Doesn't the County Sheriff's Department have somebody to handle that?"

Jed ignored him. Emmerso had probably not consulted with Jed's dad before calling in the Feds. "Self-righteous ivory-tower bastards" was how Chief Wallace characterized the Federal Bureau of Investigation in private. "Cooperation is a one-way street for them. They ride in on their high horses as though they know it all. Nothing gets them off more than making local law enforcement look like idiots." Jed agreed.

"Did you try one through four?" Brown said, and he chuckled.

Jed wanted to roll his eyes. No, he hadn't tried the most obvious password in the known universe. But he restrained the urge to make wise-ass comebacks.

"I thought you'd headed home already."

Brown harrumphed. The old-fashioned hard-ass actually *harrumphed.* "If you can call that hole-in-the-wall motel a home. No, I reviewed the unsub profile with Dr. Fleischer."

Jed's shoulders tensed up. What had the crackpot cooked up now? The so-called forensic psychiatrist's so-called profile had been as vague as it was useless. A white male. Jed could have told her that, saving a lot of time and effort. Gareth Miles was the killer. The ax belonged to him, and his fingerprints were all over the murder weapon. But hard evidence wasn't enough for Captain Emmerso, and now the FBI would have them chasing their tails.

Ignoring the FBI agent, Jed focused on the stubborn phone. He entered another code—four nines. He had tried four ones, four twos, and so on. The code failed, and the keypad locked up for thirty seconds. *Too many incorrect PINs.*

Jed sighed. "Have you worked with her before?"

The older officer stared at him. "If you mean, 'Does she know what she's talking about?' then yes. We've worked together often. Her profiles are spot-on, and that's no easy feat. Profiling isn't an exact science. It's more of an art."

Jed scoffed. "Like serial murder? According to her, that's an art form, too. She almost seems to admire them."

Special Agent Brown shrugged. "You can acknowledge a man's ability. That doesn't mean you gotta like him. And this guy still has us stumped."

As if Jed needed a reminder. Mayoral elections were six months away, which meant Jed's dad's job was on the line, too.

The serial killer had created intense pressure even before this team of outsiders had arrived to breathe down his neck. The stakes had never been higher. And this wasn't any old case. Heads would roll, but not Jed's.

He blamed Captain Emmerso. If he'd let Jed arrest Gareth Miles, Jed wouldn't be working late, struggling to unlock the phone of another dead teenage girl. Emmerso had called in the big guns to cover his ass, but that plan was backfiring. The Feds would make Newburgh PD look bad.

"You know, we had a suspect before you guys arrived," he said. "If we'd arrested him, Karla Smith might still be alive."

"Who—the first girl's father? We have nothing connecting him to the second murder, and you'll have a hard time convincing a jury that a church-going dad murdered his little girl."

Brown was right. He needed a new theory to explain Gareth's motive. Fortunately, Jed had just that.

"What about the marijuana?"

"What about it?"

"Maybe Gareth sold weed to the kids at school, and Grace was his mule? When Grace threatened to tell her mom about her dad's side hustle, he killed her."

Special Agent Brown frowned. "So, Karla was his mule, too?"

"Or a customer. Wait..." The theory unfurled before Jed's eyes. "Karla's mom had a boyfriend, Derek Allen. Maybe he was a pusher, too? What if there was a turf war between drug dealers and their daughters got caught in the crossfire?"

"You mean Allen killed Grace and then Miles killed Karla as revenge?" Special Agent Brown did not look impressed, but Jed was on fire.

"Exactly!" He'd run a background check on Allen. When he

shook that tree, all kinds of rotten fruit would fall to the ground.

The phone unfroze. Jed tried four zeros. *Incorrect PIN*. He was out of ideas. What would a fourteen-year-old use for her PIN?

"Don't waste your time," Brown said. "I'll send it to the Bureau's new digital forensics lab in Chelsea. They'll get access in no time."

Jed leaned an elbow on his desk. Maybe Brown was right. He was wasting his time. Let the Feds deal with the phone. But now the puzzle had aroused Brown's curiosity, too.

"Have you tried her birthday, that sort of thing? Most people use personal details. Numbers that are easy to remember."

"Been there, done that, in many combinations."

"And her mother."

"What about her mother?"

"The mother's birthday?"

Jed swore under his breath. He hadn't thought of that. Karla had no siblings and little contact with her father. The mother was all she had. Jed searched for the mother's records on his laptop using her social security number. He entered her birthday on the keypad. *Incorrect PIN*. He reversed it. *Incorrect PIN*. He tried the birth year. The phone unlocked.

Jed punched the air. "Yes!" he yelled.

Special Agent Brown held out his hand, and Jed low-fived it without thinking. Maybe the Feds weren't completely useless, after all.

Special Agent Brown pulled up a chair as Jed scrolled through the call list. From the call log data, they knew Karla had made her last call at 8:44 PM on Sunday, shortly before the time of her death. The same unlisted number had appeared in the call log for Grace Miles, too. All Jed needed was to find the name of the contact Karla had called.

Jed stared at the display in disbelief. "The number isn't in her contacts list. But she called the number many times over the last week."

Special Agent Brown grunted. "This was no stranger, all right. Maybe she didn't want her mother to find out about him? Have a look at her photos."

Jed selected the photo gallery and scrolled down a long list of cat photos: A Persian cat. Karla and the Persian cat; the cat and Karla's mother. What was it with people and their cat photos?

"Hold it," Brown said. "That's him. That's the one we want."

Jed's smile faltered. Not quite the result he wanted, but Brown was right. That photo was the key. They had found their unsub.

Jed looked up. Claire's desk stood empty. He hadn't seen her for some time.

"Where's Claire?"

"She left a while ago with Rob."

Jed's shoulders stiffened. "Rob?"

"Special Agent Cline."

Jed had not liked Claire spending time with the younger Fed. That was Emmerso's doing as well. "They seem to get along pretty well."

"Yeah. The ladies love him. They're probably having dinner somewhere."

Having dinner. Jed's excitement at his breakthrough waned. Jed had wanted to ask Claire out to dinner, too. But his new partner had built an invisible wall around her. She had something to hide, he was sure of it. Now Agent Rob Cline had penetrated that wall. Had he learned her secrets, too?

Whatever. Rob could keep Claire. Other women appreciated

Jed. He'd met one such woman recently, and she was both younger and more attractive. The schoolteacher, Lisa Evans, had texted him, asking whether she could help the investigation, anything at all. Jed knew immediately what she wanted. An affair with a witness in a homicide investigation might get a detective kicked back to Patrol. But Jed was no ordinary detective. Nobody had to know about Lisa. Tonight, he would follow that lead.

"Better Claire than you," Brown added. "Rob can talk forever. I wouldn't wait up."

Jed reached for his jacket. "Oh, I won't."

CHAPTER 20

"Two burgers," Rob told the waitress, his smiling eyes on Claire. "Heavy on the mayo but hold the ketchup."

The waitress waited for Claire to comment. Rob's ordering on her behalf had surprised—and slightly annoyed—her, but he had gotten it right.

"And a soda for me," she added.

"Make that two."

"How did you know?" she asked when the waitress walked off.

Rob grinned. "You haven't changed."

"You remember how I like my burgers from ten years ago?"

"Thirteen years, but who's counting."

"Did we even eat out together?"

"Twice. We only had burgers once, but it stuck with me."

"What if my tastes had changed since then?"

"Burger preference is one of the few constants in life. Must be genetic."

Claire smiled, shaking her head at his nonsensical but amusing explanation. She had chosen the burger joint, New Burgher, one of the few decent restaurants near the department. Their last meal, seven hours ago, had consisted of tuna sandwiches they'd picked up from Claire's new regular street vendor after they had visited the Smith family home.

She indulged her curiosity about her long-lost kissing partner. "How about you? How have you changed since then?"

He cleared his throat. "You know. The usual. A few extra pounds. Some false teeth."

He was spouting nonsense again, but Claire giggled. This lightness was both familiar and foreign to her. Kidding around with a childhood friend returned Claire to the carefree world she had inhabited before her family moved to Newburgh and her life had derailed.

"Is there a Mrs. Cline waiting for you at home?"

Rob held up his hand to display his ringless fingers. "Nope."

"Why not?"

"Never found the right one. They all put ketchup on their burgers." He scrunched up his mouth in disgust. His banter had crossed the line into flirting, but after a day of grieving parents and crime scene photos, Claire welcomed the diversion.

"What about you? Do you have a boyfriend?"

"Nope."

"Why not?"

She gave him a dirty look, then relented. "I keep scaring them off."

Rob laughed. He did not seem convinced. "What about your new partner?"

Claire gave him another chiding glare and a dose of his own medicine. "Jed? He doesn't have a boyfriend either, as far as I know."

"Seriously."

"Oh, we're being serious?"

"I've seen the way he looks at you. He'd like to ask you out."

"I try not to mix business and..." She considered saying "pleasure" but doubted she'd enjoy a date with Mr. My-Daddy's-the-Chief. "Other stuff," she said.

"I know exactly what you mean."

They shared another laugh.

"Let's talk about something more interesting," she said. "Let's talk about you."

"I'm not interesting."

"Liar. Tell me about hostage negotiation."

Rob took the bait. "Don't get me started. The FBI has made significant progress over the decades. Hostage situations mushroomed in the seventies. Law enforcement's default policy was to call in SWAT and shoot things up. Lots of people died. Not only bad guys. Then, somebody decided we should talk to the kidnappers."

"Really? Talk to them—who would have imagined?"

"I know. Crazy, right? Fewer people died. That was an improvement. But the real breakthrough came when we listened to them. Thanks."

The waitress had served their burgers and cans of soda. They unwrapped their food and dug in. Claire tore into her burger like, well, a hungry wolf, and the tangy taste of warm meat and fresh mayo sent her tongue to taste bud heaven.

Claire returned to their discussion of hostage negotiation. "You said the FBI listens to kidnappers?" Had she heard him right?

"Yeah." Rob took a swig of his soda. His eyes sparkled with his passion for the topic. "We used to think, 'These criminals are crazy or evil, who cares what they want. Let's just twist their arms until they reduce the ransom.' But only when we listened to them—and I mean *truly* listened—did we get the best results. Unbelievable results. Hostages sent home alive and unharmed, sometimes without their families paying even a cent."

"Wow," Claire said, her mouth full.

"Yeah. The key is empathy."

Claire sipped her soda. *Empathy*? Was he pulling her leg again? The word triggered an association.

"What's the deal with Dr. Fleischer?"

Rob shrugged. "She's great. Forensic profilers are standard now in cases like this."

Claire swallowed. "Did you see the look on her face when she saw the crime scene photos? I thought she was going to cry or run for her life. How did she get into this line of work?"

Rob chuckled. "Yeah. She's very sensitive. Empathetic. High EQ. Emotionally intelligent. Whatever you want to call it. But that's what makes her good at her job. She can get right into a killer's mind. It's the same principle behind hostage negotiation."

Claire chewed thoughtfully, pushing the images of the dead girls from her mind. "I don't want to understand them. I want to put them behind bars."

"Understanding doesn't mean liking. Empathy isn't sympathy. But to catch a killer or influence a captor, you need to know what makes them tick. We call this strategic empathy."

"Strategic empathy?"

He grinned at her again, but Claire had missed the joke.

"What's so funny?"

"You've been using strategic empathy during this conversation. More precisely, you've used empathetic listening. You repeat the last few words I say. That encourages me to open up and elaborate. Negotiating is all about gathering information. You discover what's important to me, and I feel you understand me. Then, you can influence me."

Rob's theory was making sense. She gave him a mischievous grin. "So now I can get you to do whatever I want?"

"Probably."

"Hmm. What should I make you do?" Now *she* was flirting, too. *What's got into you, Claire Wolfe?*

Rob winked at her. "A good negotiator never asks directly. Let the other side think it's their idea."

He took another bite of his burger and groaned with pleasure. "Mm, this is good."

Claire had devoured half her burger, reaching the tricky part where the next bite might spread mayo all over her face. But the torn pinkish flesh conjured images of the dead girls, and she lost her appetite. She remembered Tina's case file on the back seat of her car. Soon she'd stare at another set of photos and another dead body. Only this dead body belonged to her little sister. She put the burger down onto the plate.

"Everything OK?"

Claire hesitated. She had told no one at the station about her past. But Rob was different. He belonged to that past, and she longed to escape her loneliness.

"I had a little sister. I was sixteen years old when she died. She was fourteen. I was supposed to walk her home from school that day, but I didn't. We fought, and I..."

How much of her story did she want to share? Her eyes misted up, and she sniffed back the tears. Rob put down his burger. His eyes drank her in. He sensed her pain but didn't judge her.

"Coming back to Newburgh, seeing those dead girls... It brings it all back."

Rob gave her a sympathetic frown. "I'm sorry about your sister. What was her name?"

Claire drew a tremulous breath. "Her name was Tina."

CHAPTER 21

Claire curled up on her couch in her pajamas, the rumpled manila folder on her lap. After dropping Rob at his motel, going for a jog, showering, loading the washing machine, and fixing a cup of green tea, she had run out of excuses to put off the task she dreaded most. She placed the teacup on the coffee table, closed her eyes, and breathed in deeply. *Are you ready?*

She had imagined this moment countless times. In her dreams, she opened the folder and found nothing inside. No crime scene photos. No reports. Tina wasn't dead. She had run away. Her casket had been empty. Tina leaped into the room, still fourteen years old, and yelled, "surprise!" Mom followed her into the room holding her famous chocolate cake, the candles burning bright.

Claire had liked *that* dream. Other dreams had been less pleasant. Her mother stormed into the room, her kitchen apron drenched in blood, a carving knife in her raised hand. "Murderer!" she cried as she lunged at Claire with the knife. "Murderer!"

A shiver traced her spine, turning her skin to gooseflesh.

She drew another deep breath. *You can do this. This folder contains the truth. You have nothing to fear.*

Claire opened her eyes and extracted the documents from the folder. The first page contained a block of typewritten text. Detective Brian O'Leary's name appeared near the bottom. The detective had scrawled his signature in blue pen above his name and a few corrections in the text. In the customary dry prose of police reports, the text described the crime scene.

"At approximately 7:15 PM, the body of a teenage girl..."

Not any girl. Claire's sister. There it was, black on white. Tina had not disappeared. She had not escaped to an exotic getaway. She had died. The police had discovered her corpse hours after she had gone missing.

"...found in a wooded area off Park Street by..." Claire did a double take. Her pulse drummed in her ears. *A wooded area off Park Street.* Tina's body had turned up in the same place as Grace Miles.

That was not entirely unexpected. Tina had gone missing near Newburgh Middle School. Few places close by were suitable for the disposal of a dead body. She read on.

"The victim is fully clothed and lying on her back. She has contusions on her neck..."

Claire's breathing became faster, shallower. Again, she noted the similarity to the recent serial murders. But there was more.

"...the victim's face displays signs of severe mutilation with a blunt object."

Claire's hand flew to her mouth. Her fingers trembled on her lips. She might have opened the case file of Gracie Miles, not Tina. Claire's gut instinct had connected the murders. Now that theory was no longer a mere intuition.

Her detective's brain took over. She fingered the pages, locating the thicker folios that contained the crime scene photos. *You don't have to see those. It's not too late to close the folder.* But Claire had to see for herself. To solve her sister's murder, she would have to study those photos long and hard and analyze every brutal detail.

She examined the first photo. There was no doubt now. Despite the harsh white light of the camera flash—these photos were taken at night—she recognized the rough path in the woods and the tall willow with the forked trunk at the edge of the long shot. Claire had visited that place on her first day at Newburgh PD. Tina's body lay in the same spot as Gracie.

The girl lay on the bed of dry leaves and broken twigs. Claire recognized her sister's white Nike sneakers, her jeans, and the gray sweater. Her body lay in the same position as Gracie, too—her legs straight, her arms at her sides. She looked as though she had dozed off and might wake up at any moment. Except for the lumpy red patch where her face had been.

Claire forced her hands to move, her fingers to turn the page. The next shot, a close-up, displayed the girl's head in the stark, pale flashlight. *No. That's not Tina.* Tina had sapphire-blue eyes and a perfect dimpled smile. The chunk of butcher's meat in the photo had neither eyes nor nose—no humanity. The bloody mess of flesh and bone wasn't her sister—it couldn't be Tina!

She flipped the photo over. Her mouth trembled so badly, her teeth chattered. *Geez, Tina.* Claire had loathed her little sister. Sometimes, she had wanted her dead. But nobody deserved to die like that—to become an inhuman pulp.

Claire drew long breaths. She sipped her tea, letting the scent of ginger and sugary sweetness revive her. She had endured the worst part of the file. The rest would be easier. The next photo displayed a kitchen knife, a thin smear of blood along the edge. Her mother's knife from the kitchen of her childhood.

Claire pieced the puzzle together. The killer had attacked, Tina had tried to defend herself. She had drawn blood. *Good for you, Tina*. But the fourteen-year-old girl's brave defense did not save her.

Why had she carried a kitchen knife? Claire had seen the knife on Tina before. She had flashed the blade at Claire on their way to school. Had Tina known her life was in danger? Why had she not told Claire, her older sister?

Wetness at the corners of her eyes announced fresh tears. If Claire had only known, she could have done something. She wouldn't be sitting here, twelve years later, studying photos of her sister's dead body.

Claire held back the tears and swallowed her emotions. Crying wouldn't bring her sister back from the dead. She flipped back to the first photo. What did it tell her? What had O'Leary missed? Her eyes frisked every pixel. *Look for what's missing*.

She spotted the glint of the kitchen knife near the body's feet, and the thick, bloodied tree branch, thrown to one side. Dots of red spatter marked Tina's sweater, the leaves, and the dirt. Unlike Grace, Tina had died there in the wooded clearing.

Dr. Fleischer had speculated about an earlier murder, and Claire had found it. The killer had been less careful and experienced. He had not planned the murder well, striking Tina and mutilating her body *in situ*. Acting impulsively, the killer had selected a high-risk victim who had fought back.

Claire had to tell the team. She had found the missing murder. Tina was the killer's first victim, the twisted fantasy he kept reliving and perfecting with each subsequent murder. Claire reached for her phone, then pulled back.

Not yet. She hadn't read the reports. Once her sister joined the list of victims, Claire would have to recuse herself from the investigation. The victim was her sister. She was too emotionally involved in the outcome. When they cornered Tina's murderer, the temptation to short-circuit the justice system and squeeze the trigger would be too great.

Claire skimmed through the remaining pages: the evidence list; the medical examiner's report. Her eyes skipped from one critical detail to the next. Time of death, between four and six PM—the same time as Gracie.

The last person to see Tina alive was her classmate, Kitty Tucker. There was a name Claire hadn't heard in years. O'Leary had also interviewed Evelyn Restall, the former principal of Newburgh Middle School. Claire flipped ahead, searching for Kitty's report when she came upon a note typed up by Detective O'Leary. The title caught her eye.

Her heart skipped a beat as she read the dead detective's words. Time ground to a halt. When Claire finished reading the report, her hands were cold.

Son of a bitch. In the memo, O'Leary summed up his case against the prime suspect—the victim's sister, Claire Wolfe.

CHAPTER 22

Tuesday morning, Claire arrived at work late for no good reason. Dread stuck in her throat like a tumor as she trawled the Newburgh PD parking lot for a vacant spot. Was the late start a delaying tactic of her subconscious—an attempt to put off this difficult task?

She backed into an empty parking space, turned off the ignition, and sat behind the wheel in silence, immobile. Her adult life had revolved around solving Tina's murder, but today would be her last day on the case. The dominos were ready to fall. Her actions over the next few minutes might end her career in law enforcement and—in a worst-case scenario—take away her freedom. But Claire had made her decision and she would follow through. There was no other way.

While she'd read Tina's case files on her living room couch last night, her cup of tea had grown cold. No matter how many times she reread the reports, she arrived at the same conclusion. Claire Wolfe, the victim's sister, was the only suspect.

Detective O'Leary had visited her home several times. He had held hushed discussions with Claire's parents and kept them abreast of his progress in Tina's murder investigation.

Claire had never imagined she was a suspect—never mind the prime suspect.

O'Leary's argument was short and simple. The older sister hated the victim. She resented her young rival and was supposed to have walked her home from school. Minutes after Tina's estimated time of death, the suspect had come home with multiple bloodstains on her body. Claire had played Cain to Tina's Abel, and her motive was the oldest in criminal history. The detective lacked only the physical evidence, washed away by the suspect, to present his case.

But if O'Leary had suspected Claire, why had he not confronted her? At sixteen, a court would have tried her as a minor. Claire's mother would have demanded Claire pay for Tina's death. Had O'Leary shared his suspicions with her father? Had the detective taken pity on her? Or had he pitied her parents who, having already lost one daughter, now stood to lose both?

Claire closed her eyes and recalled the sensations of that terrible day: the sight of Tina walking away from Claire that morning, her hips swinging in her haughty, practiced strut; the pressure of the middle school's chicken-wire fence against her back that afternoon as she marked time on her wristwatch; the sting of her leg and the sticky wetness on her hands when she arrived home. She had slipped on the broken curb and gashed her leg. So Claire had told her mom, and she had spoken the truth. But blind spots obstructed her memory of that day. That thick fog of doubt and unreality cloaked all her recollections of her little sister.

With the AC off, the air in the car grew stuffy. Claire forced herself, one last time, to consider the theory O'Leary had sketched in his report. Broken street curbs weren't the only sharp edges Claire had encountered that day. Tina had carried a kitchen knife, the blade the police had discovered at the crime scene, covered in blood. Last night, Claire had cheered Tina on for using the knife in self-defense. But had her little sister carried that weapon to defend herself from Claire? Her breakfast of eggs and toast threatened to rise in her throat. Could she have killed her sister?

No, definitely not. The thought repulsed her. Claire was not a killer. She might have hated her sister sometimes, but Tina was her flesh and blood. Claire had tried to protect her. She had wanted a close relationship with her sister, but Tina always pushed her away. No, Claire could never have hurt her.

Except for that one time. Another image sprang into her mind unbidden—Tina sprawled on the kitchen floor, a dark wet stain spreading through her clothes. *No!* Claire exorcised the image from her brain. Claire had done nothing wrong. Tina had set her up. She had pulled an evil, twisted prank on her, turning Claire's sisterly concern into a weapon. Claire's fingers rubbed at the palm of her hand. She suppressed the compulsive movements. But no matter how hard she scrubbed her skin, the ghostly bloodstain remained.

Claire slammed the wheel of her car and cursed O'Leary. A brief talk with the old detective would have set the record straight. But O'Leary was gone. He had died weeks before her transfer. His death had opened the door for Claire to the Newburgh PD Investigations Bureau but closed the door on the truth she sought.

Claire had searched the case files for other leads. The ME had found no signs of sexual assault on the corpse, but Forensics had collected pubic hairs on Tina's clothes. Dr. Fleischer had talked about the serial killer's sexual fantasy. Had the murder aroused the killer? Had he masturbated near her corpse? The file contained no lab results or DNA analysis of either the blood or DNA.

Claire would follow up with the forensics lab and the ME's

office, hoping they kept records for the case. To do that, she'd need to share Tina's file with the team. This was no longer just about Tina.

A straight, bloody line connected her sister with Gracie Miles and Karla Smith. Claire was sure of it now. But if she shared Tina's file, Claire would become a suspect, not in one murder but three.

Claire knew how the wheels of justice turned. Things would not look good for her. The murders had started soon after she'd reappeared in Newburgh. The murders matched Tina's, detail for detail. Dr. Fleischer's profile for the killer had mentioned a cold and critical mother, a personal connection to the first victim, and high intelligence. Claire met all three criteria. The killer knew about police procedures and forensic science. He would inject himself into the investigation. Claire had joined the police force and pushed for the transfer to Newburgh PD for years.

There were too many coincidences. If Jed had pounced on Gareth's ax and fingerprints, then this truckload of connections would make him foam at the mouth. And Claire wouldn't blame him. She had visited both recent crime scenes. Flecks of her dry skin might have ended up in the forensic samples. Her name might appear on the crime scene log, but she'd still have a hard time proving she hadn't been there earlier.

Claire's only defense was her sex. The killer was a man, according to Dr. Fleischer. But that one detail did not prove her innocence, and a jury would lose little sleep over her conviction.

A surge of dark, ironic humor filled her, and Claire laughed. Tina's death was her parting shot, one last prank to trump all the others. *Well done, little sister*. Without even trying, Tina had framed Claire for her murder.

As she sat on the couch last night, Claire had lifted

O'Leary's incriminating report in the air by her fingertips. The solution to her problem was both simple and terrifying. All she had to do was destroy one piece of paper. The case file contained plenty of irregularities. Nobody would miss a memo about the victim's sixteen-year-old sister.

But Claire dropped the page into the folder and closed the manila cover. Destroying evidence was a crime. It was wrong. Tampering with evidence would not help her discover the truth, it would only make her a criminal.

At that moment, she made her decision. She would share Tina's file with the investigation. Claire had not killed Tina. She had not killed Gracie Miles and Karla Smith either. The wheels of justice may be imperfect but they turned. She had to trust the system. The system was all she had. The system would deliver the true killer.

Two loud knocks on the window by her ear startled Claire, waking her from her reverie. A familiar face smiled at her. Claire opened the door and got out.

"Dad, what are you doing here?" Her cheeks warmed at being discovered there, just sitting in her car.

"I was in the neighborhood and thought I'd drop by to see you. We haven't spoken since Friday."

"I know. I've been busy at work." The excuse sounded lame even to her ears. Just when she'd reconnected with her dad, she'd neglected to visit again or even call.

His expression darkened. "I know. I saw the news. The department is after a serial killer, aren't they?"

"Yeah."

There was no point in denying it. Picking up the scent, the hyenas ensured nobody in Newburgh felt safe. Claire remembered the manila folder on the passenger seat and the confession she had to make. Would her father still be happy to see her after she became a suspect in the murder of three girls, including his daughter?

"Can I walk you in, see where you work?"

"Sure." Claire collected her bag and the manila folder and led her father inside.

The squad room brimmed with people. Claire almost collided with Dr. Fleischer at the door. The dark pools of her eyes rippled with concern. Dr. Fleischer had sensed Claire's tension but said nothing, turning her attention to the man beside Claire.

"Dad, this is Dr. Sally Fleischer of the FBI."

Dr. Fleischer shook his hand. "Nice to meet you, Mr. Wolfe."

"Call me Bill. I didn't realize the FBI employed doctors."

"She's a forensic psychiatrist. The FBI is helping us with a case."

Her dad's eyes widened. "You're one of those profilers who hunt serial killers, like on TV? What a fascinating job."

Dr. Fleischer forced a smile. She was not enjoying the attention. "Yes, many people say that. Nice to meet you." She slipped out the door.

Claire made for her desk. Rob intercepted her, his eyes moving from her to the older man beside her.

"Dad," she said before Rob could say a word. "This is Special Agent Robert Cline."

"Wow, two FBI agents. I chose the right day to visit."

Rob swallowed hard. "Glad to meet you."

He shook her dad's hand. Claire grinned. Rob seemed as uncomfortable as a teenager meeting his girlfriend's parents for the first time.

"Claire, uh, does fantastic work here."

"I don't doubt that." A note of rebuke chilled Dad's voice. Had his fatherly intuition picked up on their relationship?

Claire stepped in to ease the tension. "Rob trained as a hostage negotiator."

"Really?" Her dad considered him with renewed interest. "That's impressive."

Rob shrugged off the compliment. "It was challenging work."

While her dad took in the squad room, Rob shot Claire a subtle but ironic grin. "Look at us," he seemed to say. "This isn't awkward at all!"

Then, her father's expression darkened. Claire followed his gaze. He was staring at the list of girls' names on the whiteboard.

"The papers said you'd found two girls. Are you expecting more?"

Claire cringed inside. He knew what losing an adolescent daughter meant. Claire should never have brought him into the squad room.

"No, Dad. But we've placed some girls under police protection until we catch the killer."

"Detective Wolfe," someone said behind her, his voice dripping with sarcasm. "Thank you for joining us this morning."

Jed strolled over from the captain's office, a spring in his step and a smirk on his face. Claire tensed up, remembering her decision. Once she handed Jed the manila folder, the investigation would slip out of her control.

"And just in time for our briefing. And you are?"

"William Wolfe. Claire's dad."

The smirk faded, and Jed offered his hand. "Detective Jed Wallace."

After a moment's hesitation, her dad shook Jed's outstretched hand. "I knew a Detective Wallace, years ago."

He held on to Jed's hand, and drops of sweat appeared on her partner's forehead.

"You must mean my father, Harry Wallace."

"Yes, that's him." An undercurrent of menace heated his words. Had he met Jed's father after Tina's death? "He wouldn't remember me, though." Bill released Jed's hand and spoke to Claire. "I don't want to get in your hair. I'll show myself out. Speak to you later, Cub?"

"Sure."

Her father walked off. He had aged a few years since entering the squad room. Claire turned to Jed. She needed to speak up before she lost her nerve.

"Jed, I need to—"

"Not now. We're late enough as it is. I've got an important announcement."

Claire hesitated. Last she heard, the investigation had stalled. Had Jed uncovered a new lead? Had he discovered the connection to Tina? Would he expose Claire's connection to the case before the entire bureau?

Jed raised his voice. "Gentlemen—and ladies. We've made a breakthrough."

Enthusiastic murmurs circled the room. Claire stepped back, away from Jed and the center of attention.

Jed cast a glance at Tom Brown, who stood nearby. "With Special Agent Brown's help, we gained access to the second victim's phone last night."

At the words "last night" he gave Claire a dirty look. Was he judging her for leaving work before him? Had she, in his opinion, not put in enough hours?

Jed waved the grainy print of an enlarged photo in the air. "We have a new lead."

In the photo, Karla Smith laughed. She glanced away from the camera toward an older boy with long brown hair. He locked his arms around her shoulders, the tattoo of a Chinese character visible on the pale skin of his freckled forearm. A white trail of smoke wafted from the joint in his hand.

"The male in the photo is Justin Fox, a senior at Hannover High and three years older than the victims. As you know, Karla Smith called an unlisted number several times. The number also appears on the call log for Grace Miles's phone, which is still missing. We suspect the number belongs to Fox and that he's been dealing marijuana at the school. He's officially a person of interest in both murders."

Claire blinked. Justin Fox. The white male matched Dr. Fleischer's profile. But Fox was five years old at the time of Tina's death. If he was the killer, Tina's death was unrelated to the homicides. Relief washed over Claire.

Jed glanced at her, a smug grin on his face. Did he think his smooth detective work had made her smile? Claire did nothing to dispel that impression.

"We're bringing Fox in for questioning," Jed said. "This sucker's going down."

CHAPTER 23

"Everything OK?" Rob asked Claire as he drove the blue Bureau car to their next destination.

First Dr. Fleischer, now him. Claire wished she wasn't so transparent. Just when she'd summoned the courage to share Tina's case file with the team, the investigation had changed direction. If Justin Fox had murdered the girls, Tina's case was no longer relevant. But the justification failed to appease her conscience. She'd better be careful what she said. Rob manipulated hostage takers for a living. Squeezing information from her would be child's play.

"Sure. I'm fine. Why do you ask?"

"You seemed a little...flustered."

She snickered. "*Flustered*? Old ladies get flustered. Are you calling me an old lady?"

Rob grinned but said nothing. She hadn't told him the whole truth, but he didn't pry.

Don't tell him, Claire. Rob worked for the Feds. Even if he didn't share the information with the department, he'd have to report his findings to his superiors. But after they had reconnected last night, Claire owed him an explanation.

"I've spent too many hours studying dead girls." That much was true.

Rob nodded with empathy. She had told him about Tina's death, but she had not mentioned her murder. Claire needed a change of subject.

"What do you think of our new lead?"

Rob frowned. "Too soon to tell. A lot of kids do drugs. Karla's mom didn't mention Justin, but she probably didn't know about him. I guess a lot of girls don't share their love lives with their moms. But not even recording his name on her phone—that's weird. It strengthens Jed's theory that Fox was her dealer. He probably asked her to keep his details off the record."

"I don't know," Claire said. "Dr. Fleischer said our unsub is highly intelligent. If he's been selling weed to middle school girls, how intelligent can he be?"

Rob laughed. "I guess we'll find out soon enough."

By "we" Rob meant the department. Jed and Tom had rushed to Hannover High along with two squad cars to pick up Justin Fox. Meanwhile, Claire and Rob headed to the senior's home to collect evidence. Claire didn't mind. The home visit should pass quietly. After almost sharing Tina's file with the team, Claire was glad the investigation's spotlights had focused elsewhere.

The navigation app told Rob they'd reached their destination. The thickets of wild grass and peeling picket fence reminded Claire that they'd strayed from middle-class suburbia and entered Glenville, Newburgh's poverty blocks to the west of the park. An old car tire hung from a hunchbacked Autumn Purple Ash tree. The single-level home must have looked charming in the seventies, but decades of neglect had taken their toll.

Rob pulled up behind a white Subaru. An old white Chevy

rusted in a dusty patch beside the house. "Somebody's home," he said.

The sound of their closing car doors echoed off the walls, and that tingling sense of déjà vu crawled up Claire's spine again. Another family home, another crime. Maybe this time, their net would close around the killer.

They walked up to the front door, and Rob pressed the buzzer. Hearing nothing, he rapped his knuckles on the wooden door. Feet dragged on the floorboards inside, and the door cracked open to the length of a security chain. A woman in her forties emerged from a cloud of high-tar cigarette smoke.

"If you're looking for Justin, he ain't here."

Claire flashed her badge. "Detective Claire Wolfe. This is Special Agent Cline. May we come in?"

"I told you, he ain't here."

"We need to ask you a few questions."

Justin's mother took a drag on her cigarette. "Suit yourselves." She unlatched the chain, and they followed her inside. The slack skin of her arms flapped as she walked into a living room with a large box-shaped TV the likes of which Claire hadn't seen in years.

Mrs. Fox flopped on the pillow of a wicker couch, which belonged on a front porch not indoors. Claire and Rob shared the second matching couch.

"What's he done now?"

"It's probably nothing, but he might have information that can help our investigation."

The mother scrutinized them, unconvinced. "Can't be nothing if you're here. Did the school send you?"

"No. Why would they?"

"Because he's disappeared, that's why."

A meaningful glance passed between Claire and Rob. Jed and Tom were in for an unpleasant surprise.

"When did you last see your son?"

"Last week. He's too cool for school." Mrs. Fox spoke about her son with undisguised contempt. "He doesn't listen to me. Too busy hanging out with his fancy friends in the 'real world' and buying fancy clothes. I don't ask where he gets the money. I don't want to know."

Claire remembered Dr. Fleischer's profile: White male; critical mother; older than the victims. Justin Fox met all the criteria.

"Does he have a car?"

"If you call that rust bucket a car."

"Do you have any idea where he might have gone?"

She shrugged.

"What about his father—would he know where Justin is?"

"If he does, he ain't telling nobody. Hal died when Justin was six."

Claire apologized, and Justin's mom softened.

"I knew he'd get himself in trouble someday. When you lot came knocking, I thought you'd tell me he'd gotten himself killed."

"Do you mind if we look in his room?"

"Be my guest."

Pushing her palms to the cushions, she got to her feet, hobbled to a passageway, and threw open the door of a bedroom. "Knock yourselves out."

An unmade bed hugged one of the white blank walls. The air smelled faintly of burnt rope, the scent of marijuana. This was their guy. The door had fallen off the IKEA closet, which stood empty except for a few hangars and a faded T-shirt emblazoned with the word 'Disturbed.'

They opened the drawers and poked around. If Justin had stashed drugs in here, he'd taken them with him.

"Rob." Claire pointed to a SIM card on the wooden desk. A

charred black circle in the center of the small plastic rectangle had burned away the golden circuit lines.

"Somebody didn't want to be traced."

Rob handed her a pair of latex gloves. Serial killers had motives, he had said. Did Justin believe a grandiose government conspiracy had targeted him? Was that why he killed the girls?

Rob tried the desk drawers while Claire made for the red trash bin beneath the desk. The SIM card had given her hope for more discoveries, and she was not disappointed.

"I've got something." A mobile phone lay at the bottom of the trash can. The case had purple and pink flowers. The lithium-ion battery lay beside it.

Rob moved closer and stared into the bin. "Grace's phone?"

Claire called Jed. They needed a warrant to search and process the scene thoroughly. Any doubts she had harbored about their new suspect fluttered away. Grace had spent her last hours with Justin. The trail glowed hot.

CHAPTER 24

Claire was studying at her bedroom desk when she heard the scream. The high-pitched, blood-curdling wail came from downstairs, the sound of a wounded animal. She dropped her pencil on her English workbook and dashed out of her room.

"What happened?" she cried from the top of the stairs. She peered over the railing at the empty hall. Her mom had gone grocery shopping. Her dad had left town for work. Claire was supposed to keep an eye on Tina. Where was she?

"Tina?"

The shriek sounded again. The voice came from the kitchen. Tina's voice. Had thieves broken into their home? Had her sister slipped and injured herself? Her mom would never forgive Claire if something bad had happened to Tina.

Claire raced down the stairs and sprinted to the kitchen. Tina lay on the floor, her body slumped against the kitchen counter. Blood pooled on the floor and soaked Tina's shirt and skirt. Her sister's hands pressed her belly where, from between her fingers, the handle of a carving knife protruded.

Claire ran to her little sister, who writhed in pain, her face a twisted mask of agony. How did this happen? Was the attacker still in the house? She saw no sign of an intruder.

Her helplessness terrified her. Her sister was dying, but Claire didn't know how to stop the bleeding. Tears spilled from her eyes.

"Tina!" Panic rang in her voice. "Tina! What happened?"

Tina winced. Weak from loss of blood, she couldn't speak. Claire dropped to the floor and held her little sister in her arms, blood staining her hands and clothes. "Stay with me, Tina! Don't fall asleep." An ambulance! She needed an ambulance.

Claire clambered to her feet and fumbled for the house phone on the kitchen counter. She dialed 911 but botched the digits. She hung up and tried again. Why wouldn't her fingers stop shaking?

On her third attempt, she dialed the number correctly. Tina slipped to the floor in a pool of blood. Claire had responded too slowly, and her sister was dying before her eyes. Claire's mom would kill her. Honest to God, she'd strangle Claire for this.

An automated message on the other end of the line asked Claire to wait. *Why won't they pick up already?* Claire paced on the spot, bawling into her one hand while the other pressed the receiver to her ear. Her hair was damp with sweat. Or blood.

Finally, a woman answered. "Nine-one-one, what's your emergency?"

Claire forced back her tears and drew a shallow, halting breath, the panic choking her. "It's my sister!"

Then, Claire heard another sound, and she froze.

On the kitchen floor, Tina's body convulsed, but this was not a seizure or epileptic fit. Tina was laughing. She held the carving knife in the air and giggled her head off. The blade was clean.

Tina pointed at Claire and gulped air between fits of laughter. "You...you should've seen...your face!"

Claire blinked back her disbelief.

"Hello? Is anyone there?" the operator said.

Claire put down the phone. Relief flooded her. Then, fiery rage.

"You psycho!" Claire swore. She never swore. Her mom had strong opinions about cursing.

"Watch your mouth, Big Sister, or Mom will wash it out with soap." Tina picked herself off the floor, knife in hand. She switched to her mocking, baby voice. "Did a little ketchup get your panties in a bunch?"

"You scared the crap out of me, you little...shit!"

She'd sworn again. Claire didn't care. Her demonic younger sister deserved a stabbing. But Tina sensed Claire's mood and turned on her with the knife. "What you gonna do about it, Big Sister?" she taunted, prodding Claire to make another mistake.

The front door opened, and Claire spun around. *Thank God!* Mom was home. Tina wouldn't dare attack her in front of their parents. She'd transform into a smiling angel.

Her mother elbowed her way inside, her arms loaded with paper bags. Then, she glanced at the kitchen, and the color drained from her face. The bags dropped to the floor, and glass containers cracked.

"Ow!" A loud and melodramatic cry came from behind Claire. Tina had no shame. She didn't know when to stop. Then, her sister let loose another banshee shriek, and Claire cringed. Tina was cruel to do this to Mom. But she'd get away with it.

"Claire!" their mother shouted. "What have you done?"

"Nothing, Mom. She's OK. She's playing another stupid prank."

Tina groaned and slid to the floor.

"You call that nothing?!" Her mom rushed forward, casting

a horrified glance at Claire's red hands and clothes as she passed her and crouched over her wounded daughter.

Tina pointed at Claire and yelled, "She stabbed me!"

Enough was enough. "I did not! She's made that up, Mom. Look, she's not even hurt."

Claire knelt beside her mother and reached for the knife. But the blade had torn through her sister's jeans and buried itself in her thigh. Claire grabbed the handle, but the knife wouldn't budge.

Tina yelped with pain. "Get her away from me! She's trying to kill me!"

"What? No! She's lying!"

Claire hadn't stabbed her sister. Had she? What had happened? Suddenly, Claire had no idea.

Mom snarled at Claire. "Get away from us, you evil girl!" She pulled Tina close, supporting her in her arms. "Tina, can you get up?"

Tina's voice was small and scared. "I don't know, Mom."

"On three." Their mother counted to three and lifted Tina to her feet. "I'm taking you to the hospital. Claire, you just...stay here. I'll deal with you later."

Her mom held Tina by her arms, supporting her. They were halfway to the front door. Claire followed, wanting to help.

"Mom!" Tina bawled. "She's coming for me!"

"Stay back!" Her mom raised her hand in the air, like a priestess warding off demons with a crucifix. "Just stay back!"

They disappeared out the door. Moments later, a car engine started, and they departed. Claire stood rooted to the spot, her hands red and sticky, her head spinning. What had just happened?

CHAPTER 25

Wednesday morning, Claire placed a bouquet of lilies on Tina's grave. Rob stood at her side, silent. The flowers had seemed fitting. This was the first time Claire had visited her sister since the funeral. What had taken her so long?

Gray clouds veiled the sky. A nippy breeze tugged at Claire's coat. A male voice droned on about heavenly kingdoms. The funeral service in another section of the graveyard had begun. Below the tombstone statue of a winged angel, her sister's epithet read, "An angel born of heaven. Gone too soon." Her mother had chosen the words. She'd only seen the angel in Tina.

A morbid thought came to Claire. What remained of her sister's body after twelve years in the ground? For weeks after the funeral, Claire had refused to accept her sister's death. Ironically, the crime scene photos in Tina's murder book had resurrected Claire's incredulity. She could not deny the blood and gore, but the mutilated corpse had not displayed her sister's face. Again, that childish hope swelled in her breast. Was Tina still alive? If so, whose body lay beneath Claire's feet?

Claire said, "So killers do attend their victims' funerals?"

Rob nodded. "Detective novels got that one right. Serial killers especially. Seeing the suffering their actions have caused gives them a sense of power and control. 'Look at what I did.' Well, some kinds of serial killers."

Claire turned from her sister's old grave, and they watched the funeral of Gracie Miles. Her family and friends, all in black, stood in silence. The second ring of well-wishers kept a respectful distance. Seventy people, Claire estimated. Half probably only knew Gracie from the news.

How many had attended Tina's funeral? Claire couldn't recall. She only remembered the earth swallowing her polished casket and the nauseating thump of dirt clods landing on the wooden lid. And O'Leary. Pudgy, old Detective O'Leary with his brown fedora and graying hair. He had eyeballed Claire at the funeral. Had he suspected her even then?

"Think he'll show?"

Rob scanned the crowd. "Not if he's smart, but the urge might be too powerful."

By now, Justin knew the police were onto him. Detectives had interviewed his classmates, teachers, and neighbors. The department put out a BOLO with Justin's description. His phone, now offline, had last connected with a communications tower on Monday morning within ten miles of Newburgh Middle School.

Had he been scouting his next victim? When Rob raised that possibility, Captain Emmerso had asked Captain Rodrigez of Patrol to assign another two officers to the school. The police protection allocated to the girls on Claire's list already weighed heavily on the department's resources, but nobody wanted to find another dead girl. Newburgh PD was pulling out all the stops for the Middle School Strangler, as the media had dubbed the killer. Until the department reeled him in, other proactive policing tasks would have to wait.

"Her classmates have shown up," Claire said. She recognized them from her visit to the middle school with Jed a week ago. It felt like a month ago.

The schoolgirls whispered among themselves. Some wiped at tears, others hid awkward smiles. At their age, death was a distant rumor. Unbelievable, the way Tina's death had been to Claire.

The service concluded, and the attendees dispersed. Still no sign of Justin Fox. Maybe their suspect was smarter than she had thought. Claire and Rob approached the family and waited for their turn to console them.

Claire looked Gareth and Candace Miles in the eyes. "We're sorry for your loss."

Candace, her face hidden behind dark glasses and thick makeup, nodded. She gripped her son, Paul, by his shoulder, and they made for the parking lot. An update about the investigation would have to wait. Their daughter's death had only now become a reality. Claire would stop by their home later. Who knew, maybe by then they'd have located the murderer.

Rob's hand closed on Claire's elbow. "Over there."

She followed his gaze. A man in jeans stepped from behind a tree and pulled the hood of his gray sweatshirt over his head. He shoved his hands into his pockets and rushed toward the group of schoolgirls as they cut through the grassy lawns toward the parking lot.

Claire and Rob moved toward the man. They had about twenty seconds before he reached the girls. Rob pointed to the side, and Claire nodded. She would approach from behind while Rob outflanked him to cut off his escape route.

Claire called Captain Emmerso on her phone and picked up her pace.

"Are you still at the funeral?" he asked.

"We have eyes on a suspect, sir. Not sure it's Fox, but if it is, we'll need backup and roadblocks around the cemetery."

"I'm on it."

She tucked her phone back into a pocket and drew her weapon, holding the Glock low to draw as little attention as possible. Adrenaline pumped through her veins while she jogged toward the suspect, closing the distance. Claire knew these sensations well from other hot pursuits. The world came into sharp focus. Every muscle in her body coiled, ready for action. Only she and her prey existed. Everything else faded into the background. During the thrill of the hunt, the true nature of life emerged in its pure and primal essence.

In her peripheral vision, Rob raced ahead, cutting across the grassy knoll. The hooded head stalked onward toward the girls, oblivious. The tunnel vision of this predator's hunt blinded him to theirs.

Fifty yards now. Claire doubted he'd attack the girls in public and broad daylight. But if cornered, Justin might take a girl hostage. Claire had to catch him unawares.

Twenty yards. Autumn leaves crunched beneath her feet. The man broke into a trot. Had she made too much noise? At any moment, he might bolt. If she lost him, he wouldn't show his face again. She had to take him down now.

The man veered sideways and said something. He reached out toward the girls. What did he have in his hand? Claire raised her firearm. One girl glanced at the man, fear on her face. Then, she spotted Claire behind him and the gun in her hand.

"Stop!" Claire cried. "Police!" She aimed the gun at the center bulk of his torso.

The man froze in the tall grass. Claire had never shot anyone in the line of duty. She would, if necessary. But she couldn't risk injuring the girls behind him.

The man spun around, a stray lock of hair escaping the hood. It was the boy from Karla's phone, Justin Fox. The whites of his eyes flashed as he took in Claire's gun.

"Put your hands on your head. Slowly."

The girls behind him squealed with terror. Fox raised his arms. His hands were empty, warding her off.

His mouth opened as though about to speak. Then, he bolted.

Claire swore under her breath and sprinted after him. The kid was young, but he wasn't in good shape. He changed direction every few steps. Did he think she'd shoot him in the back?

She charged ahead, the muscles in her legs prickling. The teasing pain, an old friend from Claire's running routine, signaled the endorphins would soon kick in. Justin's shoes kicked up grass and dirt. He looked over his shoulder, and she sensed his fear. He reached the parking lot, but he was no match for her.

Claire holstered her weapon and pounced. Time slowed. Her shoulder connected with his back just as his legs flew sideways from beneath him. Another fast-moving body had slammed into the suspect in a second mid-air collision.

Time caught up. Claire landed on Fox's heaving body, and the kid groaned beneath her.

"You OK?" she asked Rob, who still hugged the kid's legs. Red scratches marked his hand where the gravel of the parking lot had grazed his skin. His sideways tackle had hit the kid at the same moment Claire intercepted him from behind.

"Yeah."

Claire panted, riding the adrenaline rush. Rob held the kid down while she cuffed his hands behind his back.

"Where d'you learn to run like that?" Rob asked her.

"Track team." When the kid groaned again, she added, "Shut up and stay down."

Rob searched the suspect for concealed weapons. "Well, what do you know?" He held a plastic bag of tightly packed joints. "Justin Fox, you are under arrest."

"I did it," the kid said. "OK? I did it."

Claire wanted to kick him in the ribs but held back. She pulled out her phone. Miraculously, the device had survived her fall. She called Dispatch to send patrol officers, then dialed Captain Emmerso.

"Sir, we got him."

CHAPTER 26

Claire studied her suspect on the computer monitor in the Newburgh PD observation room. The camera in the interrogation room's corner showed Detective Jed Wallace sitting at a small square table. The door opened. A patrol officer escorted Justin Fox into the room, then left. The teenager sat opposite Jed, leaning back in his hard chair and smirking Claire did not pity him. *I did it.* Justin Fox had confessed. Confessions gave the district attorney an easy conviction. But as the adrenaline of the chase subsided, Claire's disgust for the killer mixed with uncertainty. Fox had provided no details. Had he confessed to murdering those girls or some other crime?

On the screen, Jed riffled pages in a folder on the interrogation room table.

"I'm Detective Wallace. Do you want some water?"

Justin glared at Jed but said nothing.

"He seems relaxed," Claire said.

"Yeah," Rob said.

The FBI agents had crammed into the small observation room with her.

"That's not unusual for serial killers," Dr. Fleischer said.

"After getting away with multiple murders, they think they're smarter than law enforcement. They believe they'll never get caught, and even when they do, they figure they'll talk their way out of it and beat the system."

Claire, Rob, and Dr. Fleischer resumed their silent analysis of their suspect's body language. That nagging intuition itched again. With his hood off, revealing his hippie-length hair and a soft, pretty face, the kid didn't appear to be capable of multiple brutal murders.

"I'd never have tagged him as a killer," Claire said. "I guess I was expecting a monster. This kid's a wimp."

"Few serial killers are physically imposing. They choose easy prey—the weak and defenseless. Prostitutes. Isolated elderly women."

"Little girls," Claire added.

On the screen, Justin Fox stretched his shoulders. Jed tried to build rapport with the suspect again.

"How far have you gotten in school?"

The door of the observation room opened, and Captain Emmerso entered. "Detective Wolfe, Agents. Excellent work on capturing the suspect."

"Thank you, sir."

"I understand he confessed during his arrest?"

Claire hesitated. "He didn't give any details."

Emmerso grunted and studied the suspect on the computer monitor. "Let's see what he says now."

In the investigation room, Jed's chest rose and fell as he sighed. He was losing his patience.

"Are you under the influence of drugs or alcohol?"

More silence. Giving up on rapport, Jed got to business. He placed a recording device on the table, mentioned the date and the names of those present, then pushed a clipboard and pen toward the suspect.

"You need to sign that."

Again, no response. Fox didn't even look at the Miranda form.

"Smart-ass," Agent Tom Brown muttered and shook his head. Was that an insult or a compliment? By saying nothing, Fox deprived them of ammunition. Could he be their highly intelligent killer, after all?

Jed lifted a plastic evidence bag in the air containing a single joint. "We found these in your bedroom and car." At last, surprise registered on Fox's face. "You parked down the road from the cemetery. But we're not here about drugs, are we? We're interested in the crime you confessed to—the murder of two girls, Grace Miles and Karla Smith."

Justin's cheeks reddened, but his jaw clenched tight. "We found Grace's phone in your bedroom. Your prints are all over it."

"Are they?" Captain Emmerso said.

Claire answered. "Still being processed."

Jed continued. "You burned her SIM card to prevent us from tracking her to you. That's Obstruction of Justice. You'll spend a long time in prison."

Justin's nostrils flared, but his lips remained sealed.

"This is going nowhere," Captain Emmerso said. "Agent Cline, you're the negotiator. Why aren't you in there?"

Jed had insisted on interrogating the suspect personally, but the others said nothing.

Rob hesitated. "That's your call."

"Go on, then."

Rob handed his gun to Tom and made for the door. But he was too late.

Jed stood and collected his folder. "Have it your way." He walked out. "Book him," he told the officer at the door.

Tom returned Rob's gun. "Maybe next time, hotshot."

Jed burst into the observation room. "He's our guy!" he told Captain Emmerso.

"How can we be sure?"

"We'll have his prints soon. A DNA swab might tie him to trace evidence from the crime scene. Meanwhile, we can hold him for possession. Fifty grams of marijuana."

"Thank goodness for that. What do you think, Dr. Fleischer?"

The forensic psychiatrist frowned. "I had expected him to be older, but the profile is only a guideline. I wish he'd say something. We need to get into his head and figure out what he's thinking."

Jed scoffed. "Take your time. Once he's locked up for life, you'll have years to pick his brain."

"Assuming he's the killer. So far he hasn't confessed to that."

"He will. He's our guy."

Dr. Fleischer glanced at Rob. "You spoke with the mother?"

Rob said, "She doesn't think much of him. His father died when he was six. He's a textbook case of early childhood emotional deprivation."

Dr. Fleischer nodded. "He could be the killer. The drugs might have played a part, too, either to lure his victims or as a feature of his sexual fantasy."

Captain Emmerso squinted at the psychiatrist. "Doctor, if I recall correctly, the victims showed no signs of penetration."

"In serial murder, intercourse is often absent from the crime. The murder fantasy replaces normal sexual interaction. The killer might masturbate during the crime or much later. You'll want to search his home for trophies or mementos."

"Like Gracie's phone?" Claire suggested.

"Yes." She hesitated. "Although he wouldn't have thrown his memento in the trash. He'd want to keep it for later to relive the crimes. Did you find jewelry or identity cards belonging to the victims?"

"No, nothing like that."

Dr. Fleischer frowned. Something wasn't adding up, and Claire wasn't the only one harboring doubts about their new suspect.

"Search his phone," Dr. Fleischer said. "He may have photographed the victims before or after killing them."

"We'll do that," Jed said. He turned to the captain. "He'll talk, eventually. I can feel it."

Captain Emmerso nodded. "Good work, everyone. Soon we'll know if he's a keeper."

They dispersed to their tasks. Claire dropped off the DNA swab at the forensics lab, then returned to the squad room to type up her report of the arrest.

"Yes!" Jed blurted, startling Claire at her laptop.

He sprang to his feet and danced the disco, stabbing his hand at the ceiling like John Travolta's character in *Saturday Night Fever*. The other detectives watched him with amusement.

Mahoney stroked his chin. "Let me guess. You found your dick?"

Jed was too elated to take offense.

Claire stifled a laugh. "I'm betting the fingerprints match our suspect."

"Fingerprints *and* DNA, baby," Jed crooned. "Love me some D-N-A!"

"We have a DNA match?"

"Mm-hm. Skin particles found under Grace Miles's fingernails match Fox's DNA."

Claire blinked. She hadn't expected that. They had placed Justin Fox with Gracie shortly before her death, and her phone had surfaced in his bedroom. Their suspect's brief confession tied the case with a gift ribbon. They had caught the killer.

Jed danced over and high-fived her. "Let's tell the captain and call the DA's office."

After breaking the good news, Claire looked for Rob in the squad room. She'd last seen him a few hours ago. Had the Bureau called him to another case now they had the Middle School Strangler in custody? Would he have left without saying goodbye?

Her email app pinged. Captain Emmerso had assigned her a robbery. Soon, the detectives would put the murders aside to focus on other crimes. Claire leaned back in her chair. Another unsolved case needed her attention. Tina's murder. Kitty Tucker was the last person to see Tina alive. What had become of her?

Rob and Tom entered the room, all smiles.

"We just heard," Rob said. "Congratulations."

Jed rose to his feet and shook their hands. "Thank you. Your emotional support made all the difference."

Tom rolled his eyes but patted the detective on the shoulder, his long-suffering smile hinting that the FBI agent was used to others taking credit for his work.

Rob sidled over to Claire. "Ready to celebrate?" A playful note had entered his voice.

"That depends. How are we celebrating?"

"Oh, I know the perfect way."

CHAPTER 27

Claire smirked at Rob. "*You* are a sissy."

Tears streamed from his eyes. In his hand, he held a knife. "It's the onions, honest."

He stood beside her at the kitchen counter, an apron over his sweater and jeans.

"Now you're just making excuses."

They had stopped by his motel to pick up fresh clothes, then shopped at the local Walmart Supercenter for groceries before heading back to Claire's house. He'd showered, changed into civilian clothes, and got to work in the kitchen. Claire hit the shower, too. The thought that Rob had stood naked in the stall only minutes before gave her shower a sensual quality.

By the time she had dressed, he had set the kitchen table with a red cloth and two wine glasses. Now he chopped onions into uniform little chunks and swept them into the frying pan, which responded with a satisfying hiss. He sautéed the onions expertly, then added chicken pieces he'd basted in a tray. There was something sexy about a man who cooked. She drew near and inhaled the pleasant scent of his aftershave on his freshly showered body.

"I never learned to cook," she confessed. "You make it look easy."

Rob grinned. "Some like to do, some like to watch. I won't judge you."

They traded innuendos like a long-time couple. Around Rob, Claire was a carefree teenager again, the decade of anguish and heartache evaporating into the night. She couldn't believe they'd reconnected only two days ago—two intense days they had shared as comrades in arms. But tonight, Claire wasn't feeling very sisterly.

A sudden doubt marred her enjoyment of the moment. *What are we doing?* The multiple homicide case was at a close. Quantico would send Rob far away to assist other investigations. After tonight, Claire might never see him again. She pushed that depressing thought aside. They'd make their last night together very memorable.

Claire walked over to the table, opened the bottle of wine—a task that, unlike cooking, she had mastered—and poured two glasses of red. She handed one to Rob.

"Thanks." He accepted the glass and took a quick gulp.

The scent of cooking chicken got her juices flowing. "Mm, smells good."

"Here." He scooped a spoonful of diced chicken and blew on the steaming broth. Claire opened her mouth for the spoon. He watched her closely as she chewed and swallowed.

"That's good. But now I want more."

She moved closer to him, and their hips touched. Desire flashed in his eyes. The warmth of his body radiated through his clothes, and her resistance melted.

Claire placed her wine glass on the counter and turned off the stove. She bunched his sweater in her fists and pulled him close. "Let's skip to dessert."

Later, in bed, she rested her head on his bare chest. His

heartbeat raced in her ear. Outside, thunder rumbled. Rain poured down, washing the city clean. Rob stroked her hair. Claire soaked up the warm contentment. She was at peace with the world and herself. She wanted to bottle this feeling and save it forever.

"I was thinking," he said.

Claire could guess where this was going. She smiled. "About the elephant in the room?"

He chuckled. "Yeah. It's a different elephant this time. I was thinking..."

Again, she interrupted him. "That we should stay in touch?"

"Hey, don't jump to the punch line. I've been rehearsing this speech for hours. Hear me out."

"OK, I'm all ears. But give me the abridged version."

"Here goes. You should join the FBI."

Claire chuckled. "The Behavioral Analysis Unit in Quantico?"

"Why not? You're smart. You've just caught your first serial killer. And we'll see each other every day."

"Unless we get shipped off to different cases across the country."

"I've got that figured out, too. We'll partner up. I'll convince the unit head. You'll like Chief Alda. She's really smart."

"She? I'm jealous already."

He chuckled. Rob was spouting nonsense again and he knew it, but he was also telling her he wanted them to stay together.

Claire played along. "Sure. Where do I sign my name? Wait. There's one other problem."

"The FBI can't afford you? I know. But we'll make an exception. Name your price."

"The real problem is Tom. I've seen the way he looks at you.

He won't give up on you that easily. That guy's going to fight me to the death."

Rob laughed again, and his chest shifted. As the passion and pleasure faded, grim reality set in. No matter what Rob said or wanted, soon their paths would part.

"This case tied up so quickly."

"I know."

Claire wasn't just mirroring his regret at having to say goodbye. Another murder case weighed on her mind, but sharing that burden required exposing a part of herself she'd kept bottled up for years. Maybe it was time she uncorked that bottle. Thanks to Rob, she had rediscovered a glimmer of her old self. She owed him the whole truth. And with their serial killer in police custody, there was no harm in sharing her dark past.

"There's something I need to tell you."

"Uh-oh. Let me guess. You're a guy?"

"You would have noticed that by now." She sat up on her elbows. "I'm serious."

He sobered up. "Go ahead."

"This stays between you and me."

Rob crossed his fingers. "Scout's honor."

Here goes. "I told you about my sister. There's more to that story. Tina was murdered."

"Here, in Newburgh?"

Claire nodded. "Her case was never solved. She's the reason I became a cop."

"You joined the Academy and transferred here to solve her murder?"

"Yup."

"Wow. Claire Wolfe, you are such a badass."

"Thank you. I think. Then, those girls turned up dead. Gracie and Karla. Fourteen years old. Blonde-haired and blue-eyed. Just like Tina. It sounds stupid now, but I had hoped we'd find Tina's killer at the bottom of that rabbit hole."

"Wow."

"Yeah. Crazy, right?"

"No, not crazy. But Justin Fox was five years old then."

"Exactly. Fox didn't kill my sister."

"Don't be so sure. Have you seen the five-year-olds these days? They're monsters."

Claire slapped him on his naked, firm stomach.

"Ouch. OK, I deserved that."

"You did." She rested her chin on his chest again, savoring this fleeting moment of contentment. "I can't leave Newburgh. Not yet. I've still got work to do."

CHAPTER 28

A thunderclap struck outside as Detective Jed Wallace answered the door in his shirtsleeves. A young blonde woman with round golden glasses stood on the threshold of his home, a bottle of white, bubbly wine in her hand. Judging by her bare feet and shapely, naked legs, she wore nothing else underneath her trench coat.

"You've been a bad boy." Lisa Evans placed her free hand on his chest and shoved him backward. "I'm going to send you to the principal."

Jed had texted Lisa about the breakthrough in the case, and this was exactly the response he'd hoped to receive. He grinned. "You'd better punish me yourself."

She pulled a pin from the bun behind her head, and her silky hair fell to her shoulders. Walking into his arms, she kissed him, hard and hot. He took the bottle from her hand, placed it on a nearby surface, and slipped his hand up her thigh. He'd been right about her dress code. Lisa knew how to drive him wild.

The teacher slapped his hand away and disengaged, giving him another playful shove. "Beware, Detective. My punishment comes in one flavor—strict." She swung the door shut behind her and unbuttoned her coat.

Jed swallowed. "Mercy."

Lisa had not been kidding. By the time they finished, Jed was breathing hard and dripping sweat. Bite marks decorated his body. He'd had no idea the schoolteacher's petite frame packed so much passion when he'd first hit on her at Newburgh Middle School. Now, he was glad he had.

He lay on his back, panting. Scenes from that day flashed over the dark screen of his bedroom ceiling: Justin Fox on his way to the holding cell; Claire Wolfe smiling at Special Agent Rob Cline; the crime scene photos of the two dead girls.

He preferred not to use their names. Words such as "decedents" and "victims" helped him pretend the corpses were objects, not actual young girls. The twist in the investigation had surprised him. He'd built a case against Grace's father when Justin Fox had turned up. Still, Jed found the crimes hard to fathom. Fox was just a kid, only three years older than his victims. He had known both girls. How could he have killed and mutilated them?

Lisa rested her chin on her hands and watched him like a purring cat. "Thinking about the case?"

"Mm-hm."

"We'll all sleep easier knowing you caught the guy. I'm very grateful."

"I can see that."

She jabbed him in the ribs. "I'm serious. Gracie was in my class. She was like my kid, too. I can't believe anyone would hurt her."

My thoughts exactly. Jed had told Lisa how the killer had murdered and mutilated the girls. How *Justin Fox* had murdered and mutilated them. And yet...

"What's the matter?"

Jed shouldn't discuss the ongoing investigation with a civilian. But the victims were a part of Lisa's life, too. "I don't know. Something doesn't seem right. Fox is just a kid."

Lisa sighed. "High school kids shot up Columbine."

"Yeah, but this kid didn't go on a rampage. These were separate, well-planned killings. I just don't see how he pulled them off."

Her brow creased. "Didn't he confess?"

"He did."

"Then, that settles it." She gave him an attentive, feline stare. "What does your girlfriend think?"

Where had that come from? "What girlfriend?"

She smirked. "Your partner, silly. Detective Wolfe. She's kinda cute, don't you think?"

Was Lisa jealous? "Don't worry, she's not my type. Let's not talk about her."

Lisa sat up, the sheet falling from her chest, and straddled him. "I know the perfect way to clear your mind."

Jed smiled again. Lisa seemed like a shy schoolteacher, but she sure knew how to get him started.

Lisa moved her hips, grinding into him. She lifted her arms in the air and curled her hair into a bun on top of her head. From that angle and without her glasses, she reminded him of the first dead girl. He shifted sideways, and she toppled beside him, startled by his change in mood.

"What's the matter?"

"Nothing," he lied.

The ghostly reminder had turned off his libido and dug up memories he couldn't face again. Yes, there was more to this case than met the eye. But what?

CHAPTER 29

Thursday morning, Claire walked into the squad room to the sound of shouting.

"This is bullshit, and you know it!"

The man's voice boomed through the closed door of Captain Emmerso's office.

Mahoney looked up from his desk. "Morning, Detective. I believe you're wanted in there." He gave Claire an apologetic grin. "You, too," he added, as Rob came up behind her.

Although she and Rob had driven to work together in Claire's car, they had decided for the sake of appearances to enter the station a few seconds apart. From Mahoney's raised eyebrows and the knowing smirk he shared with Nakamura, Claire and Rob had fooled nobody.

"You sure?" Rob asked.

"Afraid so. Captain's orders."

Had their suspect's lawyer descended upon the station? They entered the captain's office. Emmerso leaned backward in the chair behind his desk. Jed and Tom sat with their backs to the door while a tall dark-haired stranger in an expensive suit bounced on his feet with rage. The captain took advantage of the new arrivals to cut him off.

"Detective Wolfe, Special Agent Cline, this is Dennis Lewis, our DA."

Claire inclined her head and stood to the side. An exchange of pleasantries was unwelcome in this discussion. The district attorney ignored them and resumed his tirade.

"Show me the effing evidence!"

His voice seemed to possess only one volume level—an infuriated roar. Claire was glad Dr. Fleischer wasn't in the room.

"We have his fingerprints," Jed said, but the DA cut him off.

"On the murder weapon?"

"On the victim's phone."

"The phone means nothing. Anybody could have handled her phone. That doesn't make him a murderer."

"We have his DNA at the scene of the crime."

"DNA from what? Semen? Blood?"

Jed deflated. "Skin flakes."

Dennis Lewis scoffed. "Let's do a little thought experiment, Detective. If he had gotten close enough to handle her phone, could he have sat next to her? Who knows, they might even have—shudder the thought—touched. Last I checked, making out with somebody wasn't a felony." The DA pulled at his hair. "Jurors want murder weapons, motive, eyewitnesses. They want a story. This isn't an affidavit for a search warrant. Probable Cause isn't enough. We need Beyond Reasonable Doubt. You should know this by now."

He let out a frustrated groan, then regained his composure. "The entire state is watching us. Two young girls are dead. Parents are pushing for school closures. Voters want justice."

Claire folded her arms, unimpressed by the blatant use of

political considerations. Like the mayor, the DA faced reelection within the year.

He continued. "We can't afford to get thrown out of court for lack of evidence. Your rumor of a confession and half-ass evidence won't get us past the preliminary hearing."

A knock at the door saved them from further verbal abuse. Officer Del Freeman poked his head inside the office and addressed the captain. "Sir, the suspect says he wants to talk."

The officers shared a sigh of relief.

"Thank you, Officer. Take him to the interview room."

"You'd better get a full confession on video," Dennis Lewis warned them, "before you call me down here again." He stormed out of the office.

"Agent Cline," Emmerso said. "As an FBI negotiator, I think you—"

"Sir," Jed interrupted. "If you don't mind. I started the interview. I know I can finish this."

The captain weighed the request, then relented. "OK, Detective."

Twenty seconds later, Claire, Rob, and Dr. Fleischer joined the captain in the observation room. On the computer monitor, Jed sat at the table of the interrogation room when the uniformed officer led the suspect inside.

Take two. She hoped this time Justin Fox would cooperate and close the case for good. The teenager sat heavily and leaned over the table, his back bent, his fingers fidgety.

Jed slid the clipboard and pen across the table. Fox grabbed the pen and signed his name on the dotted line. One night in the holding cell seemed to have broken him.

Jed placed his recording device on the table and pressed record. "I understand you're ready to come clean."

"How can you keep people in that hole?" Fox said. "It isn't fit for humans."

"Your cellmates didn't make a fuss."

"They were drunk." The kid shuddered at the memory. "They puked all over and shat on the floor. I spent the *whole night* in that stinking room."

"Yeah, well, you reap what you sow."

"But I didn't do anything." Fox hugged his chest. "I didn't kill Gracie or Karla."

Jed stared at him, his lips parting in shock.

"Oh, crap," Emmerso said.

Claire seconded that thought. Her heart seemed to drop into her boots. This was the worst possible scenario. Fox had recanted. And if he hadn't killed the girls, then Tina's case was still relevant to the investigation. Rob glanced at her, but Claire kept her eyes on the computer screen.

Fox was on the verge of tears. "We were friends."

"That's not what you told us yesterday. You said you did it."

"I lied!"

"Why would you confess to murders you didn't commit?"

Fox clamped his jaw shut.

"We're losing him," Emmerso said. "If he asks for his lawyer, it's game over."

The captain was right. Once lawyers got involved, the process would drag out. They'd face the arraignment and preliminary hearing with the little information they'd gathered so far, and they'd have to choose between galloping ahead, lances raised, and dropping the murder charges.

Captain Emmerso said, "You're up, Agent Cline. For what it's worth."

Rob handed Tom his gun and rushed out of the room. On the screen, the interrogation room door opened. Rob walked up to Jed and whispered in his ear. The detective turned red, then stood abruptly and stormed out of the room. Rob took Jed's seat. Justin Fox sized up his new opponent, his arms still folded over his chest.

The observation room door flew open, and Jed entered, breathless. "Captain Emmerso, I just need a few more minutes."

The captain put his fingers to his lips and watched the screen. Rob sat opposite Fox in the interview room.

"Hi, Justin. My name is Rob." He'd used their first names, taking an informal approach.

Fox kept his mouth shut.

Rob grinned. "How's your leg?" He had given Fox the bruises by tackling him at the cemetery.

The kid still made no response.

"My hand still hurts like hell."

Fox snickered despite himself, satisfied that he'd injured the FBI agent.

"You must think we're the bad guys, and I get that. But we're not trying to set you up. The evidence seems to show you killed those girls. Your fingerprints are on Gracie's phone. Your DNA is on her dead body."

Jed swore. "He's leaking our evidence. Captain, we need to stop this!"

"I didn't kill anybody!"

Fox had spoken, and all eyes focused on the monitor.

Rob hardened his tone. "So you say. But how are we supposed to believe you when you won't tell us what happened?"

Fox pressed his lips together again. Rob stared at the kid in silence. Ten seconds passed. Then, ten more. The silence was excruciating.

And Fox broke. "I picked Gracie up after school, OK? I took her back to my place."

In the observation room, the officers traded excited glances.

Claire couldn't believe her ears. The suspect had placed himself with the victim close to the time of the murder. Justin Fox was officially the last person to see Gracie alive.

"Your place?"

Rob was echoing the suspect's last words, encouraging him to elaborate. *Strategic empathy.*

"My mom's. We always hung out there so her folks wouldn't find out about us. That terrified her. We'd hang out and smoke some w..." He caught himself in time. "Some *stuff.* Then, she'd go home. I loved her, man. When I heard she was dead, I was all broken up."

"Broken up?"

"Yeah. I mean, it was my fault. I wasn't supposed to be selling the...stuff, you know? Because of me, they killed her."

"They killed her?"

"The Gutter Boys."

"The Gutter Boys?"

Fox gave him an incredulous look, then relented. "You're not from around here, are you? The Gutter Boys deal in weed, crack, you name it. Newburgh is their turf. If they found out I'd been selling on the side, they'd kill me, like they killed Gracie. That's why I had to go into hiding."

"Into hiding?"

Rob's empathetic listening was working like a charm.

"They're not idiots. If they found Gracie, they'll find me. I was freaked out, man. Karla called me up the other night. She was running low on...stuff. She wanted me to pick her up. I said I was lying low and couldn't see her. Then—bang! She's dead! The Gutter Boys got her, too, I'm telling you. I figured they must have traced her phone, so I trashed Gracie's SIM, too. She forgot her phone at my place the day she died."

Fox sobbed. "I loved her, man. Karla, too. Now they're both dead because of me. I was so relieved when you guys said you were cops. The station's full of cops. The Gutter Boys can't touch me here. But then you said I murdered Gracie and Karla… You can't put that on me. I didn't kill them!"

"It's OK, Justin. I understand. We'll figure it all out together. You take it easy now. Nobody will hurt you here. The officer will take you back to the holding cell, but we'll speak again soon."

Rob had rejoined the officers in the observation room.

"So much for our confession," Captain Emmerso said. "Good job on the interview, Agent Cline. I guess we're back to square one."

Rob said, "What do we have on the Gutter Boys?"

"They're not our murderers. Two of our detectives are dismantling their ring with the DEA as we speak. The Gutter Boys are on the run. They couldn't wage a turf war even if they wanted to."

Rob hooked a thumb toward the interrogation room. "Justin doesn't seem to know that."

"Apparently." But Emmerso wasn't eager to throw their only suspect back in the water. "We've got his prints and DNA. He just admitted to collecting the victim from school on the day of the murder. That matches the ME's time of death. He could have killed the girls, then invented this conspiracy theory to cover his tracks."

"You could make that case," Rob said. "But the DA is right. Justin's story fits the facts. A jury will think he was in the wrong place at the wrong time. The killer is still out there."

Emmerso nodded. Despite the pressure, he wouldn't shoehorn Fox into a murder charge. Emmerso was a good man. He'd do the right thing.

The captain said, "What do you think, Detective Wallace?"

Jed had remained uncharacteristically silent during the discussion. Rob had outdone him in front of his boss, and Jed's ego must still smart from the humiliation. This case was his baby. He'd been pressing for a resolution from day one, starting with the first victim's father. But even Jed couldn't deny the new reality.

"He's right. The kid's telling the truth. Picking up the victim doesn't make him a murderer."

Claire gaped at Jed, then closed her mouth. After his single-minded pursuit of Gareth Miles, she had not expected him to back off now. Again, she had misread her new partner.

Jed noticed her look and shrugged. "I did stupid things when I was his age, too."

Emmerso turned to Dr. Fleischer. "Anything to add?"

The doctor shook her head.

"OK, then. We'll hand him over to the DEA. Detective Wallace, the other girls are still under police protection, right?"

Jed swallowed hard. "I'll tell Patrol to renew the schedule."

Claire's mouth dropped open a second time. "We pulled their police protection?"

Jed blushed again. "I released Patrol when we arrested Fox. Captain Rodrigez kept complaining about a lack of resources."

Claire couldn't believe the screwup. Without police protection, the killer had easy access to the girls. And if the girls' families thought the murderer was in custody, they wouldn't see him coming either.

"Fix that, pronto."

"I'm on it, sir." Jed left the observation room.

"Dr. Fleischer," the captain said, "I'd like you to review that profile again, see where it points us. We need new ideas."

"Sure."

Again, Rob glanced at Claire, but she refused to make eye contact. Claire knew what he was thinking, but suddenly she wasn't ready to share Tina's file. Rob had given his word he'd keep her secret, and she'd hold him to that promise.

"Thank you, everyone."

The officers exited the observation room. Claire made for the door, but Rob touched her arm, and they lingered behind.

"Claire," he whispered. "It's time you shared your information with the team."

Claire steeled herself with a deep breath. "I'm not—"

"Listen, Claire. I know you might get dropped from the case. But think about it—do you have a choice?"

Rob was right. This was her chance to aim the department's resources at finding her sister's killer. Keeping silent now was tantamount to obstructing the investigation. And if Tina's file got out later, her silence would not reflect well on her.

But still, Claire's heart pounded. Rob didn't know about O'Leary's report. Once Claire became a prime suspect, Jed would remove her from the case.

She studied Rob's eyes. By telling him about Tina's murder, she'd placed him in an impossible situation, too. But he left the decision in her hands.

And Claire knew what she would do. She'd decided days ago. A wave of relief washed over her. Rob was right. She had no choice.

CHAPTER 30

Gastric juices burned a peptic ulcer in the lining of Captain Emmerso's stomach as he stood outside the door of his boss's office. He was about to get his ass handed to him.

Chief Wallace often dropped by Emmerso's office to share his displeasure with the Investigations Bureau's performance. Emmerso thought of those visits as drive-by shootings. A summons to the chief's office meant matters were much worse—a summary execution.

Years ago, Emmerso had seen a humorous illustration that compared an organizational hierarchy to birds sitting on the branches of a tree. The birds at the top crapped on the birds below, who, in turn, crapped on the birds below them.

The drawing had amused him. He'd always believed that his job was to shield his subordinates from the rain of crap from above. How else were they supposed to do their jobs? This meeting would test his resolve.

Emmerso knocked on the chief's door, sucked in a deep breath, and braced for the mother of all crap storms. He should have brought an umbrella.

"Sit down," Chief Wallace said. His voice was surprisingly calm, and an amused smile crept over his bulldog face. Was he looking forward to dressing down his captain? Did he derive sadistic pleasure from exerting power?

Emmerso did as he was told. He reviewed his mental notes for the meeting—a laundry list of excuses and mitigating circumstances: He'd called in the FBI to assist with the case; his detectives had cooperated fully with said agents; they had followed their expert advice; and the chief's son, Detective Wallace, had led the team. The blame for the investigation's current stalling did not lie squarely on his bureau's shoulders.

"I don't need to tell you how bad things are," Chief Wallace said.

Emmerso did not fall into the trap of false hope. This was just the prelude.

"Or that they look even worse from the outside."

Emmerso discarded his mental notes. There was only one wise move during a crap storm of this intensity—keep your mouth shut.

"In fact," Chief Wallace continued, his voice rising, a vein throbbing at his temple, "things are so bad—"

A knocking at the door cut him short.

"What is it?" he yelled.

The door cracked open, and Detective Jed Wallace poked his head inside. Emmerso had never been happier to see the detective.

"Sorry to interrupt, sir." Emmerso was uncertain which "sir" Jed was addressing. The detective paused, unsure of how to proceed. "I was looking for Captain Emmerso."

"And now you've found him. I expect you have something very important to tell him."

The detective hesitated again, glancing from his boss to his boss's boss. Emmerso had assumed the chief intimidated his son less than the others. Perhaps he'd been wrong.

"Spit it out, Detective. Captain Emmerso keeps no secrets from me. Isn't that right, Captain?"

"Yes, sir."

Emmerso prayed that the detective had brought good news about the case. He could use some good news right now.

Jed rediscovered his tongue. "Detective Wolfe just handed me this." He displayed a manila folder, the cover wrinkled and discolored by many years. "It's the case file for a twelve-year-old homicide. Detective Wolfe thinks the case might fit our current serial killer."

He let the words sink in, his eyes on the chief. This was good news. *Very* good news. Claire had found a promising new lead.

"And?" the chief prompted. He did not seem comforted by the turn of events. Was he unwilling to let Emmerso escape his thrashing?

"The victim was Tina Wolfe. Detective Wolfe's younger sister."

The revelation hit Emmerso like an unexpected left hook. So that's why the detective had wanted to discuss the matter with him in private. Claire had become entangled in the case.

"It seems," Jed continued, "that Detective Wolfe has been investigating the old case in her spare time."

Emmerso swallowed hard. Detective Wolfe had run her private investigation without his knowledge. If the chief had thought Emmerso had lost his grip on his unit's activities before, this new debacle settled the matter. His mental forecast upgraded the crap storm to a crap hurricane.

"I see," the chief said. "And what do you make of this, Detective?"

Jed seemed surprised at the question. "Well, sir, the case is twelve years old. It doesn't seem relevant to—"

"Really?" Chief Wallace interrupted. "I wouldn't be so sure. This new information might lead us to a new suspect and allow us to, pardon the expression, kill two birds with one stone."

"Yes, sir." Jed turned to leave.

"Oh, and Detective."

"Yes, sir?"

"I suggest you go through the materials very carefully. Make sure we arrest the right suspect this time. Understood?"

"Yes, sir."

Jed closed the door behind him. Chief Wallace stroked his goatee, and Emmerso waited for his sentencing. Had Jed's newsflash averted the storm or had Emmerso merely slipped into the deceptively calm eye of the tornado? One wrong move and the storm would sweep him away.

"Captain?"

"Yes, sir."

"You've got work to do, don't you?"

"Yes, sir."

"Don't let me keep you from it."

Emmerso didn't need to be told twice. He shot from the chair and fled the room. He'd had a close encounter with a menacing force of nature and survived to tell the tale. Next time, he might not be so lucky.

CHAPTER 31

Filled with trepidation, Claire entered the photocopy room. Her future lay in Jed's hands. An industrial copier machine spat sheets of paper, duplicates of Tina's case files. Jed stared at the growing pile of pages on the humming machine and didn't see her coming.

That afternoon, Jed had not seemed happy about linking their investigation to a twelve-year-old cold case. His face had become rigid with surprise when she'd confessed that the victim was her sister. But he'd promised to run the idea by their superiors. From the flow of documents out of the copier, Claire deduced that he'd been true to his word and that their superiors had agreed to pursue the new lead. Their superiors were either very open-minded or desperate for progress.

"Hey," she said.

Jed looked up. "Hey. I'm sorry about your sister."

Claire brushed his concern away. "It was a long time ago."

"Still, it must be hard to see the crime scene photos." He turned his attention back to the copier machine.

Had he read the report about Claire yet? Judging by his response, he had not.

Fear chewed on her nerves. Claire had a personal stake in the case. Any competent defense attorney would claim that her involvement had tainted the investigation. Driven to avenge her sister's death, she might have tampered with evidence to secure a conviction. The safe bet would be to drop her from the case. The frustration of being shut out at this critical point would be unbearable, but the uncertainty was driving Claire crazy. Either way, she had to know. She bit the bullet.

"Jed." Her voice sounded brittle and vulnerable to her ears. "Am I still on the case?"

He bunched his eyebrows together. "Of course." He grinned. "I've known you only a week, but you're a professional. I'm not worried you'll lose your objectivity, and neither is the captain."

The unexpected compliment threw her off-balance. She wouldn't have to argue her case. Jed had taken her side. "Thank you, Jed."

"Don't mention it. If it was my sister, I'd want to be on the front lines of the investigation. The chief knows, too. It's cool."

Claire didn't know what to say. "Let me help."

She separated the wads of paper into several complete case files, then paused. "The photos are missing."

"Dr. Fleischer has them. The forensic reports, too. She wanted to get a head start on analyzing the crime scene and adjusting her profile. Let's get everybody up to speed."

A minute later, the team gathered in the squad room for a briefing. Rob smiled at her as she walked in with Jed, and Claire brushed a stray lock of hair from her face, suddenly self-conscious. She had done the right thing. But what would everyone think of her after reading O'Leary's report? Would Rob feel differently about her, too?

Captain Emmerso gave Claire an empathetic frown before addressing the assembled officers.

"Listen up, everybody. Thanks to Detective Wolfe, we have a new lead on the Middle School Murders."

Claire and Jed handed out the pages of Tina's file, and the captain turned over the discussion to Jed.

"The victim's name is Tina Wolfe," Jed said after he had summed up Tina's murder scene. "And if you were wondering, yes, she was Detective Wolfe's younger sister."

All eyes focused on Claire. Heads nodded with understanding, and the bureau's clowns kept their jokes to themselves.

"The crime scene photos will follow soon. Dr. Fleischer, any thoughts?"

"Yes." The forensic psychiatrist looked animated for the first time in days. She held up a photo of Tina's body in the wooded clearing. "This homicide fits the first murder perfectly. The victim profile, MO, and signature facial mutilation are identical. We're dealing with the same unsub. His execution of the murders has improved over the years."

Dr. Fleischer displayed a close-up of the corpse. "The killer was less prepared back then. Note the spatter on her clothes and surrounding greenery. He killed and mutilated her at the crime scene. The round contusions on the neck are finger marks and indicate manual strangulation. He strangled the victim with his hands and mutilated her face with a tree branch he found at the murder scene. In the later murders, he prepared nylon rope and an ax."

She beamed at her audience. "This is the earlier murder we had searched for and probably his first kill. Our unsub likely had a personal connection to the victim. He murdered her on the spur of the moment. A stressor—a setback at work or in his family life—triggered the homicide. But he'd fantasized about this crime for some time. Acting out that fantasy whets his appetite for more. The subsequent murders were his attempts to reenact this first murder, to perfect it, to relive the fantasy and the sense of control the crime gave him. The location of the Miles murder proves that. He deposited Grace's body in the same location as the first victim."

Mahoney raised his hand. "Then why leave the second—I mean, the third victim at a construction site?"

"The woods were a recent crime scene. Returning there was too risky. But he's grown more confident, killing with higher frequency."

"But why wait twelve years?"

"Who says he waited?"

Claire shuddered. A killer had been stalking Newburgh for twelve years undetected. Or had he?

Nakamura said, "Or something prevented him from killing during that period. Maybe he was incarcerated for a different crime and only recently released from prison?"

"Good point," the psychiatrist said. "Detective Wallace, you'll want to review recent parolees with a history of sexual crimes."

Jed folded his arms. "We did. None of them match."

"Did the third ViCAP query return anything?"

"We widened the scope for both time and location but still drew a blank."

"He's been killing, though. Either he disposed of the victims very well or he got distracted, experimenting with other fantasies. Now he's returned to where it all began. He's learned a lot since that first murder. He plans and cleans up. In the first murder, he left blood and pubic hairs. He took a lock of Tina's hair as a trophy. Very reckless. Trophies can link him to the crime. He kills the girls in a safe location, then dumps the bodies away from the murder scene. No trophies, no spatter, no hairs or fingerprints. Nothing to link him to the crime."

"What about the ax?" Jed asked. "Why steal the father's ax to kill the daughter?"

Claire was wondering the same thing, but Dr. Fleischer didn't seem bothered by that detail.

"He selected the ax on purpose to distract law enforcement. We'd assume this crime was an isolated murder and fail to protect the other girls on his list."

Claire thought of the girls' names she'd written on the whiteboard. The killer was monitoring them, too. She only hoped their police guards would reach them before the killer did.

"He thinks he's superior," Dr. Fleischer continued. "He's rubbing our noses in our failure to catch him, taunting us. Here I am, still free years later. Still killing."

The forensic psychiatrist's body swayed to an inaudible rhythm. She was inside the killer's head, conjuring his thoughts like a shaman communing with the spirits of the dead. Then, she snapped out of her trance.

"Search for dead girls, strangled or otherwise, and with other signs of mutilation. This man hates his mother and, by proxy, all women. The anger is clear in the mutilation. He's destroyed their faces, their humanity. This is a textbook serial killer. We're looking for an intelligent white male. At the time of the first murder, he was in his mid-teens to early twenties. He might have started with rape before he moved to murder. Now he's well-versed in forensic science, too."

Captain Emmerso took the reins again. "Detectives Mahoney and Nakamura, let's review that list of local sexual offenders again. Detective Wallace, contact the school. Ask about any temporary janitors or gardeners they employed over the years."

The detectives nodded.

"We've all got reading to do."

Claire raised her hand. "The case summary lists a Kitty Tucker as the last to see Tina alive, but there's no report of her interview. She's still in Newburgh. I can visit her and see what she remembers."

"Good. OK, everyone, we'll speak later."

The officers dispersed to their tasks. Claire hurried to the whiteboard and found a marker pen. She added Tina Wolfe at the top of the list, above Grace Miles, then drew a line through the name.

Who says he waited? Their list of victims contained three crossed-out names. How many names would Claire cross out before they caught this killer?

A hand touched Claire on the shoulder. Dr. Fleischer stood beside her, the crime scene photos under her arm. "I'm so sorry for your loss." The psychiatrist's eyes sucked her in like bottomless pools. "There's nothing like the bond between sisters. Her death must have devastated you."

Claire stiffened at the talk of sisterly love. Could the psychiatrist sense the truth—that Claire had despised her sister? She forced a smile. "Thank you. I wanted to ask you something. You always talk about a white, male killer. How can you be sure of that?"

The doctor smiled. "Serial murders are usually intraracial. Seeing that the victims are all white—"

"What I mean is, could the killer be a woman?"

Dr. Fleischer gave her a conspiratorial smile. "Female serial killers are rare. Women go on killing sprees or murder people under their care. Usually, they kill for some tangible gain. The periodic sexual fantasy murder is a male-dominated field."

A nervous laugh escaped Claire's lips. "I hope the feminists won't take that the wrong way."

The psychiatrist gave her an ironic grin. "Oh, they do. You'd be surprised."

Dr. Fleischer made for her conference room with the photos, and Claire exhaled a breath of blissful relief. Then, she chided herself for even asking the question. O'Leary could go to hell. Her mother, too. Claire hadn't killed Tina or anyone else. *Female serial killers are rare*. Did that explain why Dr. Fleischer hadn't mentioned O'Leary's report on Claire, and why Captain Emmerso had kept her on the investigation?

Claire returned to her desk, opened her laptop, and glanced at the digital clock on the screen. 6:15 PM. It was getting late. If Kitty Tucker was a working girl, she'd be heading home by now. She found the details for Kitty Tucker and dialed her mobile. The number connected, and an energetic female told her to leave a message. Claire read her new number off her business card and asked Ms. Tucker to call back as soon as possible.

Kitty Tucker. The name had seemed familiar, but Claire couldn't picture her. Tina hadn't invited friends over much. Her death must have affected her friends, too. Now Claire would drag Kitty back in time to memories she'd rather keep buried. But if Kitty was the last person to see Tina alive, she'd probably have useful information. Yes, Claire decided. Kitty was the key.

"Detectives," a woman said.

Claire and Jed looked up from their desks. Dr. Fleischer stood over them, pensive.

The warmth drained from Claire's face. Had the psychiatrist discovered O'Leary's report on her? Would she bar Claire from the case? Serial killers often inserted themselves into the investigation, and Claire had worked hard to do just that.

"Yeah?" Jed said.

"Grace Miles died last Wednesday, Karla Smith on Sunday."

Jed shrugged. "Are those days significant?"

"No, but the murders were four days apart. Today is Thursday."

Claire's heart rate sped up. "Four days since the last murder."

Dr. Fleischer nodded, her expression grim. "I can't say for

sure when the killer will strike again. But If I were a betting girl, I'd pick today."

CHAPTER 32

Dana Wood applied red lipstick in her bedroom mirror. She had borrowed it from her mom's makeup bag. Tonight would be the best night of her life.

She had designed the perfect birthday gift for Dean Ward. On the card she'd written the regular birthday greetings, wishing him health and happiness and that all his dreams come true. But into the card, she'd also slipped a rectangular voucher which she'd printed on her computer. The romantic curly script entitled the bearer of the voucher to one kiss. Not too pushy, not too vague—the hint was the perfect way to nudge Dean in the right direction. Tonight, they'd share their first kiss, and Dean would fall in love with her.

But first, she had to jump a few hurdles. Dana put the lid on the stick and grabbed her phone. Lena answered on the second ring.

"What's up?"

"All dressed up and ready to go. Dean's going to love his gift, I know it."

"Aren't you still grounded?" Lena was such a downer.

"Depends on who you ask. My dad still won't let me out, but

the cops left yesterday. As far as they're concerned, I'm as free as a bird."

"Are you sure about this? Your dad will *not* be happy if you sneak out."

"Let me worry about my dad. Lori's going to make her move on Dean tonight, I can feel it, and I will not let her steal him from me!"

"Lori. Are you kidding me? She still has braces!"

"She has her ways. And I've seen how she looks at him after school. Your mom's still taking you to the party, right?"

"Yeah?"

"Can I get a ride with you?"

"Uh, sure. But don't be late."

"I won't be late."

"If we have to wait around, my mom will call yours, and we'll both get busted."

"OK, I get it. Don't tell her anything. I'll just show up. If I'm not on time, leave without me. But I'll be there."

Someone called outside her room. "Dana!" It was her dad.

"Gotta go. See you soon."

She ended the call and cracked her door open an inch. She didn't want her folks to see her all dressed up. Her mom would be furious if she learned Dana had used her precious Givenchy without permission.

"Dad," she said. "I'm tired. Going to bed early."

"There's someone here to see you."

Who had come over so late on a school night? Had Dean stopped by to take her to his party? No, that was impossible. Dean didn't know she existed. After tonight, he'd never forget her.

She poked her head out the door.

The black uniformed officer smiled at her from the bottom of the stairs. "Hello, Dana. Nice to see you again."

Not again! Officer Freeman had guarded her front door every night and hadn't let her leave the house. The smiling shadow annoyed the hell out of her. She was fourteen years old, for crying out loud. She didn't need a babysitter! Yesterday, he'd left the house, and Dana had rejoiced. Finally, she could live her life again—and just in time for Dean's party. But tonight of all nights, Officer Freeman was back. Would the cops please get off her back already?

"Hi, Officer," she said.

He squinted at her. "You look different."

Shoot! He'd noticed her makeup.

"Goodnight, Officer. I'm going to bed." She closed the door.

This was bad! Dana had to move fast. If her folks knew she was gone, they'd get worried and start calling around. If they found out she'd snuck out, her dad would crash Dean's party and drag her home. Dana would rather die.

"G'night, honey," her mom said.

"G'night!" Dana turned out the light.

Her mom's footfalls passed her door, but she didn't come in. Her mom wasn't a kisser. Thank God for that. With the cop downstairs, her folks would drop their guard. *Perfect*. She counted to twenty, then fumbled in the dark for her phone and stuffed it in the tiny handbag with the sequins she saved for special occasions. Slowly, she slid her window open and stepped onto the roof. Holding her high heels in her hand, she padded over the cold tiles in her stockinged feet.

As a little girl, Dana had been a tomboy. She had climbed trees and caught frogs. Tonight, her tomboy skills would save the day. She tiptoed to the edge of the roof and climbed down the trellis. The wooden slats creaked underfoot. In a few years, she'd be too heavy to use that escape route.

Her feet touched the ground, and she crouched at the edge of the wall. The cop wasn't at his post yet. Through the living room window, he sipped a steaming mug and chatted with her father, that annoying smile still on his face.

Dana seized her opportunity. She hurried down the side-walk. When she'd passed the neighbors, she slipped on her heels and trotted toward Lena's home. Getting back into her bedroom would be harder, but she didn't care. After tonight, she'd hold Dean's heart in her hand. Her parents could ground her as long as they liked.

She glanced at the time on her phone. *Rats!* She had two minutes to reach her destination, or Lena's mom would leave without her.

Besides the clicking of her heels on the sidewalk, other foot-falls joined them. The rapid patter of running shoes on concrete followed her. A woman, by the sound of it. A lot of their neighbors exercised at night. The Trumans from across the street jogged every evening. They didn't have kids, and Mrs. Truman always stopped to chat with Dana.

The footfalls gained on her—only one pair of feet. Mrs. Truman was jogging alone tonight. Dana kept her eyes on the prize. She had to avoid a conversation with her yappy neighbor, who might ask why she was out alone so late. Dana checked the time on her phone again. The device was also an excuse to ignore her neighbor and her pesky questions.

As the jogger passed her, a streak of white crossed her vision, and the jogger bumped into her. Dana's phone dropped to the sidewalk with a crack. She wanted to say, "Hey, watch where you're going!" but she couldn't speak. She couldn't breathe either. Something thin and tight cut into her neck.

Mrs. Truman pulled her backward, off her feet, and dragged her into a dark gap between houses. Dana couldn't see her face, but she smelled her sporty deodorant. This wasn't Mrs. Truman. Her neighbor would never attack her.

"Help!" she tried to scream. "Somebody help me! Officer

Freeman! Over here!" Her lips moved, but only a soft, spluttering whisper escaped her mouth.

A heeled shoe slipped from her foot as she struggled in the shadows far from the streetlights. Nobody could see her. Nobody would hear her either.

She groped at her neck, but the cord was too tight and cut into her skin. She reached behind her to claw her attacker's eyes out, but her hands flailed in the cool, empty air. Her lungs burned. Her head throbbed. Exhaustion numbed her body. Her skin tingled all over. The world faded to black. Dana would never kiss Dean Ward. She would never kiss anyone ever again.

CHAPTER 33

A floorboard creaked in the hall while Claire was in the shower. Her heart skipped a beat, and she turned off the tap. There it was again—the sound of furtive movement. Somebody was in her home.

The shower after her nightly jog had done Claire a world of good. The jet of hot water had massaged her neck and shoulders. Her legs still ached, but the physical training had lifted her spirits. For the first time since reading Tina's file, Claire found peace. She had shared Tina's file with the team, and the sky had not fallen. Now she could pursue her sister's killer with the full resources of law enforcement behind her. She only hoped she'd beat the killer to his next victim.

Mahoney and Nakamura had interviewed five more gardeners and janitors who had worked at the middle school. All had alibis for the first murder. One janitor was only twenty-one years old and hardly capable of killing Tina twelve years ago. A sixth janitor was still unaccounted for. Patrol officers were monitoring them. Under police surveillance, the killer wouldn't dare strike again. Or would he?

The sound of movement in her apartment had shattered Claire's tranquility. She wrapped a towel about her midsection and pulled her Glock from her holster among the pile of clothes.

Gun in hand, she listened at the bathroom door. Silence. Was the intruder listening for her movements, too? She turned the showerhead on again and resumed her vigil at the door. Over the hiss of falling water, a floorboard creaked again. Her skin prickled.

If the killer had penetrated the investigation, he would know the detectives' names. With a little research, he'd discover Claire's home address. As the net closed around him, was the killer taking the fight to her?

Claire placed a trembling finger on the doorknob. Then, she flung the door open and aimed her weapon. A man stood in the hall.

"Whoa! Is that how you greet all your guests?"

Claire lowered her gun. "Most guests ring the bell."

Rob hooked a thumb toward the front door. "Most people don't leave their front door open. I thought somebody had broken in."

Claire stood there a moment, confused. "I locked the door when I got home. I always do."

Rob shrugged. "Not this time."

Claire blinked at him. She had locked the door. Why would he lie about that? The short answer: he wouldn't. Claire must be mistaken.

"May I come in?"

She grinned at him, brushing aside her memory lapse. "Please do."

He glanced at the towel over her midsection and stepped closer. Her wet, exposed skin prickled again but for an entirely different reason. She had wondered whether Rob, after reading

O'Leary's report about her, would ever look at her the same way. Now she had her answer.

Desire flashed in his eyes, and Claire's body responded. She wanted him.

"I should put some clothes on," she said without conviction.

He took another step forward, and their bodies touched. "Don't bother."

Later, Claire lay beside him in her bed and sighed. "Had I known you were coming over, I wouldn't have gone for a run. That's two workouts in one night."

Rob stared at the ceiling, lost in thought. "You did the right thing, you know."

Claire's mood sank. For the last half hour, she'd forgotten about serial killers, dead girls, and O'Leary's report. Now Rob had reminded her.

She fidgeted with the bedsheet. "I wasn't sure you'd stick around after reading the file."

He glanced at her, confused. "Why not?"

She raised her eyebrows at him. "After O'Leary's report?"

"Which one?"

Now he was playing stupid. She sat up on her elbow. "The one about me, the sister."

Rob's eyes shifted as he scanned his memory. "I read the file from start to finish. There's nothing in there about you."

A dark pit opened in Claire's gut. She had read the report. O'Leary had singled Claire out as a suspect in her sister's murder. She had held the page in her hands. The icy fingers of dread wrapped around her heart. *Was the report a figment of her tormented imagination?* Once again, Claire was a confused and terrified teenage girl in her mother's kitchen, covered in blood and doubting her sanity.

"Claire, are you OK?" Rob sat up and gazed at her.

Tears trickled from her eyes and wouldn't stop.

He stroked her hair. "It's OK, Claire. Everything'll be OK."

"I must be going crazy" Tears distorted her voice.

"You're not crazy, Claire. You're an intelligent, talented woman."

She shook her head. "I've been imagining things—nonexistent reports, locked doors that I left open."

He chuckled. "Everyone forgets things, Claire. You're only human. And as for the report, I'm sure there's an explanation. Dr. Fleischer had the photos and forensic reports. Maybe she held on to that report, too."

Claire laughed through her tears. Of course! He was right. That's probably what had happened. She leaned into his arms, and he held her for a long time.

"Everybody keeps telling me how sorry they are." Claire hadn't planned on sharing this with Rob, or with anyone, but the words demanded an outlet. Adrift at sea, she clung to Rob, her lifesaver. "They say losing Tina must have devastated me. But it didn't. The truth is I hated Tina. I wanted her dead."

"Kids say that about their siblings, Claire, but they don't mean it."

"Oh, I did. I hated her and her stupid pranks. She kept turning my parents against me."

"What did she do?"

Claire took a moment to gather her thoughts. She did not want to sound delusional *and* deranged. Then, she told him about the day Tina pretended someone had stabbed her with a carving knife. Claire described how Tina had laughed when a traumatized Claire had called 911. Then, when their mother had come home, Tina had stabbed herself in the leg and accused Claire of trying to kill her.

"My mom never believed me. Sometimes, I'm not even sure what happened myself."

Claire cried into Rob's neck. She expected him to push her

away and run from her, but he didn't. He just listened and stroked her hair.

"Wow. Your sister was a piece of work. But you are not crazy, Claire."

She looked into his eyes. "How can you know that?"

"Tina abused you psychologically, Claire. Trust me. I know about these things. Gaslighting is a major weapon in an abuser's arsenal. Undermine the victims' grip on reality. Make them doubt their sanity. Then, they're helpless, and the abuser takes control."

Rob's analysis made sense, although Claire had never looked at her sister's behavior that way. Tina's dark, twisted mind games followed a pattern. And Claire was not alone. Others had suffered like her, and strangely, that knowledge comforted her.

She rested her head on his chest. "Did they teach you that at the BAU, too?"

He drew a deep breath. "No, I learned that the hard way. My mom drank. When I was a kid, she'd come home from work, empty a bottle of wine, and beat me up."

Claire studied his face. Rob had been her friend at school. She had visited him at his home, but she had never guessed what he'd gone through.

"The words hurt the most. She'd say I was a burden, that I'd ruined her life. I was just a kid. I felt so guilty. And so angry. In the morning when she sobered up, I'd confront her. Why did she hit me? How could she say that to me! Guess what she said? It never happened. She'd never touched me or said those things. I had imagined it all."

"I'm so sorry, Rob."

His eyes moistened. "At first, I thought she didn't remember. Maybe she was too drunk, and she'd blacked out. But it happened again and again. Each time, she'd deny it. And she just kept on drinking."

Rob sniffed and licked his lips. "I was so angry at her and so confused. Lucky for me, my school had a good psychologist. Slowly, the truth sank in. My mom remembered. She remembered everything. But she'd never admit she'd done anything wrong. It was easier to make me doubt my sanity. Eventually, things got so bad, I went to live with my dad."

Claire caressed his chest. Rob had seemed so calm and confident. She'd never imagined the hurt he carried inside.

"I'm sorry you had to go through that."

"Yeah, me, too. But if I hadn't, I wouldn't have become interested in abusive personalities. I studied psychology and abnormal behavior, and that path led me to the BAU." He kissed her on the forehead. "If my mom hadn't abused me, I wouldn't be here with you today."

Claire snorted. "Remind me to send her a thank you note."

Rob fixed dinner, and they ate a tuna casserole at the kitchen table.

"This is great," she said. "What's the secret?"

"Tabasco sauce."

Claire's phone rang. She swallowed another mouthful and answered.

"Detective Wolfe?" a woman said.

"Speaking."

"This is Kitty Tucker. You wanted to speak?"

Claire flashed her eyes at Rob. "Hello, Kitty. Thank you for getting back to me. I'll come over in a few minutes if that's convenient." She grabbed a pen and paper from the kitchen counter.

"I'll be back late tonight. Can we speak tomorrow over breakfast?"

"Sure, that will be perfect."

"Let's meet at Tammy's at nine AM."

Claire jotted down the address of the coffee shop. "Perfect. I'll be there."

Claire hung up and high-fived her lover.

"She sounded very cooperative," Rob said.

Claire stared at her notes. "I have a good feeling about this. I think we'll finally get some answers."

They ate in silence for a while. Tomorrow morning, Claire would open a window on the day Tina died. She was one step closer to putting her sister's ghost to rest. But one detail stuck in her mind like food caught between her molars. Kitty had chosen a public venue for their meeting. Was she afraid to meet in private? Claire's wandering thoughts evaporated. Rob was staring at her, his eyes serious.

"What?"

"What will you do when this is over?"

It was a good question. Claire had dedicated her life to bringing Tina's killer to justice. But once he was behind bars, what then? Her goal had always seemed so far away that Claire had never considered the day after. Would she stay in Newburgh? Would she even stay in law enforcement? The future was a blank page.

Claire lowered her fork to her plate. "I have no idea."

CHAPTER 34

"Are you ready to order?" the waiter asked the next morning. It was the second time he'd stopped by their table with that question.

Claire had no appetite. Her stomach cramped at the thought of food. She felt like a convict awaiting sentencing.

Rob had dropped off the Bureau car at the motel, and they had continued to their breakfast date at Tammy's. The coffee shop's Parisian cafe theme required the servers to wear striped aprons and little red berets. The detective and FBI agent looked like an ordinary couple enjoying breakfast.

Claire shook her head. "We're still waiting for our friend."

"Another coffee?" the waiter suggested.

Rob pointed to an item on the menu. "On second thought. I'll have the eggs."

The waiter jotted down the details and shuffled off.

Rob answered Claire's glance with a shrug. "I'm hungry."

Claire read the time on her phone again. Kitty was twenty minutes late. She hadn't called either. Jed had—twice. Claire had let her phone ring to voicemail. Her partner was probably wondering why she hadn't arrived at work yet. She'd call Jed back later. Her contact might show up at any moment.

"It's probably a flat tire," she said.

Ron frowned. "Or an alarm clock failure?"

"Do they still make alarm clocks? I thought everyone used their phones."

"What can I say? I'm an old-fashioned guy."

Fresh out of snarky replies, Claire dialed Kitty's number. She was banking on Kitty to provide a new lead. Too much was riding on this meeting.

Kitty's number rang, then cut to voicemail. Claire didn't leave a message.

Rob's breakfast arrived. By the time he wiped the plate clean, Claire's premonition had become a large stone in her gut.

"Something's wrong," she said. If anything had happened to Kitty, that door to the truth would close forever.

Rob tossed a bill on the table. "Time for a house call?"

Claire drove them to Kitty Tucker's address, a modern, single-level mansion with tall French windows, slanted roofs, and a water fountain. Kitty had done well for herself.

"Nice place," Rob said. "Think she's home?"

Claire glanced at the closed door of the double-bay garage and the thick blinds that blocked the windows. "Time to find out."

Claire parked across the street. The doorbell played a soft jingle she didn't recognize that echoed inside the home. To the side, the water fountain gurgled. Not all of Newburgh was poor or middle class.

Claire pressed the button again. Somewhere inside, a dog barked—a small dog judging by the high-pitched yap. Who looked after Pooch when Kitty was away? Did she have a live-in maid?

"Think she got cold feet?" Rob said.

Claire couldn't make sense of it. Kitty had sounded so cooperative on the phone last night. The premonition weighed heavily in her gut again. Had the killer beaten them to the house and silenced Kitty forever?

Small, padded feet shuffled behind the door. Then, Claire heard something else. A woman's voice whispered for the dog to keep quiet. Kitty was alive and well. She was pretending not to be home.

"Ms. Tucker," Claire called. "It's Detective Wolfe. I'm here with Special Agent Cline. We missed you at Tammy's this morning. Are you OK?"

The person behind the door said nothing.

"We just want to ask a few questions. It's about an old school friend of yours, Tina Wolfe."

Still nothing. Was Kitty suddenly reluctant to speak to law enforcement? Claire played the emotional card. "Tina was my sister."

Not a sound from within. Rob leaned over and whispered in Claire's ear.

Claire repeated what he said. "It seems you've changed your mind about helping us."

Rob put his finger to his lips. Claire shifted on her feet. She counted the seconds as they rolled by. The silence was unbearable. This was stupid. Claire turned away from Kitty's house, ready to retreat to the car, but Rob held her arm.

"I'm sorry, I can't help you," a woman said behind the door. Kitty's voice. "Go away!"

Progress! And Claire had almost given up. Rob held up two fingers, and Claire understood.

She repeated Kitty's last two words. "Go away?"

"I already spoke to the police."

Claire stifled an amazed laugh. Rob's technique worked. Her phone vibrated. Jed again. She silenced the call.

"You spoke with the police?"

"I have nothing more to say. This isn't easy for me. Please, just leave me alone."

Rob leaned in and whispered in Claire's ear again. It was a lot to remember. And, man, he was laying the guilt on thick! Rob nodded for her to speak up.

"Two more girls have died these past few weeks, just like Tina," she said. "The killer won't stop. How can we leave when what you know could save innocent lives?"

There was a long silence. Was Kitty sobbing? Did the memory of Tina's death still hurt or was something else holding her back?

"I'm sorry," she said, eventually. "I can't help you."

Footsteps sounded behind the door, then faded. Kitty had walked away from the door.

Rob chewed his lip. Kitty had beaten an FBI negotiator. The result did not bode well for their investigation. Her sudden refusal to cooperate made no sense. If the killer had gotten to her, he wouldn't have left her alive. Unless Claire had misunderstood the situation. Had Kitty played a role in Tina's murder?

Claire's phone vibrated again. Jed. Claire had some explaining to do.

"Hey, Jed."

"Claire, where are you?" His voice sounded distant. He was calling from his car. "I've been trying to reach you all morning."

"Sorry, I was following a lead. What's up?"

"I'm texting you an address. Meet me there."

Claire met Rob's gaze. Had Jed discovered another crime scene? Dr. Fleischer had warned that the killer might strike again yesterday.

"Another body?" Claire asked, dreading the answer.

"Not yet," Jed said. "But another girl is missing, and she's on the list."

CHAPTER 35

"How could this have happened?" Claire pressed her foot to the accelerator and sped toward the address Jed had sent her. "The girls were under police protection."

Rob said nothing. Police officers were only human, and the killer had slipped through their nets. Still, Claire hoped they'd find another explanation for the girl's disappearance—an explanation that did not involve murder.

Two squad cars and three unmarked sedans parked outside the house. Claire pulled up behind Jed's department-issue car, and she and Rob raced to the open front door.

Officer Del Freeman stood inside, dark rings under his eyes.

"What happened?" Claire asked him.

"Dana was in her bedroom when I started my shift at eight PM. She said she was going to bed early, but it looks like she snuck out." The officer hung his head. He must feel terrible.

"Where's Detective Wallace?"

"Upstairs, in her room."

A man and woman stood in the hallway, hugging their chests.

"You must be Dana's parents."

They nodded, their features wrinkled with fear for their daughter's well-being.

Claire introduced herself and Special Agent Cline. "You've probably answered this before, but could Dana be with a friend?" If the killer had lured her away, the parents might have noticed.

The mother answered. "We called all of her friends this morning when she wasn't in her room. Lena lives down the street. She's her best friend. Dana had arranged to get a ride with her to a birthday party of a boy from school."

"She went to a party?"

"Not with our permission. We had grounded her."

"When did Dana get to Lena's?"

"She didn't. Dana didn't show, so Lena went to the party without her."

"What time was that?"

"About 8:15."

Claire recorded contact details for Dana's friend.

"Detective, is Dana OK?" the mother said.

Claire considered the question. The killer had murdered the girls shortly after their disappearance and dumped their bodies in the night. The lack of a corpse did not mean their daughter was still alive. And her chances of survival were very slim.

"Let's hope so."

Claire didn't like this. Gracie and Karla had hung out with Justin Fox, who was still in police custody. What, besides her physical appearance, connected Dana to the other girls?

"Did Dana know Grace Miles or Karla Smith?"

Mr. Wood glanced at his wife, who shrugged. "Karla was in Dana's class, but they weren't close. We only know about Grace from the news."

The worry lines on Mrs. Wood's face deepened as the penny

dropped. It was her daughter's turn to appear on the evening news.

"Excuse us."

Claire and Rob climbed the stairs. Jed and Tom stood outside the girl's bedroom. Inside, Brandon Yang, the forensics tech, swept for evidence.

Jed turned to the newcomers and lowered his voice. "No drugs yet. No foreign prints or signs of a struggle."

Tom pointed at the open window. "Looks like she climbed out onto the roof, then down the trellis. She must have slipped out right after the patrol officer arrived. Sneaky little thing."

Rob said, "Did the neighbors see her?"

"Patrol officers are doing the rounds now and searching the route to her friend's."

"Detective Wallace," a man said behind them. "We've got something."

Officer Adam Jenkins, the redhead Claire had met at the first crime scene, leaped up the final two steps.

"We found these down the road."

The officers and agents huddled around his phone as he flipped through photos: A girl's red-heeled shoe on the sidewalk; a small smartphone with a cracked screen.

"There's no blood. No sign of a body either. She might still be alive."

"Good work, Officer," Jed said. "Come with me."

Jed descended the staircase, and the others followed. He approached the parents.

"Mr. and Mrs. Wood, do you recognize any of these?"

The parents studied the photos on the phone, and Dana's mom covered her mouth. "That's one of Dana's shoes."

"And that's her phone," the father added.

The mother sobbed, and her husband held her. A killer had

intercepted their daughter, and the cracked phone screen did not bode well for her survival.

"We'll be right back."

Jed stepped out the front door. Claire did the same. A third girl had disappeared, and the investigation had no leads. First Grace and Karla, now Dana. Claire stopped in her tracks, and Rob almost collided with her. He gave her a quizzical glance.

She counted the girls on her fingers. "Grace Miles. Karla Smith. Dana Wood. That's the order of the names we drew up at the station." Claire tried to remain calm. "It's almost as if the killer..."

Rob completed the thought. "...is using our list?" He seemed amused, not concerned. "You think the killer has a mole in the department?"

"Or he's one of us." Claire glanced back at the Wood residence, where Officer Freeman stood on the front steps, rubbing the back of his neck.

"That sounds a little paranoid, don't you think?"

"There are fifteen names on that list! What are the chances he'd pick her next?"

"But there were only two more girls at Newburgh Middle School. We thought he'd widen the range of his attacks; we were wrong. There was a fifty-fifty chance the killer would target Dana next instead of the other girl."

Claire shook her head. Other irregularities in the case were slotting neatly into her theory.

"Tina's file was missing from the archive when I first asked for it. Officer Freeman's dad runs the archive. He found the file behind a cabinet in the basement. Somebody was trying to hide it."

"Claire—" Rob said, but she plowed on.

"Kitty's interview is missing from the folder and so is the full ME report."

"What are you saying, Claire—that the department is aiding and abetting a serial killer?"

Put that way, her suspicions did sound paranoid. "I don't know. But the killer is always one step ahead. He's been watching the girls' homes and waiting for an opportunity to strike again. He might not wait another four days."

Rob stretched his back and frowned as he considered the possibility. "It doesn't matter. The fourth girl is under guard."

"So was Dana Wood."

"She sneaked out on her own. You can't fault Patrol for that."

Claire wasn't sure anymore. The department had called off surveillance of the girls' homes before. Could they make the same mistake twice? She pulled out her phone and dialed a number.

"What are you doing?"

"Calling Dispatch."

"Newburgh Police Department," a woman said on the phone.

"This is Detective Claire Wolfe." She read in her badge number. "Who is stationed at the home of Amy Collins right now?"

A keyboard clattered on the other end of the line. "That would be Officer Freeman."

"Officer Del Freeman?" Claire shot Rob a glance.

"Correct."

Claire glanced at Dana's house. "I'm looking at Officer Freeman right now. He's at the home of Dana Wood. Who was supposed to be here now?"

The plastic keys chattered again while the call attendant checked. "That can't be right. Officer Freeman is listed at both locations. I'll send a squad over right away."

Claire swore and disconnected the call.

"What's going on?" Rob asked.

Claire dialed another number. "Freeman's supposed to be guarding Amy Collins."

"Geez! Where is she?"

The number rang. "I'm about to find out." The call connected. "Ms. Maynard, please. This is Detective Claire Wolfe." An electronic jingle played while the secretary transferred Claire's call.

"Hello. Detective Wolfe?"

"Yes. I have an urgent question. Is Amy Collins at school now?"

"One moment."

An electronic jingle played again while Claire waited. "She's checking."

The tune cut out. "I just spoke with her teacher. Amy didn't come to school today. We assumed she stayed home. Some parents are playing it safe until things quiet down. Is she OK?"

The floor dropped from Claire's stomach. She squeezed the phone. "Do you have her home number?"

"Yes, of course."

Claire wrote it down and called the number. Fifty feet down the road, the other officers stood over Dana's lost shoe and shattered phone, unaware of the unfolding drama. Claire waited in agony while the number rang. Each passing second might mean the difference between life and death.

Finally, the call connected.

"Hello?" said a woman.

"Mrs. Collins, this is Detective Claire Wolfe of the Newburgh Police Department. Is Amy at home?"

"Yes."

Claire nearly collapsed to the ground with relief.

"She came down with the flu yesterday. Is this about those girls? We heard you'd caught the murderer."

"The investigation is still ongoing. A police officer is on the way to your home."

"Has something happened? Is Amy in danger?"

"It's just a precaution. Another girl has gone missing." She'd hear about Dana on the news soon anyway. "I'm on my way over, too, Mrs. Collins." She ended the call and headed for her car.

Rob ran to catch up with her. "Right now?"

"Right now." Claire climbed into the driver's seat.

Down the street, Jed looked up at her. Claire would call him on her way to fill him in. Rob got in the passenger seat.

Claire started the engine. "No more girls are dying today."

CHAPTER 36

Amy Ellen Collins wanted to die. Her throat was on fire, and demons pounded away inside her skull as though her brain was a bongo drum. She lay on the living room couch beside a mound of used tissues that partially blocked her view of the TV. Her body had become a mucous factory and totally grossed her out.

The phone rang in the kitchen, and her mom answered. Amy didn't pay attention to the conversation. Her fluey brain focused on an episode of *Boy Meets World*. But her ears pricked up when her mom's voice dropped to a secretive whisper. Secretive whispers always got Amy's attention, flu or not. Her mom put down the phone.

"Who was that, Mom?"

Her mom walked over. Fear pinched her face. She'd looked that way a few days ago when the police officer had shown up at the house. At first, it was cool to meet a real-life police officer. Officer Hernandez was cooler than Officer Black. He'd allowed her to take selfies with him. But soon the novelty of her police guard had worn off. Her ever-present shadow was supposed to keep her safe, but she felt like a hunted animal.

The day her police guard left, Amy had come down with the flu. Just her luck! Nobody was trying to kill her anymore, but she had missed Dean Ward's birthday party all the same.

Amy's mom stood over her with that worried expression. "The police are on their way."

Amy groaned. "Not again. Didn't they catch the guy?"

"I thought so, too." She frowned at the mound of tissues. "Tidy up before they get here." She glanced at Amy's pajamas, which she had worn three days in a row. "And change into some clothes."

"I'm in the middle of an episode!"

"*Now*, Amy. They'll be here any minute."

"Give me a break, Mom. I'm sick."

Her mother picked up the phone again. "Either get dressed or stay in your room."

"Fine! I'm going upstairs."

She grabbed her box of Kleenex and trudged upstairs while her mom dialed a number. Last week, Amy had been scared out of her mind. She had seen Karla Smith every day at school. Like Amy, Karla was quiet in class, but they'd never really connected. News of her murder had freaked Amy out. A serial killer had murdered two girls from her grade within a week, and the police uniform outside her home did little to calm her fears. With all this stress, no wonder she had caught the flu.

Amy stomped on each step as she went upstairs, then stopped to eavesdrop.

Mom spoke softly into the phone. "Another girl has gone missing." She had called Amy's dad. "They didn't say, but she's in her class."

Amy's mouth fell open. *Dear Lord, another girl is missing.*

"Yes, right away." Mom put down the phone, locked the back door, and engaged the security chain.

Amy tiptoed to her room and closed the door behind her.

Here, she was safe. A breeze blew in from outside. Her mom must have opened the window to freshen the air.

Amy climbed onto her bed and leaned against the wall, propping a cushion behind her back.

Another girl is missing. First Grace Miles from 8B. Then Karla. Who was the third girl?

Everybody at school was talking about the murders. Cops had become a common sight at Newburgh Middle School, but only two girls had police guards posted at their homes: Amy and Dana Wood.

Amy's best friend, Mandy, had been so jealous. "So, I'm not good enough for the killer, huh? Not pretty enough to die?"

Amy had told her to shut up. All this talk of death terrified her. Dana Wood. It must be her. Dana was a stuck-up bitch, but nobody deserved to die young. Poor Dana.

Outside, a siren wailed, the sound of an ambulance. Amy reached for Fluffy, the stuffed polar bear her grandma had bought her at SeaWorld.

Years ago, when her parents had gone out and the babysitter had fallen asleep, Amy had snuck into her parents' room to watch TV. Her parents never let her watch late-night TV, even when she couldn't sleep. In the film, a girl was at home alone. A masked killer with a knife had hunted her from room to room. Amy had run back to her bed and couldn't fall asleep all night.

Had Amy become that girl in the house? She stared at the white wooden door of her bedroom. Any moment now, the door would splinter, and the masked killer would burst inside with his knife.

Amy shut her eyes and hugged Fluffy. The wail of the siren grew louder. Not an ambulance, a police car. Her mom had said the police were on their way. They would keep her safe. They'd catch the man in the mask and throw him in jail. Then, Amy would never be afraid again.

The siren was right outside her window now. Tires squeaked on the road, and the siren cut out. Doors opened and shut, and feet hurried to the front door. Her mother's voice rang out downstairs, and footsteps stomped on the staircase. Someone was running up the stairs.

Amy loosened her grip on the bear and opened her eyes.

She gasped. A figure stood over her. The police were too late. The killer had found her. Instead of a knife, the woman aimed a large handgun at Amy's head.

Amy hugged Fluffy tight and held her breath. She was going to die.

CHAPTER 37

Bella Winters stared at the blinking cursor on her computer screen. The surrounding cubicles buzzed with ringing phones and busy keyboards. *The Newburgh Herald's* wordsmiths were rushing to meet the deadline for Sunday's expanded edition. Bella bit her fingernails. Her feature story on the Middle School Strangler was missing a certain...something.

She'd coined the moniker after the second murder, and other newspapers had adopted the term. Now she wished she'd invented something more evocative. The Middle School Strangler conjured images of an enormous noose around the Middle School's red-brick buildings. The cartoonish image was unlikely to strike fear in the heart of her readership. Fear sold newspapers.

Over the past week, she had written about the murders from every angle: The senseless death of a fourteen-year-old schoolgirl; an exposé of police incompetence; a harrowing tale of serial killers on the loose. Bella loved serial killers. Nothing sold newspapers like serial killers.

But the killer hadn't struck since Monday. The police had arrested a suspect but delayed pressing charges. Bella's job would be much easier if the investigative officers were more cooperative. Caught in a news drought, yesterday's article had discussed the household names of serial killer notoriety. Compared to the Ted Bundys and Sons of Sam of the world, the Middle School Strangler displayed a poor work ethic. To be fair, he was just getting started. But if he didn't pick up the pace soon, Bella would have to resort to some R&R. In her business, that meant covering stories of rape and robbery.

Bella chided herself for her callous attitude toward heinous crimes. Her job had eroded her sensitivity to human suffering. She hadn't started out so jaded. Eight years ago, she'd been a young journalist eager to change the world. As the *Herald's* rookie crime reporter, she'd visited Newburgh PD daily to meet with the Public Information Officer and review police reports. She'd quickly lost her naivety about the state of humanity. The magnitude of the evil humans piled on each other boggled the mind. She'd also learned that the chances of an investigative journalist cracking a murder case using the scraps the cops threw the media approached zero.

On the bright side, she'd met some useful contacts at Newburgh PD, and she liked to think she played her part in fighting crime. For example, her article about police incompetence had stirred the boys in blue to place some Middle School girls under police protection. Could that have slowed the killer down? Ironically, the little good her writing did for the world made her job harder.

In her feature story for the Sunday edition, she delved deeper into the human-interest angle of the murders. She had set out with low expectations—what experiences or achievements of note could a girl of fourteen have racked up? But after interviewing their families, her attitude had changed. The girls and their families were nothing alike. Grace Miles had belonged to a middle-class, Church-going family. Karla had grown up with a single mother and had kept mostly to herself. Two unrelated families, united by the senseless deaths of their beloved daughters. Bella had gotten to know Gracie and Karla very well, and cracks had appeared in her cynical outer crust.

"How's our feature coming along?" a man said.

Steve leaned his arm on the wall of her cubicle and stole a glance at her screen. His other hand cradled a coffee mug. She'd never seen the editor-in-chief without his caffeine hit, which he refilled constantly. He liked to joke that he drank only one cup of coffee a day, and that cup lasted from morning to evening.

"Almost done?" A question mark had crept into her voice, betraying her misgivings about the story.

"But?"

"I don't know. It lacks...urgency. I left space for a few paragraphs."

"Well, you've got twenty-four hours to fill them."

"I was planning on taking Saturday off."

Steven chuckled as he moved on. "I've heard that before?"

He knew Bella too well. A perfectionist, Bella had squandered many a weekend polishing her prose and chasing that one last story lead. No wonder she was still single at thirty.

She reached for her cell phone and texted Deborah Jones, her contact at the Newburgh PD Dispatch. "Any updates on our mutual friend?"

"Mutual friend" was their code phrase for the Middle School Strangler. They used the secret vocabulary to ensure Deborah didn't lose her job if her supervisor ever discovered their conversations. Bella appeared in Deborah's contact list as "Mom 2." Bella compensated the phone jockey for her inside information with a Hershey's hamper and a 24-pack of Diet Dr. Pepper every other month.

Her phone buzzed when Deborah's text arrived. "Hotcakes."

Bella sat up at her desk. "Hotcakes" meant new information, hot from the oven. She typed away. "Another bird gone?" Had they found another victim?

The response arrived in seconds. "No. But a bird has flown."

Bella scrunched her nose and tried to decipher the message. She and Deborah had to coordinate their code words one day. Did she mean the girl wasn't dead, only missing? If so, a body could turn up at any moment. Bella typed away. "Name?"

The next response contained two letters. "DW."

Bella pulled up the Excel sheet she'd compiled of the names of the eighth-grade students at Newburgh Middle School. DW matched two names: Dean Ward and Dana Wood. Bella searched online for Dana Wood and knew what she'd find: a fourteen-year-old girl with blonde hair and blue eyes. Maybe Bella hadn't slowed the killer down, after all. Maybe her news coverage had egged him on. After her long meetings with the bereaved families, she hated to think she might have contributed to a young girl's death.

A small notification box at the bottom of the screen announced a new email. She clicked the square. The sender was not on her contacts list. The string of random characters that comprised the Gmail username meant the sender was either a spammer or an anonymous informant. Her email address was easily available on the *Herald's* website, and many of her contacts used burner email accounts to protect their privacy. But the subject line grabbed her attention. It contained two words: Dana Wood.

The hairs on the back of her neck bristled. Very few people knew Dana was missing. In all her years covering major crimes, never had a murderer contacted Bella.

The body contained a one-line message and a single attachment. Her pulse sped up. She double-clicked the video file and braced for the worst.

The clip lasted for only three seconds, but its meaning was clear. Her feature story would have to wait. Bella had found her sense of urgency.

CHAPTER 38

"Move!" Claire yelled at the car in front of her. A halo of white hair above the headrest was the only sign of the driver. If the old lady moved any slower, she'd be a rock. Claire tried to overtake, then swerved back into her lane to avoid a head-on collision.

Rob held on to his seat with both hands. "I can drive if you like. I did a defensive driving course at Quantico."

Claire ignored the hint. "No time. Grab the light from behind your seat."

Rob twisted around, reached behind the passenger seat, and retrieved the emergency strobe light. "I always wanted one of these." He untangled the spiral power cord. "How does it work?"

"Just throw it on top. The magnet and suction pad keep it from falling off."

Rob rolled down his window, placed the half-sphere on the roof, and plugged the power cable into the cigar lighter socket.

Claire pressed a button on the controller, and the device let loose a banshee yelp while the strobe light tinted the windshield in alternating blue and red. Rob covered his ears, then closed the window over the cord.

"I think I've gone deaf."

He rubbed his ears. Under other circumstances, Claire would have laughed. But she was intent on reaching her destination. The old lady pulled over to the side of the road.

"Thank. You!" Claire yelled while she overtook the slowcoach.

"What did you say? Speak louder. I can't hear you."

"Not funny, Rob. Amy's at home and unprotected. This is the killer's last opportunity to complete the target list."

Claire stepped on the accelerator to overtake another car.

"Watch out!" Rob said.

Claire swerved into her lane, narrowly avoiding a high-speed and untimely death. Her heart pumped adrenaline. Good. She was ready to act. Amy Collins would not die today—Claire forbade it.

"*I* drew up that list," Claire said. She needed to explain her urgency. "I put those girls' names on that board, and now they're dead."

"Claire, it's not your fault. You didn't get them killed. You were doing your job."

He was right. Her reaction wasn't rational. But the killer had murdered Claire's sister, and since she'd returned to Newburgh, he'd claimed three more girls. Claire would do anything to save Amy Collins from joining them. Only one thing was certain—the killer wasn't slowing down. He seemed more determined than ever.

"Snatching Dana outside her home was risky," Claire said. "The killer must have known a police officer was at her home. Why is he pushing his luck?"

"It's not uncommon. After killing a few people, serial killers become overconfident. They think they're superior to law enforcement and will never get caught. That carelessness often leads to their arrest."

The car tires squealed as Claire took a sharp corner. "Let's hope that works for us today."

She pulled up outside the Collins address, a two-level colonial, and Rob jerked forward in his seat when she slammed the brake pedal. Claire turned off the ignition, and the siren cut out. She jumped out of the car and leaped up the stairs of the front porch.

Her staccato knocking on the wooden door summoned a pale-faced, middle-aged woman with short red hair.

Claire flashed her badge. "Mrs. Collins, where is Amy?"

"Upstairs."

Claire walked inside and ran up the staircase, not waiting for Rob to catch up. Stickers of colorful butterflies covered the first door around a nameplate with the word Amy. As Claire raised her hand to knock, an explosion erupted inside the room. Claire knew that sound well. It was the report of a gunshot. She drew her Glock and burst inside.

A girl lay on the bed, slumped against the wall, a white fluffy bear on her lap. A drop of blood trickled from a black hole in her forehead. Her eyes stared at Claire, unseeing. A crown of red spatter colored the wall behind her.

Movement drew Claire's gun barrel to the open window. A black-clad figure straddled the windowsill and stepped onto the roof. The woman held a gun. A tuft of blonde hair sprouted from under her ski mask. A jolt of recognition immobilized Claire. *No, it can't be her!* The moment of shock passed. The killer was outside, padding across the roof tiles, escaping.

Claire aimed her gun and pumped the trigger. The glass pane shattered, the wooden frame chipped and splintered. Claire raced to the window, shoving her head and shoulders outside to improve her range, but the killer had disappeared.

Claire raced toward the door and almost slammed into Rob. His eyes moved from the dead girl on the bed to the smoking gun in Claire's hand.

"On the roof!" she said. "She's getting away!"

They sprinted downstairs, taking the steps three at a time, guns drawn. Amy's mother held her hands to her ears and stared at them open-mouthed.

"Stay down here!" Claire yelled. *No time to explain. Get the killer. Stop her now.*

They poured out of the house. "Go left!" she called to Rob.

She turned right, checked the street for the fleeing gunwoman, and circled the house, her gun trained on the roof. Dry leaves crunched underfoot. Claire halted, straining her ears for the sound of her prey's movements. That predator focus honed her senses. The murderer was not going to escape.

Hearing the whisper of crunching leaves, Claire charged ahead, reaching a backyard and a low wire fence. Clotheslines stretched between poles. Bedsheets, shirts, and blue jeans billowed in the breeze. Claire walked through the clothes, her gun aimed in both hands, scanning, searching. A dark figure stepped around the building, gun in hand. Claire swiveled, her finger on the trigger, then she froze. Rob lowered his gun, and so did Claire.

Rob shook his head. He'd seen nothing. The killer had evaporated into thin air. But Claire had recognized her, and now Claire's guts clenched with shock.

No. That's impossible.

CHAPTER 39

Police officers and forensic technicians bustled in and out of the living room. They brushed past Rob but paid him no attention. He was invisible, like a ghost.

An otherworldly fog clouded his senses. Claire was speaking to somebody nearby, but he could not process her words. The Doomsday crack of gunfire still rang in his ears. The scent of burned powder and spilled blood lingered in his nostrils. A half hour after the shooting, his heart still thumped. Horrible images haunted his mind's eye: A young girl slumped on a bed with a hole in her head and a circle of red on the wall behind her; Claire Wolfe staring at him, wide-eyed, her lips parted with shock, the wild tendrils of her dark hair grasping at her face, while a wisp of smoke rose from the barrel of her gun.

Rob had studied countless murders. He'd visited many crime scenes. But he had never stood this close to a victim when the bullets hit their mark. Until today.

"A black jumpsuit," the Internal Affairs officer, Alan Driver, said. He repeated Claire's words and scribbled them on his notepad.

"And a black ski mask," Claire added.

Mrs. Collins sat on the couch and wailed. Her husband was still on his way home from work. Police officers had sealed the neighborhood and were searching every car and pedestrian in a half-mile radius.

Yellow police tape blocked the entrance of the home. Captain Emmerso stood by the front door and shared a hushed conversation with a pensive Chief Harry Wallace. The department had set up a command post outside, a black RV jammed with computers and communications equipment. From the command post, officers coordinated the roadblocks and the new homicide investigation. Because, this time, an officer had discharged her weapon at the scene, Internal Affairs had joined the team.

The chief nodded as he listened to Captain Emmerso, but his eyes drifted to Claire, and they filled with suspicion. Rob could guess what he was thinking. Was Detective Wolfe a cold-blooded murderer?

"Are you sure it was a woman?" Officer Driver asked Claire.

"She had breasts. And long blonde hair." A note of anxious frustration sharpened her tone. She'd gone over this before.

"I thought she wore a ski mask?"

Claire pointed to her neck. "Some of her hair stuck out underneath."

"Did you recognize her?"

Claire hesitated. "As I said, she had a mask."

Rob watched Claire's expression closely. What was she holding back?

Officer Driver looked at him. "Agent Cline, did you see the shooter?"

Which one? "No. She'd already escaped onto the roof. We went downstairs and gave chase, but she was gone."

Feet on the staircase announced a female forensic tech in a surgical suit and sanitary covers over her hair, hands, and feet.

"Which one of you discharged the weapon?" she asked.

"I did," Claire said.

"How many rounds?"

Claire placed her hand on her Glock 22 in its holster. "Five."

"I'm going to need the gun as evidence."

Alan Driver said, "I'll collect the gun from Detective Wolfe at the station." He turned back to Claire. "We'll get you a replacement weapon right away. You'll take off the next few days as administrative leave."

"Administrative leave?" Claire's voice rose an octave with frustration. "We're in the middle of an investigation."

Driver grinned. "So am I. Try to take it easy. Do you want an attorney present for your full interview?"

"No."

"OK. The department will arrange for you to meet with a psychiatrist, too. You can look forward to some desk work until we complete our investigation." He spoke to the forensic tech. "Lee, swab them both. And we'll need photos, too. Make sure their clothes are fully visible."

"Yes, sir," the forensic tech said.

Driver gave Claire a grim smile. "We're done for now. Do you need to call anyone—family or friends?"

"No, I'm good."

"OK. I'll get an officer to drive you to the station."

"Don't bother. My car is outside."

Officer Driver gave her an apologetic frown. "I'm afraid we'll need that, too. Evidence."

"Oh. Right."

He gave her an expectant glance. "Can I have the keys? We'd prefer not to break the locks."

"Right. Sorry." Claire handed over her car keys. "I'm a bit shaken up."

"That's understandable."

Rob wanted to put his arms around her and hold her tight, but he held back. This was no time to reveal that their relationship had become intimate.

Officer Driver bagged the car keys in a plastic evidence bag and wrote Claire a receipt. "I'll see you at the station."

The Internal Affairs officer left the crime scene. Lee, the forensic tech, photographed them and swabbed their hands for gunpowder residue.

Tom and Jed entered the house, ducking under the police tape, and headed toward the chief and captain. Claire and Rob drew near to the bosses, too.

"What do we have?" Commander Emmerso asked them.

Tom shrugged. "At least two sets of footprints. It's hard to tell who's who. Forensics should take a closer look."

Jed's phone rang. All the officers watched him intently as he answered. Had they netted the killer?

Jed listened to the caller. "I see. OK, keep me posted." He hung up. "Nothing. The killer might be holed up within the perimeter."

Emmerso nodded. "We'll go house to house if we have to. Did you put out that BOLO?"

"Yes, sir."

Tom said, "I wouldn't get our hopes up, Captain Emmerso. We have few identifying details on the killer, and she's probably disposed of the weapon by now."

Claire spoke up. "We should notify the airport."

The officers turned to Claire and Rob.

Tom flashed his teeth in a humorless grin. "And stop every blonde-haired woman from leaving the state? I don't think so."

A man in a suit appeared in the doorway, his face white. His eyes took in the assembled officers, then found Mrs. Collins on the couch. He stepped underneath the crime scene tape, rushed to the sobbing woman. Amy's father had arrived home.

Chief Wallace sighed. "The press is waiting for our statement. We'll leave you to do your jobs."

The bosses left. Jed gave the others a brave grin, then walked over to the victim's parents. While he spoke, shock and disbelief reflected in their eyes. The couple was in their fifties. Amy had been their only child. What consolation could they hope for? Rob put his thoughts of tragedy on hold. He had a killer to catch.

Claire watched the parents and rubbed the palm of her hand. She was eating herself up inside. Her intuition had warned that something bad was going to happen. But they had arrived seconds too late.

"We're heading back to the station," Rob told Tom, and Tom nodded.

Rob and Claire exited using the front door and made for the nearest patrol cruiser. Halfway there, Claire halted. She looked Rob in the eyes.

"It was Tina."

"What do you mean?"

"The shooter. It's her."

Rob glanced over his shoulder. Nobody was close enough to overhear their conversation. "Tina's dead, Claire."

"What if she's not?"

Rob had to tread carefully. Claire was under a lot of strain.

"Tina died twelve years ago, Claire. She'd be twenty-six now. You probably wouldn't recognize her."

"I did."

"Then why didn't you tell Officer Driver?"

"Because he'd think I'm crazy."

Rob wanted to support her, but she wasn't making sense.

Claire gazed at him with stony defiance. "What if the mutilation wasn't a sign of anger or hatred? What if the mutilation was simply to hide the victim's identity?"

"So, Tina faked her murder—when she was fourteen years old?"

She clenched her jaw. "Tina or somebody else."

"And now she's back, killing girls with the same MO because...?" He trailed off.

Claire's shoulders sagged. "I don't know why. But I know what I saw."

A patrol officer stood outside her cruiser and nodded at Rob. On the other side of the street beside the command post RV, Chief Wallace and Commander Emmerso faced the crowd of newshounds and their microphones. They shouldn't catch Rob and Claire arguing outside the murder scene.

"C'mon. Let's go. We'll talk later." He smiled at the patrol officer. "Can we bum a ride to the station?"

"Sure."

In the squad car, Rob's thoughts sank into darkness. He knew what he had seen, too. He'd never forget that image. The dead girl on the bed. The hole in her forehead. The wet, red flower on the wall behind her. And Claire standing there, a smoking gun in her hand.

CHAPTER 40

"What's the likelihood our killer is a woman?" Emmerso asked Dr. Fleischer.

After returning from the crime scene that afternoon, he had summoned the FBI agents to his office to make sense of the recent developments. The killer had murdered a fourth victim, and the third girl was still missing. Everything they knew about the killer had flown out the window. And judging by the press conference outside the recent victim's home, public confidence in law enforcement had hit a new low. Their investigation needed a breakthrough more than ever.

The assembled detectives and agents watched Dr. Fleischer, who shifted on her feet.

"Unlikely but not impossible. Female mass killers usually claim multiple victims in one event. They don't go for the sexual fantasy of serial murder. If our killer is a woman, I'd suspect mental illness. But these murders were well-planned. The killer has changed MO and is taking more risks. It's almost as though he's rushing to check off items on a hit list. The murders are more like...assassinations."

"*Assassinations*?" Agent Tom Brown didn't hide his disbelief. "As in organized crime?"

The psychiatrist shrugged. "Hits disguised as serial murders."

Agent Robert Cline said, "Why would organized crime want to execute fourteen-year-old girls?"

"Good question."

Emmerso sighed. His search for answers only raised more questions. "Detective Wolfe said the killer is female. Agent Cline, can you corroborate that?"

The agent shook his head. "I didn't see the killer."

"Do you have any reason to doubt Detective Wolfe's words?"

Agent Cline shot him a surprised glance. Surprise or guilt? Did Cline doubt Claire's version of the events, too?

A loud knock on the door put their discussion on hold. Detective Mahoney poked his earnest face into the room. "Captain Emmerso, there's someone to see you—a reporter from *The Newburgh Herald*."

Emmerso bristled. *The Newburgh Herald* had printed that piece about police incompetence. "Tell Ms. Bella Winters we already made a statement to the press today."

"Sir, she says she has a message from the killer."

Stunned looks circled the officers and agents. Was this the breakthrough they had needed?

"What kind of message?"

The door swung inward, and a thick mane of auburn, blow-dried hair barged into the room. "A video clip," Bella Winters said. "Dana Wood is alive."

CHAPTER 41

Captain Emmerso played the three-second video clip on the reporter's flash drive again. Gathered around his desk chair were Dr. Fleischer, the two FBI agents, and Detective Jed Wallace. Bella Winters of *The Newburgh Herald* made herself at home in the visitor's chair.

"It's her," Jed said.

"Are you sure?" Emmerso asked.

On the screen, a girl squirmed on a cement floor beside a copy of this morning's *Newburgh Herald*. Cable ties secured her hands behind her back, and a black canvas bag covered her head. The girl groaned. She could be anyone.

Jed pointed to the girl's feet, tied together at the ankles. One of her feet ended in a red, high-heeled shoe. "The other shoe turned up on the street near her home along with her phone. The parents identified both as belonging to Dana."

Emmerso gave the reporter an appreciative glance. "Ms. Winters, thank you for coming to us right away."

Bella Winters inclined her head. Emmerso had assumed the reporter had shown up at the station to fish for information. She'd not balked at portraying Newburgh's finest in a negative light before. Why would she stop now? But if she'd cared only about newspaper sales, she would have published the information without consulting the police. The video clip produced new hope for finding the missing girl alive. Maybe there was hope for humanity after all?

"The video came with a message," Bella added for the benefit of Jed, who had returned to the station minutes ago. "If we don't publish the video within twelve hours, he'll kill her."

Emmerso noted Bella's use of the male pronoun but didn't correct her. There was no need to leak their new lead to the press.

"Did he make any other demands—ransom money?" Emmerso asked

"No, nothing."

"What do you think, Special Agent Brown?"

Brown frowned. "Do as he says, but we'd like access to that email. Our folks at Cyber might be able to identify the sender or his location from the video file."

"No problem," Bella said.

"Thank you again, Ms. Winters," Emmerso said. "We'll take things from here. Agent Brown, please follow that up ASAP."

Special Agent Brown and the reporter left the room, closing the door behind them.

"Everyone, please have a seat." He waited for them to settle. "Dr. Fleischer, I'd offer you a penny for your thoughts, but considering psychiatric rates these days, I think that would cost a lot more."

Dr. Fleischer gave him a dry grin. "Either way, you won't get your money's worth, Captain."

"Why the video? Is the killer taunting us?"

"That's possible. He—or she—might enjoy the attention and the sense of control. But the killer is intelligent. The message might be a diversion, too."

"A diversion from what?" Jed asked.

"The killer was on her way to Amy Collins when she sent the email. She knows the girls are under police protection. Maybe she wanted to divert police resources from protecting Amy to finding Dana. She didn't bank on Ms. Winters holding the information."

"If the killer wanted a diversion," Emmerso said, "she should have sent that email earlier and set a tighter deadline."

"You're right. I'm open to other ideas."

Special Agent Robert Cline spoke up. "Who coordinated police protection for the girls?"

Emmerso turned to Jed, who answered.

"Officer Jessica Long." The FBI agent gave him a puzzled frown. "You may have seen her in the squad room. Blonde hair. Blue eyes."

Agent Cline raised his eyebrows, and Emmerso knew what he was thinking. Officer Long matched Detective Wolfe's description of the shooter. Had she sabotaged the girl's police protection intentionally? Was she the murderer? Emmerso nipped that conspiracy theory in the bud.

"Human error happens, Agent Cline. Assigning blame won't help us catch the killer."

Dr. Fleischer rolled her shoulders and clasped her hands. She looked miserable. This case was getting to her.

"You know," Emmerso said, waxing philosophical, "I always thought forensic profiling was a psychic superpower. One glance at the crime scene and you'd know the color of the killer's socks and his favorite brand of toothpaste."

Dr. Fleischer sighed. "Hollywood has raised expectations. It's a hard standard to meet consistently. We usually provide actionable information. But to be fair, this is an unusual case."

"How so?"

Dr. Fleischer scoffed. "Where do I begin? Identical murders

separated by over a decade. A female serial killer caught red-handed. And don't get me started about the irregularities."

Now she had his full attention. "What irregularities?"

She hesitated, then seemed to decide she had nothing to lose. "I studied the case files. Some reports are missing in the Tina Wolfe murder."

Emmerso eyed Jed. "Which reports?"

Agent Cline folded his arms.

The psychiatrist hesitated again. "The summary lists Kitty Tucker as a witness, but there is no transcript or summary of her interview."

"What else?"

"The crime scene provided traces of blood and pubic hair, but the file contains no forensic analysis. Either the detective in charge was sloppy bordering on negligent or somebody tampered with the files."

Somebody. Emmerso steepled his fingers. Claire had checked out the case file, but she had mentioned no missing reports.

"Are we still dealing with one perp?"

"I think so. The crimes are too similar. Besides the killer, only a handful of law enforcement officers knew the full details of Tina's murder."

"But the killer strangled the others. The new victim doesn't fit his MO. Would a shooting fulfill his murder fantasy?"

Dr. Fleischer shrugged. "Maybe. Maybe not. But there's a simpler explanation. The unsub had intended to strangle and mutilate Amy Collins, too, but the detectives interrupted the commission of the crime. So, the killer improvised, rushing the job and changing his MO to escape capture. The accelerating kill rate shows that he's become more confident. But I've never seen anything so dramatic. Serial killers usually wait weeks, months, or even years between victims. The mental pressure builds as the thrill of the last murder wears off. When the compulsions become overpowering, the killer strikes again."

She trailed off, lost in thought. Emmerso didn't dare interrupt.

Dr. Fleischer shook her head. "Something isn't adding up. The killer is speeding ahead. It's as though he's trying to fill a quota on a tight schedule."

"That hit list you mentioned earlier?"

The doctor nodded. "What if we're not dealing with a serial killer at all, but a psychopathic murderer who understands serial killers?"

Jed raised his eyebrows. "What's the difference?"

Dr. Fleischer ignored him. "Female serial killers are rare, but female assassins are not."

"You mean like...a spy?"

"Not espionage, Detective. Organized crime."

Emmerso shifted uneasily in his chair. They had circled back to the Mafia hypothesis. This new direction explained the crimes but failed to reassure the captain. He was not looking forward to the chief's reaction to his next progress report.

Jed cleared his throat. "There's another possibility. I spoke with the forensic tech at today's crime scene. What she said made no sense at the time, but now..."

"Spit it out, Detective."

"Well, Dr. Fleischer said the killer has deep knowledge of forensics and police procedures. Highly intelligent, she might insert herself into the investigation."

"Go on."

"Forensics retrieved three bullets in the victim's bedroom—one in the wall behind the victim and two more in the window frame."

The gates of Hell opened beneath Emmerso's feet. "The shots fired by Detective Wolfe?"

Jed nodded. "Detective Wolfe said she fired five rounds at the killer as she escaped onto the roof. At least one bullet must have passed through the window. We're still waiting for a full firearms analysis, but for now, one thing is certain."

"And that is?"

Jed licked his lips. "The same type of gun fired all three bullets—a Glock 22."

CHAPTER 42

"What do you mean 'nothing'?" Rob yelled at the desk phone that night.

Bella Winters had forwarded the killer's video to Tom's contact at the FBI Cyber Division an hour ago, and Rob had banked on their magicians divining the girl's location. The fourteen-year-old would die if they didn't find her in time, and the investigation's one solid lead had hit a brick wall.

"You heard me," the young cyber tech said. Tom had put him on speakerphone in the squad room. "Whoever made the video is a pro. They stripped the MP4 file of all headers. The email address is a burner, as you suspected. You can subpoena Google for their IP logs for the Gmail account, but judging by the video, the sender would have used a VPN and Tor to stay anonymous."

"Check that, all the same," Tom said, calming the tone of the conversation. "We'll be in touch later."

"OK. I'll hand it over to the next shift."

"So much for Cyber," Rob said when Tom disconnected the call.

Tom pointed to the freeze-frame of the girl from the video clip. "Looks like a basement to me. That would explain the lack of ambient noise. The killer probably stored the dead bodies there before dumping them."

"What are we supposed to do—search every basement in the city? By the time we find her, she'll be dead."

The long hours and the emotional stress of the morning's shooting had worn Rob out. He was grumpy, his nerves stretched thin. He wished he could hand this case to the next shift, too. Working from Claire's desk without her in the squad room felt wrong. Stuck at home, she was probably climbing the walls. Claire was slowly becoming a suspect in her homicide investigation. And she had no idea.

Emmerso called the squad room to attention. "As you all know, we have a hostage situation on our hands. A small army of Feds is on its way to lend a hand."

A small army of Feds. Rob and Tom exchanged meaningful glances. Newburgh PD had called in reinforcements.

Emmerso continued. "We'll work shifts over the weekend. Detective Nakamura is drawing up the schedule so be sure to send him flowers."

Few officers chuckled. The mood in the room had darkened.

"Get some rest while you can. We're all on call. That's it for now."

The officers sidled over to Detective Nakamura at his desk.

"One at a time, boys and girls," he said.

Mahoney leaned back in his chair. "That's the price of popularity, partner."

"Special Agents, Dr. Fleischer," Emmerso said. "My office."

Rob and Tom exchanged more meaningful glances. First Emmerso had added Bureau resources, now he'd called them to his office. Was the department unsatisfied with their performance? Detective Jed Wallace followed them into Captain Emmerso's room and closed the door behind him.

Captain Emmerso perched on his desk. "We think our department has been compromised."

Rob stiffened. *Here it comes.* He turned to Tom, hoping his partner would object to the speculation, but Tom kept his eyes on the captain.

"Detective Wallace," Emmerso said, prompting the investigator to explain.

Jed folded his arms. "Here's what we know. The victims died in the same order as the list on our whiteboard."

The chill spread down Rob's body. Claire had made the same observation, but he had brushed aside her suspicions.

Tom said, "You think the killer has a mole inside the department?"

"Or the killer works here."

The cold flush filled Rob's body. Earlier, Jed had mentioned the three bullets found in Amy Collins's bedroom. The handgun that had fired them—the Glock 22—was the police department's standard service weapon. Rob's premonition was materializing. Did Jed suspect his partner had committed the murders?

Emmerso said, "That's why we're discussing this in my office. Our suspicions must stay in this room."

Jed seemed to have convinced the captain already. Rob had to stop that train from leaving the station. And he had to speak up without exposing his relationship with Claire.

"Hold on," he said. "Two of the girls died before we made that list. That leaves only Dana Wood and Amy Collins. There's a fifty-fifty chance the killer would have—"

Captain Emmerso cut Rob off. "There's more. Please hear him out."

Rob backed down, and Jed continued.

"As Dr. Fleischer noticed, someone removed documents from the Tina Wolfe case files. I followed up with Officer Freeman at the Archive. Only one person checked out the files during the past few years—Detective Wolfe."

Rob said, "Maybe the documents were missing from the start? Did you check with the lead investigator?"

"Lieutenant Brian O'Leary died over a month ago."

Rob groaned inside. With O'Leary dead, they'd never know for sure what the original folder contained. This was not looking good for Claire.

"Besides possessing the files, Detective Wolfe also fired five rounds at the most recent crime scene, claiming she had tried to stop the killer from fleeing the scene."

Rob could not let that pass. "*Claiming*? Do you think she's lying?"

"Agent Cline, did you see the killer?"

"I missed her by a few seconds."

Jed grunted. "Agent Brown, you searched the surroundings of the house for traces of the killer. How many sets of tracks did you find?"

Tom hesitated. "Two, but the backyard was dry and—"

"Two tracks account for Agent Cline and Detective Wolfe. Did you find any sign of a third person outside the house?"

Tom inhaled deeply but kept his eyes on the detective. "No."

Jed turned back to Rob. "Which leads to the next question. Why were you and Detective Wolfe at the Collins home to begin with?"

The sudden cross-examination caught Rob off guard. They didn't think he had a hand in the murder, too, did they? "As soon as Detective Wolfe discovered that Amy Collins was home and without police protection, she feared the killer would get to her."

"And she did."

Rob clenched his jaw. "Yes, *the killer* got to her."

"Why didn't she call a squad car on her police radio to meet at the girl's home? A patrol vehicle might have been closer."

"She did."

"And yet she rushed to the girl's home right away."

"Detective Wolfe sensed that the girl was in immediate danger. She trusted her gut instinct, and she was right. Surely you don't think..."

Rob looked from Jed to Captain Emmerso to Dr. Fleischer in disbelief. They had all worked with Claire. Had they turned on her so quickly?

Rob aimed his question at Jed. "Do you think your partner killed those girls?"

"I've known her a week," the detective said. "You've spent more time with her over the past few days than the rest of us combined."

His upper lip twitched as he spoke the words. Did he know about Rob's romance with Claire? Rob glanced at Tom, who still avoided eye contact. Rob had not slept in his motel bed the past few nights. Had Tom told Jed? Was Jed jealous? Asking that question would expose Rob's entanglement with Claire and land him in the same mess. Rob let the silence work for him.

Jed continued. "Detective Wolfe first applied for a position at Newburgh two years ago. Did you know that? Her first day on the job, she went after Tina's case file."

"Tina was her sister, Detective. Wouldn't you do the same if you were in her shoes?"

Jed shrugged. "I wouldn't have withheld her file from the investigation for a week."

"Her sister died twelve years ago. Maybe Detective Wolfe thought a twelve-year-old murder wasn't relevant to the case?"

Jed grinned. "And when she moved back to Newburgh twelve years later, more girls turned up dead just like her sister. That's quite a coincidence, don't you think?"

Rob had no answer for that.

Captain Emmerso spoke up again. "Agent Cline, I respect Detective Wolfe and, to be honest, I like her. But we can't ignore the evidence. Dr. Fleischer, what do you think—is Detective Wolfe serial killer material?"

The psychiatrist glanced from Rob to the captain and back. "She's intelligent and physically capable. Obviously, she is familiar with forensics and police procedures. She had a close personal connection to the first victim. In my profile, I specified a male. But a female killer isn't out of the question. In the short time we've spent together, Claire has displayed empathy and emotional intelligence. But psychopaths can be very deceptive."

The image of Claire in Amy's room, the discharged gun in her hand, flashed in Rob's mind again. Had Claire fooled him, too?

Jede continued. "I've traced Detective Wolfe's movements. Her whereabouts during the first and second murders are unknown. She moved to Newburgh a week before she started work at the department. That gave her enough time to surveil the girls and plan her attacks. She was present during today's murder, and she seems to have been at home alone last night when the killer snatched Dana Wood from the street."

Rob swallowed hard. Claire hadn't been alone last night. He had been with her. But if he confessed to spending the night with her, his credibility—and his career—would be in question.

He racked his memory of the previous night. Claire had gone for a run before he'd arrived. Was that enough time to kidnap an unsuspecting young girl? Had Claire kept Dana in her basement right under his feet?

No! Claire wasn't a cold-blooded murderer. She was the victim of several bizarre coincidences.

Emmerso took charge of the discussion again. "Detective Wolfe is innocent until proven guilty. But we need to rule her out as a suspect. Detective Wallace, we'll need an affidavit for a search warrant."

"A search warrant?" Rob blurted.

"Yes, Agent Cline. The entire city is searching for Dana Wood. We can't leave any stone unturned. Let's hope we find her before it's too late. Dr. Fleischer, what else we should specify in the affidavit?"

"Trophies and mementos. Look for clothing or jewelry that belonged to the victims. Hair, too. The killer would use them to relive the murders and fantasies."

"Good. Detective Wolfe is on administrative leave for the next few days. I expect she'll cooperate. But this conversation stays here. She knows nothing of our suspicions, and I want to keep things that way. Do not reach out to her. If she contacts you, tell her nothing. Understood?"

They nodded, and the captain ended the meeting. As they filed out of his office, Jed touched Rob's shoulder, and they hung back to speak in private.

"Listen. This is hard for me, too. I like Claire, and I'm sure you do, too."

He searched Rob's eyes, and Rob held his breath. Did Jed know about his relationship with Claire? Not even Tom knew about their childhood connection. Nakamura and Mahoney had seen Claire and Rob arrive at work together. Had they spread a rumor?

"But we have to think of Dana Wood and put our personal feelings aside. Her life depends on us. If she's still alive, every second counts. That's why I'd like you to join the search first thing tomorrow morning."

Rob nodded. "No problem."

"Good." Jed stepped closer, a little too close for comfort. "We'll be the first ones through her door."

CHAPTER 43

Dana Wood awoke in the dark. Her shoulder hurt, and her neck stung. She lay on a cold, stony floor, her hands tied behind her back. The inky black space smelled of damp. Where was she?

A twisted cloth filled her mouth. No matter how hard she pushed, her tongue could not expel the disgusting, wet wad. Hot air blew in her face when she breathed out of her nose. A bag covered her head, and her cheek chafed on the rough canvas. How had she landed up here?

She had snuck out of her bedroom window, climbed down the trellis, and hurried to Lena's house, to Dean Ward's party. Then, she remembered: The footsteps behind her; the tight cord around her neck; the burning sensation in her lungs; and the sudden realization that she was going to die.

Only she had not died. Not yet. She had passed out, and her attacker had brought her here. She had to get free. At all costs, she must escape. Her life depended on it.

She scrambled to get to her feet, but her legs refused to cooperate. A tight, thin cord bound her ankles. Like an inch-worm, she flexed her legs and bare feet, but her efforts only shifted her body in a circle on the rough floor. She lay there, panting into the canvas bag.

Her stomach ached with hunger. How long had she been there? Had the attacker abandoned her there to starve to death?

Her breathing sped up. A dizzy cloud descended on her mind. *No, don't pass out again. Calm down!* She drew slow, deep breaths. *You are not going to die. You will get out of here.*

She thought of the other girls: Grace Miles and Karla Smith. They'd turned up dead soon after they'd gone missing. How much time did she have left?

A sound from above froze her solid. The whine of water in pipes, and the rain of a showerhead. Someone was here with her. No, not here. Up there. She was in a basement! Dana congratulated herself for figuring that out. She could do this. Her attacker was taking a shower in the house above. Good. Nobody would hear Dana as she struggled to break free.

Dana kicked her feet again, spinning in a circle. Her fingers brushed a strap, and she gripped the object in her hand. A shoe. A high-heeled shoe, one of the pair she had chosen for the party. Did that help her? Yes! She could use the sharp end of the heel.

She rolled onto her stomach. Then, she lifted her head, dug her knees into the floor, and bent at the waist. She had inched backward, her chest pressing painfully against the cold rough surface. That didn't matter. She repeated the movement over and over until her foot bumped into something solid. She explored the surface with her toes. A wall. If she could free her hands, she'd be able to untie her legs, rip the canvas bag from her head, and run away.

The shower noises fell silent. Dana rotated the shoe in her hands, careful not to let it drop. Her fingers explored the seams of the leather pieces. The heel wasn't sharp enough to cut, but if she could rip the shoe apart, she might find a nail or expose a sharp edge. Something. Anything. She gripped the shoe and pulled for all she was worth, but the glue held tight.

A door opened in the house above. Not the door to the basement. Another door. A woman spoke, and then a man. Dana could not make out the words. Did the attacker have an accomplice or a visitor—a visitor who had no idea his host kept Dana in the basement?

Dana cried out despite the gag. "Help! Help me! Please! I'm down here! In the basement!"

Only muffled grunts escaped her mouth. Boards shifted in the ceiling.

The woman raised her voice. She was shouting now. Had the visitor heard Dana? Was he confronting the attacker? The man responded, his tone soft and apologetic.

Dana screamed for all she was worth. "Here! Down here! Please, help me! Help! Me!"

CHAPTER 44

Someone knocked on the front door as Claire got out of the shower Friday night.

"Just a minute," she hollered.

She had hoped Rob would stop by tonight. Claire's administrative leave had cut her off from the investigation. The infuriating powerlessness was driving her insane, especially considering the surprising recent development.

The television news had played a clip that the killer had sent to *The Newburgh Herald*. Dana Wood was alive. The footage of the hostage had set off a frenzy of media speculation. Was the video the windfall the investigation needed to figure out the girl's location? Claire had urgent questions of her own. Would the video vindicate Claire's belief that Tina was behind the murders?

Claire toweled off quickly and pulled on a fresh set of clothes. Greeting Rob while wrapped in a towel again would send the wrong message. After the day's tragic madness, Claire was in no mood for romance. But she longed for an update from the front lines of the investigation.

Her hair wrapped in a towel, she padded through the hall

barefoot and opened the front door. Rob stood on the welcome mat in his plain FBI suit. He'd come straight from the station. Like the others, he was working overtime. Guilt needled Claire for waiting on the sidelines.

Rob seemed exhausted and tense, and Claire feared the worst.

"Have we found Dana?"

He shook his head. Claire's shoulders sagged, and she released the breath she'd been holding. "We got nothing from the video?"

"How do you know about the video?"

She didn't like the suspicious tone of the question. "It's on the news."

"Oh, right."

He made no move to enter. She needed to lighten the mood and loosen his tongue.

"At least this time, I remembered to lock the door." She tipped her head toward the kitchen. "Want some dinner?"

Rob lingered on the doorstep. "No. Thanks." Why was he keeping his distance?

"Feel free to come in."

Rob gave her a quick, cool smile, then stepped inside and closed the door. He glanced around as though he'd never visited her home before, never cooked her dinner in her kitchen, or made love to her in her bed. What was the matter with him? The morning's murder scene must have shaken him badly. She didn't blame him. After the adrenaline rush of the pursuit had faded, the vision of Amy, dead on her bed, haunted Claire, too.

Claire found a bowl and spoon and fixed herself a gourmet meal of Kellogg's Special K. Rob stood in the hall and didn't join her at the table. Did shock and frustration explain his behavior, or was something else on his mind?

"The video must have given us *something*," Claire said.

He shook his head. "The Cyber Division had a look. The killer knew what she was doing."

"She," Claire repeated. The investigation had taken her report of the killer seriously. The day was not a total loss. "So, Dr. Fleischer updated her profile?"

"Yeah. We're searching for a female killer now."

"Good." Claire chewed her cereal.

Rob watched her closely, and his tense scrutiny got on her nerves.

"Did you tell them I think it's Tina?"

During her run that evening, Claire had regretted not sharing her suspicions with Captain Emmerso. Sure, she would sound crazy. But if Tina had faked her death, the investigation would need to change direction and explore other leads.

"No."

Claire nodded. She shoveled another spoonful of cereal into her mouth. Rob didn't want to sound crazy either. Fair enough. She needed to pierce the wall of ice that had shot up between them.

"I've been thinking. You were right. A teenage girl can't disappear on her own. Tina must have had help."

"Claire, why would anyone help her fake her death?"

"I don't know. I'm just trying to make sense of it all."

Rob studied her empty bookshelves and the framed posters the owners had hung on the walls. What was he hunting for? And why was he suddenly so tight-lipped?

"I saw the search party on Park Street." Claire had wanted to speak to the volunteers, but she'd held back. Internal Affairs might not like her interfering in an ongoing investigation.

"Did you go for a run last night, too?"

The question sounded like an accusation. What was he implying?

"You know I did. I run most nights. Running clears my mind."

"Clears your mind?"

He held her gaze. There it was again, that icy allegation in his voice. She didn't like his line of questioning.

"Rob, is everything OK?"

He held her gaze. "It's been a hellish day."

"Yes, it has." She scooped up the last flakes from the bottom of the bowl.

"You must feel pretty shaken, too."

Claire dropped the spoon in the empty bowl. "I guess."

"You guess?"

"Yes."

"How did you know Amy was in immediate danger?"

"I didn't. But my hunch paid off."

"It paid off?"

Claire opened her mouth to speak, then stopped herself. Rob was repeating her last few words.

"What is this—strategic empathy? Am I a suspect now?" Claire had meant that as a joke, but Rob didn't laugh. A fire ignited in her chest. "Rob, am I a suspect?"

He stared at his feet. "Things aren't looking good, Claire. Forensics found the slugs. They all came from a Glock 22."

Claire bolted to her feet, the kitchen chair clattering to the tiled floor behind her. "You think I killed Amy—that I shot her in cold blood?"

"No, of course not. I'm only saying how things seem. The bullet striations should set the record straight."

Claire scoffed. "Are they so desperate that they're trying to pin the murders on me?"

"They're only trying to make sense of the facts. You drew up the list of victims, and the killer has been checking them off one by one."

"The entire department saw that list. The cleaning service, too."

"But they weren't in Amy's bedroom moments after her death."

"I was there because I'm a cop and I have good instincts."

"Those girls only started turning up dead the moment you moved back to Newburgh."

"I did not kill those girls!"

"What about Tina? You hated her. You wished she was dead."

Claire's mouth fell open. The betrayal almost stopped her heart. "You told them. What I shared with you in bed. You told them!"

"No, Claire. I didn't say a thing."

"But you think I killed her."

"If I thought you killed anyone, I wouldn't be here."

"Then why are you here?"

He paused and drew a breath. "I had to know for sure."

"Screw you!"

"Claire—"

"No, screw you! I've dedicated my life to finding Tina's killer, and now you're building a case against me?"

"I'm not building a case against you."

"Then, who is?"

A noise came from the floorboards, a vague rumble. "What was that?"

"Water pipes. It's an old house."

Rob glanced at the basement door.

Claire feigned embarrassment. "Silly old me. I forgot. Dana Wood is in the basement. Why don't you say hello? Go on. Check the basement. That's why you're here. Knock yourself out."

"I don't need to. She's not here. You're not a killer."

"Glad to hear it, Special Agent Cline. Now get the hell out of my home!"

Rob nodded and let himself out.

Claire stood rooted to the spot, her chest heaving, and her mind racing. Rob was the last person in the world she'd expect to turn on her. But he wasn't alone. Claire knew how these things worked. The department needed a new lead suspect, and they had chosen her. If they were building a case against her, she'd need evidence to clear her name. Seeing as she hadn't killed the girls, that shouldn't be difficult.

She reviewed the few weeks since she came back to Newburgh. When the victims had disappeared, she'd either been at home or out jogging, alone. Claire swore under her breath. She had no alibi. In the investigation's eyes, she had both the means, motive, and opportunity. And today she had discharged her weapon in Amy's bedroom moments after her murder. The DA had a story to sell to the jury. Claire was the department's new hire. Newburgh PD could hang her out to dry without looking bad. The dirty cop would take the fall for all their failures.

One other conviction solidified—Tina had help from inside the department. Her collaborator had staged her death, and now he and Tina were setting Claire up for murder. And they would cover their tracks. If Claire turned herself in, nobody would believe her. Not even Rob. She'd have nobody left to prove her innocence.

Claire rushed to her bedroom and grabbed her new standard-issue Glock. In her underwear drawer, she located a box of cartridges. Administrative leave or not, Claire had to conduct her investigation, alone.

CHAPTER 45

"Is this really necessary?" Rob asked Detective Jed Wallace, early Saturday morning. He eyed the half-dozen SWAT officers behind them who stood, weapons drawn, outside Claire's front door. He felt like a traitor.

Jed unfolded the search warrant from his pocket. "She may have murdered four girls, including her sister. We're taking every precaution."

The stocky Latino SWAT commander, Sergeant Vincent Morales, drew near. "Detective, we're in position and ready to engage the target."

The target. Overnight, Jed had turned Claire from a colleague into a suspect. During the pre-mission briefing, the SWAT sergeant had noted the positions of his men along the street and in neighboring properties to prevent Claire's escape.

"Thank you, Sergeant. We're going in."

The SWAT sergeant rejoined his men. Jed knocked on the door and backed away as though he expected Claire to shoot her way out. This was ridiculous. Claire was not the Middle School Strangler. Their time and resources were better spent searching for Dana Wood elsewhere.

Rob dreaded the look of hurt and betrayal on Claire's face. Would she ever forgive him? After years apart, they had rekindled their spark. Now he'd lose her again, and this time probably forever.

Jed had given him no choice. A refusal to take part in the search would call his loyalties into question. If Jed found out Rob had visited Claire last night, he would kick Rob back to Quantico immediately for an official censure. Let the detective enjoy his posturing. The search would prove Claire's innocence. Rob didn't doubt that for a second.

Jed knocked on the door again, louder and longer. "Detective Wolfe," he called. "This is Detective Wallace. I'm here with Special Agent Cline. We have a warrant to search your property."

No movement came from within. Was Claire asleep? Had she slipped out for an early morning jog? How did Claire Wolfe spend her free time? He had known Claire Wolfe the teenager well, but how well did he know Claire Wolfe the homicide detective?

Jed nodded at Sergeant Morales. The sergeant waved, and two SWAT officers with a battering ram approached the door. Two seconds and one deafening bang later, the door swung open on its hinges, and the other SWAT officers poured inside, rifles drawn.

Rob and Jed drew their weapons and followed them inside. Claire would need a new door lock. A cereal bowl sat on the kitchen table where she had eaten dinner last night. He was glad he hadn't taken up her offer to eat with her. Two dirty bowls would have raised questions that would lead right back to him.

The SWAT officers returned, Sergeant Morales in the lead. "The house is clear. Basement and perimeter, too. Detective Wolfe must have left earlier. I think we're done here."

Rob relaxed. He would not confront Claire face-to-face. The officers had found no sign of the missing girl either. Why did a small part of him feel relieved?

Jed thanked the SWAT officers, and they filed out of the house. He handed Rob a pair of latex gloves.

"You take the kitchen. I'll get the black light and do the basement."

Rob nodded. A black light would reveal traces of organic residue invisible to the human eye. Jed was looking for bloodstains. But the black light would also reveal semen. If Jed used the light in the bedroom, would he find traces of Rob's DNA?

Rob searched the kitchen moving clockwise, as always. He opened drawers and rummaged around the utensils. He'd used the spatulas and pans to cook dinner for Claire. This invasion of her privacy gnawed on his conscience, but he had talked the talk and now he had to walk the walk. He found no severed heads or other serial killer mementos. *Surprise, surprise.* Where was Claire? Had his visit last night spooked her, prompting her to flee her home?

Jed made a racket in the basement. He'd been down there a long time. What had he found? His heart pounding, Rob headed toward the basement, the place he'd expect to find the missing girl if Claire was guilty. She wasn't. But he had to silence his doubts for good.

Rob descended the steep staircase. Except for a single cardboard box on a low shelf, the basement was empty. There were no suspicious stains on the concrete floor. Jed wrapped an electric cord around a rectangular box. He was packing away the black light and luminol spray.

"Find anything?"

"A few burned light bulbs."

"Hmm. That's probably not a federal offense."

Jed scoffed. "Not yet. But somebody cleaned up well."

He was implying that Claire might have kept the girl there. She might even have processed the dead bodies in the basement, too. But the ultraviolet light would expose nothing if she'd sanitized the room, leaving no trace of her crimes.

Rob sniffed the air. He couldn't deny the faint scent of disinfectant. "Claire moved in recently. The landlord must have cleaned up."

Jed trudged up the stairs. "Maybe."

Upstairs, Rob entered Claire's bedroom ahead of Jed. He'd rather the detective didn't find any remnants of his time with Claire. Fresh, smooth sheets covered the queen-sized bed. Either Claire hadn't slept in her bed last night or she'd tidied up first thing in the morning. Had she expected a search party?

He dropped to his knees and peered underneath the bed. Opening the closet drawers, he dug through Claire's socks and underwear. A few scribbles from a county judge, and men with guns invaded your private space, guilty or not. Claire might walk in any moment and catch them in the act.

Rob peered behind the t-shirts and sweatpants. He felt around for hidden objects. He found nothing. A homicide detective wouldn't use the obvious hiding places. He pulled out the entire drawer and checked the underside. Nothing.

"Need help with the mattress?" Jed stood in the bedroom doorway.

"Uh, sure."

They flipped the mattress, checked the underside and the bed frame. They tested the parquet for loose panels and tapped the walls for concealed storage spaces. Still nothing.

"The living room is clean." Jed sounded disappointed. "I'll do the bathroom. There's a spare bedroom, too."

"Then I guess I'll do that."

The spare room contained an old desk with a pile of detective novels and sticky drawers. One by one, he removed the drawers and turned them over. Nobody could accuse him of not being thorough.

His fingernail caught on the underside of the third drawer. A large envelope was taped to the plywood surface.

Rob peeled away the tape and peered inside the envelope. Two sheets of paper lay within. He recognized the signature at the bottom of the first page. His gut tightened as he skimmed the document. When he read the second police report, he wanted to puke.

Dear God. Claire, what have you done?

CHAPTER 46

Claire walked up to the house on Birch Street and glanced over her shoulder. Right now, Newburgh PD was searching her home. She was pretty sure nobody had followed her. But for all she knew, officers might be waiting inside to arrest her. Claire knocked twice. She had no choice. To prove her innocence and solve Tina's murder, she had to take risks.

That morning, she'd watched from a distance as armed men had broken into her home. Her blood had boiled at the thought of them rummaging through her intimate possessions. What hurt most was who had led the assault—Jed, her partner, and Rob, her lover—two men she had trusted with her life. To be fair, Rob had tried to warn her. If he had not stopped by last night, she would have answered her door dressed in her pajamas when the SWAT team came knocking.

After Rob's visit, she had gathered a few essentials and let herself into a vacant home down the street. The lights were never on when Claire passed the home during her nightly runs. A stack of unopened mail at the front door had confirmed her suspicions. The Baxters were away for some time, and she'd enjoy their unknowing hospitality. Claire couldn't exactly crash at her parents even if she'd wanted to. The uniforms would look for her there.

Rob had not lied. The department thought she was the killer. The officers at her door had carried enough firepower to kill a dragon. All of Claire's life, people had judged her. Her mother. Detective O'Leary. Now Newburgh PD had joined the list. People made up their minds about her then cherry-picked facts to support their verdict. But the world was upside down. The dragon lay not in her home but inside Newburgh PD. Claire was the damsel in distress. And this damsel would breathe fire if she had to.

Claire knocked on the door again and hoped she wasn't too late. The For Sale sign pegged into the front lawn by Golden Touch Realty had a Sold sticker across the front. To get the police dogs off her trail, Claire needed to give them a stronger scent. But if the house's occupant had left town already, Claire's private investigation would grind to a halt.

Inside the home, a pair of feet shuffled, and the door opened as far as the security chain allowed. A middle-aged woman with blow-dried hair and thick makeup scowled at her.

"Whatever you're selling, I'm not interested."

Claire flashed her Newburgh PD badge and smiled. "Mrs. O'Leary, I'm a detective from Newburgh PD. May I have a quick word?"

Claire played it safe in case her name had appeared on the morning news. O'Leary's widow eyed the officer on her doorstep for two long seconds. Then, she smiled, unlatched the chain, and let Claire inside.

"Thank you."

"Would you like some coffee? I know all about detectives and their coffee." A grandmotherly sparkle glinted in her eye. Mrs. O'Leary seemed to have decided that the young female officer might make an interesting conversation partner.

"I'd love that."

The living room was an empty shell. Faded rectangles on the walls remained where pictures had hung. Claire followed her hostess to the kitchen where she filled an electric kettle with tap water.

"You got me just in time. I leave tomorrow morning."

"Tomorrow morning?"

"Tallahassee, Florida! We found a lovely retirement village by the sea. What a shame that Brian didn't get to enjoy it. He'd planned the move for over a year."

"For over a year?" Rob's interview technique was working effortlessly.

"He was looking forward to early retirement. He'd had enough."

Claire hadn't realized detectives could afford an early retirement or a home by the sea. The kettle hummed as the water heated.

"You're new to the department, aren't you?"

"That's right. I started last week."

"I knew all the detectives once. We went to all the barbecues. Or at least we used to."

"Used to?"

"We stopped a few years ago. Brian saw the officers enough at work. He didn't need to spend his off-hours with them as well." She chuckled.

O'Leary had planned an early retirement and kept his colleagues at a distance. A red flag waved in Claire's brain.

The kettle boiled. Mrs. O'Leary poured the coffee and handed Claire her mug, one of only two that remained.

"The job wears people down," Mrs. O'Leary continued, becoming somber. "Brian used to love it. But then something changed. Cookie?" She offered Claire a Tupperware container of chocolate chip cookies.

"Thank you." The Baxters had cleaned out their fridge and freezer before leaving, and Claire had eaten a package of dry crackers for breakfast. The cookie paired well with the coffee. "What changed?"

"In his last few weeks, he wasn't himself. He put on weight. Oh, Brian was never in good shape, but he'd started drinking, too. He scared me sometimes. Kept going on about how he'd sold his soul to the Devil."

"The Devil?" Another red flag waved. Weeks before retirement, O'Leary's conscience had eaten at him. And then, he had dropped dead.

"Just the ghosts of the past, I guess. He'd spent so many years staring at violence and death. I don't know how he carried the burden all these years."

Now that the widow had warmed to Claire, she pushed her luck.

"Mrs. O'Leary, did Brian ever discuss his cases with you?"

"No. Just as well. I have no stomach for violent crime."

Claire nodded, sipped her coffee, and reached for the cookies again. "May I?"

"Please! You go ahead."

Claire chewed her second cookie. "I'm working a case. Fourteen-year-old girls found murdered."

"Oh, the Middle School Murders. I've been following that on the radio. I sold the TV last week. So shocking. Those poor, poor girls. I can't imagine how terrible this must be for their families."

"The case is very similar to one your husband worked twelve years ago. You wouldn't happen to remember anything about that?"

"Like I said, Brian never spoke about his cases with me."

Claire nodded and reached for her third cookie. The visit had not supplied the breakthrough Claire had hoped for, but at least she'd supplemented her meager breakfast. Where could she go next?

"You should ask his old partner. I'm sure he'll have the details."

"His old partner?"

Mrs. O'Leary sipped from her mug, then nodded. "Twelve years ago, Brian partnered with Detective Wallace."

Claire watched O'Leary's widow closely. Was she confused or suffering from dementia? Twelve years ago, Jed was a teenager.

Mrs. O'Leary noticed Claire's expression and chuckled. "Not Jed Wallace. His father, Harry. You must know him. He's the chief of police now."

CHAPTER 47

Rob leaned against the squad room wall, his arms folded over his chest. Claire's desk stared back at him, empty and ominous. He'd always trusted his instincts. How had he misjudged Claire so badly?

The team gathered for another briefing, but the officers avoided her chair. He didn't blame them. The seat's previous occupant, Lieutenant O'Leary, had died of a heart attack. The current occupant was a serial killer. That desk was jinxed. Had he truly known Claire? Was the woman he had loved a ghost—an apparition formed not of flesh and blood but conjured out of thin air by Rob's romantic confirmation bias?

Captain Emmerso stood by Claire's desk and cleared his throat and won their undivided attention. A gloomy silence fell over all present. The rumor had spread.

"Today we discovered additional evidence that sheds light on the first murder, that of Tina Wolfe. I'd like to thank Special Agent Cline of the FBI for his help in searching Detective Wolfe's home."

Rob avoided the officers' eyes. He wished he'd never joined this case. And he wished he'd never met Claire.

"We had suspected that pages were missing from the first victim's file. Now we've vindicated those suspicions. Detective Wallace has the details."

Jed held sheets of paper in plastic covers. The missing case files from one murder investigation had become evidence in another.

"Agent Cline discovered two reports taped to the underside of a desk drawer in Detective Wolfe's home. In the one report, Detective O'Leary notes his suspicions that the victim's sister, Claire Wolfe, had murdered her sister, Tina. According to the victim's mother, Claire had hated Tina. On the day of the murder, Claire was supposed to walk her sister home from school. She arrived home without her sister but had bloodstains on her hands, leg, and face. Claire claimed to know nothing of Tina's whereabouts. Her mother also claimed that Claire had tried to kill her sister once before, stabbing her in the thigh with a kitchen knife. The wound had required stitches but had caused no long-term damage. Claire had said the incident was a prank, and the mother kept it quiet."

Some officers present shook their heads in disbelief at the violence Claire had inflicted on her little sister. Rob had heard that story before. He had taken Claire's side, dismissing Tina as an abusive narcissist. But O'Leary's report offered an entirely different interpretation of the incident, and Rob had not known who to believe. Until he'd read the second document.

Jed displayed the second page of evidence. "The other report details O'Leary's interview with Kitty Tucker, a friend of the victim and the last person to see her alive. Kitty said the victim feared her older sister, who had threatened to kill her. Tina had taken a knife to school for self-defense. When the witness last saw Tina, she was walking with her sister toward the Park Street woods. She never saw her friend again."

"I don't get it," Mahoney said. "Why didn't O'Leary charge her with the murder?"

Nakamura grunted his agreement.

"That's a good question," Jed said, "and one I'd love to ask Lieutenant O'Leary. Other documentation appears to be missing from the file, specifically a forensic analysis. O'Leary might have lacked sufficient physical evidence to place Claire at the crime scene. That's speculation. Considering the recent murders, I'm not sure it matters anymore."

Jed bowed his head. "Over the past few weeks, we got to know Claire and to like her. I never suspected her of any wrongdoing and I'm her partner. Maybe Lieutenant O'Leary simply couldn't believe Claire could have murdered her sister in cold blood."

Heads nodded as the weight of the revelation sank in. A sworn police officer had killed those girls. One of their own, Claire had moved among them, armed with a standard-issue firearm and the resources of modern law enforcement. What had prevented her from one day using her brutal nature against them and turning their department into a bloodbath? They had all survived a close call with violent death.

Jed continued. "I've asked Dr. Fleischer to update her profile in light of the new evidence."

The psychiatrist stood and addressed the room. "If Detective Wolfe is the killer, which seems likely judging from the recent evidence, then we're dealing with a very unusual case. Detective Wolfe's recent behavior suggests that she might not be aware that she committed these crimes."

Confused murmurs circled the assembled officers. Rob couldn't believe his ears either. Was she suggesting that Claire was insane?

Nakamura spoke up first. "What, like a split personality or something?"

"Dissociative identity disorder, formerly known as multiple personality disorder."

More murmurs animated the crowd.

Rob spoke up. "That disorder is very rare."

The psychiatrist was undeterred. "As I said, this case is an outlier. Her mind may have suppressed her criminal persona, which occasionally takes control and hides every trace of her crimes from her conscious self. It's the only theory that matches all the evidence."

"Assuming this is true, Doctor, what other symptoms would she have displayed?"

"Memory lapses. Unexplained absences."

Rob's insides knotted. Claire had forgotten she'd left her front door open. She had doubted her recall of childhood events. Rob's personal experiences had primed him to identify those episodes as gaslighting and emotional abuse. But what if Sally was right about Claire suffering from mental illness? A split personality explained those details, too.

He opened his mouth to speak, then closed it. How would he explain his access to Claire's deepest, darkest childhood secrets? *Oh, and by the way, I've been sleeping with our prime suspect. No biggie. I'm still perfectly objective.*

His impulse for self-preservation was not the only reason he remained silent. A part of him rejected the accusations out of hand. *No way. Claire is not a killer. And she is not crazy*. But was that his professional opinion talking or merely his desire to save his lover?

Jed stared at him, and Rob kept his eyes on Dr. Fleischer. He couldn't trust his body language to hide his inner turmoil.

"One thing I can't figure out," Jed said, still studying Rob, "is how Detective Wolfe knew we were coming this morning."

Rob didn't move a muscle. Aiding and abetting a murderer was a felony. Jail time would destroy his career in law enforcement and render him unable to help Claire clear her name.

Mahoney saved his skin. "Detective Wallace, I think a SWAT team showing up on her doorstep might have given the game away."

Many of the officers laughed, but Jed didn't seem impressed with the joke. "She was long gone by the time we arrived."

Nakamura said, "She might have slipped out early and seen you on her way home."

"Whatever. Either way, she fled the scene. In my book, that's an admission of guilt."

"I don't understand," Mahoney said. "She's got a split personality, right? Her conscious self has no idea about the reports her evil self stashed in her home. So why would she run for it?"

"That's a good question, Detective," Dr. Fleischer said. "Her criminal side always lurks in the corner, so to speak. When it senses imminent danger, it takes over. Claire would experience this as a lacuna in her memory. She'd fill the gap with rationalizations or confabulated memories. Both can be very convincing, even to outsiders. Remember, she's very intelligent."

The knot in Rob's insides twisted again. Claire believed the killer had a mole within Newburgh PD. Had she created that conspiracy theory to protect her conscious self from her murderous inner demons?

"All attempts at locating Detective Wolfe have failed," Jed continued. "Her car is in evidence, and she has disabled her phone. We've put out a BOLO. If she contacts any of you, let us know. Keep her on the line as long as possible. She's killed four girls so far, and she still has Dana Wood. We can't let her take another innocent life."

Jed's words echoed in Rob's head as Tom drove him and Dr. Fleischer back to their motel. By visiting Claire last night and tipping her off, he had allowed her to avoid arrest. If she killed again, he would share the responsibility for her crimes. He had already failed to prevent Claire's dark side from killing Amy Collins. Now Claire was a wanted woman. He had to convince her to give herself up or, when taken into custody, she might get hurt—or killed.

Dr. Fleischer thanked them for the ride, and Rob and Tom returned to their shared room—their sacrifice to save taxpayer dollars. Rob was looking forward to a long, hot shower, Chinese takeout, and some well-earned sleep. Where was Claire spending the night? What was she eating for dinner?

He flopped on the single bed, the springs squeaking beneath him. He picked up the motel phone. "Want some Chinese?"

Tom hung his suit jacket in the closet and turned around. "How far are you taking this?"

Rob's gut tensed again. Tom was onto him.

"Chinese food? All the way."

He'd used humor to evade the question but failed to amuse Tom.

"I'm not blind, Rob. As much as I enjoy having the room to myself at night, is it wise to get mixed up with the lead suspect in a multiple homicide? Detective Wolfe is pretty and smart and all, but you heard Sally. Claire might be a deadly nutcase, too. Don't forget the Golden Rule."

Despite everything, Rob snickered. Every agent knew the FBI's Golden Rule, "Don't Embarrass the Bureau."

"Don't worry, Tom. I won't embarrass the Bureau."

"This isn't funny, Rob. Are you willing to risk your career for her?"

Rob said nothing for a few seconds. There was no point in denying his affair with Claire. Tom wasn't threatening to rat on him, but Rob had placed his partner in an awkward position.

"I won't do anything stupid."

Tom laced his voice with sarcasm. "Great. I'll sleep much better."

"I'm touched, Tom. I didn't realize you cared so much about me."

"Don't flatter yourself, Agent Cline. I'm used to your snoring, that's all. Can't seem to fall asleep without it. I'll take the sweet-and-sour chicken."

Rob ordered the food while his partner beat him to the shower. Sneaky old fart. This long and tiring day had ended, but his mind found no rest. Despite the mounting pile of evidence, the investigation's new direction unsettled him. His unease went beyond his relationship with Claire. Something about the new evidence bothered him. But that itch remained just beyond the reach of his conscious mind.

His cell phone rang. The call came from a private number, and he answered on the second ring.

"Rob," Claire said. "It's me."

CHAPTER 48

"Where are you?" Rob's voice asked.

Claire sat on the edge of the Baxters' couch, the burner phone trembling in her hands. The Nokia dumbphone had no GPS to track her location, but law enforcement could still triangulate her position using the cellular network data. Was Rob concerned for her welfare or trying to hunt her down?

"Somewhere safe," she said.

Claire had trust issues at the best of times, and that morning, Rob had raided her home looking for incriminating evidence. She had little reason to rely on him. But tonight, she placed her life in his hands. He was her only hope.

"Listen, I need to tell you something—"

"Claire—"

"Just hear me out. I discovered something important today."

"What?"

"We've been asking the wrong questions. The right question is, 'Who was O'Leary's partner?'"

Rob said nothing for a few seconds. "The case files don't mention a partner."

"Exactly!"

"Not all detectives have partners. Maybe O'Leary worked alone."

"He didn't. Guess who his partner was?"

"I have no idea." Was he growing impatient with her?

"Harry Wallace."

"As in Chief Harry Wallace?"

"The same."

Claire could kick herself for not figuring it out sooner. Her dad had told Jed he'd met Jed's father in the past, but Claire hadn't connected the chief to Tina's murder investigation. Rob did not sound impressed by the information.

"So, the chief of police is our mole? Claire, this has to stop."

He was close to hanging up on her, she could sense it. "I'm not making this up, Rob. O'Leary's wife told me."

"You spoke with her?"

"At her home today, and just in time. She's moving to Florida. O'Leary bought a house by the sea for his early retirement. How do you think he can afford that on a cop's salary?"

"I don't know. Maybe he invested his money wisely over the years. Where's this going?"

His unwillingness to think out of the box frustrated her, but she had to remain calm. "Don't you see? Harry Wallace worked Tina's case, but his name appears nowhere in the files. Key reports are missing from the folder, including the forensic report. Doesn't that raise any red flags?"

"Why would the chief tamper with evidence?"

"I'm still working on that. The case files contained no forensic analysis. Maybe they didn't process the trace evidence because Tina wasn't dead. O'Leary's wife said he started drinking before his death. He told her he'd made a deal with the Devil. The cover-up of Tina's murder was chewing on his conscience."

Rob went silent for five excruciating seconds. "Claire, you need to turn yourself in."

Anger flared in her chest at his suggestion, but she played dumb. "I'm on administrative leave, not under arrest." She knew what Rob had done that morning, but she would make him confess.

"Claire, you left your home and disabled your phone. You know we searched your house."

"Then, you know I have nothing to hide."

She waited for him to admit that she was right, but he didn't.

"We found them, Claire."

"Found what?"

"The missing reports."

"Where?"

"In your home."

"My home?" Her heart pounded. What was he talking about? This couldn't be true.

"The report about you, Claire, and how O'Leary suspected you in Tina's murder."

Claire spoke so fast she spluttered. "I told you about that report. It was in the case file I handed over. You know that."

A cramp formed in her gut. She remembered holding the damning report in her fingers. How easily she could have destroyed the fragile page. But she hadn't destroyed the evidence. She had returned the report to the folder. How had they found it in her home?

"What about the other report, O'Leary's interview with Kitty Tucker?"

Claire's lungs filled with new hope at the mention of that name. Kitty Tucker was the last person to see Tina alive and the key to Tina's final moments.

"Kitty's interview wasn't in the file, Rob." Now curiosity

pushed her anger and frustration aside. "Did Kitty see Tina after school?" Claire gripped the phone tightly. Kitty's testimony would settle the matter.

"Yes, she saw her leave school."

"Was she alone?"

"No."

"Then who was she with?" Why was he stalling?

"With you."

"What?"

"With you, Claire. Tina left school with you."

"That's not what happened. I waited for her, then I went home."

"It's your word against Kitty's."

"She was lying."

"Why would she lie about that?"

"I don't know. Maybe she played a role in Tina's disappearance, too?"

"On her own or with Chief Wallace? He's part of the conspiracy, remember?"

"Don't mock me, Rob." She fumbled for the right word. "Don't *gaslight* me. I know what happened that day. Don't make me doubt my sanity!"

This was Rob's cue to apologize, but he didn't, and the truth pierced her heart like a bullet. *He thinks I killed her.*

"For God's sake, Rob, I didn't take the reports. I never even saw Kitty's interview. I'm not a murderer!"

"Then how do you explain the facts?"

Claire grasped at straws. "Somebody must have planted them."

"Who—Chief Wallace?"

"Maybe. I don't know. During the search this morning, anybody could have pretended to find the documents in my house. 'Hey, everybody, look what I found.'"

"That's not what happened."

"How can you be sure?"

"Because I found them, Claire. In an envelope taped to the underside of a drawer."

A chill invaded Claire's cheeks. This couldn't be true. Rob must have made that up. She remembered what she had done. She knew what had happened.

Claire grabbed at another straw. "Then, somebody must have planted them earlier for you to find. Two nights ago, I didn't remember leaving the door open. That's when they did it!"

"Claire, listen to me for a second. Dr. Fleischer spoke to us today. What she said explains the memory lapses and confusion."

"I am not confused!"

"She explained why you don't remember hiding the reports, why the shooter you saw suddenly disappeared, and why you believe there's a conspiracy. They're all symptoms of the same underlying condition."

"No!" Claire sprang to her feet and paced the Baxters' living room. He was questioning her sanity again. "I didn't imagine the shooter, Rob. I saw her. She climbed out of the window—"

Rob cut her off without mercy. "Then why did nobody else see her? Why did she leave no tracks outside?"

"The tracks weren't clear, Tom said it himself. We must have trampled hers."

Rob sighed on the other end of the line.

"I am not crazy, Rob. I did not kill my sister or those girls."

Her anger faded as terror clawed at her heart. She sank to the couch. Could Rob be right?

"You joined the force." His voice was calm and even. Was this the voice he reserved for kidnappers and terrorists? "You came back to Newburgh. All that time, you told yourself you were here to solve Tina's murder. But coming back to Newburgh triggered something inside, something you've hidden from everyone, including yourself."

A tear trickled down Claire's cheek. "I didn't kill Tina. I didn't kill those girls. How could you think that!" But doubt slithered into her mind like a poisonous snake.

"Claire, we can help you. But you need to turn yourself in. The entire city is looking for you. They'll bring you in at any cost. I don't want them to hurt you, Claire. I care about you."

"No, you don't. If you did, you'd never say these things!"

"Come to me. We'll go to the station together. I promise we'll figure everything out."

"You bastard! How can you do this to me?"

"I'm on your side, Claire. How am I supposed to help you if you won't let me?"

The room spun around her. Claire needed air. She summoned her last burst of energy. "Screw you, Rob! I don't need your help. I'll do this myself."

She disconnected the call and slumped on the couch, her chest heaving. *Lies*. Rob had told terrible, hurtful lies. Dr. Fleischer had seemed sensitive and intelligent, but she was just like the others. Claire was not crazy. Claire had not killed her sister or those other girls. Tina had.

But that slippery, slimy snake refused to leave her mind. Claire slammed her hands over her ears to block the questions. But she could not shut out the hissing voices. *This is all your fault*.

CHAPTER 49

Lightning crackled overhead late that night as the shovel bit into the black earth. Raindrops pelted the back of Claire's neck, but she pressed the shovel deeper with her foot. She didn't mind. Sweat had soaked through her shirt already. Since 2 AM, she had toiled away in the cemetery, alone and under cover of darkness, like a deranged Dr. Frankenstein. Now she stood waist-deep in the hole. Maybe Rob was right—maybe she was crazy.

She emptied the shovel onto the mound of dirt and surveyed her handiwork. The stone angel lay on its side between the graves. *Not much further now.* Claire had seen Tina. She was alive. And soon Claire would have proof.

A car engine rumbled, and Claire ducked into the shallow grave. Beyond the trees at the edge of the cemetery, the glow of headlights swept along a road, then faded from view. Who was up at this hour? Kids returning from a party? Criminals? Or Tina on her way to dump Dana Wood's body?

Claire got back to work. She had borrowed the shovel, crowbar, and heavy-duty flashlight from the Baxters' garage and loaded them onto Mrs. Baxter's mountain bike. The unlit flashlight sat beside the open grave. She had used the light sparingly. Nocturnal activity in the graveyard would draw attention, and Claire was a fugitive.

Anger fueled each thrust of the spade. All these years, Claire had wrung her hands over Tina's death. She had dedicated her life to finding her sister's killer when all along Tina had been alive and well. Claire vented her frustrations on the wet, raw earth, slicing the ground with the shovel and dumping dirt over the wall of the trench.

Had Claire known this from the start? At Tina's funeral, Claire had refused to believe her sister was dead. She had dismissed her feelings as denial, the first stage of grief. Now the blonde assassin at Amy's window had proved Claire right. Tina was alive and well. Her pranks had escalated in boldness over the years and graduated into murder. Claire had to stop her once and for all.

She wiped wet strands of hair from her eyes. Rainwater pooled in the pit, turning the dirt to mud, which seeped into Claire's shoes. The sludge was easier to penetrate but heavier to lift, the shovel making sucking noises each time. The wind sent frozen fingers through Claire's soaked shirt, chilling her to the bone.

Metal crunched against wood. The shovel had hit a hard, flat surface. Claire fell to her knees and cleared the mud from the casket. Her fingers traced the rounded edges of the box. She worked faster, hacking at the remaining dirt that held her target.

A tap closed in the heavens. The rain slowed to a drizzle, then petered out. Someone up there was cheering her on, watching on the edge of a proverbial seat while she confirmed her suspicions. An empty casket was all Claire needed to redirect the investigation. If Tina wasn't dead, Claire had not killed her. O'Leary had stalled the case and buried the files because he had known the truth. Tina was alive.

Claire labored to expose the coffin. Questions crowded her head. What had become of her sister? Had her brazen stunts gone too far? Had Tina messed with the wrong people, outlaws who had forced her into a life of violent crime?

Claire's anger at the deception washed away any sympathy for her long-lost sister. Somebody was framing Claire for multiple homicides. Whatever trouble her sister had gotten herself into, Claire was not going to prison for murder.

Moonlight peeked through the clouds and gleamed on the casket's surface. After twelve years in the ground, the wood had lost its original sheen. Claire reached for the crowbar but hesitated. An empty coffin would not clear her name. A state prosecutor would claim Claire had removed her sister's corpse. But Claire would know the truth. She would decapitate that slithering doubt, and her confidence in her innocence would make all the difference.

She wedged the crowbar into the edge of the lid and pulled with all her strength. Wood splintered, rusted nails gave way, and the cover jerked upward. The moon hid behind the clouds, shrouding the grave in darkness once again. Claire jammed the crowbar into another corner of the coffin, separating the heavy cover from the box, and she heaved the lid aside. A strong chemical stench rose from the box, and her stomach tightened with foreboding. The coffin was not empty. Claire scrabbled for the flashlight and turned it on.

The cone of harsh, yellow light fell over a human body in a white dress. The girl's arms and legs rested at her sides, motionless. Her body seemed oddly deflated, her chest completely still, and her skin a ghostly gray. A white cloth covered her face, disturbingly flat and even.

Claire's breath came in fast, shallow bursts. She forced her analytical mind to take over. After twelve years in the ground, Tina's flesh should have decomposed, leaving a bag of bones and sinew. Was this a girl-shaped dummy, a synthetic placeholder for the missing human body?

No. Claire recognized that chemical stench. Formaldehyde. The funeral home had embalmed the corpse before burial. The cold climate and extensive use of preservatives had stifled the growth of bacteria and severely limited the decomposition process. This was no life-sized doll. But was this Tina?

Her fingers trembling, Claire reached for the still corpse. She lifted the fabric of the dress over the narrow shins, exposing the smooth, pale legs. The flashlight beam moved to the thigh and the white ridge of a two-inch scar, the stab wound of a cleaving knife.

Claire dropped the flashlight. She pushed away from the coffin, her back to the wall of the grave. Her chest shuddered as she sobbed. Tina had not killed Gracie or Karla or Amy. She had not kidnapped Dana. Her sister was dead. Her dead body lay in the casket at Claire's feet. The answer raised another question. Who had Claire seen escaping through Amy's bedroom window? Who—or what?

CHAPTER 50

Claire towered above the world in her father's strong arms. His hands were hard, his skin rough. The thorns on his chin prickled her fingers. She longed for her mother's soft touch, but Mommy had gone away. Two days had passed since Claire had seen her last. Today, finally, she would see her again.

Her father carried her down a brightly lit corridor. There were many doorways. The rooms contained beds and flowers and balloons. Men and women in white cloaks and blue uniforms passed them by. Some of them smiled at Claire. She clutched a large pink balloon by its long, shiny ribbon. The balloon was not for her. It was for her new sister. Claire didn't mind. She'd been waiting for her sister to leave her mommy's tummy for a very long time. Finally, she'd get to play with her little sister. They would be best friends.

Her father entered a room and walked up to a bed behind a tall curtain. Mommy lay on the bed. She smiled at them, her cheeks red, her hair a jumble of golden curls. Daddy lowered Claire to the bed, and Mommy hugged her. Claire wrinkled her nose—her mother's familiar flowery scent was now mixed with sweat—but she said nothing.

"Where is the baby?" Claire asked. Her mother's belly rose beneath the bedsheets. Had the baby not come out yet?

"She's sleeping. But she'll be here soon."

Claire nodded but didn't understand. Her parents talked, and Claire played with the pink balloon, tugging the ribbon, then letting the balloon float to the ceiling.

A woman in blue clothes wheeled a cart into the room, and her parents spoke excitedly. The woman reached into the tub on top of the cart and lifted a doll into the air. No, not a doll, a creature in white pajamas. The creature's face was pink and wrinkled, the eyes narrow slits. Tiny fingers curled into tiny fists. Golden tufts of hair poked from beneath the white cap on its head. The woman handed the creature to Claire's daddy.

"This is your sister, Claire," he said. "Her name is Tina."

Claire turned to her daddy for reassurance. Her sister was not the smiling baby she had imagined. Claire held out the ribbon of the balloon, but the creature didn't accept her gift. The creature didn't even look at the balloon or her big sister.

Then, Mommy shifted on the bed, opened her shirt, and pulled out her breast. Claire had not seen her mother's breasts in a very long time, and now the nipple was large and red. Her daddy lowered the bundle to the bed, and her mommy held the baby to her exposed teat. The creature made sucking noises, and Mommy winced, then smiled.

An uneasy feeling gripped Claire. Her mother no longer let her drink from her breast. She got angry when Claire tried. But she let the pink creature drink, even though it hurt her. That wasn't fair.

Mommy glowed with joy. Her fingers stroked the tufts of golden hair beneath the cap. "She's got my hair. And my eyes."

The words made Claire anxious. "Me, too, Mommy. I look like you, too."

Her mother's smile faded. "No, you don't. Not like she does." Mommy gazed at the creature with love, the love that had belonged to Claire. "This one is mine."

A hot sensation shot through Claire's body and warmed her face. She hated the pink creature. She *shouldn't* hate the creature, but she did. Claire wished the creature would go back inside her mommy's tummy.

Her feelings shamed her. She had been so excited to meet her sister and she had wanted to be her friend.

Claire looked to her daddy. "Can I play with her now?"

Her father chuckled. "She's too small to play, Cub. But she'll grow up quickly, you'll see. You'll play together then. And you'll help us take care of her. We're Wolfes. We look out for each other, don't we?"

Claire nodded. Her world had changed. She'd have to share her mommy with her sister. That was OK. Soon, she and her sister would become the best of friends. Claire would take care of her. Always.

CHAPTER 51

Claire's home was a mess. Closet doors stood open in the kitchen. Utensils and cleaning supplies cluttered the counter. The Newburgh PD bloodhounds were thorough but not considerate. Claire stepped over orphaned drawers on the living room floor. She abhorred disorder in her personal space, but that morning the chaos didn't bother her. She wouldn't have to endure the mess for long.

Last night, after filling in Tina's grave and heaving the tombstone's angel upright, she had returned to the Baxter home. In the shower, she rubbed the dirt and caked mud from her flesh and hair. On the couch, she downed half a bottle of Jack Daniel's she'd found in the liquor cabinet. No matter how she analyzed the facts in her mind, she kept returning to the same conclusion.

Rob had been right. Her mother, too. Claire did not remember killing her sister, but all the evidence led back to her, and cold, hard facts did not lie. Her tidy, focused life was an illusion. She had rushed back to Newburgh not with a righteous urge for justice, but the opposite. Her every deed had aimed at destroying evidence and tying up loose ends. The return to her hometown had reignited buried, twisted impulses. And those impulses were insatiable. Having killed her only sister, Claire had drawn up a list of sister substitutes and murdered them one by one.

She didn't ask why. You don't ask why a virus kills its host. You destroy the sick cells and halt the virus in its tracks. A part of her was very sick but that part was inoperable.

In the morning, Claire woke up on the couch with a nasty hangover. As if on autopilot, she brushed her teeth, dressed, and walked over to her house.

In the spare bedroom, she found the drawer. A corner of duct tape still adhered to the underside. Here Rob had found what she had hidden from herself.

Claire should have figured this out earlier. Her subconscious had sprinkled enough hints in her path: Her impulse to destroy O'Leary's report; the thirst for blood she'd sensed while chasing Justin Fox; the secret hatred she'd carried in her heart for Tina. Claire had not paid attention, and now three more girls were dead. But it wasn't too late to save Dana.

Dana Wood was alive—captive, starving, and frightened out of her mind, but alive. Claire did not remember abducting the girl. She had no memory of the video she had sent to *The Newburgh Herald*. And try as she might, Claire could not recall where she had taken Dana. That secret remained locked within her deviant brain.

Claire turned the desk drawer over in her hands. She ran her fingers over the remains of the duct tape. She had hoped that handling the drawer would open a door to her repressed experiences. But no matter how hard she strained her mind and racked her memory, nothing registered. No mental images or sounds surfaced. Claire slid the drawer into the desk. She had figured the attempt would fail, but she'd had to try.

Claire peered into her bedroom. The mattress sat askew on

the bed frame, also courtesy of Newburgh PD. She had shared that bed with Rob. At least she had snatched a few moments of happiness before her world had imploded.

Claire returned to the living room and sat on the edge of the couch. She drew a few deep breaths, trying to remain dignified to the end. Failing to locate Dana, only one course of action remained. Claire posed a clear and present danger to society. She needed to act now before her dark side took over and killed again.

She reached for her Glock. Claire had considered giving herself up as Rob had suggested but didn't see the point. If she couldn't access her memories, others stood no chance. Dana was probably dead already, and Claire would live out her days in a padded cell.

Claire refused to rot in a cell. She'd perform one more selfish deed to end them all.

"I'm sorry," she said. She hoped Tina could hear her words. Gracie Miles, too. Karla Smith. Amy Collins. And Dana Wood, her *last* victim.

The Devil may have infiltrated her mind, but that mind depended on a body. And when her body died, Claire would drag the Devil back to Hell with her.

She placed the barrel of the gun in her mouth. Her thumb touched the trigger. One hard squeeze and she'd end the nightmare. The anguish, the killing, the struggle. She should have done this years ago when she'd received her first service weapon. One act of self-sacrifice would have saved four innocent lives that had barely begun. Claire closed her eyes.

Don't think about it. Just do it. Do it now!

Claire drew her final breath and eased the trigger down with her thumb.

The phone rang. Her home phone. Claire opened her eyes, the gun barrel cold and hard on her lips. Nobody had this number, except for the station. Was Rob trying to reach out to her? Would he try to dissuade her from ending her life? They might have had a future together. Did she owe him an apology or an explanation or, at least, a goodbye?

Claire pulled the barrel from her mouth and reached for the phone.

"Hello," a woman said.

Wonderful. Saved by a telemarketer.

"Hello," the woman repeated, upset. "Is that Detective Wolfe? This is Kitty Tucker."

Claire's heart almost stopped beating. *Kitty Tucker*. Despite the woman's audible discomfort, Claire recognized her voice.

And in that instant, Claire knew. She hadn't killed Tina. Otherwise, Kitty would never have called. And if Claire hadn't killed Tina, she hadn't killed the other girls either. Kitty Tucker had a lot of explaining to do.

CHAPTER 52

That morning, Jed Wallace parked outside a two-level house in suburban Newburgh. He rarely worked Sundays, but these were extraordinary times. Detective Claire Wolfe, his former partner and a suspect in multiple homicides, was still at large. Jed blamed himself. He should have realized who she was a long time ago. Now he wouldn't rest until he'd corrected that mistake.

He walked up to the front door. A television chattered inside. He pressed the buzzer.

Jed had known no Wolfes from Boston. But Claire hadn't grown up only in Boston. Had she told him the full truth, he would have dug deeper. He would have discovered her connection to Tina Wolfe. Armed with that information, he would have wrapped up the homicides easily and saved innocent lives.

Jed shook his head at his stupidity. To think that he had liked Claire. He sure had crappy taste in women.

He stretched his back while he waited for the Wolfes to answer. Somebody was home. Were Claire's parents harboring her? Claire wasn't that stupid. But the parents might provide a lead to her whereabouts. He pressed the buzzer again.

A man yelled from upstairs, "Diane, can you get that? It's probably Claire."

So, they knew their daughter was in town. Did they know she was a fugitive? Furniture creaked, and feet shuffled toward the door. A middle-aged woman with messy gray hair opened the door and squinted at him. Jed smiled.

"I'm Detective Wallace from Newburgh PD." He flashed his badge. "I'm looking for Claire Wolfe."

"She isn't here."

Make that *very crappy taste* in women. Did he want this old hag to be his future mother-in-law?

"Do you know where she is?"

The woman blinked at him as though he'd asked her to calculate the square root of minus one. She lowered her voice. "Have you tried Hell? Check there first."

This woman was a piece of work. "This is a serious matter, ma'am. I'm investigating several murders. Three young girls." He didn't mention her late daughter, Tina. There was no need to upset her.

"Young girls?" The woman considered this. "Sounds like our Claire. She killed her sister, too, by the way. Did you know that?"

Jed pulled out his recording device. Whatever leads he had hoped to glean at the home of Claire's parents, he had never expected to discover a witness for the prosecution. "Mrs. Wolfe, are you telling me your daughter, Claire, killed Tina Wolfe?"

Claire's mom shrugged as though this was common knowledge. "Not that you'll do anything about it. I told the investigating officer, but he didn't do diddly-squat. O'Leary was his name. Brian O'Leary."

A man materialized behind Mrs. Wolfe, barefoot and in jeans and a wifebeater. "Who is this?"

Jed offered his hand. "Mr. Wolfe. Good to see you again. I was just speaking with Mrs. Wolfe about Claire."

Bill Wolfe ignored the outstretched hand. "Diane, please go upstairs."

The wife trudged back inside.

"What are you doing here, Officer?" Bill asked.

Jed bristled at the man's commanding tone. People were usually more respectful when talking to a badge.

"I'm looking for Claire."

"You mean Detective Claire Wolfe."

"Not anymore, sir. She's currently under investigation for multiple homicides."

"Homicides? You're mistaken. Claire is no murderer."

Jed gave him a knowing grin. "Your wife seems to think differently."

"My wife is unwell, Officer, and I don't appreciate you taking advantage of her poor health. We've suffered enough. I won't have you or anyone else digging up painful memories or throwing around accusations."

"Yes, well, this is a murder investigation. We need to be thorough."

"Claire isn't here. We haven't seen her since last week when I visited her at the station. You remember that, don't you?"

"Yes, I do." Jed peered around Claire's father at the dark interior of the home. He didn't believe the man for a second.

"Do you mind if I take a quick look around?"

"Yes, I do. Now get off our property and leave us alone. *Please.*"

"I can come back with a search warrant—"

Jed's mobile phone buzzed in his pocket and cut him off. The call was from Newburgh PD Dispatch. "Excuse me." He answered.

The female call attendant spoke urgently. "Detective

Wallace, we just received a tip-off about Claire Wolfe's whereabouts. SWAT is ready for a briefing."

"Send me the address. I'm on my way." Jed disconnected the call. "I have to go. We'll continue this conversation later. Have a nice day, Mr. Wolfe."

The weekend just got better and better.

CHAPTER 53

Claire looked over her shoulder as she walked past the water fountain outside Kitty's mansion. She'd had her hopes dashed there before. This time she might fall into a trap.

She rang the bell, and a dog yapped inside. Was Kitty Tucker home? Would she refuse Claire entry again? In plain sight of the street, Claire had never felt so vulnerable. She gave Kitty the benefit of the doubt. Her call had saved Claire's life. For now.

Kitty Tucker had dialed the number Claire had left on her answering service, the number on her Newburgh PD business cards. Seeing that Claire had disconnected her cell phone, the Newburgh PD communications system had routed the call to Claire's home line. Kitty had promised to tell Claire the full story of Tina's last day but refused to elaborate on the phone. She sounded afraid but not of Claire.

Had Newburgh PD used Kitty as bait to capture Claire? Kitty's testimony had incriminated Claire. Claire, the psychopathic killer, would want to silence Kitty just as she had suppressed the record of her testimony in Tina's murder file. Were a dozen officers waiting inside to arrest her, or was Kitty ready to tell the truth—a truth that would both clear Claire's name and expose Tina's true killer?

High heels clattered on a tiled floor behind the front door. "Quiet, Lulu," Kitty said.

As the lock turned, another possibility sent a wave of panic through Claire's body. Was Kitty Tucker the black-clad killer Claire had seen at Amy's window? Had she told O'Leary she'd seen Tina leave school with Claire only to divert suspicion from herself? Claire had worried about walking into a police trap. Had Tina's killer lured her into her deadly web?

As the door opened, Claire's fears disappeared. The pretty, delicate woman in the doorway had salon-dried black hair that fell to her shoulders in immaculate plumes. Her makeup was perfect, and her beige business suit probably cost more than Claire's monthly wage. Ignoring the trappings of wealth, she and Claire looked a lot alike. This pampered young woman was no serial killer.

A Maltese poodle crouched beside her owner's fancy pumps and growled at the stranger. Her cheeks flushed and her mouth tight, Kitty sent a concerned glance past Claire at the outside world. She jerked her head for Claire to enter, and she complied.

Kitty Tucker shut the door and turned three heavy locks. Claire stood in an open expanse of glossy white floor tiles. There were no police uniforms in sight. *So far so good*. The lights were on, the curtains closed. Either Claire's host was neurotic about her privacy or she understood the danger of their situation and the need for secrecy. *Even better*.

"Wine?"

"No, thanks." Claire almost added "I'm on duty" by force of habit, then remembered she was now a fugitive from the law.

"I'll get you some anyway. Trust me, you'll need it."

Kitty had an airy, bored manner of speaking, even when terrified. She charged ahead on her tall heels, and Claire followed, the Maltese snuffling her boots. They passed living rooms of leather couches, oriental rugs, and paintings with elaborate golden frames. Tina had chosen wealthy friends. Kitty was a stepping stone to the dream life Tina had envisioned for herself.

Claire's hostess slipped on her heels, almost spread-eagling on the expensive tiles, then regained her balance and continued on her way. Kitty had gotten a head start on the alcohol.

The kitchen was enormous, white, and modern. On the island, Kitty poured red wine into a large wine glass and topped up another, which was nearly empty. She perched on a stool and waited for Claire to sit beside her.

"You don't look much like her," Kitty said.

"Like Tina? No, we are very different."

Kitty smiled and took a long draft from her glass. "You speak of her as though she's still alive. I still can't believe she's gone even after all these years. Sometimes I think, 'What would Tina have said about that?' or 'What would Tina do in this situation?' She seemed too full of life to die like us mere mortals. Death was too boring, too clichéd for Tina."

"I know exactly how you feel."

Claire gave her hostess a quick polite smile and sipped her wine. But Claire had not risked her neck to reminisce about her dead sister.

"This is all your fault, you know?"

Kitty's sudden accusation startled Claire. Had she invited Claire over to aid her or confront her? "What do you mean?"

"You made me do this. You made me feel guilty about those other girls. I hear one of them is still missing. They think she's still alive, the poor thing. This has to stop."

Where was she going with this? Claire leaned forward, suddenly angry at Kitty for her report to O'Leary.

"You told Detective O'Leary that Tina was afraid of me, that I picked her up from school the day she died."

Kitty pulled her head back in disbelief. "I did not!"

"That's what he wrote in his report of your interview."

"Then the report is a lie. I told him the truth. Tina didn't like you. She didn't like many people. But that day she had someone else in her crosshairs. An older boy."

An older boy. The tension in Claire's body evaporated. Kitty's revelation changed everything. Claire had not killed Tina, and she was not crazy. And now she had a new lead. A boy had killed Tina.

But Kitty's information contradicted other facts about the murders. A woman had killed Amy. Claire had seen her in the girl's bedroom. Had Claire mistaken the killer's sex after all, or was this case more complex than she realized? She discarded all of her assumptions.

"He'd been flirting with her for days," Kitty continued, "trying to pick her up. But his family wasn't rich or powerful enough for Tina, so she decided to teach him a lesson. She had a knife on her—can you believe that, a knife! Tina was fearless. I think I was afraid of her, too."

"So how did she end up with him after school?"

"She told him she'd planned a surprise for him after school and she made it sound sexy. They walked off toward the woods on Park Street, and that was the last I saw of her."

The picture slowly came into focus. Tina's final prank had backfired. Expecting a sexual encounter, the older boy had reacted aggressively when Tina pulled the knife, and he had killed her. Did his anger at her deception explain the damage to her face?

Dr. Fleischer's profile had indicated a white male close to

Tina's age. Killing her—and getting away with it—had aroused his appetite for murder. And twelve years later, he attacked four other girls who looked just like her.

"This changes everything," Claire said.

Kitty emptied her glass. "I hope it helps. They swept the truth under the rug before. They'll do it again."

"Who will?"

"The cops. I told Detective O'Leary what I saw. He wrote everything down, and I was sure he'd act on it. I was so naïve. He never did, of course. By the time I realized what he'd done, it was old news. What was I supposed to do? I was a teenager. I wasn't about to accuse a police officer of covering up a murder."

Claire had been right about O'Leary. No wonder he told his wife he'd sold his soul to the Devil. Over the years, the guilt over the cover-up had eaten away at him, and he drank himself into an early grave.

"Why would O'Leary cover it up?"

Kitty looked at her, bemused. "You haven't figured it out yet, have you? He covered it up because the killer's father was a cop, too. The boy's name is Jed Wallace."

Kitty might have hit Claire over the head with the wine bottle. *Jed?* Claire had her issues with her new partner, but she'd never pegged him as a serial killer.

Now she connected the dots in her mind. Jed's dad, Chief Wallace, had been O'Leary's partner at the time of Tina's death. O'Leary had buried Kitty's eyewitness account, withheld the crime scene hairs and blood from forensic analysis, and hidden the case files in the archive. In return, Wallace had rewarded him with promotion to lieutenant and a comfy early retirement by the sea.

Jed checked all the boxes of Dr. Fleischer's profile. Claire had handed him Tina's case file. Jed had ample opportunity to withhold O'Leary's memo about Claire from the team and forge an interview with Kitty. He must have planted both in Claire's home for Rob to find later. Jed was the mole in Newburgh PD. He had led the hunt for the Middle School Strangler. But all along, the killer was Jed.

Goosebumps spread over Claire's arms. *No, it can't be.* Despite the mounting evidence, her heart resisted. She had partnered with Jed. They had broken the devastating news to Gracie's parents together. Could he be the killer?

She tried not to sound incredulous. "Jed killed Tina?"

Kitty shrugged. "Tina left school with him, and she turned up dead. You tell me, Detective."

Claire found no other explanation. Jed had killed Tina. His father and O'Leary had covered up the murder. Now Jed had killed again. Kitty was right, Claire needed the wine. She reached for her glass and took a gulp.

"Jed's leading the homicide investigation," she said. "Now they're trying to pin the murders on me, including Tina's."

Kitty topped up Claire's wine glass. "Isn't that convenient? All the loose ends tied up."

Claire shook her head. This was too much. Could her partner have murdered and mutilated those girls?

"If you're having any doubts," Kitty continued. "Don't. Jed showed up at my home on Thursday night. He threatened to kill me if I told anyone the truth about Tina."

Claire blinked at her, too shocked to say anything.

"That's why I stood you up for breakfast the next morning, and why I didn't let you in. I'm scared, Detective. Terrified."

The Maltese started yapping.

"Quiet, Lulu. Keep it down." But the dog kept barking at the street. "Lulu, I said—"

A loud crackle startled Kitty, and she spilled her wine on the island counter—the crackle of a loudspeaker outside.

"Claire Wolfe," a voice boomed on the loudspeaker. "This is

the Newburgh Police Department. We know you're in there. Come out the front door. Do it slowly and with your hands in the air."

Kitty grabbed Claire's hand. Like Claire, she had recognized the voice of the speaker. His name was Jed Wallace.

CHAPTER 54

Officer Corey Peters climbed out of the rear door of the SWAT van and leaned his sniper rifle over his shoulder. He glanced at the fancy house across the street and thanked his lucky stars.

"You owe me ten bucks, pal," he told Officer Jayden Glover

"Says who?"

Peters pointed at the house across the street, a modern single-level with fancy floor-to-ceiling windows, a water fountain, and a double-door garage. A small dog yapped inside.

"That is no bank."

Their last two operations had involved bank robberies, and Glover had bet him ten dollars the next stop would make three in a row. Peters would not let him wriggle out of this one.

Glover grinned. "Look at that house, man. They own a bank!"

"Owning doesn't count, and you know it."

A familiar cranky voice interrupted their argument.

"Enough chitchat, girls," Sergeant Vincent Morales said. "Get into position."

"Yes, sir!"

The SWAT commander had assigned them tasks during the pre-operation brief at the Newburgh Police Department. Captain Emmerso had introduced the SWAT team to Detective Jed Wallace, a young officer in a plainclothes suit, who had outlined their mission. Their target was twenty-eight-year-old Claire Wolfe, a local homicide detective and now a prime suspect in the series of teen murders that had shaken the city. A tip-off to a call line had notified the department that Wolfe had entered the mansion across the street thirty minutes ago. Their mission was to take Wolfe into custody. The owner of the house, Kitty Tucker, a television producer and a key witness in the murder investigation, was probably dead already, but they might have a hostage situation on their hands.

Peters grumbled under his breath as he walked to the two-level house opposite the target mansion. He had promised his wife he'd be home in time for their daughter's fourth birthday party. But the negotiators might take days to talk Wolfe down from her tree. According to Detective Wallace, Wolfe was intelligent, armed, and extremely dangerous. She had already murdered four, possibly five, fourteen-year-old girls in cold blood. The rogue officer had no reservations about using deadly force. While their target's actions shocked and disgusted Peters, they gave him hope. The nutjob would probably screw up and get herself killed quickly, and Peters might get home in time for Drew's birthday party after all.

Peters knocked on the front door, introduced himself to the neighbors, and found a clear view of the target house from the window of a kid's bedroom. He pulled up a white wooden chair, placed a padded blanket on the windowsill, and rested Old Trusty, his Remington Model 700 sniper rifle, on top. He peered through the scope, and the crosshairs passed over the broad, tall windows of the mansion.

Dirty cops. Those twisted psychos gave law enforcement a

bad name. *Child killer*. He thought of his daughter and felt sick to his stomach. On the other hand, the mission was a welcome break from his routine. He'd never taken down a child killer before. Claire Wolfe. The target's name made the operation feel like a hunting trip.

The crosshairs paused over a gap in the curtains behind the French windows. A framed painting hung on an interior wall. "Hello," he said.

The killer had screwed up already, giving Peters an unobstructed view of the inside. Yeah. He'd be home in no time.

CHAPTER 55

Rob floored the gas pedal, and the Bureau car gunned down the street. The photo of Claire the department had released to local TV stations had paid off when a neighbor had spotted her entering Kitty Tucker's home. If Rob missed this hostage negotiation, he'd never forgive himself.

"Are you sure you're up to this?" Tom said from the passenger seat.

Tom preferred to drive, but Rob had grabbed the car keys as soon as Captain Emmerso had called.

Rob kept his eyes on the road. As the closest FBI negotiator on call, he had no choice but to confront Claire. Rather him than somebody else. Claire might listen to him and surrender quietly. But Claire was stubborn, on the run, and haunted by conspiracy theories. He only hoped he arrived before she did anything desperate.

Rob negotiated a corner at high speed.

"Don't worry. I won't do anything stupid. You'll have to put up with my snoring for much longer."

Rob's humor camouflaged his guilt, too. He had told Claire he'd found Kitty Tucker's report in Claire's house. Now Claire had turned up at Kitty's home. Did she think Kitty was part of the conspiracy against her? Or had Claire's murderous split personality decided to eliminate Kitty? If anything happened to Kitty or Claire today, it was his fault.

He rounded one last corner and slowed. A SWAT officer holding a semi-automatic rifle blocked the entrance of the street. Rob flashed his FBI badge, and the officer waved him through. The street looked like a disaster zone. Three police cruisers, two black SWAT vans, and an ambulance straddled the sidewalk. A half-dozen men with black tactical gear and snub-nosed military-grade rifles took cover behind the vehicles and watched Kitty's home.

Rob pulled up behind a squad car and made for the huddle of Newburgh PD commanding officers. Captain Emmerso, Chief Wallace, Detective Jed Wallace, and the SWAT sergeant looked at Rob and Tom when they drew near.

Emmerso handled the introductions. "Sergeant Morales, meet Special Agents Tom Brown and Robert Cline. Agent Cline is an experienced hostage negotiator."

The sergeant shook their hands. "Agent Cline and I met this morning outside the target's home. This isn't quite how we planned to spend our weekend, is it?"

"Not at all," Rob said.

Tom asked Captain Emmerso what they'd missed.

"Detective Wallace called a few times for her to come out, but we haven't received a response."

"Have you tried calling the landline?"

"No answer. Detective Wallace, let's see what our FBI negotiator can do."

Jed grimaced but handed Rob the loudspeaker. Now Rob had ousted him from a key task twice, and the detective did not hide his irritation. "I hope you can do better. It's probably too late to save Ms. Tucker anyway. By now, Wolfe is disposing of her body."

"Let's not jump to conclusions."

Jed scoffed. "While you're at it, ask her where she buried Dana Wood. The video was a diversion. She got us chasing our tails while she closed in on her next victim."

Rob let the topic go. He had more urgent goals than persuading the detective that Claire wasn't a homicidal maniac. To be honest, Rob wasn't certain of that himself.

"Whenever you're ready, Agent Cline," Chief Wallace said. "Show us how it's done."

Rob glanced at Kitty's mansion over the roof of a squad car. Drapes blocked the tall windows. A small dog's yapping was the only sign of life within. He reviewed his mental toolbox of negotiation techniques. First, he had to get Claire talking.

He put the megaphone to his mouth, and his voice blared across the street. "Claire, it's Rob. We know you're in there. We just want to talk. Please call me."

Rob watched the house for movement. He checked his phone for network reception and waited. A minute later, he repeated his call. Negotiations took time. But they required communication. If he couldn't get her talking soon, the chief might decide that Claire had already fled the scene or killed herself. The SWAT team would storm the house, and in the confusion, anything could happen. Rob cranked up the pressure.

"Claire, how are we supposed to listen to your side if you won't even speak to us?"

As if in answer, a loud crack rang out—the report of a high-velocity round breaking the sound barrier—and Rob's body tensed. Glass tinkled behind him. They were under fire. Instinctively, Rob hit the ground, his heart pounding. Claire had finally answered his call...with a bullet.

CHAPTER 56

Crouching low, Claire peeked between the drapes of Kitty's living room window. The street swarmed with police cars, SWAT vans, and gunmen. Tactical soldiers waited in position behind the vehicles. Claire had collaborated with SWAT teams in Boston. Highly professional, they would have surrounded the house by now. Claire was trapped.

The megaphone squealed a third time over the incessant yapping of the Maltese. "Claire Wolfe," Jed's voice declared, "we know you're in there. Come out slowly with your hands in the air. This is your last chance."

Jed had killed Tina and the other girls. He had threatened Kitty's life and now he seemed ready to deliver.

Claire considered her options. The SWAT team would monitor all the exits. If the force outside included a K9 unit, hiding would be futile. She was running out of time.

"We must do as he says," she told Kitty, who crouched beside her, wine glass still in hand. "We'll surrender."

Kitty almost choked on her recent mouthful of alcohol. "Are you crazy? Jed will kill us both!"

Claire hazarded another peek out the window. Behind the

cover of a squad car, Captain Emmerso and Chief Wallace spoke with Jed and a SWAT commander. Another car pulled up, and two men in suits got out. Rob and Tom Brown.

"It doesn't work that way. The FBI has arrived. They'll try to get a conversation going. If we go peacefully, you'll be OK."

"What about you?"

"I can't let them lock me up. They think I'm criminally insane and that I came here to kill you. But seeing you, alive and well, will work in my favor. Your testimony changes everything. Just keep your hands in the air and do as they say."

"But how will you get out?"

Good question. The SWAT team would be watching the neighboring properties, too. "I'll figure something out."

The loudspeaker crackled again, and this time Rob spoke. He asked Claire to call him and talk things out. A part of her saw his involvement as a betrayal. But he didn't have a choice. He was an experienced FBI negotiator. This was his job. And Rob's presence comforted her. He would not allow things to spin out of control.

"Don't make me go out there," Kitty begged.

"You hear that voice? That's Special Agent Robert Cline. You can trust him. He's a good man. Tell him everything you told me, and this nightmare will be over."

Kitty did not look convinced. "I don't know. Jed's dad is the chief of police. They buried Tina's murder for over a decade. They'll do anything to silence me."

"Even the chief has to answer to the Feds."

Outside, Rob called her name again.

"We can't stay here, Kitty. If we don't respond, the SWAT team will break in and—"

"What?" Kitty interrupted, outraged. "Break in—to my home?" In her drunken state, she seemed more concerned about her fancy home than her life.

A loud crack rang outside and the sound of breaking glass. Claire dove to the floor, pulling Kitty down with her. Lulu jumped up and down, barking her head off.

"What the hell!" Kitty said. "Now they're shooting my place up, too?"

Claire listened, her body tensed for action. The shattering glass came from *outside* Kitty's home. A SWAT team would never open fire unprovoked. Had an edgy officer discharged his weapon by accident or was Kitty right? Would Chief Wallace do anything to ensure his son beat a murder rap?

"That asshole has gone too far!" Kitty yelled. "I'm going to give him a piece of my mind. C'mon, Lulu!"

Kitty shot to her feet. Her high heels clattered on the tiles as she marched toward the front door, Lulu charging beside her and growling.

"No, Kitty!" Claire said. "Get down!"

But Kitty wasn't listening. She strode toward the door. Then a window shattered, and Kitty's head exploded.

CHAPTER 57

Rob crouched on the sidewalk beside the squad car, his body rigid, and the blood freezing in his veins. For a long, terrible moment, silence reigned. Even the dog's yapping had ceased. Two shots had rung out overhead. The first seemed to have come from Kitty's house, the second from behind him. Rob was caught in the middle of a shootout. What the hell was going on?

"It's over," Sergeant Morales said. The SWAT team leader's helmet had bulletproof glass and a built-in microphone. He scanned the Tucker home with binoculars.

"What do you mean?"

"Our sniper took the shot. The target is down. Head shot."

Rob couldn't believe his ears. *They shot Claire in the head. She's dead.* Few of the hostage situations he had managed had ended in bloodshed and none so quickly. But if Claire had fired on the officers, she had signed her own death warrant.

The realization hit him again, harder. *Claire is dead.* Rob climbed to his feet, his grief giving way to rage, which he vented on the SWAT sergeant. "What the hell just happened?"

Sergeant Morales lowered his binoculars, not losing his

cool for a moment. "The target tried to take out our sniper. He returned fire."

He hooked a thumb at the house behind them. Jagged shards of glass hung from the second-story window where a SWAT sniper peered down the scope of his rifle.

"Outstanding work, Sergeant," Chief Wallace said. He and Captain Emmerso got to their feet and brushed off their clothes. "I'm glad this is finally over."

"It's not over yet, sir," Captain Emmerso said. "That girl is still missing."

The chief turned to the SWAT sergeant. "Get inside the house. We need to search Wolfe for any sign of where she put the girl. And Captain Emmerso, you'll need to explain how you hired that psycho to begin with."

"Yes, sir." Emmerso turned to the SWAT commander. "Sergeant, for all we know, Wolfe might have rigged the house with explosives. Take every precaution."

The SWAT sergeant spoke into his microphone. "Team, get your gear. The door might be wired. We're going in."

Tom patted Rob on the shoulder but said nothing. Rob stood rooted to the spot in a numb state of disbelief while the world swirled around him. SWAT officers pulled protective vests from the back of a van and headed for the front door. This was unreal. Chief Wallace got into his unmarked car and drove off. Was he satisfied that the situation had resolved or was he distancing himself from the crime scene? Rob looked around for Detective Jed Wallace. Rob had last seen him shortly before.

Sergeant Morales spoke into his microphone. "Move out!"

The clump of soldiers at the front of the house inched forward behind their shields. Two of them ran ahead with a battering ram when a soft mechanical whine drew Rob's attention to the double garage at the side of the house.

"Hold your positions," the sergeant said.

The garage doors opened, and a Maltese poodle sprinted into the street. Rob's heart galloped, clutching at hope. Was Claire alive? The door rose, and a large red car, all curves and glass panels, rolled out silently. The Tesla turned onto the street and drove off. The woman behind the wheel looked straight ahead as she passed by. *Claire!*

The sniper's bullet had missed. But Claire's life was still in danger.

"She's in the car," Sergeant Morales said. "Block the road!"

The SWAT officers guarding the road held their ground and raised their rifles. But Claire didn't slow. Soon she would run them down. Rob opened his mouth, but before he could cry out for them to stop, they opened fire.

Bullets pelted the car's nose and shot out a tire, but the vehicle continued its forward motion. The officers backed away from the approaching vehicle, firing with every step. Failing to stop the car, the officers aimed higher to disable the driver. The windshield shattered, the fractured glass turning milky white. But still, the vehicle continued toward the shooters.

Rob watched in horror, his brain frozen. How had Claire escaped injury? Was she wearing Kevlar?

The car accelerated suddenly and veered toward the house. Jumping the curb, the car slammed into the water fountain, toppling the heavy statue and mounting the prone sculpture with a crunch of metal parts. The car came to a halt, front wheels spinning in the air and water spraying from the broken fountain.

"Hold your fire," Sergeant Morales said.

Water surged over the sidewalk. The SWAT officers approached the vehicle slowly, their rifles at the ready. Rob stared at the driver's door, willing it to open, willing Claire to step out, her arms raised in surrender. But there was no movement from the driver's seat. The SWAT officers lowered their weapons. The battle was over.

Rob's mind thawed. He ran to the wrecked car and pushed through the throng of SWAT officers. The bullet-riddled car resembled an old target in a firing range. Through the empty windowpane, he glimpsed the woman within. Or what remained of her. Claire slumped forward in the driver's seat, her seatbelt tight against her body. Blood and gore matted her hair and stained her torn suit jacket and shirt red. Clusters of bullet entry wounds mangled her face.

Rob stumbled backward. He looked away, his hands raking his hair. Claire was gone. He had lost her forever.

CHAPTER 58

Emmerso smelled blood the moment he entered the house. SWAT officers swarmed within the Tucker mansion. The shootout had lasted seconds and injured none of their officers. They had been lucky. Things could have turned out much worse. But unanswered questions plagued the captain's mind.

Sergeant Morales drew near, pulling up the visor of his helmet. "The house is clear. No sign of the missing girl."

The news didn't surprise Emmerso. If Claire had come here to assassinate a witness, she wouldn't have dragged Dana Wood, her teenage hostage, along for the ride.

"Where's the body?" Emmerso asked. "Kitty Tucker," he added when the SWAT sergeant blinked at him in confusion. Emmerso considered the copious amounts of blood on the marble tiles of the entrance hall. "Seems like she died here."

Sergeant Morales shrugged. "We checked every room, sir. There's no sign of Tucker. The only dead body is out there." He meant the Tesla on the water feature with Claire Wolfe's corpse in the driver's seat. "And the blood might be Wolfe's," Morales added. "The impact with the window must have changed the bullet's trajectory and injured her badly."

"Or missed her completely." Claire had still driven out of the garage for her last stand.

But what had Claire done with Tucker's body?

"Maybe Tucker wasn't home?" Morales suggested.

"Maybe." Emmerso doubted that. The tip-off caller had seen Tucker open the door for Claire. "Thanks, Sergeant. We'll take things from here. Forensics won't like us disturbing the crime scene more than we have."

Sergeant Morales nodded and hurried away. Emmerso had called Forensics already. The two techs were minutes away. They needed the extra hands to clear that corpse from the street as soon as possible.

Meanwhile, they should start their investigation. Emmerso glanced around for Detective Jed Wallace. He hadn't seen the detective since Agent Cline had taken over the negotiation.

A familiar voice called his name, and Jed walked inside at a brisk pace. *Speak of the Devil.*

"Detective Wallace, I was just looking for you."

The detective lowered his gaze to the floor. "I...needed the bathroom. Badly."

"I'm sorry about Detective Wolfe. Despite everything, she was your partner."

The detective nodded and swallowed hard. "Yeah, I guess she pulled the wool over all our eyes. Has SWAT searched the house?"

"Yes. No sign of the girl. We'll search Wolfe for leads to the girl's location as soon as Forensics arrives. Meanwhile, walk me through the scene."

Jed extracted a digital recorder from his pocket. "The killer must have attacked Kitty in the hall shortly after she entered, about fifteen feet from the front door. There's a large pool of blood two feet from the window."

"That's possible, Detective. But we still haven't located Ms. Tucker's body."

"Oh." The detective seemed anxious.

"But let's roll with that scenario. Why would Kitty let her in?"

"What do you mean?" The question threw the detective off balance, making him both anxious and confused.

Emmerso felt for him. It was hard enough to discover your partner was a murderer. Retracing her crimes, play-by-play, was even worse. Emmerso was struggling to accept the new reality, too.

"There's no sign of forced entry. Look at those locks on the door. The decedent must have feared for her safety. She wouldn't have opened the door to anyone."

Jed nodded. "I guess Wolfe talked her way inside, then killed her."

"How?"

Jed studied the hall. "There's a lot of blood on the floor but no casings. The tip-off didn't mention any gunshots. She must have used a knife. Either way, she moved the body." He pointed. "Those blood smudges show the direction in which she dragged the victim. Toward the garage." He paused. "She must have put the body in the trunk."

Emmerso smiled. Jed was warming up.

"We'll test that theory soon enough." Nobody had touched the car for fear of contaminating the crime scene. "Let's move on for now," Emmerso added. "A round was fired at the SWAT sniper across the street."

Jed pointed at the broken window. "She must have fired from here, breaking the window."

"With a Glock? No wonder she missed." Emmerso

inspected the punched-out window and the shards of glass. "And why is there more glass inside than out? This is our sniper's work."

They turned toward the wall opposite the window. Blood spatter speckled the wall and an expensive-looking painting.

Jed adjusted his narrative. "Wolfe must have fired from a different location. Our sniper hit her right here, the same spot where she killed Tucker. Injured and desperate, she stole Tucker's car after dumping her body in the trunk."

Emmerso grunted. That story didn't feel right either. "OK, time to test our theory."

He stepped outside, ducking underneath the yellow police tape. Emmerso had a theory of his own that required validation. The pockmarked sports car perched on the water feature at an unsettling angle. Somebody had turned off the water mains, but the sidewalk was still damp. Special Agent Tom Brown spoke with the SWAT sergeant. Special Agent Rob Cline sat on the curb, his hands in his hair. The Fed had worked closely with Detective Wolfe and he'd taken her death badly, worse even than Jed. Brandon Yang and his fellow forensic tech snapped photos of the car.

Emmerso stepped over the line of yellow tape tied between traffic cones and sent a glance at the woman slumped in the driver's seat. She was still wearing her detective work clothes. Emmerso turned to the Forensic techs.

"Thanks for getting here quickly."

Yang placed his gloved hands on his hips and shook his head at the wreckage. "What a waste."

"Yeah," Jed said. "That's a brand-new car."

Yang shot him an annoyed look. "I was talking about the driver."

The comment had surprised Emmerso, too.

Jed shrugged. "It's poetic justice."

"How so?" Emmerso asked.

The detective pointed at the remains of the driver's head. "She ended up just like the girls she killed."

Emmerso nodded. Something inside the car glinted in the afternoon light, catching his eye.

"May we open the trunk?" Emmerso asked the tech.

"Sure."

Yang handed him a pair of latex gloves. Emmerso put them on and popped the trunk. It was empty.

Jed swore. "Wolfe must have dumped the body in the house."

"Then why didn't we find her there?" Emmerso said.

He moved back to the front of the car, reached inside the glassless driver's window, and lifted the corpse's arm by the jacket sleeve.

"What is it, Captain?"

Emmerso turned. Special Agent Rob Cline had materialized at his side. He looked beat and disheveled, but hope glimmered in his eyes. Emmerso let go of the lifeless woman's sleeve.

"Agent Cline and Detective Wallace. You both spent time with Detective Wolfe, didn't you?"

The two men exchanged anxious glances, wondering where the question was leading. Every so often, a captain needed to exhibit his detective chops. It kept his men sharp.

"Yes, sir."

"Did she wear nail polish?"

Jed said, "Not that I noticed."

"What about earrings?"

Agent Cline answered. "No, she didn't."

"I figured that much." Emmerso pulled the gloves from his hands. "Gentlemen, we've found Kitty Tucker."

CHAPTER 59

Dana squirmed in the darkness. She'd slept in short fits, waking every few minutes from the pain in her shoulder and thigh. The cable ties had worn her wrists and ankles raw and tender. She rolled onto her belly, rested her chin on the stony floor, and breathed through the canvas bag on her head. How long had her captors held her there?

She had peed six times. The first time, she had almost died from terror. Feet had descended the steps. Hands had unzipped Dana's jeans and yanked them to her ankles, along with her panties. Dana froze with shock. Her captors were going to rape her. But they didn't. The hands dug under her armpits, lifting her off the floor, then lowering her naked behind onto a plastic bucket.

The relief at emptying her bladder had overwhelmed her. Without a word, her captor had raised her again, returning her to the floor and pulling her clothing into place. Then, Dana had begun the next long period of dark discomfort.

Twice, her captor had shifted the edge of the canvas bag over Dana's nose, removed the gag from her mouth, and placed a straw between her lips. Dana had drunk the sugary liquid greedily until the woman yanked the straw away. Then, back came the gag, and down came the bag. Once, she had glimpsed shelves on the walls, and boxes, but nothing else.

She hadn't eaten solid food in a long, long time. Days, probably. Her captors wanted her alive but not strong enough to escape. The other girls had turned up dead shortly after disappearing. Did her captors have other plans for her?

Dana sobbed, her tears soaking the canvas bag. She'd never sneak out again. She'd never go out again, ever. Dana would be a good girl. She'd listen to her parents. *Oh God, I will. I promise. Just let me go home, please!*

The door opened above. Feet padded down the steps. The footfalls were heavier than before. A man. He descended the stairs with slow, confident strides, and he stood over her. He didn't smell of flowers like the woman but of peppermint and eucalyptus—a man's aftershave. What did he want with her?

He touched her shoulder, and Dana flinched. She shifted onto her side and curled into a fetal position. Was he going to kill her now? Would he hurt her first? Rape her?

Large, hard fingers clamped over her arms and lifted her to her feet. Her legs were asleep from the long hours on the chilly floor. She could barely stand on her bare feet.

"Please don't hurt me," she cried, but the gag muffled her words. "I'll do whatever you want."

This was it—the end. Terror mixed with curiosity. Was this how Grace and Karla had spent their last moments?

The hands gripped her waist and hoisted her into the air. A bony shoulder slammed into her stomach, winding her. Carrying her like a sack of potatoes, he climbed upward, her body flopping painfully with each step. He was taking her upstairs. Dana had hated that basement, but now she wanted to stay, alone and far from the man.

"No! Please don't!" But the gag turned her pleas into the

pitiful mewling of a doomed animal on its way to the slaughterhouse.

CHAPTER 60

That evening, Rob took a hot shower in his motel room and prepared to break the law.

The steaming water soothed his aching muscles like a rejuvenating rain. *Claire was alive.* The woman in the Tesla had worn Claire's clothes, but her name was Kitty Tucker. A sniper's bullet had destroyed her brain minutes before Claire had propped Kitty's body behind the wheel. Claire had not killed Kitty. She had faked her own death and remained, once again, one step ahead of the Newburgh PD. Rob wanted to kiss her... and curse her.

For fifteen terrifying minutes, he had lost her. He had mourned her death and he would never forget that heartache. But he couldn't fault her for duping him.

Her close brush with death had been his fault. He had told her about Kitty's report, leading Claire to risk a visit to Kitty's home. And when the SWAT officers opened fire on Kitty's car, Rob had looked on helplessly.

During the After-Action Review with Captain Emmerso, the officers had pieced together the sequence of events. The sniper's bullet had killed Kitty instantly. Claire dressed Kitty in her detective clothes and strapped the lifeless body into the driver's seat. Then, she activated the Tesla's autonomous-driving feature and opened the garage doors. Adding an ironic touch, Claire had selected the Newburgh Police Department as the car's destination.

In the shootout's aftermath, the SWAT officers had relaxed their surveillance of the property. Claire had slipped into the backyard and scaled a wall, escaping through a neighboring home. What she was wearing now, nobody knew. She had dumped Kitty's bloodstained clothes in her washing machine. The manhunt continued. And this time, Rob would not let Claire down.

He turned off the shower and toweled down. He still had more questions than answers. Why had Claire fired at the SWAT sniper? In hindsight, the gambit had paid off. The distraction had prepared the way for her escape. But the move could have gotten her killed.

"She's a homicidal nutjob," Detective Jed Wallace had said. "That's why she opened fire."

This time, Rob had kept his objections to himself. Claire was a crack shot. The officers on the street had provided easier targets than the sniper in the upper-floor window. Claire had missed on purpose.

There were other discrepancies. Forensics had found a .22 caliber bullet buried in the bedroom closet behind the SWAT sniper. Claire's standard-issue Glock 22 used .40 caliber bullets.

Jed had found an explanation for that, too. "She must have used a .22 LR conversion kit to extend her range and use high-capacity magazines." And although that was possible, it didn't explain the next problem.

The bullet's trajectory didn't match the ground-floor window of the house across the street. A simpler explanation placed the shooter outside the Tucker home. But that solution only triggered more questions.

Claire had suspected a conspiracy. Rob didn't believe that Tina had faked her death, but could Newburgh PD have covered up the murder? Chief Wallace had partnered with Detective O'Leary. Case files had gone missing only to appear in Claire's home during a search the chief's son had led. And Jed's mysterious disappearance from the crime scene immediately before the shooting began only fed Rob's speculations. Claire's conspiracy theory was no harder to swallow than her supposed split personality.

"Just because you're paranoid doesn't mean they aren't after you," read the quote from Joseph Heller's *Catch-22*. For the sake of his sanity, Rob had to dig deeper. Claire's life depended on it. As far as Newburgh PD was concerned, Claire was a highly dangerous fugitive. She could expect no help from her fellow officers. No help they'd provide willingly.

Rob wrapped the towel around his waist and glanced at the small device on the bathroom counter. A red dot flashed within concentric circles on a map. Coordinates and vectors updated on a side panel. Rob's target was on the move. *Where are you going tonight?*

Rob pulled on fresh clothes and pocketed the device. Tom lay on his motel bed and scrolled down a feed on his phone. Rob swiped the car keys from the bureau by the TV.

"I'll be back later."

Tom stared at his phone. "Don't do anything I wouldn't do."

Rob skipped his usual witty response. He left the motel room and got in the Bureau car. Tom would definitely not do *this*. But Rob refused to sit back and do nothing.

He turned the key in the ignition and placed the tracking device on the dash. As he reached for the gear stick, the rear door opened, and the barrel of a gun pressed against the back of his neck. He froze, his hand still on the stick.

The car door closed. Without moving his head, he glanced at the rearview mirror. The headrest blocked the intruder's face but not her locks of blonde hair.

"Don't turn around," she said.

CHAPTER 61

Raindrops splattered on the windshield. Rob's heart galloped. A gun barrel pressed against the base of his skull. Death might be moments away. And yet he felt the urge to sing. He knew that voice.

"Claire—" he began.

"Shut up and listen," Claire said. "I didn't kill Kitty Tucker. Your effing sniper did."

Claire had dyed her hair blonde. And she was angry. After the raid on her apartment and her close shave with death, she had every right to distrust him.

"I know."

"And I didn't shoot at anyone."

"I know." The pressure of the barrel eased for a moment, and he tried his luck. "But who did?"

"I don't know. What matters is this. Jed was the last one to see Tina alive. Kitty told me that before she died."

"Jed Wallace?"

"He was at her school. He'd been hitting on her. The day she died, Tina told Kitty she was going to teach Jed a lesson. Tina left school with Jed. She probably pulled a knife on him.

But her prank backfired, Jed killed her, and his father and O'Leary covered it up. Jed must have forged Kitty's report and planted it in my house."

Claire had done it. She had found the missing pieces to the puzzle.

"So Tina's dead after all?"

Rob imagined Claire clenching her jaw in the silence.

"I was wrong about that. She's dead. I dug up her body to be sure."

"Geez, Claire!"

Her clipped tone betrayed her desperation. "I know you think I'm crazy, but—"

"Not anymore. I believe you." To help her, he had to regain her trust.

Sarcasm filled her voice. "Did the gun at your head convince you?"

"I didn't believe you before, Claire, but I do now."

She scoffed. "It doesn't matter. My only witness is dead, and the only record of her testimony contradicts what she told me. I'm screwed."

"No, Claire. We can still turn this around."

"Let me guess. You just need to drive me to the station?"

"Not the station. But let me take you into custody. Stay with Tom until I get hard evidence."

"And how will you do that?"

He raised his right hand slowly and pointed at the homing unit on the dash. "I put a tracker on your partner's car. If he leads us to Dana, we'll have him."

"We?"

"You're not alone, Claire. We can do this together. I'll protect you."

"Like you protected me this morning?"

"I was trying to keep you alive."

Claire said nothing. She didn't lower the gun either. Would she trust him again or did she think he was leading her into a trap? If he still thought she had a murderous split personality, he'd say anything to disarm her. And she'd do the same in his shoes.

"Get out."

"What?" The rain had picked up, becoming a steady drizzle.

"Don't make me shoot you."

"You'd shoot me?"

"Losing an ear won't kill you."

Rob had pushed his luck far enough. He opened the door, climbed out, and stepped away from the car, the rain battering his head and matting his hair. Claire got out the back, her gun still aimed at him. She looked a lot like the photo of her sister Tina.

"Tell Captain Emmerso what I know. He's a good man. He'll do the right thing." She got into the driver's seat.

"Let me come with you."

She closed the door and drove into the night. The taillights vanished in the dark as the rain trickled down Rob's neck and seeped into his shirt. He turned back to the motel. She'd taken the Bureau car. Tom was going to love this.

CHAPTER 62

Raindrops streaked through the beams of the headlights in the dark. Claire glanced at the red dot on the tracking unit as the car ate the road. She was a fugitive in a stolen FBI car. The odds were stacked against her.

Her conscience twinged at abandoning Rob in the rain, but she'd had no choice. He said he believed her, and she wanted to trust him. But tracking Jed's car was a risky move and probably illegal. Rob was a sworn officer of the FBI. Duty would require him to surrender her to the authorities until they resolved the facts. The powers that be would overrule his good intentions and place Claire in mortal danger. Again.

The winding road passed through a wooded area without streetlights. The red dot had stopped moving at a spot under a mile away. Claire was not familiar with this part of the city. She had no idea what lay ahead. Why had he stopped here? If Jed had noticed the tracker, he'd be waiting for her.

Her stomach still convulsed at the memory of that morning. Kitty had collapsed on the tiles like a limp doll.

"No!" Claire had cried. "No!"

She had crouched over Kitty's lifeless body. The sniper's

bullet had carved a large hole in the side of her head, shattering her skull and spraying blood and brain matter on the wall behind her. Lulu whined softly and sniffed at her dead owner's fingers and the spreading pool of blood.

Kitty had been brave. She had shared the information Claire needed to solve Tina's murder and clear her name. But without Kitty's testimony, Claire was just another conspiracy theorist—a murderously insane conspiracy theorist.

Claire had forced the horror of Kitty's corpse and her own impossible situation from her mind. Any moment, a SWAT team would burst inside. To escape, Claire needed a diversion.

She stripped down to her underwear and changed Kitty's corpse into her work clothes. The dead girl looked eerily like Claire. She carried Kitty to the garage, propped her in the driver's seat of her brand-new Tesla Model X, and fastened the seatbelt. The electric sports car came with a self-driving feature. Her lifelong interest in cars had finally paid off. *Thanks, Dad*. Claire started the car, plugged in the first address that came to mind, and, after muttering an apology to her hostess, she opened the garage doors, and Lulu sprinted outside.

Back in the house, she tossed Kitty's bloodstained clothes in the washing machine and waited for the shooting to end. When silence reigned again, she snuck out the backdoor barefoot and still in her underwear. Her gun clutched in her hand, she scaled the wall of the neighboring home and found a black sweatsuit on a clothesline.

Claire could not afford another confrontation with law enforcement. She had to go underground. In the Baxters' bathroom, she found a canister of blonde hair dye, and now the face in the mirror looked uncannily like Tina.

The wipers squeaked across the windshield. Claire slowed to a stop on the dark wooded road. She had passed the red dot on the tracker display. Jed must have taken the access road she had passed on her right. Was this where he lived or was he visiting grandma in the woods? Either way, she might run smack into her old partner. Claire welcomed that possibility. She was done running. This time, Jed had picked on the wrong girl. This time, a Big Bad Wolf was after *him*.

Claire pressed her foot to the accelerator. After a half mile, she stopped on the side of the road. With the butt of her Glock, she smashed the taillights. *Sorry, Rob. It's for the greater good.* Then, she got inside the car and doubled back.

Turning onto the dirt side road, she cut her headlights and rolled forward. She could do with Kitty's silent Tesla right now.

Two hundred yards in, a ranch house appeared in the moonlight. Jed's silver Dodge Stratus parked outside behind an old white Mazda 3 hatchback. A light burned in one room.

Claire stopped the car and killed the engine. Was this the private facility the killer had used to hold the girls? Had Jed led her to his murder den?

The face of Dana Wood rose in Claire's mind. Her body had not turned up yet. She might still be alive. Jed knew Claire had spoken with Kitty and learned the truth. Sensing Claire's noose closing around his neck, had he returned to his den to kill Dana and dump her body?

Claire checked her new Glock—she had fifteen rounds in the full magazine and one more in the chamber. She eased the car door open and proceeded on foot. In her black gear, Claire moved like a shadow in the dark. Raindrops pelted her head. She picked her way forward around dead twigs, the rhythmic patter of the falling rain swallowing the crunch of gravel beneath her feet. A chill breeze rustled the leaves in the tall trees and shifted her damp hair. On a branch high above, an owl hooted.

She drew alongside the house and peered into the illuminated room—a kitchen with old cupboards of faded wood.

Cans of food and dirty dishes cluttered the counters. She saw no sign of Jed. But the white hatchback meant he wasn't alone.

Claire made her way along the side of the house, her gun pointed downward, her finger off the trigger. An accidental discharge might alert her target and end Dana's life.

She listened at the kitchen door. Hearing nothing, she tried the handle. The door was unlocked—a lucky break or an inviting trap?

Claire inched the door open and cringed at the soft squeak of the hinges. She passed through the kitchen, the rubber tread of her wet shoes making sucking noises with each step. The wind howled through the trees, and the cabin's wooden planks sighed like an old ship in a sea storm.

Claire moved into the darkness of a corridor, listening while her eyes adjusted to the gloom. Her heartbeat thumped in her ears.

Step by step, she continued down the corridor, peering around corners, shifting her weight slowly to make as little sound as possible.

Voices. A man and a woman. The man raised his voice. A shot rang out, and Claire flattened her back against the wall. But she was not under attack. The explosion came from below, from a basement.

Had Jed shot the girl? Claire was alone. She had no backup. A call to the police department from her burner phone would get her arrested for murders she had not committed. She'd left Rob miles away in the rain and without the tracker. He would have arrested her, too, trusting the justice system to find the truth. But the system had let Tina down. Claire could rely only on herself.

She stepped toward the sound. A thin rectangle of light revealed a door beneath a staircase. A basement door. The killer kept his victims down there. The basement walls would swallow the screams, and visitors wouldn't wander in there by mistake. Claire only hoped she wasn't too late.

She pressed her ear to the doorjamb. Something whimpered within. Someone. Using the wall as a shield, she reached out her hand and turned the handle. The door glided open.

Claire rounded the doorframe, her gun aimed ahead in both hands, blinking as her eyes adjusted to the light. She stood at the top of a cement staircase. A naked yellow light bulb hung from the ceiling. The basement was littered with packing boxes, old chairs, and low wooden bureaus.

The man in the gray suit at the foot of the stairs stood with his back to Claire. Jed held a gun in one hand, a black ski mask in the other. He stood over a woman in a black jumpsuit, who lay in a puddle of blood. She had blonde hair.

Claire's breath caught in her chest. The dead woman was not Tina, but Claire knew her. They had met outside Gracie's eighth-grade classroom. Lisa Evans, the middle school teacher, lay dead on the floor. She was the blonde killer who had fled out of Amy's bedroom window, and that spark of recognition had convinced Claire her sister was alive. She had noticed the chemistry between Jed and the teacher, but she'd never imagined they were partners in murder. Jed had come to the ranch house to tie up the loose ends, and he'd started with his accomplice.

A moan drew Claire's attention to another figure. A girl lay facedown on the floor behind Jed. Cable ties bound her wrists and ankles. A black canvas bag covered her head. Dana Wood was alive!

Claire aimed her Glock at Jed's center.

"Drop it!" she cried. "Drop the gun now."

CHAPTER 63

Jed turned around and looked up at Claire. His gray tie hung off-center, revealing the buttons of his rumpled white shirt. He seemed surprised to see her...and scared.

"Claire?"

Her new hair color had unnerved him. Had he thought Tina's ghost had risen from the grave to avenge her death? In a way, she had.

"I said put it down!"

Slowly, Jed crouched, placing the gun on the floor.

"Kick it away and put your hands on your head."

Jed complied. Carefully, Claire descended the steps.

"So, this is it?" he said. "Are you going to kill me like Tina and the other girls?"

His nerve outraged Claire. To the very end, he heaped lies upon lies. But nobody would gaslight Claire again. She doubted neither her sanity nor her senses. Jed would pay for the murder of Tina and the other girls. But first, Claire had to ensure Dana's safety.

Reaching the bottom of the stairs, she stepped around Jed,

the gun trained on him. Claire pulled the black hood from the bound girl's head. Pale and thin, the girl flinched.

"It's OK, Dana. I'm with the Newburgh Police Department."

The girl's body shuddered as she wept with relief. Claire found a pair of kitchen scissors on a bureau and cut the cable ties.

"Can you walk?"

Dana nodded and wiped tears and mucus from her face.

"Go upstairs. Get out of the house. There's a blue car on the dirt road. The doors are open. Wait for me there."

Dana took Claire's hand and rose to her feet. She ran up the stairs and disappeared into the house without looking back. Claire should have brought food for the girl. Soon Dana would get treatment and start the long road to recovery.

Jed scoffed. "So, now you're the hero?"

"It's over, Jed. You might as well tell the truth."

Jed raised his voice. "What do you know about the truth, Claire Wolfe?"

She had riled him. That was good. Let him talk in anger. She needed to hear the words.

"The day she died, Tina left Newburgh Middle School with you. Kitty Tucker told me that before your sniper blew her brains out."

"That was an accident. We were after you."

"Oh, I know. You were itching for a shootout, weren't you? Kitty told me you threatened to kill her if she talked. You forged the report of her interview with O'Leary and planted it in my home. You couldn't let the truth get out, so you had her killed."

"Kitty brought that on herself. She should have shut the hell up."

Claire plowed on. Jed would not talk his way out of this.

"But that wasn't the first time a Wallace had tampered with evidence, was it? Your father made sure you didn't become a suspect in Tina's murder. He buried the evidence against you. He eliminated Kitty's testimony and his name from the case files."

"Leave my father out of this. There's no proof—"

Claire interrupted him. "O'Leary's wife remembers. Her husband partnered with Detective Harry Wallace back then. O'Leary started drinking before he died, saying he'd made a deal with the Devil. It seems his conscience finally got to him. Makes you wonder why Chief Wallace promoted him and where he got that nest egg for his retirement. Your father bought his silence. And when O'Leary had second thoughts, you silenced him forever."

Jed's mouth twisted with disgust. "You're sick, Claire. Brian was my friend, my mentor. I had nothing to do with his death!"

Claire had gotten under his skin, and she pushed harder.

"But you killed Tina. You wanted her, didn't you? After school that day, she led you to the woods, but then she resisted. She pulled a knife on you, and you killed her. And why not? Daddy had your back."

"I did not kill her!"

"Then, why the cover-up?"

"Because nobody would believe me!" Jed's shoulders sagged, and he lowered his eyes to the floor. "You're right. I left school with Tina. I had a crush on her, all right? A stupid teenage crush. Tina was so pretty and confident. She said she wanted to show me how much she loved me." Jed inhaled a tremulous breath. "I was too naïve to understand what she was doing. In the woods, she got down on her knees and unzipped my jeans. She..." Jed choked up at the memory. "She took me in her hand. But then she put a knife to my balls." Jed glared at Claire, his face red. "She said she was going to teach me a lesson I'd never forget. The psycho drew blood! I almost passed out. Then, she laughed and let me go. I ran the hell away from her. But I did not hurt her. I didn't even know she was dead until later."

Claire had no patience for his lies. "Tell it to the judge."

"Don't you see? They had my pubic hair and blood at the scene. Kitty saw me with her!"

"So it's OK to destroy evidence?"

"The evidence told the wrong story! You know how these things work. They had my DNA. The courts would convict me of murder and send me to a reformatory. If my dad hadn't intervened, Tina would have ruined my life."

"The way you ruined hers?"

Hatred filled Jed's eyes. "Don't act so innocent, Claire. You wanted her dead. You hated her guts. O'Leary wrote it in his report. You'd tried to kill her before. And that day, you found your opportunity. You saw us go into the woods. You saw me leave. Then, you cornered her there and strangled her."

"I was never there, Jed."

"You ungrateful little bitch." His chest heaved. "My dad buried the investigation to protect me, but he also protected you. I'm the only reason they didn't press charges against you. A trial would have raised too many questions. But I'm done protecting you."

"Protecting *me*? You tried to kill me. If you'd had your way, I'd be in the morgue with Kitty."

"I warned her not to get involved. Kitty should never have talked to you. I can't go to prison, Claire. I'm innocent!"

"No, Jed. Innocent people don't forge and plant evidence. They don't kill people."

"Unlike you." Jed's smile chilled Claire to the bone. "Grace Miles. Karla Smith. Amy Collins. Do you even remember killing them?"

"I didn't kill those girls, Jed."

"Are you sure? You're sick, Claire."

Claire shook her head to free her mind of confusion.

"I'm done with your lies, Jed." Her words spilled out louder than she had intended. "You're the sick one. Even after you joined the force, you couldn't get Tina out of your head. You needed to control her again. You needed another Tina. That's where Lisa Evans came in. You seduced her, and she became your accomplice. But after a while, delivering your victims wasn't enough for her. She beat you to Amy Collins. Was that your sick idea of foreplay? But your girlfriend screwed up. I saw her at the scene of the crime, and you had to act fast. You turned the investigation against me. You planted evidence to frame me for Tina's murder. Soon, you'd connect me to the other girls, too. But I was already onto you. I had spoken with Kitty and discovered the truth. You panicked, trying to silence me and Kitty. When that didn't work, you cashed out. Two scapegoats are better than one. You'd blame me for Tina, and Lisa for the other girls. And *you* would play the hero. You'd kill Lisa and free Dana. You'd say Lisa was *my* accomplice. And with her dead, it's your word against mine."

Claire stood there panting, her speech complete. She had broken through his web of lies. He would never gaslight her again.

His vicious stare could pierce steel. "You got one thing right. It's my word against yours."

"No, Jed. It's your word against you." Claire pulled the Digital Voice Recorder from her pocket. "You placed yourself with Tina at the time of her death. You admitted to forging and planting evidence to incriminate me. You killed Tina and those girls. Your father covered it up. And you're both going down."

His Adam's apple shifted up and down. He hadn't seen that coming. But Claire didn't expect his next words either.

"You're just like your sister, aren't you? A sick, crazy bitch."

Claire shrugged off the insult. Words wouldn't save him from justice.

But he wasn't done. "This is entrapment. You brought me here tonight."

"What are you talking about?"

"You texted me the GPS coordinates, Claire. Otherwise, I would never have found this place. I had no idea Lisa was involved in the murders until I walked in on her now and she pulled a gun on me. You orchestrated it all."

Claire clenched her teeth. Her mother's voice echoed in her ears. *Murderer! This is all your fault.*

Claire's lips trembled. "Liar! My phone is offline. I destroyed the SIM. There's no way…"

Jed put his hand in his trouser pocket, and Claire curled her finger around the trigger.

"Don't shoot," he said. "I'm getting my phone. See for yourself."

This was another trap. She had not texted him. But he seemed so sure of himself. Was he a psychopathic liar or was he telling the truth?

Jed held out his phone. "Here. Take a look. This proves you're behind this."

Claire glanced at the phone in his hand. *No, he's lying. He must be.* She hadn't sent him here. Until tonight, she hadn't known the ranch house existed. He was distracting her so he could make his move—to kill her and destroy her recording. But she had to know for sure.

"Put the phone down."

"What's the matter, Claire? Afraid you'll find out what you really are?"

"I said, put it down!"

But Jed didn't. His arm became a blur, and the phone flew at Claire's face like a poison dart.

CHAPTER 64

Dana Wood threw open the door of the house and ran into the night. She had to get away from that place and those people.

The tall black silhouettes of trees reached for the moonlit skies. She leaped down the porch steps on wobbly legs and sprinted down the gravel road as the policewoman had told her. Sharp stones tore at the soft soles of her bare feet. Rain pelted her body and soaked her hair. But she didn't stop or slow.

She sucked in the fresh air and the scent of wet pine needles and stumbled forward. Dana was free and out of the basement, but the terror refused to leave her heart. Was she truly safe?

She glanced over her shoulder at the shadowy ranch house. Nobody was following her. But the policewoman had held a man at gunpoint. He had already shot and killed another woman. She lay dead at his feet in a puddle of blood. Was her savior in danger, too? Dana needed to call for help. But how?

A blue car emerged from the gloom. She opened the passenger door, climbed in, and engaged the central locking. The interior of the car was only a little warmer. Rain drummed on the roof. She hugged her chest and shivered in her soaked clothes. Through the waterlogged windscreen, the house was a warped black monster.

She searched the car for a phone. In the glove compartment, she found a user manual, a pack of cigarettes…and a large black handgun.

Her hands trembled as she handled the heavy weapon. She'd never touched a gun before. Before the night was out, she might need to fire one. The thought terrified her. She dropped the gun back in the glove compartment.

Should she go back inside and help the policewoman? No! The officer had told her to wait in the car. She hadn't dressed like a police officer. A woman had kidnapped her. A woman had tended to her in the basement. But was her captor the dead woman on the floor or the woman who claimed to be a cop?

A loud, sharp noise rang out, and Dana screamed. The second time she heard the blast, she clamped her hand over her mouth. Gunshots! She had heard two more gunshots from inside the house. The dark monster shifted beyond the watery windshield. Was her savior dead? Was Dana safe in this car?

No place was safe anymore. Dana opened the door and stepped back into the rain. She ran down the gravel road, away from the car and the house, and into the night.

CHAPTER 65

Claire groaned. Her shoulder burned. She lay on her back on the cement floor of the basement. Battered and stunned as though coming to after a car smash, her body refused to move.

As Jed's phone had launched toward her face, time had slowed to a crawl. A reflex in Claire's lizard-brain urged her to catch the phone, but Jed had dived sideways, his hand reaching for his gun. Claire resisted the urge, ducked the hurtling phone, and adjusted her aim as Jed hit the floor and rolled over, gun in hand. She squeezed her trigger. But fire flashed from Jed's weapon, too. Pain exploded in her shoulder. Her legs collapsed beneath her, and she landed hard.

Silence reigned for what seemed an eternity. Had she hit him? Claire hoped to God she had killed him. She was in no state to defend herself. The gun had slipped from her hands. She reached her left hand to her right shoulder. The fingers came away wet and sticky. Blood. A lot of blood. She needed medical attention. All thoughts of doctors fled when the sound of scraping rose from the other end of the basement.

Jed grunted. "You shot me, you bitch!"

Claire rolled her head from side to side and smiled. She'd hit him. No matter what happened next, she'd shot the bastard.

Get up! a voice whispered in her mind. Tina stood over her, fourteen years old and dimple-cheeked. *Claire, get up.*

You're not real. You're dead.

No, I'm not. I'm right here. Inside you.

"But you hated me. We hated each other."

Sadness filled the apparition's face. *That wasn't our fault.*

More scraping sounds. Jed was getting to his feet.

Get up, Claire! Finish him before he kills you, too.

Claire strained her neck and searched behind her for the gun. She found only packing boxes and bureaus.

Sorry, Tina. I failed you. I found your killer, but I couldn't stop him.

The vision of Tina scowled at her. *Don't you dare give up!*

Claire held her breath and with a superhuman effort, she rolled onto her good shoulder. Lisa Evans's corpse stared at her. Her dead fingers still held a Glock. Jed had killed one woman tonight. Claire would not be number two.

"That was for Tina," she yelled, and she shifted toward the dead teacher.

"I told you, bitch. I didn't kill Tina!" Jed shuffled to his feet.

Move, Claire! Move!

"But I wish I had!"

Claire was inches from Lisa's hand.

Screw it! Claire gathered all the fight she had left and lunged forward. Ignoring the searing pain in her shoulder, she pried the gun from the dead woman's hand and crawled behind a bureau.

A shot fired, and wood splintered behind her. Jed wouldn't let her leave this place alive.

"It doesn't have to end this way," she called.

Claire ejected the Glock's magazine and checked the

rounds. Ten bullets left. She'd have to make them count. Drawing a deep breath, she focused her thoughts. Jed's Glock 22 stored fifteen rounds in a full magazine. He'd fired at least two already. That left thirteen shots. He could afford to make more mistakes.

"Yes it does, Claire."

Claire raised her arm, grinding her teeth at the pain, and extracted her arm from her black sweatshirt. Then, she dangled the sleeve beyond the bureau. Two shots exploded behind her. One tore a hole in her sleeve. Eleven rounds left. He wouldn't fall for that trick twice. And he probably had a spare magazine. *Crap!*

Claire reached out and pulled a packing box near. Inside she found a baseball cap, a pair of sunglasses, a knotted mess of women's necklaces, and a pile of Polaroid photos, but no weapons.

In one photo, a young woman sat on a chair. Wearing only frilly black underwear, she cocked her head at an unnatural angle. The hangman's noose around her neck held her body upright. Claire gasped. The woman was dead. There were more photos of other victims. Jed had killed others, and he had not stuck to young girls. How many innocent lives had he snuffed out? But Claire had no time to study his mementos. She needed to survive.

"You're going to prison, Jed," she called out, trying to buy time. "This has to stop."

"It stops with you," he shouted.

Claire leaned toward the other side of the bureau and poked the baseball cap beyond the edge. Nothing happened. Either Jed was still focused on the other side or he'd learned his lesson. She repeated the action with the sunglasses. Reflected in the lenses, a shoe protruded from behind a box.

Claire didn't hesitate. She placed the Glock in her injured

hand and rolled over. Holding her hand steady on the floor, she fired three shots, then retreated, her shoulder on fire. The yelps of pain made the torture she endured worthwhile.

"That was for Gracie."

Jed swore. "Psycho…bitch!"

Claire had wanted to anger him, and she'd succeeded. There came the sound of more shuffling. Then, a footstep. And another. Jed was limping toward her. Once he rounded the bureau, Claire would be a sitting duck. She had seconds to even the odds.

She slid the glasses to the other side of the bureau. In the reflection, Jed stumbled toward her, one hand over a dark patch in his abdomen, the other holding his gun. He raised the gun, and the sunglasses shattered, the frames rocketing away.

Claire braced herself. The footsteps grew closer. A few more and he'd have a clear shot. Claire wasn't going to wait around. She slid to the floor, flat on her back, grunting at the effort and excruciating pain. Then, she aimed at the single light bulb above, closed her eyes, and fired.

At the sound of shattering glass, she rolled out from behind the bureau again, her arms extended above her head, her eyes wide open. The world spun cartwheels around her as she tumbled on the cement floor. The recording device pressed into her ribs. Jed towered over her, a black form blinded in the sudden darkness. Pain throbbing in her bloody shoulder and down her arm, Claire pumped the trigger until the magazine emptied and the firing mechanism went to lock back. Her body bumped into Lisa's corpse and halted.

Claire waited for her verdict. Guilty or innocent? Dead or alive?

Jed's knees thumped to the floor, then his body followed. Claire lay in the dark on the cold floor, listening to her ragged breathing. It was the most beautiful sound in the world.

CHAPTER 66

In the middle of the night, Emmerso walked up to the large white door of a familiar colonial house. The emergency lights of the squad cars on the street painted the tall pillars in blue and red. The chatter of police radios marred the still night air. The rain had ceased, but a new storm was brewing. His few prior visits to the home had excited and honored Emmerso. Today, his heart ached. The sooner he got this over with, the better.

He pressed the buzzer, and "Yankee Doodle" played inside the home. Dogs barked in the backyard. Emmerso had woken the residents, and he gave them time to make their way to the door. They would not get much sleep tonight. They might never sleep well again.

Emmerso had been working late at his desk Sunday when the call had come in. He was still writing his report of the day's debacles. As if the shootout at the Tucker home wasn't bad enough, the Feds had called to inform him that Claire Wolfe had stolen their Bureau car, a blue Toyota Corolla, at gunpoint. Chief Wallace would go ballistic. This was not the inter-agency cooperation Emmerso had promised.

A half hour later, his phone had rung again, the display registering a private number. If the voice of the caller had surprised him, her message had confused him. Claire Wolfe requested an ambulance and a forensics team. She provided a set of coordinates instead of an address for her location. The day's events were not over, and Emmerso's report would have to wait.

Within five minutes, he had arrived on the scene along with three patrol units. Detective Claire Wolfe sat on the front porch of the ranch house. At first, Emmerso didn't recognize her. She had cut her hair and dyed it blonde. Claire allowed the officers to cuff her before administering first aid for her gunshot wound to her shoulder. She told them about the crime scene in the basement and the box-loads of evidence for many additional murders. Then, she played her recording.

The crime scene matched her story, but Emmerso delayed judgment, deciding not to underestimate her again. He made a few calls. Dana Wood, rain-soaked and terrified but alive and whole, had dialed 911 from a gas station two miles away. Patrol sent a cruiser to pick her up. The girl corroborated Claire's story. Only then did he remove the cuffs and apologize.

The large wooden door of the colonial opened. Police Chief Harry Wallace stood in a white bathrobe over gray pajamas and squinted at his subordinate. "Do you know what time it is?"

"Yes, sir."

"This had better be good."

"I'm afraid it's bad, sir. Very bad."

The chief looked at the squad cars outside and seemed to sense that his house of cards had collapsed. Emmerso had asked the officers to wait on the street curb. For the next few minutes, Wallace was still the chief of police—*and* his boss.

Emmerso had spent the past four hours reviewing the evidence and consulting with both Internal Affairs and the FBI.

He had woken Dennis Lewis, the district attorney. All had agreed that because of the delicacy of the matter and the very clear evidence of wrongdoing, they would have to act immediately. Incontrovertible was the word the DA had used. He loved his long words.

Emmerso and Lewis had conferenced Judge Andy Weiss into their call and requested a telephone warrant. They had decided against telling the chief of his son's death right away. The combined blows of losing his place in society, his freedom, and his only son might push him over the edge.

"Is this about Jed?" Chief Wallace asked.

"Among other things. We'll escort you to the station. That's all I can say for now."

Wallace rubbed his nose but didn't put up a fight. "May I... pack a few things?"

Emmerso sent Officer Hernandez inside to make sure the chief didn't destroy evidence or take his own life. They did not use the cuffs.

At the station, Wallace denied none of the allegations. When he heard of Jed's death, his bulldog cheeks trembled, and his eyes moistened. Learning of the many other murders documented in the ranch house basement, he shook his head, and his eyes glazed over.

"I never believed he killed that girl," he told Emmerso, his voice unusually soft and defeated. "Never imagined he was capable of this."

Emmerso fixed him a cup of coffee and allowed him as many calls as he liked. At least he'd been able to afford the broken man some privacy in these difficult moments.

Despite the harsh treatment his boss had piled on him, Emmerso took no pleasure in delivering the tidings. He was just doing his job. It wasn't his fault.

CHAPTER 67

While Tom packed his suitcase late Tuesday morning, Rob sat on his motel bed, fully dressed but unable to face the day. Images of the basement crime scene stuck in his mind.

He and Tom had arrived late at the ranch house on Sunday night. Seeing as Claire had stolen the Bureau car, they had hitched a ride with a Newburgh Patrol squad car.

Rob had rushed to the ambulance as a paramedic wheeled Claire inside. Blood reddened the bandage on her shoulder, and she had an IV attached to her arm.

"Are you OK?"

"I will be. Sorry about the car."

"Forget about it." Later, he learned of the damage to the Toyota's taillights.

She gave him a weak smile, and her eyelids drooped.

"You need to rest," he said. "We'll catch up later."

"In the glove compartment," she whispered.

"What?"

"The tracker."

As the paramedic closed the ambulance door, Rob digested

Claire's words. The tracker Rob had planted on Jed's car would have raised the uncomfortable question of why an FBI agent had tracked a Newburgh PD homicide detective. Despite her injuries, Claire had located the tracker and moved the incriminating evidence to the glove compartment of the Bureau car before the police had arrived at the scene. Claire had saved his skin.

In the basement, forensic techs processed the two dead bodies, while Captain Emmerso called the shots. One victim had been Claire's partner and the lead detective on the case.

Detectives Mahoney and Nakamura filled in the FBI agents on the details. Jed had killed the woman, Lisa Evans. The middle school teacher had taught both Grace Miles and Amy Collins. Claire had walked in on Jed after the murder, freed Dana Wood, and recorded his confession before killing him in self-defense. She had survived the shootout with a gunshot wound to the shoulder. Jed had confessed to being alone with Tina at the time of her murder and to tampering with evidence to incriminate Claire.

Claire had done it. Not only had she cleared her name and saved Dana Wood's life, but she'd also uncovered a trove of evidence—photographs and other souvenirs—linking Jed and his accomplice to many other murders. But when Mahoney reviewed the timeline of the evening's events, Rob's gut tightened.

"How did she know Jed was here?" Rob asked Mahoney, raising the one question that might link him to the crime scene.

"She followed his car."

"Oh."

"Yeah, I know. The entire department was searching for her, and she was shadowing the lead detective. She's got grit."

"That she has."

Claire had covered for him again. It was a small white lie,

considering the enormity of what had transpired. But the ease with which she'd brushed over that inconvenient fact and moved the tracker gave him pause. What other inconvenient facts had she brushed over? The more he thought about the case, the tighter his guts twisted.

"You should pack." Tom's voice roused Rob from his reverie. "Our flight leaves at one PM. We'll head for the airport from the station."

"Or we could stay. There's a pile of evidence for more serial murders in that basement. The BAU will want us to stay on."

Tom zipped his suitcase shut. "That's Chief Alda's decision to make after we present our report. For now, we're done here."

Tom was right, of course. The unit chief would decide their next priority now that the current case had concluded. But was their work done here?

Tom sighed. "Go on, Rob, spit it out. What's eating you?"

Rob glanced at his partner. "A serial killer couple?"

Tom shrugged. "One serial killer and one sidekick. Many killers have accomplices. We get to go home, and Dr. Fleischer gets to write another book. Her unsub profile was right on the nose. Everybody's happy."

"And Jed just happened to start killing more fourteen-year-old girls the moment Claire came back to town?"

Tom gave that detail more thought. "His daddy was chief of police. Maybe he knew Claire was coming. This was his big opportunity to close Tina's case and frame Claire."

Rob's smile turned sour. "Claire implied that Jed might have killed O'Leary to keep him silent, but he denied it."

"He denied everything, Rob. Some killers deny their crimes to the bitter end. But, you're right. O'Leary probably died of natural causes. So what?"

"I don't know. Something doesn't feel right."

"Come on, Rob. You know how it is. Reality is messy. There are always loose ends."

"Yeah, I guess so." Rob remembered something. "In the recording, Jed said Claire had texted him the coordinates of the ranch house. He denied knowing about the place before that."

"Rob, you've got to stop believing every word he said."

"Did they find his phone at the crime scene? That claim should be easy to disprove."

"The phone was smashed to pieces."

Jed had thrown the phone at Claire to distract her. The phone could have broken on impact. Or Claire could have destroyed the phone after she'd killed Jed.

"Don't beat yourself up over it," Tom added. "Plenty of online services allow you to send text messages and choose the sender number. Jed could have sent it to himself to cover his tracks."

"If somehow he knew she was coming after him."

"Maybe he saw her following him?"

Only she hadn't followed him. She had followed the tracker Rob had planted on Jed's car. But only Rob and Claire knew that.

"What about the shooter?" Rob asked. "Somebody fired at the SWAT sniper opposite Tucker's house. Was that Jed Wallace, too?"

"Must have been. He could have slipped away and taken the shot from behind the home. With the right rifle, a .22 can do the distance. He wanted to kill both Wolfe and Tucker, and the firefight he started almost succeeded."

Rob nodded. That would explain the bullet's trajectory and Detective Wallace's sudden disappearance before the shooting began.

"Like I said," Tom concluded, "the real world is messy."

Rob turned the facts over in his head. Tom was right. Dr.

Fleischer's serial killer profile matched Jed Wallace with uncanny precision. And yet, a few days ago, the killings had resembled the work of an assassin or a split-personality killer.

Jed had confessed at gunpoint, placing himself at the scene of Tina's murder. But being there didn't prove he had killed her.

Claire was highly intelligent. She matched most of the other profile specifications. And as he'd seen, she could be cunning and devious. What if Claire had known about Jed's meeting with Tina from the start? Could Claire have killed those poor girls only to reopen Tina's homicide case and frame Jed for all three murders?

Rob shook the crazy thought from his head. Who's the conspiracy theorist now? Having a gun pointed at your head sure changes your opinion of a person. But Claire wasn't just his colleague. She meant much more to him. And this shadow of a doubt was eating him up.

"I'm staying."

"I'm getting tired of covering for you."

"You don't have to. I'll take a few vacation days. See the sights."

Tom scoffed. "Yeah, right. Newburgh is a major tourist destination."

Rob shrugged off his partner's sarcasm. He couldn't leave. Not yet. He had to know for sure.

CHAPTER 68

The squad room fell silent when Claire walked in early Tuesday afternoon. Mahoney and Nakamura looked up from their desks. A knot of patrol officers stopped their conversations. All eyes focused on her. Had they been expecting her? She stood there in plain clothes, her arm in a sling, and tried to divine their mood from their expressions.

Yesterday, she had killed their long-time colleague and incriminated his father, the chief of police. Police officers were notorious for closing ranks in the face of external threats. Did they see her as a traitor?

Mahoney stood, his face grim. Then, he clapped slowly. Clap. Clap. Clap. Nakamura stood, too, and joined in the applause. One by one, the other officers added their hands to the chorus. Dirty cops gave the force a bad name, and she had rooted out two in one day. On second thought, their initial silence had a simpler explanation. The last time she'd set foot in the squad room, her hair had been black.

Mahoney walked over and offered her his hand. Claire responded with her left. Handshakes would take time as well. At the sound of the commotion, more officers poured into the room, and soon a crowd of well-wishers huddled around her. Claire searched for Rob but found neither him, Tom, nor Dr. Fleischer. Had they returned to Quantico without saying goodbye? At the ranch house, Rob had said they'd catch up later, but he hadn't shown up at the hospital yesterday or at her home. Where was he?

"When are you getting back to work?" Nakamura asked.

"I'm not sure. I got lucky, the bullet passed right through, but it's going to take some time until I can get back in the saddle. Don't ask how long it took me to get dressed this morning."

Mahoney beamed at her. "Well, if you need help getting dressed, I'm happy to lend a hand."

Nakamura swatted him over the head. "Get back to work, you pervert."

Claire laughed. Life in the department had moved on. Both of her standard-issue guns were in evidence lockers, and the Internal Affairs investigators were busy dissecting bigger fish, thanks to her. It would take many long months until she'd hit the streets again. That was just as well. She needed some downtime to heal and to think about what came next.

Captain Emmerso emerged from his office with a brown paper bag in hand. "Welcome home, Detective. I'm glad you made it."

The captain had asked her to come in today to show her face, and she suspected he wanted to say a few words for closure. After all, they had lost a detective and their chief. There would be a lot of changes at Newburgh PD. Claire hated being in the limelight, but she agreed to a brief visit anyway. The prospect of seeing Rob again gave her an extra incentive.

Captain Emmerso raised his voice. "Everybody, listen up! In our line of work, we see more than our share of death and misery. It's always comforting when we save an innocent life.

Two days ago, Detective Wolfe did just that. She saved Dana Wood's life, at great personal risk. She also discovered a sizeable amount of evidence on several other homicides. So you can thank her for the overtime you'll be doing, too."

The captain waited for the laughter to subside, then he drew a deep, tremulous breath. Claire had been right about him. Emmerso was a good man.

"Detective Wolfe—Claire—on behalf of our bureau and the department, thank you for your service. I also feel the need to apologize. To be doubted by your fellow officers is a terrible thing. For whatever reason, we didn't believe in you when we should have. I'm sorry we weren't there for you when you needed us. Now for the part you all came for." He pulled a bottle of scotch from the paper bag. "Detective Mahoney, you can do the honors. I think you know your way around one of these."

Nakamura smirked. "He sure does. But he has trouble finding his way back out."

The officers chuckled and doled out plastic shot glasses.

Captain Emmerso raised his glass. "To Detective Wolfe. We look forward to having you back on duty as soon as you're ready."

The officers cheered and emptied their shot glasses. Claire raised hers but didn't drink. She stared at Jed's empty desk. Barely two weeks ago, Jed had welcomed her to the department. He'd made her coffee. Now she'd put him in the morgue and sent his father to jail. All the time they had investigated the murders together, Claire had never suspected him of any wrongdoing. Maybe her intuition wasn't as reliable as she had thought?

"I almost forgot," Captain Emmerso said. "We got you something. Deborah?"

A uniformed black officer approached with a bouquet of pink roses. Claire accepted the flowers, and her eyes moistened.

"Speech," Nakamura said.

The others joined his chant. *Speech! Speech! Speech!*

Claire raised the flowers in defeat. "You'll need a lot more whisky to get a speech out of me." Her comment won her a few chuckles. Then, the expectant silence sucked at her mind. Did she want to get something off her chest? Jed had been her partner. Claire had killed him in self-defense, but she'd still have to live with his death. Then again, he was a killer. He'd murdered Claire's sister and got what he deserved. Claire could never see past that. No, she would not mention his name.

"Let's leave it at 'thanks' and call it even."

Mahoney raised his glass, which had magically refilled. "I'll drink to that!"

"OK, everybody," Captain Emmerso said. "Back to work. Detective Wolfe," he added. "In my office."

Claire rested the flowers on her desk, followed her boss to his room, and closed the door behind her. Captain Emmerso perched on the edge of his desk.

"How are you holding up?"

Claire considered the question. Suddenly, the idea of returning to work unnerved her. Nightmares had woken her in the middle of the night, returning her to that basement and the terror of imminent death. And now that she'd found Tina's killer, Claire was no longer sure she belonged in the world of law enforcement. But that was a lot to unload on her boss.

"I'll be OK."

"Let me know if you need anything?"

"Yes, sir."

"The court proceedings will take months. By then, I hope the dust will settle and we'll get back to normal. Well, a new normal. Recent events have left a vacuum in the department, but they also created opportunities." He eyed her meaningfully.

She knew what he was hinting at. The department needed a new chief and another detective. Depending on how the positions shifted, the department's new heroine might be up for promotion. Her stomach cramped at the thought.

Captain Emmerso seemed to sense her discomfort. "Don't think about that now. Rest up, heal. Take your time. You deserve it."

"Thank you, sir."

She let herself out.

A vacuum. That described the feeling inside her perfectly. Rob stood by her desk, studying the flowers. Her spirits lifted.

"Agent Cline, I was beginning to think you'd left town without saying goodbye."

Rob looked her up and down, his eyes lingering on the white sling. "I thought I'd stop by on my way and say goodbye. Our flight leaves in a few hours."

The surge of optimism ebbed. Rob was leaving. Would he stay in touch, or had their ordeal damaged their relationship beyond healing?

"You kept the hair," Rob said.

Claire touched her head self-consciously. "It's hard to wash out, especially with one arm."

He shoved his hands in his pockets. "You look good."

"Thanks." An awkward silence developed between them. "I...wanted to apologize," she said.

He raised his eyebrows.

"About the taillights. I hope the FBI won't dock your salary."

"Forget about it. Tom signed for the car, anyway."

She laughed. "And I wanted to apologize for pulling a gun on you."

He grinned, but a stiffness had crept into his movements, and he avoided her eyes.

Claire would have to work hard to fix that. She pushed her luck. "Do you still think I should apply at the FBI?"

"Do you want that?"

Her confidence faltered. *Did she?* Her facade collapsed. "I don't know what I want anymore."

Right now, she wanted him to hold her, to feel his body against hers, and to hell with what the other officers thought. She needed him to say he loved her and that everything would be all right.

Rob stepped forward and hugged her. She closed her eyes and inhaled his scent. But his body was rigid, his arms wooden—the friendly embrace of two colleagues who had shared a brief, intense working experience and were now parting ways. A tear formed in the corner of her eye. She had lost him. Who should she blame? Jed? Tina? Fate?

He stepped away. "I should go."

She sniffed but did not cry. His last memory of her would not be of tears. "Have a good flight. Say hi to the others for me."

He nodded and walked away, out of the squad room and out of her life.

Claire should get going, too. She had a lot to think about and a lot of television to binge-watch. But before she became a couch potato, she had to make one last stop. Claire had fantasized about this visit for twelve years, and now she'd make that dream come true.

CHAPTER 69

Butterflies stirred in Claire's belly as she drove to her parents' home in her rental car. For the first time in twelve years, the thought of facing her mother did not fill her with dread. On the contrary, she was looking forward to delivering the good news. Claire had found Tina's killer. He had paid the ultimate price for his crimes. Her sister's spirit would finally find rest. Claire and her parents would start a new chapter in the Wolfe family story.

Driving with an injured shoulder was more difficult than she had expected. She turned the wheel with her left hand and winced every time she glanced over her shoulder. The side mirrors were her friends. She parked on the curb and composed herself for the encounter.

Claire got out of the car, walked up the short path, and found the front door ajar. She froze, her police training priming her for action. Had someone broken in? Claire reached for her gun, then winced. The movement brought both physical pain and the frustrating realization that she had no service weapon. She would call for backup, but she had yet to buy a new phone. The door drifted open at her touch.

"Mom?" she called. "Dad?"

Her voice would spook petty thieves and send them running. Hearing nothing, she stepped inside. The TV was off. Mom wasn't on the La-Z-Boy. Had her parents gone out and forgotten to lock the door? That kind of forgetfulness seemed to run in the family. Yes, that explained it. Claire exhaled a relieved breath and closed the door behind her. She had panicked over nothing.

In the kitchen, she opened the fridge, hoping to find a drink. They were out of beer. Her mother must have drunk them dry. Claire still had one good arm. She'd fetch a six-pack from the basement. The idea of helping around the house and restocking the fridge felt therapeutic, a sign she had rejoined the family for good.

Claire opened the door beneath the staircase, flipped on the light switch, and trudged down the basement steps. Once a jumble of boxes and discarded furniture, the cement floor below was spotless and uncluttered. Her dad had cleaned the place out since the last time Claire had ventured there. That explained all the junk she'd found upstairs in her old bedroom. Strangely, the basement looked much smaller than she remembered. That made sense. Last time, she'd been a teenager.

Instead of mothballs, the air smelled of disinfectant and order. Rows of raised steel-edged storage shelves lined one wall. In the central void sat a small square table with a red disposable tablecloth, a sealed bottle of champagne, and two polished wine glasses. A white gift box tied with a red ribbon claimed the center of the small, square table between the two foldable chairs.

Claire grinned. For the second time that morning, tears formed in her eyes. This gift was for her. Her father must have seen the news on television and planned a private celebration.

Little did he know, the homicide case had also solved Tina's murder. But why had he chosen the basement, of all places? Had he wanted to surprise her or did he want to keep her mother from emptying the champagne bottle on her own?

Claire chuckled at the thought. After hearing the news, maybe Mom would finally sober up. She still had a few decades left in her. Claire would help her clean up her act and get back on her feet.

Claire was halfway down the stairs when she realized they'd need a third chair for her mom. She climbed back upstairs when a scratching sound came from below.

She stopped and listened. There it was again, the soft scurrying of tiny legs. Did they have a rat problem?

Claire descended quietly, step by step. The sounds came from the shelves, from one of three storage boxes. Claire drew near. If a rat had fallen into the box, Claire could evict the pest easily.

The scratching continued. She peered through a horizontal slat cut along the side of the box. Something moved within. Thin, silken lines glittered inside the box, catching the light from the ceiling lamp. Dark misshapen blobs hung from the lines, the shells of flies entombed in the web, their bodies sucked dry.

A thick hairy leg crossed the opening of the slat, startling Claire. Then, another insect leg crossed the window, and a third. The legs led to a dark swollen abdomen. Claire stood rooted in place and stared at the largest spider she had ever seen. "Watch out for the spiders," her mother had said, but Claire had not believed her. The immense arachnid before her seemed to glow in the lamplight, a luminous pink.

"Claire."

She spun around. Her father stood at the top of the staircase.

"Geez, Dad, you scared me." Her heart galloped.

He spread his arms and smiled. "Surprise!"

He closed the basement door behind him and descended the steps. Claire chuckled, forgetting the spiders.

His face bunched with concern. "You're hurt."

Claire wiggled her injured arm but did not wince at the pain that shot through her shoulder. "What, this? Just a scratch. I'll be as good as new in no time."

He stepped closer and touched the sling on her arm. "You took a bullet?"

There was no point in denying it. "A clean shot. No surgery needed. Another story for the grandkids." She glanced at the set table. "You heard the news?"

Her dad smiled. "The papers mentioned you by name."

"My stalker never tires. Where's Mom?"

"Resting. Her meds knocked her out. It's just the two of us."

"Oh." Claire tried not to look disappointed. Not serious. She'd share the news with her mother later.

Dad lifted the champagne bottle and picked at the silver wrapping over the cork. "Have they promoted you yet? I hear they need a new chief of police."

Claire laughed. "My captain hinted at some possibilities. But I'm pretty sure I'm not a candidate for top cop."

"Not yet." With a loud pop, the cork hit the ceiling and bounced on the floor. He filled two glasses and handed one to Claire. "To Newburgh's best detective."

Their glasses clinked, and they sipped the sweet, bubbly wine.

He smacked his lips. "Harry Wallace had it coming. Just like O'Leary."

Claire's smile faltered. His mention of the officers' names rattled her. Then, she remembered. O'Leary had investigated Tina's death. He had updated Claire's parents on the investigation's progress. That's how her father had met Harry Wallace.

Her dad must have read about O'Leary's death in the papers, too.

"Great job, Cub."

The champagne bubbled into her bloodstream, making her pleasantly tipsy. Claire hadn't eaten yet. She had hoped to have lunch with her family, happily reunited after the solving of Tina's murder.

"Dad." She put her glass down on the table beside the gift box. "This wasn't just another case. The man who killed those girls also killed Tina. I closed Tina's case. The man responsible for her death is dead. Jed Wallace, Chief Wallace's son."

Her father's eyes glistened with pride.

"Did you kill him?"

The question unsettled her, returning her to that fateful night in the ranch house basement. Claire nodded. Her father's chest expanded as he inhaled. The knowledge that his daughter's murderer had died for his crimes would not bring Tina back, but the fact consoled him.

"How did it feel?"

She gave her dad a quizzical glance. What a strange question. Claire had not wanted to kill Jed. He had given her no choice. Afterward, standing over his dead body, she had tasted that primal, animal exhilaration of having defeated a mortal enemy. There she stood, while his blood spread in a dark pool on the floor. That killer instinct had both excited and shamed her.

Claire avoided her father's eyes. "Mixed feelings, I guess."

His lips trembled. "You always remember the first time."

What had gotten into him? Had her father read that line in a detective novel? Firefights with villains seemed glorious in crime fiction, but the reality was far more disturbing. Claire would have to live with what she had done. Years from now, she'd still analyze each moment of the gunfight, searching for something she could have done differently. If she'd aimed lower, Jed might await trial instead of burial. Had she secretly wanted him to attack her and force her hand? Claire needed a change of subject.

"What's in the box?"

"A gift to celebrate your achievement."

"May I?"

"That's what it's there for."

Claire claimed the box. It was light for its size. She gave it a shake. Something shifted within. A gift card? She untied the ribbon and removed the lid.

The box contained a short lock of blonde hair, tied at either end with elastic bands. The hairs on the back of her neck prickled, and the floor seemed to fall away beneath her feet. But her conscious mind refused to register her deduction.

"I don't understand."

"This belongs to you now, Cub. You deserve it."

"Dad, what is this?" Her voice contained an urgent demand. *Tell me I've misunderstood. That isn't a killer's trophy. Tell me that isn't Tina's hair!*

"You've always been one step ahead," he said. "It took me much longer to understand what I am—what *we* are. You knew right from the start."

"Dad—"

"It's OK, Cub. It's just you and me here. You can be yourself. We're the same. We're a pack." He chuckled, his voice ringing with wonder. "Your mother was right. Tina was hers, but you, Claire, you are mine."

He stepped closer, his hands gripping her upper arms. She wanted him to stop, to take back the words, but he kept on talking.

"Even as a teenager, you knew what needed to be done."

Twelve years of guilt and pain bubbled to the surface and burst from Claire's mouth. "I didn't kill Tina."

"I know, Cub. But you wanted to. You tried to."

Claire remembered the knife stuck in Tina's leg, the blood spreading over the kitchen floor. Her mother had told him. She had told him Claire had tried to kill Tina. But instead of horrifying him, the story had pleased him. He'd misunderstood. Claire hadn't tried to kill her sister. Claire wasn't the girl he thought she was. And now her legs turned to jelly, as the repressed deduction rose in her mind in all its terrible detail.

"Jed didn't kill Tina," she muttered.

Her father shook his head, slowly.

Claire grasped at straws. "Lisa Evans, the teacher—she killed her!"

"Lisa is new to the pack."

The pack. A gang of bloodthirsty wolves prowled the streets of Newburgh. But how did he know this, and what was his connection to that deadly pack?

He continued. "Lisa killed the last two and captured the third once we understood what was needed."

"What was needed?" Claire stepped backward but could not escape his powerful grip. She clung to the idea of the father she had known and loved, refusing to believe he'd played a role in the murders. "How could Karla and Amy need to die? Why would Lisa need to kidnap Dana?"

"Why?" His voice was tender. His eyes glimmered with love and admiration. "For you, Cub. Because you told me to."

CHAPTER 70

Blood pulsed in Claire's ears. Her father's hands clamped harder onto her upper arms. The basement air was hot and stifling. She couldn't breathe. *This can't be true!* Claire hadn't ordered the kidnapping and murder of those girls. Had she?

"We kept Dana Wood right here in this basement." Her father sounded nostalgic.

Claire shuddered. Newburgh PD had searched the city for Dana frantically, when all along, the girl had been in this basement beneath Claire's childhood home. And somehow, it was all her fault. Was Dr. Fleischer right—had a murderous split personality taken over Claire's life?

"Dad," she pleaded. "Why would you think I wanted that?"

"I'll show you."

He released a hand from her arm to retrieve an open shoebox from a shelf. Claire didn't want to look. Once she found proof of her murderous self, her life would be over. But she couldn't resist her desire for the truth.

The box contained two everyday objects: a red high-heeled

shoe—Dana Wood's missing pump—and a folded sheet of yellow paper.

"Go on. Read it."

Claire reached into the box, unfolded the note, and the room spun around her. The page contained two words written in Claire's handwriting. Karla Smith.

Claire had jotted down the girl's name the night she had visited her parents. But the note in her hands was not the page she had written in her parents' kitchen. The two words were yellow indentations in a dark sea of pencil shadings. This sheet of paper was the page directly underneath the one Claire had torn from the notepad.

"Indented writing," her father said. "It's an old forensic technique. I'm a slow learner but steady. When I saw you'd used the notepad, I knew you'd left me a message."

The page trembled in Claire's fingers. There had been a terrible misunderstanding. Her father had reconstructed the writing from her note and interpreted the name as a call to murder. But why?

"I found your other messages, too, Cub. When you left for the police academy, I read the books you left me. Police procedure. Crime scene investigation. You were right. People like us must always be one step ahead of the law. That's why you became a cop. That's why you applied to join Newburgh PD years ago."

Her detective's mind snagged on that detail. "How did you know I'd applied at Newburgh PD?"

Her father grinned. "The way I knew everything else that went on inside the department. Lieutenant Brian O'Leary."

"Why would O'Leary tell you that?"

Her father scoffed. "Once he'd covered up Tina's murder, he was vulnerable. I told him I knew what he'd done, and I leveraged the crap out of him. We developed a mutually beneficial relationship. Tina's was the first case he buried, but not the last."

Claire had known O'Leary was dirty. She'd known he'd covered up Jed's role in Tina's death. But she'd had no idea O'Leary's tampering with evidence had extended beyond Tina's case.

The roots of Claire's hair tingled. "The ranch house. The souvenirs from other murders."

Her father's crooked grin confirmed her suspicions. "In his old age, O'Leary grew a conscience. During one of his drunken rages, he called me and threatened to talk. He didn't know who he was dealing with."

"Lisa killed O'Leary, too?"

"There was no need. The booze took care of him. And just in time. He'd figured out what we would do after his retirement. You would join Newburgh PD, and another girl would die. Her death would match Tina's closely. Newburgh's homicide detectives would look for a serial killer, and a serial killer they would find. Jed Wallace would go down for both murders. And the town's savior would be Detective Claire Wolfe. With you rising through the ranks of Newburgh's finest, the pack would be unstoppable. The city would be ours."

Claire tasted vomit in her throat. The yellow page dropped from her fingers. She hadn't called for murder. She had no evil inner self. And the man before her wasn't her father. She had never truly known this man at all.

"We had thought to stop with Grace Miles. Arranging that was risky enough. But your note inspired me to go further. You knew best, being inside the investigation. The Wallaces wanted to keep Tina's case buried. They tried to pin this murder on the girl's father. A second dead girl would force them to consider serial murder and widen the scope of the investigation. You were right."

He tossed the box back on the shelf.

"Even so, I didn't go far enough. To gain the most from the murders, we needed more eyeballs on the investigation. Dead girls are one thing, but a kidnapped girl is solid gold. Imagine the fear and outrage. Imagine the media coverage and the glory you'd reap when you swooped in to save the day. Your star would rise faster."

Claire could not believe what she was hearing. Her voice trembled as she spoke. "You killed those girls and kidnapped Dana...to further my career?"

"Don't be modest, Cub. The idea was yours. That day I stopped by the station, you introduced me to the Fed from hostage negotiation. You showed me the names on the white-board. I may be a slow learner, but I'm not blind. And this isn't just about your career, Cub. This is about the pack. The pack always comes first."

A fiery streak of anger broke through Claire's terror. This man had killed the idea of her father, the only island of warmth and comfort in her cold, miserable childhood. He patted himself on the back for murdering young girls while spreading the blame to her. Claire wanted no part in his criminal pack.

"The pack comes first? The way Lisa Evans came first?"

His jaw clenched at the criticism.

"Lisa dug her own grave. Her job was to deliver the girls and get out of the way."

Claire's detective mind filled in the blanks. "The girls knew her from school. They trusted her enough to get in her car."

He nodded. "After the first two girls, Lisa acted out. Against my instructions, she got involved with Jed Wallace to get inside information on the investigation. Lisa was jealous of you. She wanted to show she could take your place in the pack. And she was reckless. She shot the Collins girl in her bedroom—while you were in the house. Her sloppiness almost ruined everything. The investigation turned against you, forcing you to go underground. Jed Wallace came by the house looking for you. The idiot had no idea Dana was here, right under his feet. I couldn't let him frame you for the murders. I wouldn't let him hunt you down like a dog."

"The sniper," Claire said. "You shot at the SWAT sniper."

Bill Wolfe smiled. "The pack takes care of its own. A police radio scanner gave away your location. I had to improvise. The shot was a diversion to draw attention away from the house and allow you to escape."

"Your *diversion* got an innocent woman killed!"

The appalling fact seemed to amuse him. "It helped you escape, didn't it? But next time, we might not be so lucky. The game had to end. I moved the girl to the ranch house and set a trap for Jed Wallace."

A dark crevasse seemed to open beneath Claire's feet. "You texted him from my number. You sent him to the ranch house." Claire reeled at the realization. Jed hadn't lied. He had threatened Kitty to silence her, but he had never intended to murder her. To the end, Jed had believed that Claire had killed Tina.

"He had you in his sights, Cub. I had to stop him. And Lisa had to clean up the mess she'd made. I gave her a fighting chance. If she killed Jed, good. The scene would show that the girl had broken free and shot Jed, her captor. Sadly, the girl would die, too, and Jed would take the fall for all the murders. But if Jed killed Lisa, well, sometimes a wolf dies to save the pack. And with the killer in hand, nobody would blame you."

"But they'd still charge me with Tina's murder. Jed forged a document, making me the last to see her alive. And your diversion killed the only person who could contradict him."

That revelation left him wordless for a moment. "I didn't know that, Cub. It doesn't matter. I didn't know you'd show up at the ranch house either. But you did, Claire, and you saved the day. You rescued the girl and got rid of Jed forever—a resolution even better than the one I had intended."

Claire swallowed hard. She had killed Jed thinking she was defending herself from Tina's murderer. But Jed had thought the same about her.

"Jed said I killed Tina. He thought Lisa was *my* accomplice."

Did her father think Claire had killed Tina, too? Was that what had driven him to murder the others—to protect her?

Her father laughed. "Those idiots were so obsessed with covering Jed's tracks, they never figured out who killed Tina."

"I'm not a killer." Her voice was small and weak.

"You are now."

"I shot Jed in self-defense. I never wanted to kill him. I would never hurt Tina."

Her father's knowing smile chilled her to the bone.

"Don't deny it, Cub. You wanted Tina dead. She was choking you like a weed, blocking out the light. You tried to kill her once before, but you were too young to follow through. So, I acted for you."

"*No.*"

Claire sobbed. She wanted him to stop. His words stabbed her through her heart. Diane had told him about that day in the kitchen. He, too, believed Claire had tried to murder Tina. But that was Tina's sick prank!

"I knew exactly how you felt, Cub. Tina was her mother's daughter. Diane blamed me for ruining her life. Her failures were all my fault. She made every waking moment a misery. Eventually, I'd had enough. But she didn't deserve a quick death. She needed to suffer as she had made me suffer. So, I took away the one thing she treasured most."

Tears formed in her father's eyes, not tears of sorrow but of joy.

"Diane had worked so hard for that birthday party. Tina

was her baby. She'd wanted everything to be perfect. And it was perfect."

His lips trembled as he relived the memory of that day.

"I saw Tina's school from the car, saw Jed follow her. Tina, the little whore, was giving it away, just like her mother. But I had wanted to get Tina alone. The boy had messed up my plan. I was about to give up and go home when he bolted from the woods like a bat out of Hell. I couldn't believe my luck. Jed had set up the perfect murder. I found Tina in the clearing. The smug little slut was smiling to herself. How she jumped when she saw me!"

He imitated her teenage voice.

"'He tried to rape me, Daddy!' She was lying to my face. I wrapped my hands around her throat and squeezed. The look on her face while the life drained from her was priceless. The little bitch hadn't seen that coming. Afterward, I panicked. I hadn't planned how to dispose of her body. Tina stared up at me with her mother's eyes, taunting me. I heard Diane's voice in my head. 'You can't even do this right!' So, I grabbed a broken branch and wiped her face away."

He stretched his neck, and the vertebra clicked.

"I killed two birds with one stone that day. Diane got what she deserved, and you, finally, could flourish. Diane fell apart, as expected, and I had a front-row seat. Her pain didn't fade with time. It worsened every day. Tina's death was the gift that kept on giving."

He looked Claire squarely in the eyes, content. "We've won, Cub. Nothing can stand in our way."

Claire shrank from him. "There is no 'we'. I am not like you."

He stared at her, suddenly aware that Claire had not warmed to his tales of murder.

"But you left me the books. You transferred to Newburgh.

You came home and left me that note. You told me you'd learned my secrets, Cub, and that you'd come back to close Tina's case."

"To bring her killer to justice. Not to cover up her murder with others!"

The warmth in his eyes flickered out. He sized her up, a predator tasting a scent in the wind. Was she a member of the pack or lunch?

"Don't be afraid, Cub. You don't have to pretend anymore. You're with the pack now. Nothing can stop us. Soon, this city will be ours. I have plans—big plans..."

Claire shook her head. Warning lights flared in her mind. *Tell him what he wants to hear!* Claire was alone in the basement with a murderer. Unarmed, injured, and with her heart breaking, she was too weak to fight. *Say anything so you can get away and call for help.* But the haunted child inside her needed him to know the truth. Tina's death was not her fault!

"No, Dad," she said through the tears. "You got it wrong. Tina was the evil one, not me. I never tried to kill her. She stabbed herself to make me look bad. I wanted none of this. Those clues and messages are all in your head. You've got the wrong girl."

His hands tightened on her arms. "No, Cub. In your heart, you wanted her dead!"

"Maybe I thought that, Dad, but I never meant it. Losing her wrecked my life. I wish she'd never died."

"Enough!"

Her father's brow knotted while he processed her words and considered his options. He'd killed Tina. Twelve years later, he'd killed Gracie, too. God only knew how many others he'd murdered in between. But was he capable of killing his favorite daughter?

He gripped her arms, and pain flared in her shoulder again.

He'd decided. He stared right through her. Claire recognized that look—the thousand-yard stare of a murderer on the edge of the abyss.

Claire had to get out of there. She might be younger and fitter, but in her current state, she was no match for him. And this man was her father. Every cell in her body revolted against hurting him. If a drop of fatherly love remained in his sick, sick heart, maybe he'd spare her life?

"I won't tell anyone," she lied. "Whatever you've done, you're still my father. We never had this conversation."

Slowly, he shook his head. "There's too much at stake."

He squeezed her shoulders, and she winced. Tears trickled from her eyes.

"Dad, please, no!"

"I'm sorry, Cub."

He spun her and wrapped his arm around her neck. Claire couldn't breathe. His bicep pressed against her carotid artery, cutting off the flow of blood to her brain. Within seconds, she would lose consciousness. He was killing her. Her father was strangling her in the basement of her childhood home. The betrayal stung. The lack of air triggered her fight responses.

Claire had trained in hand-to-hand combat. She had battled criminals in the streets and shot down attackers. Claire would not die like a sheep.

She swung her elbow into his belly, and his grip loosened. Claire leaped sideways, breaking free, and raced for the exit. Her shoes pounded the steps as she climbed toward the basement door. A hand caught her foot, and the steps disappeared from underneath her. She landed heavily on her injured shoulder. White spots of pain exploded before her eyes. She rolled on the floor, gasping, her head reeling.

Claire tried to get up, but cruel hands shoved her downward, and she sprawled on the cement floor. Knees pressed into her back, pinning her down. A thin, hard cord tightened around her neck and yanked her head backward. Again, Claire couldn't draw breath. Her pulse throbbed in her throat. She clawed at the rope, but her fingers could not grasp the thin ligature.

"This is breaking my heart, Claire."

She kicked back with her feet. Her heel jabbed his body, knocking him off-balance, but the blow didn't break his death brace. His breath blew hot on the nape of her neck.

"I didn't want you to die like this."

Oh, I won't. She kicked off her pump, launching it forward. Her fingers scrambled over the smooth floor and closed over the shoe. Then, she slammed her good hand backward, aiming the heel at his face. He groaned and reeled back. But his heavy bulk remained on top of her. He pulled so hard on the rope that blood droplets prickled on the skin of her neck.

Claire's muscles cried out for oxygen. She thought of Tina, of Gracie, and Karla. Claire had found their killer but stumbled into his web. She had failed them. She had failed Jed, too. And soon, she would join them.

"No!" her mind cried. "This can't be the end!" But her lungs burned, and her limbs became heavy. The edges of her vision frosted over.

The basement steps towered above her. She had climbed those steps a thousand times but she would never climb them again. The world swam around her. The sounds of her struggle and her father's effortful breathing faded.

And the heavens opened.

A light shone from above. A human shape appeared in the light, wrapped in a dazzling aura. The form reached for her. *Tina, is that you?* Was Tina greeting her in death? The figure raised its arm, and fire belched from its hand. Then, Claire was falling, and the darkness swallowed her.

CHAPTER 71

Claire woke up and immediately wished she hadn't. Her head throbbed, and her neck stung. She shifted on the bed, and a fire ignited in her shoulder. The unfamiliar room had green walls, and bright light poured from the windows. Claire shuttered her eyes and groaned. She wasn't dead. Death wouldn't hurt so much.

A machine beeped. A plastic bag hovered over her head, suspended from a metal hook. Liquid dripped into a tube that snaked over the bedsheets, ending in the bandage on her arm. She was in the hospital. What had happened to her?

She had gone to share the good news with her parents and... The beeping of the monitor sped up as she heard her father's words and the ghost of a cord tightened around her neck. He had tried to kill her. Somehow, she had escaped.

"You're awake," Rob said.

He got up from an armchair in the corner, his hair messy. Looking as though he'd just woken up, he smiled at her.

"What...?" she began, the questions tumbling out in confusion. "How...?"

He shushed her. "Easy now, just rest."

The terror returned. After what her father had told her, he'd come back to finish the job. Claire would never be safe again. She tried to sit up, the effort sending jolts of pain through her shoulder and hammers at her brain.

"I can't stay here!"

Rob sat on the edge of her bed and eased her back down. "It's OK, Claire. Take it easy."

"My father, he'll come for me—"

"He won't. You're safe now. I promise."

"You don't understand!" She reached for the needle in her arm, but Rob held her hand still. "He told me everything, he'll—"

"He's dead, Claire. I'm sorry."

She froze. Her father was dead. No, not her father. Her true father had died long ago. That father might never have existed.

"There's a guard outside."

Claire glanced at the door. Was the guard to protect her or to keep her from leaving? If her father had died, he'd taken his confession with him. Whoever had found Claire would have found Tina's hair and Dana's shoe in the basement. Would Newburgh PD charge her for her father's crimes?

"Am I under arrest?"

Rob grinned. "No, you're not under arrest. You're under observation for your injuries. But if you're into handcuffs, I can arrange for that."

He was flirting with her. The old Rob was back. She had thought she'd lost him forever. Maybe she had died and gone to Heaven, after all. But none of this made sense.

"I don't understand."

Rob sighed. "I have a confession to make."

Claire moaned. "I've heard enough confessions. They always end with somebody trying to kill me."

"Not this time." He held a small metallic disc between his

fingers. The object resembled the battery of a wristwatch. "Homing signal and miniature recording device. Another handy FBI toy." When she didn't respond, he added, "I slipped it into your jacket pocket when we said goodbye."

Claire recalled the stiff hug they had shared in the squad room.

"It's voice-activated and very sensitive," Rob continued. "It picked up your conversation with your father."

Relief washed over Claire. Then, sorrow. Her brave facade crumbled. Her chest heaved, and she sobbed uncontrollably.

"My father," she muttered. That loving father figure, who had given her hope in her darkest hours, had been an illusion. "He was a monster."

Rob squeezed her hand. "Psychopaths are experts at hiding their true nature. And from what I've heard of Tina, that apple didn't fall far from the tree."

Claire wiped her eyes. "He's all I had. I feel so...alone."

Rob stroked her hair. "You're not alone, Claire. You'll never be alone. I promise." His eyes moistened. "Please forgive me."

"Forgive you?" What had he done to hurt her? Claire searched her hazy memory for clues.

"For not believing in you. I swear to you, Claire, I will never doubt you again."

The sting of that betrayal arose in her mind. For a short time, he had thought she was a cold-blooded murderer. Could she ever trust him again? The sharp reversals of raging emotions sapped her strength. *Enough!* Claire had survived two brushes with death. *Be thankful.* She let go of all resentment.

"If you had trusted me blindly, you wouldn't have followed me. I'd be dead now. Besides, I can't blame you for that. I doubted me, too. I guess I'll have to forgive us both." Again, Claire drifted in the terrifying void. "How do I move past this?"

"You'll be fine. *We'll* be fine."

He had switched from "you" to "we." She glanced at him through fresh tears and hazarded a smile. "Does that mean you're going to stick around?"

"We have a basement full of evidence for more serial murders. That'll create a lot of work for the FBI. I'm not going anywhere."

CHAPTER 72

Dressed in her running clothes on a Saturday morning, Claire put her hands on her hips and surveyed her handiwork in the entrance hall of her childhood home with pride. She never imagined she'd ever do this. The move was painful but necessary, and she'd made peace with her decision.

"Where do you want these?" Rob asked. He had just walked in carrying two suitcases, which contained all of Claire's worldly belongings. Claire had shed the sling, but her shoulder was still tender. She was in no shape for heavy lifting, and Rob had offered to help.

"Bedroom."

He nodded and trudged up the stairs. They had spent the earlier part of the morning clearing out the two children's bedrooms. Now a dozen brown packing boxes crowded the hall and awaited interment.

"Morning," Rob said upstairs.

Claire braced herself. Now for the hard part.

Her mother descended the stairs in her threadbare robe, her expression surprised and appalled as though she'd woken to find her home overrun by garden gnomes.

When she spotted Claire, she halted on the staircase. "Who is that?"

"Rob, my...boyfriend." Claire was still adjusting to the word. She was adjusting to a lot of things lately. Some changes were more pleasant than others.

Mom reached ground level and glanced at the packing boxes. "What are these?"

She reached inside an open box and pulled out a frilly bedsheet with red hearts and an old Barbie doll.

Her mother snarled. "These are Tina's things."

"*Were* Tina's things," Claire corrected. "Now they're just taking up space. We're donating what we can and throwing out the rest. A van is on its way to collect."

Mom tossed the Barbie back in the box. "You can't do that."

"Oh, we're just getting started, Mom. Renovators are coming over later to take measurements."

"Renovators?"

"Oh, yeah. We're going to tear down the wall between Tina's room and mine."

Her mother blinked at her in open-mouthed horror.

"I'll need the space. I'm moving in, Mom. Until you're back on your feet. We all need to adapt."

Scowling, Mom aimed a trembling finger at her daughter. "How dare you! You murdered my daughter. You murdered my husband, too. Now you're taking over my home?"

Claire placed her hands on her hips and returned the stare. Only weeks ago, Claire had fled her mother's tirades, but today she stood her ground. During her week of rest and introspection, she had talked things through with Rob. Claire and her mom were both victims of Tina and her father. But Claire refused to remain a victim, and it was time her mother got with the program, starting now.

"Go ahead," Claire said. "Blame me. That's what you've

always done. Blame me for Tina and Dad. Blame me for ruining your life and destroying your career. You know what? I blame you, too. I blame you for setting sisters against each other with your stupid favoritism. I blame you for making me think I was never good enough or deserving of your love. The truth is, I am worthy of love. I always have been. But you were too busy feeling sorry for yourself to love your own daughter."

Claire caught her breath.

"How dare you—"

Claire raised her hand. "I'm not done yet." She had rehearsed this speech a hundred times and, by God, she was going to finish. "If I blame you for that, I should also blame you for the rest. I blame you for giving me the drive to prove myself. I blame you for the determination I had to survive the police academy to graduate top of my class. I blame you for turning me into a kick-ass officer and an excellent homicide detective."

Claire was panting now, adrenaline stoking her body. The words poured out from the open wound in her soul, the wound that had started to heal.

Her mother gaped at her, out of words and accusations. *Good.*

Claire jerked her thumb behind her at the kitchen table, where plates of fried bacon, scrambled eggs, toast, and a pot of coffee waited. "Now go eat your breakfast and get dressed. I'm dropping you off at the hair salon in an hour."

Mom gaped at Claire for five more seconds. Then, she closed her mouth, walked past her daughter, and sat at the kitchen table. Claire stretched her shoulder and smiled. The chat had gone better than expected. Claire liked her new self. She could definitely adjust to that.

"Oh, and by the way, you were right about the spiders—huge suckers. I got rid of them. You don't have to worry about that anymore."

In the basement, Claire had found the canisters of spray paint her father had used on the spiders. Pink and red. At least now her mom knew she wasn't crazy. And without the meds her father had used to sedate her, Mom could become a new person, too, so long as she cut back on the alcohol.

A horn honked outside. The collection van had arrived. Rob descended the stairs and hefted a box. He'd had the sense to wait upstairs while Claire and her mom had their little moment. Claire opened the front door for him, and he paused on his way out.

"You OK?" he whispered.

She nodded. He pecked her on the cheek and stepped outside.

While her mother ate in silence, Claire placed the framed photo of Tina on the kitchen counter. Tina smiled at her, her cheeks dimpled, and a sparkle in her blue eyes. Claire had kept her promise. She had found her sister's killer and brought him to justice. And she had let the hurt go. Tina was her sister. That bond ran deep. By hating Tina, Claire had scorned a part of herself. And that part had given her the strength to survive. Wherever Tina was, Claire hoped she had found peace. It was time they both moved on.

CHAPTER 73

Claire lifted the dolphin-shaped knocker on the door and let it drop. A hollow sound echoed within the home. She'd never be able to fill that void but at least she could offer closure.

Gareth Miles opened the door. The lines beneath his eyes were less visible. He'd been sleeping better, but that dull glint of sadness never left a bereaved parent's eyes.

"Please, come in."

She thanked him and entered the home. This Sunday, Claire had selected a fresh suit for the visit instead of her weekend clothes. For Claire, this home was a sacred space, like a church, and she'd dressed accordingly.

Candace Miles stood in the entrance hall wearing an elegant blue frock. She had also dressed up for the occasion. Paul held her hand and stared at their guest. His creaseless trousers and button-down shirt seemed too large for his thin, boney frame. They had buried Gracie weeks ago, but today felt like her real funeral.

Candace shook Claire's hand with rigid formality. "Thank you for coming. Shall we sit?"

She ushered Claire to the living room couch and armchairs, where plates of cookies and sliced fruit waited. They sat. Gracie's mom offered Claire a glass of soda, and she accepted. With the drinks poured, Claire began.

"I need you to keep what I'm about to tell you secret."

"Of course," Gracie's parents said as one.

"Should Paul go to his room?"

"Mom!" the boy protested.

"That won't be necessary." Claire would share no gruesome details, only facts to help the bereaved family find comfort in the wake of their daughter's death.

Claire returned the boy's grateful smile.

"The killers had planned Gracie's murder for some time."

"Killers," Gareth said. "Plural?"

"Yes. They had surveilled Gracie in school and singled her out purely because of her physical appearance. Nothing Gracie had done had led to her death. There was nothing you could have done to prevent it either."

The parents nodded. Claire wanted to make sure Gracie's parents wouldn't carry that burden of guilt for the rest of their lives. If only Gareth had dropped her off at the school gates. If only they had discovered her drug use or boyfriend.

Claire continued. "In solving this case we discovered evidence connected to other unsolved murders. It seems the killers committed many other homicides in Newburgh and beyond. If they hadn't targeted Gracie, we might never have made that connection or rooted out criminal elements that had infiltrated the Newburgh Police Department."

"Wow," Gareth said. "We heard they arrested the chief of police, but we didn't connect that with Gracie."

"He wasn't involved in Gracie's death, but an older related case."

Gracie's parents nodded solemnly. The information would

not resurrect their daughter, but her death had helped the forces of good in the world. Gracie's death was not meaningless.

Claire sipped her soda. "Do you have any questions?"

"We started a fund," Candace said. "A non-profit organization to help children struggling with substance abuse. Our church has raised money for a helpline and safe house for children at risk. We're calling it the Grace Miles Memorial Fund."

Claire smiled. The Miles family had found a way to honor their daughter's memory. In the decades to come, children saved from the bottomless pit of addiction would thank God for Grace Miles. Claire's eyes moistened.

"Did you kill them?" the boy blurted. His face wrinkled with fury.

"Paul!" The mother blushed at her son's behavior.

"It's OK. That's a valid question. Law enforcement officers shot the perpetrators dead during their capture."

The boy inhaled deeply, and his shoulders relaxed. Claire forced a smile and rubbed the palm of her hand. Rob had killed Gracie's murderer, Claire's father. Claire had blood on her hands, too. She had killed her partner, Detective Jed Wallace, in self-defense. He had tried to frame her for Tina's murder. He had contributed to the death of Kitty Tucker, but he was not a cold-blooded murderer. He had not deserved to die, and Claire couldn't help but wonder—if she had done things differently, would Jed be sitting beside her now?

"Now, tell me more about Gracie."

They talked for a half hour. Gracie had loved to draw, and she had won a science fair project in sixth grade. She had loved making fudge and showed great promise in ballet class. Gracie had dreamed of traveling the world with her dance company and bringing smiles to people's faces. Now, her memory would do just that.

As she turned to leave, Claire shook Paul's hand and ruffled his hair. "It's not your fault."

"I know." His face crumpled again, and tears slipped from his eyes.

When Claire stepped onto the street, Rob was leaning against her white Ford Focus, looking casual in his civilian jeans and sweater. "How'd it go?"

She joined him beside the car. "As good as expected."

"What now?"

He wasn't asking about the rest of their day. He was asking what Claire planned to do with the rest of her life.

Claire drew a deep breath. *Good question.* She had chased Tina's ghost for so long that the blank page of the future terrified her. For the past few weeks, Claire had avoided that question, and Rob had provided plenty of distractions. Last night, they had made love in her childhood bedroom. They'd made love in the shower where, twelve years ago, she had washed blood from her leg. One by one, Claire was painting over those old, painful memories with new, better ones.

Some memories were easier to paint over than others. The revelation in her parents' basement had shaken Claire to her core and scrawled thick, black question marks over her future. Claire had grown up in that household but failed to see the monster that lurked beneath her father's skin. Did that deadly failure of judgment disqualify her as a homicide detective? And considering her family history and genetic makeup, was Claire fit to serve in law enforcement?

Soon, this city will be ours. Her father's words haunted her thoughts. No, not her father. Bill Wolfe. *I have plans—big plans...* Claire didn't know what his plans were. She couldn't imagine how he had roped Lisa Evans into his murderous pack either. A large part of her didn't want to know. She massaged the palm of her hand. Her work in Newburgh was not done yet.

Claire shrugged. "I guess I'll go back to work at Newburgh PD."

"Are you sure?"

She put on a brave face. "Yeah. This whole homicide detective thing has rubbed off on me. And there's a load of new evidence at the ranch house. Plenty of unsolved murders. Newburgh PD needs all the help it can get."

"Yes, it does. But you could always leave that to somebody else."

Claire grinned. "And let the FBI take all the credit? No way."

EPILOGUE

"This is wrong," her mother said.

Claire bit her tongue. The drizzling rain sprinkled droplets on their shoes, coats, and the coffin of untreated wood beside the fresh grave. Rob opened an umbrella and held it over their heads. She and Diane had been over this a hundred times, and Claire didn't want to repeat the argument in public.

She had kept the time and place of the funeral a secret. William "Bill" Wolfe would not get a large funeral. Claire would have preferred to skip the event. Her father deserved a slow and lonely incineration—a taste of the suffering that awaited him in Hell. But a cremation cost more, and Bill had left his wife with an empty bank account. A simple burial in a forlorn corner of Newburgh Cemetery was the most cost-effective way to dispose of the murderer's corpse.

Let's get this over with. Claire nodded at the priest. The balding young man opened his prayer book underneath his transparent rain poncho.

But Diane wasn't done. "We shouldn't bury him like some nameless stranger. We have a family lot."

Claire snapped. “He killed Tina. We’re not going to bury him next to her.”

Rob touched Claire’s arm. The priest and two undertakers eyed her with mute concern. Rob was right. She needed to restrain her temper. Claire blamed the dull ache in her shoulder and the rope burns that still stung her neck. She blamed the pent-up rage at her criminal father and her frustration over not killing the bastard with her own bare hands.

“He’s your father,” Diane hissed. “Show some respect!”

Claire counted to ten. Diane, of all people, should understand. Claire had discovered an arsenal of anti-psychotics and anti-depressants in her parents’ bathroom cabinet. Clozapine. Trazodone. Sertraline. She had no idea how Bill had laid his hands on the powerful prescription drugs or how long he’d fed his wife that dangerous cocktail. Claire flushed the drugs down the toilet. Her mother’s drowsiness and confusion cleared up in days. Within a week, she shed two pounds of belly fat. The long-term diet of drugs might have killed Diane, but did she thank her daughter for saving her life? Oh, no.

Claire nodded at the priest to continue.

“‘I am the Resurrection and the Life…’”

Her thoughts drifted on the rhythmic droning of the priest’s voice. She held Rob’s hand. His presence over the past week had saved her sanity. But tomorrow he was leaving Newburgh to chase a serial killer in Florida. He’d be away for at least two weeks. Rob’s unit chief wasn’t eager to let her top agents speculate about cold murders in a ranch house basement when they could pursue active killers elsewhere. Did Rob’s looming departure also explain Claire’s short fuse?

A tingle crawled up her spine. The hairs on the back of her neck bristled. Malevolent eyes were watching her from the shadows. She turned toward the dark forest at the edge of the cemetery, and a human shape slipped behind a large tree.

Claire watched the broad trunk, waiting for the hooded figure to emerge on the other side. But the mysterious observer remained hidden.

The sound of metal cutting into soil rang out as the undertakers shoveled dirt into the grave. The priest had concluded the ceremony, the coffin had disappeared into the hole, and Diane sniveled beside her.

Rob whispered in Claire's ear, "It's time to go."

She released his hand, but instead of following him and Diane to the car, she stepped away from the umbrella and headed for the forest.

"Claire?"

She marched toward the tree. Had a reporter gotten wind of the funeral—or a violence junkie, hoping to witness a serial killer's funeral? She'd teach him a lesson. Claire broke into a jog. Another possibility clamped steel fingers over her gut. Was the watcher connected to her father's dark past? Had the hooded man turned up to pay his respects to Bill Wolfe?

Claire drew her service weapon and winced at the pain in her shoulder. Dead leaves crunched under her boots. The Glock aimed in both her hands, she rounded the tree. She glanced left and right, then stared into the branches overhead.

Rob caught up with her. "What is it?"

Claire stared at the pile of broken leaves behind the tree. The figure who had stood there watching only moments ago had slipped away.

She holstered her weapon. "Nothing."

ACKNOWLEDGMENTS

Behind every novel there is a long line of very talented and supportive people.

Sgt. Patrick O'Donnell, retired, of the Milwaukee Police Department reviewed an early draft of the novel. His feedback on the everyday workings of police departments helped make the story as authentic as possible.

My team of awesome beta readers provided valuable comments and corrections. They are: Maura Bauwens, Tracy Big Pond, Kimberly Bottini, Heather Bryant, Ben Draiman, Corie Draiman, Claudia Levi, Lynn Lujan, Candice Lutz, Jennifer Medina, Lara Morrison, Roger Proctor, Amy Sexton, Roxx Tarantini, Shreya Vijay, Billie Wichkan, Kai Wills, and Beatrice Yeow.

My excellent editor, Emmy Ellis, made the novel shine, and her insightful tips will guide my future writings.

Teresa Collins, my trusty and talented proofreader, ensured the final manuscript is error-free and ready for publication.

I thank you all from the bottom of my heart.

~ Jamie Millen

ABOUT THE AUTHOR

Psychopaths. Stalkers. Killers.

Jamie Millen writes about the people you hope never to meet in real life...but probably already have.

If you enjoy crime thrillers packed with nail-biting psychological suspense, unforgettable characters, and breathtaking twists, you've come to the right place.

Visit JamieMillen.com/Claire to download free stories, sneak peeks, advanced chapters, and more.

Printed in the USA
CPSIA information can be obtained
at www.ICGtesting.com
LVHW090743310124
770467LV00003B/275